# FROM HERE TO YOU

## THE COMPLETE SERIES

JULIE STOCK

CLUED UP PUBLISHING

FROM HERE TO YOU SERIES
Copyright © 2015 Julie Stock
ISBN: 9780993213526
All rights reserved.

Cover Design: Oliphant Publishing Services
Editing: H&H Editorial Services/Helena Fairfax
Proofreading: Wendy Janes

*To Simon, Hannah and Laura.*
*Thank you for believing in me and for constantly reassuring me*
*through all the ups and downs of this new writing life.*

# FROM HERE TO NASHVILLE (RACHEL'S STORY)

# ABOUT THIS BOOK

**Can Music Really Bring People Together?**

Rachel Hardy dreams of being a successful country music singer in Nashville's Music City, four thousand miles away from her lonely life in Dorset.

When Jackson Phillips, an independent record label owner, encourages her band to audition for a nationwide 'Open Mic' competition, she decides they have nothing to lose.

But when she starts to fall in love with Jackson, the stakes suddenly get higher, and she finds herself with a great big dilemma on her hands. Should she abandon her dream and take the easy way out or should she leave the life she has always known behind and take a gamble on a man who has personal demons of his own?

**Follow Rachel and Jackson as they learn to trust in love again and to see whether music really can bring them together.**

# CHAPTER 1
## POOLE, DORSET, ENGLAND

**Rachel**

'It's time for our last session of the evening now, folks. We're proud to present to you the next big thing in UK country music. Please give it up for local band Three's Company!'

The crowd applauded in response and I took a deep breath to try and stop my heart from racing as I walked over to the microphone. It didn't matter how many gigs we did, I still felt nervous every time. With a quick glance round I checked that Sam, the guitarist, and Matt, the drummer, were ready. I tossed my hair over my shoulder and moved my guitar into position, running my fingers gently over the strings to reassure myself before the growing audience.

The boys played the opening bars of Lady Antebellum's 'Need You Now' and I relaxed, letting my voice take over and lead the way. As the song ended, the crowd gave another good round of applause so we went straight on to our second number. About halfway through, I spotted a man watching me intently. He was tall, with broad shoulders and he had a healthy-looking tan. His dark brown hair curled invitingly around his face and his jaw was covered by a fine layer of stubble. He smiled encouragingly so he didn't put me off my stride and reluctantly I looked away. But I was intrigued.

By the end of the song, the crowd was singing along. More and more people had started to come in, drawn by the sound of our music, which boosted our confidence still further so I felt the time was right for some introductions.

'Hi, we're Three's Company and it's great to be here tonight.' I had to pause and wait for the cheers to subside. Smiling, I carried on, 'I'd like to take a minute to introduce the band. Sam's on guitar and that's his brother, Matt, on drums.' They both grinned and gave a little wave. 'I'm Rachel and next up, is a song of mine called "My Turn".'

I settled myself on the stool at the front of the stage, making sure I was comfortable before playing the introduction so that I could focus and get my first public performance of this song perfect. I'd written it with my mum in mind and I only wished she could see me sing it now.

*'All my life, I've been waiting, waiting for my turn,*
*Wondering how much longer it's gonna be...*
*And when it comes, I'm gonna make sure I take it,*
*Make the most of it, live my turn to the limit.'*

---

I didn't look up until I reached the end of the song and when I finished singing, there was complete silence in the pub, feeding my fears for a brief moment. This was swiftly followed by thunderous applause though and I could not believe the crowd's reaction.

When we broke for the interval, I rushed to hug Sam and Matt, flushed with our success. Standing at the crowded bar a few minutes later with my heart still pounding and a huge smile on my face, I suddenly felt the hairs stand up on the back of my neck.

I turned slowly to find myself staring up into the most beautiful pair of brown eyes I'd ever seen. The gorgeous man who'd been watching me earlier now stood before me and my breath caught as I studied him close up. He towered over my petite frame, his soft, wavy, dark brown hair falling over his forehead, hands slung low in his pockets and cowboy boots peeking out from beneath his jeans.

'Er, hi,' I managed to stutter out, reminding myself to breathe.

'Hey there,' he drawled in the most luscious American accent. 'I heard you singing and I wanted to find out more about who that fabulous voice belonged to.' He smiled and as he did, I noticed the way his lips turned up invitingly at the corners.

'Thank you. I'm glad you liked it,' I replied, trying to appear calm and to bring my focus back to his eyes.

And then he chuckled. God, he knew how to make a chuckle sound sexy. He oozed confidence too, with his broad shoulders pulled back and his head held high.

'You British, you're so damn polite,' he said, raising his eyebrows. 'You sounded great up there.'

'Yeah, the crowd had a great vibe tonight. I can't quite believe it.'

'Well, you have no reason not to; the proof's all here. I loved your own song by the way. You have a real talent there.'

I blushed then, an honest-to-goodness shade of pink that made him chuckle once more, locking eyes with me as he did, so I knew the compliment was sincere.

'I'd love to hear more of your singing. Have y'all any more gigs coming up?'

'We've got another one next Tuesday at a local pub down on the quayside. Do you know where that is?'

I gave him a cheeky smile, feeling like I'd somehow been transported to an alternate universe where I flirted with handsome Americans all the time, and he rewarded me with a playful grin by return. Wow! His grin was almost sinful. I didn't know how much longer my legs would support me, after the excitement of being on stage and now this unfamiliar feeling of attraction. I took a step back and reached out to hold on to the bar behind me.

'Well, I'm staying with my cousin, Tom. He's the bartender here so I'm sure he'll help me get to the *quayside*, whatever that is.' He tilted his head to one side endearingly and frowned a little as he considered the possibilities.

'It's down at the waterfront.' I smiled again, picking up on his confusion. 'Tom lives a couple of doors away from me actually so he knows how to get to most places.'

'Great, I'll look forward to it. I'm Jackson by the way, Jackson Phillips.' He held out his hand towards me.

'Rachel Hardy,' I responded, placing my hand in his. The warmth of his skin against mine set my pulse racing once more, as he held my hand and my gaze for what seemed like an eternity.

By this time, Tom had made it over to us. 'What can I get you two to drink?' he asked, bringing us both back to reality. 'Fantastic set, Rachel, by the way. The crowd loved it.'

I asked for a lime and soda, as did Jackson. When Tom brought the drinks back a moment later, Jackson insisted on paying for them and I took a long sip while I collected my thoughts.

'Where are you from then, Jackson?' I turned to face him and found him already looking at me, with that intensity that had caught my attention when I was singing.

'I'm from Nashville. Do you know it?'

I coughed and spluttered as I tried to swallow the sip of drink I had taken at just the wrong time. He reached out to pat me on the back, looking concerned by my reaction.

'You okay?'

'Sorry,' I managed, 'it's just that was the last thing I expected you to say. I've always dreamed of going to Nashville.' I could only hope that my face didn't have a silly teenage look on it.

'Well, it's good to have a dream to work towards and I can heartily recommend it to you. I'm over here for Tom's wedding to Meg at the end of the month, I'm going to be his best man.'

As I cast my eyes over his perfectly toned body, a sudden wicked vision of Jackson in a morning suit appeared before me. I must have given myself away because he was now looking at me quite differently. My face warmed under his scrutiny. Thankfully, my best friend, Jenna, chose that moment to come over and introduce herself.

'Rachel, found you at last!' She pulled me in for a quick hug, forcing me to tear my attention away from Jackson for a moment. 'You guys sounded brilliant out there. All those practice gigs over the last few years have paid off, you know. I felt really proud of you all, even those two brothers of mine.'

'We did a pretty good job tonight, didn't we?' I admitted before turning back to Jackson. 'Jenna, this is Jackson Phillips, he's Tom's cousin and he's over here from *Nashville*.' I raised my eyebrows slightly, knowing she would get the connection. They said hello and then I had to down my drink quickly because it was time for me to get back to the stage.

I cast a final look in Jackson's direction and he tilted his head gently towards me, giving me another charming smile. His gaze followed me all the way to the stage and the attention made my stomach flutter.

We started the second half with our version of 'Killing Me Softly With His Song', keeping quite faithfully to Roberta Flack's original, before going on to some other covers, including 'This Kiss' by Faith Hill.

All too soon, I sat down at the piano to introduce our final number. I'd chosen another one of my own songs to finish with, called 'Don't Let Me Go'.

*'How can things have turned out like this?*
*I thought you'd be here forever*
*But now you've gone and I'm on my own.*
*I couldn't make you stay but promise me one thing*
*Don't let me go...'*

The crowd cheered their approval for this final song. People came up for some time afterwards to congratulate us on our success before going on their way. Finally, only Jackson remained, smiling at me and waiting for me to finish receiving all the compliments. Sam and Matt had already started taking the gear out to the van so it took a few minutes before I could introduce them to him.

'Sam, Matt, meet Jackson, Tom's cousin. He's over here from America for Tom's wedding.'

'Whereabouts in America are you from?' asked Sam, as he put his guitar carefully back into its case.

'Nashville,' Jackson explained.

'As in, Nashville, Tennessee, Music City,' I reinforced.

'Yep, the very same,' Jackson laughed. 'That's how I know you guys sound so good. I've heard a few bands in my time,' he said.

'Nice to meet you and thanks,' Sam replied, shaking Jackson's hand.

'Hello, Jackson, glad you enjoyed the gig,' Matt said, a bit breathless after packing his drums away. 'Rachel, sorry to interrupt but do you want a lift home?' he continued. 'Jenna's waiting in the van.'

'No, I'll walk back as it's such a lovely evening, but thanks anyway.'

'If you only live a couple of doors away from Tom, I can walk you back to make sure you get home safely, if that's okay with you, Rachel,' Jackson offered, looking first at me and then at Sam and Matt as if he knew they acted as my protectors.

'Is that okay with you, Rachel?' asked Sam. The sullen look on his face caught me off-guard. I was used to him being protective of me in the absence of a brother of my own, but this wasn't the same and I couldn't quite put my finger on it.

'Yes, of course,' I said, pushing my worries away. 'Thank you, Jackson and thanks guys, for an awesome performance tonight. I'll call you tomorrow for a post-gig analysis!' I gave them both a hug and a kiss and they turned to leave.

I looked at Jackson and blew out a long, slow breath.

'A penny for your thoughts?' he asked.

That made me laugh, to hear this typically English phrase coming out of his mouth. I studied his face for a moment.

'I'm not quite sure what to make of you. I've never met anyone from Nashville before and you're taking me a bit by surprise.'

'And that's a good thing, right?' His eyes twinkled. 'Shall we go?'

Jackson took my guitar for me and we walked back slowly along the quay, delighting in all the sparkling lights and the buzz from the tourists out enjoying meals on the warm summer evening. Once or twice, his hand brushed mine as we walked and I wondered if he felt the same tingling sensation I did every time our skin touched.

'Have you always enjoyed singing?' he asked.

'Oh yes, since I was young, my mum and dad encouraged it. We always had music in the house.'

'And were your parents there tonight?' he asked.

For a moment, I couldn't answer. 'My parents have both passed away,' I whispered and found myself stopping in the street.

He took my hand.

'I'm really sorry. Sorry that happened to you and for being nosy.' He groaned.

'Don't worry. It was a natural question to ask and I don't mind talking about them.'

We started walking again and he let go of my hand. I missed the warm, reassuring feel of it.

'Did they ever hear you and the band sing?'

'No, they didn't get the chance.'

'Well, they sure would have been proud of you tonight.'

To my relief, he didn't ask me how they'd died. My family's past was my burden and not something I chose to talk about very often.

Before I knew it, we'd reached my gate and it was time to say goodbye but there was still so much I wanted to say.

'Your next gig is on Tuesday, you said. What's the name of the pub?'

'It's called The Cork and Bottle and we'll be on at eight again. I'll have to make sure we play some different songs then if you might be coming,' I joked.

'I'll definitely be there.'

My heart flipped over at his confident reply.

'Great, it will be good to see you again.' I paused, uncertain of what to say next. 'Well, I enjoyed meeting you tonight, Jackson,' I said, looking up at him one last time, 'and thank you for walking me home.' I reached out to touch him lightly on the arm, letting my hand linger for a moment before pulling away.

'The pleasure was all mine. Goodnight,' he replied softly, his deep voice caressing me right till the very last minute. Then, he handed me back my guitar, turned and continued on his walk home.

Watching him go, I had the feeling that my life had just taken a turn for the better.

# CHAPTER 2

After some breakfast the next morning, I called Sam to talk over last night's concert, still buzzing with excitement from all that had happened.

'Hello, Rach, how are you feeling today?' his gravelly voice resonated down the line.

'I still can't get over how brilliantly it went for us last night, can you?'

'No, better than we could have expected really, given that we're still quite unknown.' He fell silent at the other end of the phone, making me wonder what he was really feeling. He didn't seem his usual laid-back self.

'Hey, Sam, is everything all right? You seemed a bit upset with me at the end of the gig last night and I didn't know why.'

There was an awkward pause while I waited for his reply.

'I'm feeling a bit tired, that's all and I've got a sanding job to finish today as well. I'll be fine later on, I'm sure. Do you want to meet up for a drink tonight as usual?'

'Yes, I'd like that, shall we say six o'clock?' I was sure he was bluffing but I didn't want to push him over the phone.

'See you then, bye.' He rang off quickly as though he couldn't wait to get away.

I remembered the strange look I'd seen on Sam's face last night when Jackson had offered to walk me home and a seed of doubt began to niggle away in the back of my mind.

———

As I closed my wooden gate and stepped out on to Green Road for the short walk into town to see Jenna before meeting up with Sam, I could see what a wonderful August afternoon it was. The sun was shining, warming my skin and my soul, and the sky was such a vivid blue, it made me smile. I walked along the quay, watching the boats bobbing in the harbour and the tourists eating fish and chips, studied eagerly by all the seagulls flying around overhead.

I turned right, up the cobbled High Street towards the museum and Jenna's thriving florist's shop. Outside I saw buckets and jugs full of brightly coloured roses, tulips, chrysanthemums and lilies, and pots of all shapes and sizes as well, containing everything from lavender bushes to sage and thyme. The heavenly smell outside the shop always lifted my spirits. As I opened the door, the bell tinkled and she automatically looked up to greet her next customer. Her friendly face lit up when she saw it was me and she came round the counter to give me a hug.

'Hey, you're looking very happy this afternoon! Could this have anything to do with your great gig last night and maybe a certain gorgeous hunk you met?' Jenna knew me so well, I couldn't hide anything from her.

'I can't think who you mean,' I said, trying to look nonchalant but grinning at the same time.

'And how come I don't know anything about this guy?'

'Hang on, I only met him yesterday at the gig but I knew you'd want to hear the full story,' I said and then filled her in on how we'd met.

'And he's from Nashville too, that's pretty cool.'

'I know, I could hardly believe it. He's here to be best man at Tom's wedding. They're cousins.'

We had to pause our conversation for a moment while she served a customer who had picked up one of the bouquets from outside the shop. Jenna wrapped the flowers and told the customer briefly how to look after them so they would last longer.

'What happened at the end of the evening then? I heard he walked you home.'

'You don't miss a thing, do you?' I laughed. 'He walked me home, that's all, no big deal.'

'If it's no big deal, why have you come to see me straight away, why are your eyes shining like that and why are you smiling all over your sun-kissed face?' She reached out to pat me playfully on the cheek.

'I know I'm probably getting ahead of myself a bit but I really liked him, I felt attracted to him even and that hasn't happened in such a long time, you know.' I paused to let my mind wander to the gorgeous image of Jackson I had already tucked away in my brain. 'Still, I shouldn't get my hopes up, it's not like he'll be around for long and you know what my track record with men is like.'

My face fell and my shoulders sagged as the reality set in. Jackson would be gone in a couple of weeks and that would be the end of that.

'Don't you dare feel sorry for yourself. Just because things didn't work out with Nick, it doesn't mean every relationship you have will be the same. Give yourself a chance. What difference does it make if it's only for a couple of weeks?' Jenna scolded. 'Have you made any plans to see him again?'

'He wants to come to our gig on Tuesday.'

'He sounds keen. Make sure you look your fabulous best and he'll be blown away. Changing the subject, are you seeing Sam tonight?'

'We're meeting at the pub. Do you want to join us?'

'God, no. Too knackered. I'll see you tomorrow for Sunday dinner.'

I gave her a goodbye hug and set off to meet Sam.

---

Sam was already there when I arrived, sitting at a bench outside the pub with a pint of beer in front of him and a chilled glass of rosé waiting for me on the side. He stood up to greet me, giving me one of his enormous hugs and a kiss on the cheek. He smiled at me so I guessed things couldn't be that bad.

'You definitely know the way to a girl's heart.'

Sam laughed. 'In your case, it's easy because you're a creature of habit. You *always* have a glass or two of rosé on Saturday nights in the summer, changing over to red wine in the winter, simple! If only I could predict all women so easily.'

'So you're saying I'm predictable? Charmed, I'm sure.' To my relief, our friendship seemed to be on its usual footing again.

'Only on the wine front, of course, not in any other, more significant way, I hasten to add.'

'Okay, you can stop digging, I'll let you off. What about the gig last night? We were great, weren't we? And I still haven't recovered from the audience's reaction to us.' I was babbling on, I knew, but I wanted to talk it all over with him and if I could postpone any other sort of conversation indefinitely, that would be a bonus.

'Yeah, the crowd really seemed to approve. Anyway, I thought it went better than the last show so maybe we need to think about that when booking venues in the future. No point going back to places where we didn't get a great reception.' He paused to take a sip of his beer. 'I think your voice sounded amazing last night though and that clearly made a difference.'

'I don't know that I sang any differently. I did get a real buzz from the crowd's reaction in the first half, which spurred me on later so perhaps that helped. I think we ought to play a different setlist if we can for next Tuesday so if anyone comes again, they don't hear the same stuff.'

'I agree about different songs for Tuesday. Perhaps we could chat to Matt about it to see what we can come up with. Have you written any other new songs you'd like to play? They really seemed to go for the new material.'

'I have plenty but I'd need to practise on my own and then again with you guys. Is there enough time for all that? I know it's easier for me because I'm not working at the moment.'

He pulled a face before saying, 'Don't remind me about your lovely long holidays!' I smacked him on the arm, knowing he was trying to wind me up with the 'teachers and their long holidays' rant. 'As long as you don't spring anything too difficult on us, I think we'll be okay,' he continued, giving me his usual twinkling smile in reassurance.

We fell silent for a moment, taking in the view. I noticed that the breeze had picked up a little because I had to keep brushing my hair out of my eyes and the sky was a bit overcast now. I shivered, wishing that I'd brought a jumper along.

'What about Tom having an American cousin and from Nashville too? That was a bit of a surprise.' There, I'd said it and I turned to look at him to see if I could gauge his reaction.

'Yeah, I guess,' he replied looking miserable all of a sudden.

'I take it you didn't like him then?'

'I didn't have time to decide whether I liked him or not. It seemed a bit ridiculous, that's all, someone from Nashville coming along to one of our shows, you know, and then offering to walk you home too, Mr Charming himself.'

'Hey, he *was* genuinely charming and I don't think it's that ridiculous. I don't understand why you're so irritated about it. What harm is there in having someone who has obviously seen a lot of bands in his time coming along to our gigs and being positive about them?'

'That's not the point, Rachel.' He'd gone all quiet.

'What *is* the point you're making then?'

'Look, it doesn't matter, let's drop it. Do you want another drink?' His face was gloomy with frustration.

I handed him my glass because I didn't know what to say. While he was gone, I thought about it though. He was obviously irritated by Jackson but he wouldn't say why. I had an idea that he was being even more protective of me than usual. I watched the man I'd known for years and grown up with, as he weaved his way back through the crowd towards me a few minutes later. He didn't notice any of the admiring glances his tanned, fit body received from the women he passed. He could be out with any one of those women now, I thought to myself, but he's here with me. None of those women knew that we were just friends though and that's all we ever would be in my view. Sam was like a brother to me and although I could see how attractive he was, I wasn't going to let myself be attracted to him.

'Thanks,' I murmured as he handed me my drink.

He sat down, pushing his curly blonde hair out of his eyes. Not for the first time, I marvelled at the gorgeous, self-assured man he had become. Despite all my efforts, my thoughts strayed back to *that* night. I closed my eyes in an effort to block them out. We'd never talked about it and I didn't want to start now.

'Did you get your sanding job finished today?' I asked, breaking the awkward silence that had fallen between us. He nodded but didn't say anything. I looked away, wondering how long he was going to keep this sulk up and heard him take a deep breath.

'Are you coming over for lunch with us tomorrow?' he asked, avoiding the issue.

'Yes, I'll be there.' I paused, summoning up the courage to speak again. 'Sam...I...' I didn't know how to bring the subject up without causing an argument and the look he gave me confirmed that he wanted to steer clear of it too. 'I have to go,' I said instead and stood up.

I waited for him to stand up as well, fiddling with my bag handle while he manoeuvred his bulky frame out of the small wooden chair. I looked up at him, hoping he would say something to sort things out but he just bent down, kissed me briefly on the cheek, mumbled goodbye and sat down again. I turned abruptly on my heel and walked away.

# CHAPTER 3

I wrapped my coat tightly around me as I walked to church early the next morning and, as always, my thoughts turned to my mum and dad on the way. Sunday mornings were my favourite when my dad still lived at home because we'd always indulge in a fried breakfast all together, listening to the latest songs on the radio and singing along at the top of our voices. Despite the difficulties caused by my dad's drinking, we still shared some happy times before he left and the memory made me smile. The smile faded quickly as my thoughts turned to my mum. She'd been so selfless, keeping the pain of her cancer hidden from me after my dad's early death and it still hurt to think that I had lost both my parents in such a short space of time.

As the worship began, I relaxed into it, enjoying the familiarity of the words of both the service and the hymns. Walking back to my seat after the Communion, I glanced around the pews to check for any other people I knew but had missed, smiling and nodding at one or two. For a moment, I thought I saw Jackson at the back of the church but then I shook my head slightly, thinking I must have been mistaken and it was simply that he'd been on my mind a lot since Friday.

I said my goodbyes quickly afterwards and made my way out to the churchyard, picking up the flowers I'd brought with me from my garden on the way. I always went to see my mum's and dad's graves on these Sundays, to tidy them up, to lay new flowers and to offer up some prayers. I closed the door of the church and turned towards the path, only to find Jackson standing there.

'It *was* you at the back of the church! What are you doing here?' I demanded. None of my close friends knew I came here, it was private to me and I looked away, hoping he would get the message. He raised his eyebrows in surprise.

'Specifically, I'm waiting for you but I was out walking this morning, heard the music and decided to come in to see a Church of England service for myself. It's a bit different to what I'm used to at home.' He smiled.

'Jackson, it's lovely to see you but I...'

'What is it, Rachel? Do you want me to go?'

'Yes, no, oh, this is difficult. Okay, deep breath.' He looked a bit confused as I stumbled over my words. 'My mum and dad are buried here and I've come to see them,' I explained.

'I'm sorry, I didn't mean to intrude.' Realisation dawned on his handsome face and he made to leave.

'Jackson!' I called after him. 'Would you wait for me on the bench by the gate?' He turned back and nodded. I walked off in the other direction and spent a precious ten minutes with my parents, before discreetly wiping my tears and making my way over to him. He saw my face but, tactfully, didn't mention it. By the time we left the little lane leading up to the church, I'd managed to pull myself together.

'Thank you.'

'What for?' he asked me gently.

'For being there and for understanding how important that visit is to me. It's nice to have someone here with me afterwards. I'm sorry if I was sharp with you at first.'

'I'm sorry, I realise it must be a very private thing for you.'

We made our way back to the quayside and Jackson suggested stopping for a coffee as it had warmed up a little.

'What's new since Friday?' he asked as we sat down, smiling his megawatt, shiny, all-white teeth American smile at me.

'I've been thinking about our next gig, talking over with Sam what our setlist should be on Tuesday. I'd like to try out some more new songs but I'll need to find time to practise before then.'

'That's great that you have more of your own songs. I can't wait to hear them. You might well be pushed for time though, especially if you have to work tomorrow.'

'No, I'm a singing teacher and I'm on school holidays at the moment so I have time to practise during the day but Sam and Matt do have to work of course. Anyway, it'll be okay because we've been playing together for a good few years and we can be ready quickly when we need to.' I paused to take a sip of my coffee and to take a moment to study his features. In the daylight, I could see that he was a bit older than me, probably closer to thirty, I decided. 'How about you, what do you do for a living that allows you to come to Dorset for the best part of a month?' I smiled, hoping he would tell me more about himself.

'I run a small business in Nashville which I've left in the hands of my very capable team so it's okay for me to be gone a while. I have some business interests in London so I've been up and down there a few times during my visit to earn my keep.' I noticed he didn't tell me what his business was in but I didn't want to seem rude by asking too many questions. 'Tom was telling me about a singing competition that's going on here over the summer,' he continued. 'Have you heard about it? It's called "Open Mic", I think he said.'

'No, I haven't heard about it but it sounds interesting. Do you know any more about it?'

'He said it's a nationwide competition and there's an audition process. You guys would have no trouble getting through, I'm sure.'

He glanced out to sea as he finished talking so I couldn't see his face to get any clue about how strongly he felt about this. I had the sense that he was trying to be neutral about it but I wasn't sure why.

'I'll have to look it up. Thanks for telling me about it.' I smiled.

We continued chatting for a bit longer and then walked back to the cottage. We stood face to face across the gate to say our goodbyes.

'I'll see you on Tuesday then, if not before,' he said, without making any move to go. My hair was blown by an unexpected gust of wind across my face and he gently reached across to tuck it behind my ear, touching my face with his thumb as he did.

The sensation was as electric as it had been before and I experienced a reawakening of desire within my body that I'd not felt since my days with Nick. I didn't remember ever feeling it so strongly with him though.

When I looked up at him, I was pretty sure that my eyes were giving me away.

'Goodbye,' I replied breathlessly.

It would seem like forever between now and Tuesday.

---

Jenna's family had lived in the same terraced Victorian house for as long as I could remember. Jenna was waiting on the porch when I arrived with Matt and his family and she welcomed me with open arms. We walked through the sunny, terracotta-tiled kitchen and soon everyone was gathered together in the back garden. Sam smiled at me but he still didn't seem to be quite his usual outgoing self. There was no laughing or joking about today and I worried that whatever had upset him yesterday, had not gone away completely. I decided I would try and have a quiet word with him again later. Jenna's parents both shooed me away when I offered help with the cooking so I sat down on a bench to admire the garden. Sam came over to join me soon after and I swallowed nervously in anticipation of our conversation.

We kissed cheeks and greeted each other before falling into

silence. Neither of us wanted to be the first to broach the subject of last night's conversation. Then we both started talking at once.

'You go first,' he said.

'I know I upset you last night but I still don't understand why.'

'You didn't upset me. It's just that I care for you and I don't want you to get taken in or maybe, even hurt, by some big, flashy American who won't be here for long anyway.'

He pushed his hands through his hair, looking embarrassed.

I grabbed his hands. 'Hey, I don't want to get taken in or hurt either but I can't live in a cocoon for the rest of my life. I need to move on from the way Nick treated me, I can't let it dominate me any more.'

'But is this guy, Jackson, the right person for you to move on with?' he asked, gently pulling his hands free and turning to look at me.

'I don't know, I've barely even talked to him. Who knows if anything more is going to happen?'

I couldn't tell him how much I was attracted to Jackson, it didn't feel right to talk about that kind of stuff with him.

'Be careful, that's all.'

'Listen, your friendship means everything to me but you don't have to worry about me, I can look after myself.'

I blew out a sigh of relief to think he'd only been looking out for me, nothing more, and I relaxed back into my chair. I noticed that he sat in the same hunched-up position though on the edge of his seat. I had the feeling that there was more he wanted to say but we didn't talk about it any more that day.

We rejoined the rest of the group shortly afterwards and the afternoon passed lazily in a wondrous blur of good food and wine. The band and I discussed the upcoming gig on Tuesday and agreed to have a quick rehearsal at mine the next evening after the boys finished work. Jenna and her parents all said they would come on Tuesday and we told them about the success we'd had so far. I brought up the subject of the "Open Mic" competition to sound the guys out about it.

'Do you think that's something you might be interested in doing?' I asked them.

'I'd like to know a bit more about it first, but it sounds interesting,' Matt replied and Sam nodded his agreement.

'Jackson said it's a nationwide competition and that we'd have to audition but he didn't think we'd have any trouble getting through.'

Sam stood up and walked off then, as though I'd said something to upset him again. No-one else but me seemed to notice, leaving me to struggle with my own confused thoughts about his behaviour.

Was he jealous of Jackson? If he was, he certainly had no right to be.

---

I spent most of the next day refining the songs I'd chosen to sing at the gig on Tuesday night and trying to decide on the cover songs I would sing this time. As the first band on, we planned to perform six songs again, four covers, a mix of country, rock and pop and two of my own songs, confident that this formula would work after the success we'd had on the previous Friday.

These gigs meant such a lot to me, probably more than they did to either of the guys. In my mind, it was clearer now. I had mourned my parents for four years and although that ache would never go away, it was becoming more manageable with every passing day. I liked my job but not enough to work it for the rest of my days. Since my feckless ex-fiancé, Nick, had abandoned me after my mum died, preferring to travel the world, I had no-one that held a special place in my heart. I knew the time was right for me to pursue my dream of a music career at last and I needed it now more than ever.

Later on, I fired up my computer to see if I could find out more about the "Open Mic" competition Jackson had mentioned. It seemed that it was a nationwide singing competition for unsigned singers and bands, and auditions were being held all over the country this month! I looked up where our nearest audition location was and found out there was one coming up in Bournemouth.

The downside was that it was this Friday and I didn't know if there were still places left, let alone if we could be ready in time.

On impulse, I sent off an email asking if we still had time to apply. Shortly afterwards, I received a reply:

*'Dear Miss Hardy,*

*There are still a few places left for the audition in Bournemouth on Friday if you would like to apply. Can you tell us some more about your act please? We'd love to hear from you.*

*Regards,*

*Natasha, for "Open Mic" Competition.'*

I sucked in my breath as I read her reply and although I wanted to answer at once, I knew I'd have to wait and talk to the guys before committing myself any further. When they finally turned up at six o'clock, I could hardly contain myself, bouncing lightly on my toes as I let them in. I filled them in on all the details.

'I feel excited about this opportunity. I believe that the time is right for us now, especially as the gigs are going so well. How about you?'

'I don't suppose there's any harm in auditioning,' said Sam. 'Are you up for that, Matt?'

'We have nothing to lose,' Matt agreed, smiling.

I'd have liked a more enthusiastic response from them but decided that it was a man thing and they were keeping their inner thoughts to themselves. The rehearsal went well and after the guys had gone, I sat out in the garden, thinking about all that had happened over the last couple of days. The combination of a successful gig and meeting Jackson, who had enough confidence in us as a band to encourage us to enter this competition, was an intoxicating one. Why shouldn't we go for it now?

# CHAPTER 4

The insistent ringing of the phone woke me early the next morning and it took me more than a moment to get my bearings. Groggily, I reached out for the handset on my bedside table and picked it up.

'Hello?' I mumbled, rubbing my eyes with my free hand.

'Rachel, it's Jenna, I'm sorry to call this early.'

'What time is it?'

'It's seven o'clock, you know I wouldn't call unless it was urgent. The thing is, Mary's called in sick and I wondered if you might be able to help me in the shop today? I'm desperate.'

'Okay, what else can I say but yes, but you owe me for calling me at this ungodly hour when I'm on holiday. I'll be there as soon as I can.' I grumbled but I would do anything for Jenna and she knew she only had to ask so I stumbled out of bed and into the shower, ate a quick slice of toast and set off for the town. I knew that there was a lot of preparation to be done before the shop opened as well and Jenna wouldn't be able to do it without my help.

As I set off towards the seafront once again, I enjoyed the feel of the early morning sun on my face and the gentle breeze through my hair. I would never grow tired of living by the sea, with the particular salty smell of the air and the sound of the water lapping against the harbour walls. As I walked, my mood lifted immediately, banishing the pain of the early wake-up call. I paused for a moment to take in the red, yellow and blue-coloured boats bobbing in the harbour and their shimmering reflections in the water.

The shop kept Jenna and I steadily busy throughout the morning and it was nearly eleven before we had time for a cup of tea. I left Jenna serving while I went into the back room where she kept a very small kitchen area. As I was stirring the sugar in, I heard the bell go, then, Jenna in conversation with a very familiar-sounding American.

'Jackson!' I exclaimed.

I smoothed down my hair and apron, grabbed the cups and headed back. Jackson's face lit up when he saw me which put me at ease.

'Hey, what are you doing here?' he asked in his lazy drawl, reminding me of one of the reasons I liked him so much.

'She's helping me out for the day because my assistant called in sick. She's been an absolute star,' Jenna jumped in before I could reply.

I beamed at Jackson, revealing my pleasure at seeing him again so soon.

'That's real kind of you,' he replied, keeping his gaze fixed on me. 'I hope you won't be too tired for tonight, though, I'm kinda looking forward to it, you know,' he said, making it clear that he couldn't wait to see me again either.

I couldn't bring myself to look away from him, knowing it would break the spell he had me under.

Jenna sucked in her breath. 'Oh, Rachel, I completely forgot about your gig. You'll have to go early to get yourself ready. Thanks for reminding me, Jackson. Is there anything else we can help you with?'

Jenna was ever the business woman and I had to admire her. It gave me a moment to study Jackson too, without him being aware. I noticed his muscled arms, on show today because of the sunny weather and wondered what exercise he did to keep himself looking so good. His white polo shirt fit him perfectly and I spent a pleasant few minutes imagining the toned chest underneath it.

'I came in to get some flowers for Tom's fiancée,' he admitted. 'Meg's been having a few problems with the wedding arrangements. She's getting all stressed out so I thought some flowers might cheer her up.'

I could have swooned at his feet right there. I hardly ever received flowers and it seemed like he was so thoughtful.

'You're very quiet today,' he said, drawing me out of my daydream. I hadn't even noticed that Jenna had disappeared to put a bouquet together for him.

'I had an early start and I'm out of the habit. And Jenna was doing a fine job of speaking for me anyway.' I rolled my eyes a little and he chuckled by return. 'By the way,' I went on, 'I told Sam and Matt about the competition when we rehearsed yesterday and we've decided to apply for the audition this coming Friday.'

'That's great news, I think you've made the right decision, if you don't mind me saying. Tonight's gig will be a good practice as well.'

Jenna returned then with a delightful bouquet. I could see that Jackson was impressed.

'Will you be there as well tonight, Jenna?' he asked, as she handed him back his change.

'Yes, I'll be there. In fact, I'm bringing the whole family, so we'll see you later.'

He gave me one final glance as he left and if he'd been wearing a hat, I'm pretty sure he would have tipped it at us.

---

I didn't leave the shop till four, hoping that would be enough time for me to get myself over to the pub without being late. After a quick shower, I did my make-up, applying only mascara and a hint of lip-gloss, before getting dressed. For this gig, I'd settled on a dark brown, tiered gypsy skirt made out of a light corduroy and a pale brown scoop necked blouse that tied up at the front. Lastly, my old cowboy boots completed the outfit.

I gave my long chestnut brown hair a quick blast with the hairdryer and let it fall loosely down my back and then popped in some gold hoop earrings and clipped my lucky bracelet around my wrist. Giving myself a final look in the mirror, I went downstairs to run through a quick warm-up with my guitar. It was a little after half past five as I closed the door behind me, guitar case in hand, and set off for the quay for the second time that day.

When I arrived at The Cork and Bottle, to my relief everything was all set up. I went downstairs to the stage area. Following a quick soundcheck with the boys, we were on stage by seven. We'd decided to open with a classic Carpenters' song, 'Superstar', that everyone would know and could sing along to. I tried not to let it bother me that I could only see a handful of people in the audience as I stepped up to the microphone. As the song went on, more and more people came downstairs to listen and by the end, the room was about half full.

I had a quick glance around for Jackson but there was no sign of him. I did spot Jenna with her mum and dad and they all gave me huge smiles, which was reassuring. I sat down at the piano, taking a moment to focus and was soon lost in my next song, Roberta Flack's 'The First Time Ever I Saw Your Face'. One of my favourite songs, it required all my concentration. So I was a bit taken aback when I finished and stood up to find the room full of people, with some even standing on the stairs. I smiled broadly as the applause filled the air. That was when I spotted Jackson, standing in a corner and clapping as enthusiastically as everyone else.

Next, I'd planned to sing one of my own songs. As I glanced at Sam, he winked at me and smiled. I introduced 'Love Me' as a song I'd written and waited for the crowd to settle before playing the intro-duction on my guitar.

*'This is who I am, what you see is what you get,*

*I wear my heart on my sleeve and hope you'll do the same,*
*Accept me with all my faults and don't try to make me change,*
*Just love me, love me, take me as I am, love me...'*

---

When the audience joined in with the chorus, I knew that the song was a success and the deafening applause at the end of the first half confirmed it. I couldn't believe it. I stood and watched with surprise as everyone dashed upstairs to get a drink in the interval, looking like they wanted to be sure not to miss the second half. Sam and Matt came over for a group hug and I found I had tears in my eyes. They offered to brave the scrum upstairs to get us drinks and I turned to the piano to sort out my music for the second half.

'Excuse me...' I looked up into the face of a smiling stranger. 'I loved the first half. You have a great voice.'

'Thank you, that's kind of you to say.' I blushed at my first compliment from a fan.

At that point, I remembered Jackson and looked around to see if I could find him but the room was virtually empty. Perhaps he'd gone upstairs to get a drink too. Sam and Matt reappeared a few moments later with drinks for us and Matt filled me in on the news.

'That guy Jackson's here again, did you see?'

'Yes, I saw him when I was singing.' I feigned nonchalance but I'm not sure if I got away with it.

'He's upstairs now and he said to tell you that you were fantastic. I think he thought he'd see you upstairs. Jenna's up there too with Mum and Dad and they all sent you hugs. They said they'd catch us all at the end.'

Matt was bubbling over with infectious excitement. Sam, on the other hand, was strangely quiet.

At least Jackson hadn't just left then. I saw him come back downstairs shortly afterwards and gave him a quick wave and a smile.

He pulled a funny face then from afar, grimacing and gesturing at the crowd at the same time as if to explain that it was chaos so he would talk to me afterwards.

Jenna and her parents came down a minute later and they all gave us a big thumbs up. I turned to check that the guys were in place, getting a scowl in return from Sam but a quick nod from Matt. I didn't have time to wonder what had upset Sam now but I supposed it would have something to do with Jackson being there. I shrugged and let it go for the time being.

The second half went as well, with us singing 'The Right Kind Of Wrong' by Leann Rimes, followed by 'Breathe' by Faith Hill to a great response from the crowd but it seemed like it was our own material they were waiting for and we didn't disappoint them. Our last song, 'Too Late' was a really new one and I wanted to try it out to see how it sounded.

*'I thought my time had come and gone, baby,*
*And then you just came along,*
*You made me feel special*
*Like no-one else had ever done before,*
*And just when it seemed like it was...*
*Too late, too late, too late for me*
*I found love with you*
*And now there ain't no turning back*
*'Cos I ain't never gonna let you go.'*

Once again, the crowd joined in with the chorus and there was a real buzz in the room. The applause at the end of the song went on for several minutes and then someone shouted 'encore' and we did. People came up and talked to us for so long afterwards, I thought we might never get away! It had been such a great night once again and the adrenaline continued pumping through my veins long after the crowd had dispersed to get drinks before the next band came on.

Jenna threw her arms around me and squeezed me tight by way of congratulations.

'You're an absolute star,' she cried. 'I can honestly say that I have never heard you sing so well.' I stepped back to talk to everyone.

'Wow, thank you and thanks to all of you for coming. It was so wonderful to see you all out there in the audience.'

Jenna's parents echoed her congratulations too before they all left for home. Jenna promised to call me tomorrow, nodding in Jackson's direction before she went. Finally, only Jackson remained and I went over to find out what he'd thought of our set.

'You were incredible tonight! I've never seen a crowd in a bar respond so well to a new band and I'm sorry but I couldn't get anywhere near you, there were so many people! It was wild.' He laughed a deep, rich laugh full of his pleasure at our success.

'Wow, that's really good to hear. I mean, we felt the excitement too but being in the crowd must have been even better. Thank you for coming.'

'Would you mind if I walked you home again?' he asked suddenly.

'I'd love that, thank you,' I replied, my gaze lingering on his deep, brown eyes.

# CHAPTER 5

I was still on such a high as we left the pub and didn't want to go straight home. Jackson must have read my mind because a moment later he suggested going to get a drink somewhere to celebrate the success of the gig.

A few minutes later, we were sat side by side at a table in a new wine bar I'd seen further down the High Street. I could feel the warmth from his thigh resting lightly against mine, making it hard for me to concentrate properly.

'How are you feeling now you've had time to process your brilliant success tonight?' Jackson asked me, putting his glass of fizzy water down on the table.

'It still hasn't sunk in, to be honest. We're just doing our thing and we've been doing it for a while. I can't think what's changed.'

'Have you always performed your own songs?' he asked perceptively, turning to face me. 'I think the crowd really enjoyed them tonight.'

'Yes, we have but not at every gig and maybe, only one song at most. Perhaps that's it, the audience is getting more of a feel for us from our own songs and it seems that they like them.' I smiled warmly at him, raising my eyebrows in amazement at our good fortune. I took a sip from my glass of wine.

'Do you write the songs together as a band or is it only you who does the songwriting?'

'It's mainly me but the guys help with the music sometimes. You seem to like all this stuff, are you musical at all?'

'Me, no!' He laughed out loud at the mere idea. 'No, I don't play anything and you wouldn't want to hear me sing but I do love music, it's true.'

'I happen to think that everyone can sing, even if it's only a little bit. I've heard enough people try in my teaching career to know.'

'That's right. I remember you saying you were a singing teacher.'

'Yep, singing teacher by day, would-be singer/songwriter by night.' I laughed at how crazy it sounded. I moved to brush my hair out of my face, drawing Jackson's attention to my bracelet.

'That's pretty,' he said, reaching out to take my wrist in his hand. He bent his head forward to study the charms, touching one or two of the musical ones with his long, slim fingers. I wanted to tell him about it but I couldn't seem to find my breath. He released me and turned to look deep into my eyes, inviting me to reveal more about myself.

'My mum gave it to me for my 18th birthday and I wear it for luck whenever we play.' I could feel tears beginning to form and I dipped my head, willing them to go away. As if sensing my sadness, Jackson put his arm around me and drew me close to his body. I put my hand to his chest to steady myself and let his clean, masculine smell wash over me. Neither of us spoke for a moment, just enjoying the feeling of holding each other. After a few minutes, I pulled away from him and reached for some wine to calm my beating heart. I heard him clear his throat and glanced over to see him take a long drink too. He had managed to comfort me and set my heart racing all at the same time.

'I guess you'll be preparing for the audition for the "Open Mic" competition on Friday now?' Jackson resumed the conversation.

'I'll have to confirm that tomorrow, if it's not too late. I've been really busy today.'

'I'm sure it'll be okay. Have you any more gigs lined up for me to come to?'

'Matt organises all the bookings. He probably has some plans in mind. Anyway, haven't you had enough of us already?' I teased.

'It's been a pleasure for me to come and hear you sing,' he said, leaning towards me and pressing his thigh more firmly against mine. 'As soon as you have another date scheduled, I hope you'll let me know because I've been enjoying myself going to gigs again. I don't seem to get the time any more.' He moved back again but my heart was pounding at his touch.

'I'm glad you've enjoyed them and I promise to let you know about any new dates.'

We left the bar shortly afterwards and walked down to the quay-side once more, drawn by the sound of the waves and the glowing lights. There were lots of people milling around, chatting and laughing as they enjoyed the warm summer evening. As we reached the water, Jackson took my hand in his, wrapping his fingers around mine and stroking them gently with his thumb. I was aware of how our hands fit perfectly together, as we swung them gently back and forth. We wandered slowly back to the cottage but, once again, we'd reached my garden gate before we knew it.

As we came to a stop, Jackson blurted out, 'Would you be free for dinner tomorrow night? We could celebrate your success with the gig tonight when you're feeling a bit more rested.'

I didn't even need to consider it.

'I'd like that.'

He smiled broadly and took out his phone to exchange numbers.

'Shall I pick you up at seven?'

'That sounds like a good plan,' I agreed.

He took a step towards me and gently leaned in to kiss me on the cheek. His lips barely touched my skin but it was enough to make me want more of the same. Instinctively, I put my hand where his lips had been, as if wanting to keep the kiss there, and the crooked smile he gave me was irresistible.

'Goodnight, see you tomorrow. Sweet dreams,' he called, looking back one last time before I opened the door and went inside. God, I thought, I'd only known him for a short time, but I could no longer deny it: I was in danger of falling for him and it had been a long time since I'd let myself experience feelings like that.

———

There was a knock at the door the next morning. As I opened it, all I could see were flowers in an arrangement so enormous, even the person delivering them was virtually hidden from view. The sweet smell of sunflowers, orange gerberas, creamy chrysanthemums, luscious pink roses and so many more filled the air that I couldn't take them all in.

'Oh my goodness, Mary, are these for me?' I recognised Jenna's assistant from the shop when she poked her head out.

'Yes, and there's a card attached,' she said, grinning. I thanked Mary, told her I was glad she was better and brought the beautiful flowers into the kitchen. I didn't think I had enough vases for all of them. I noticed the card tucked into the middle of the bouquet, pulled it out of the envelope and read the message.

*'Hey, gorgeous. Just to remind you that you rocked last night and I can't wait to see you again later. Until then, Jackson x'*

I almost fainted with delight. I'd never been sent such a romantic message, nor such a fabulous bouquet. I decided to text Jackson there and then to thank him. But how should I phrase it? I didn't want to be too forward but then again, maybe I did!

*'Thank you for the lovely flowers, what a wonderful surprise! Your message has left me speechless, not something that happens to me often. Looking forward to seeing you too, Rachel x'*

Next, I called Jenna.

'I just received the flowers, they're absolutely wonderful.'

'I'm really pleased you like them. When Jackson came in and ordered the bouquet for you this morning, I wanted to make them special because you deserve it.'

'Oh, Jenna, thank you for being such a good friend. I don't know what I would do without you.'

'And what about the message on the card?' she teased me. 'He must really like you. Where are you going for dinner?'

'I don't know, we didn't discuss it.'

'Sounds like Jackson's sweeping you off your feet.'

I laughed. 'I know and it feels great! Would you like me to bring you some lunch in later so you can help me plan a course of action for tonight?'

'That's a brilliant idea. Shall we say twelve thirty?'

'That's another date for today!' We both giggled as we hung up.

---

As soon as I'd put down the phone, I fired off a quick email to Natasha at the competition telling her a bit about our band and confirming that we would like to attend the auditions on Friday. Her reply came back straight away.

*That's great, Rachel. We look forward to seeing you in Bournemouth on Friday. Soundcheck is at half past five and the auditions start at seven. The auditions are not open to the public so I'm afraid you won't be able to bring any guests.'*

I bit my lip as I read through her message. It all sounded very real now and it was too late to even think about changing my mind. Anyway, I wanted the band to take full advantage of this opportunity and, in my heart, I couldn't wait for Friday to come. I decided to ring Sam on his mobile to let him know that it was all booked for Friday and to see if we could fit in a rehearsal before then. It took him quite a while to answer and I wondered where he was.

'Hey, what's up?'

Sam sounded like he was busy working. I felt a bit guilty for disturbing him but I ploughed on.

'I've confirmed that we'd like to attend the auditions on Friday. Could we fit in a rehearsal before then?'

'I'll need to talk to Matt about it as well. Can I call you back?' He didn't sound very pleased about it. My grip tightened on the phone. All at once, I'd had enough of his pettiness over the past few days.

'I won't be here later, I'm going out tonight with Jackson. You don't sound like you're that pleased anyway, so there's no point in you calling me back.'

He sighed. 'Sorry, I can't talk right now but look, you shouldn't get your hopes up about this audition. To be honest, Matt and I are only doing this for you so let's take it easy and see how it goes.' He paused. 'And why are you going out with that Jackson guy?'

'That's none of your business. And if you have nothing positive to say, I'll let you get back to your work.'

I ended the call and threw my phone to the other end of the sofa. Why did he have to say that he and Matt were only doing this for me? Sam's poor attitude made me more appreciative than ever of Jackson's support. At least he was showing an interest.

---

Around midday, I set out for town to see Jenna, eager to get some fresh air to clear away my bad mood after the call with Sam. I walked into the shop twenty minutes later, carrying two huge sandwiches from the deli. We went out to the back room to eat and catch up, leaving Mary in charge of the shop.

'First of all, congratulations again on the gig last night. You guys were fabulous and the crowd loved you,' she began. I nodded, a bit embarrassed by all the praise. Then she went on, 'Secondly, have you decided what to wear tonight?'

'You mean from my vast wardrobe of top fashion designs?' She nodded back at me. 'Well, no, I haven't. It is a bit tricky when I don't know where we're going.'

Just then, my phone buzzed as it received a text. When I looked at it, my eyes widened in surprise.

'It's from Jackson.' I read it out to her.

*'Do you like seafood? If you do, I'm standing outside a great looking place on the High Street. Let me know what you think.'*

'He must be outside Simply Seafood. Quick, let him know,' she said.

*'I love seafood. Are you at Simply Seafood? I'm with Jenna at the moment, if you want to pop in. Otherwise, see you later and thanks.'*

'No kiss then?' Jenna teased, looking over my shoulder.

'Well, he didn't do one either and I don't want to be too flirty.'

'Why the hell not?'

A few minutes later, the doorbell tinkled and I held my breath, wondering if it was him. Jenna poked her head round the corner from the back room to check and then disappeared. When she reappeared, she had Jackson in tow. His huge frame filled the room, leaving little space for anyone else. It meant he had to stand incredibly close to me though, definitely a bonus.

'Thank you again for the lovely bouquet,' I began, looking up into his handsome face. 'That was kind of you. I can't remember the last time someone gave me flowers.'

'I'm especially glad I did then, if it's been so long.' He was close enough to touch but I didn't think it would be right in front of Jenna so I had to satisfy myself with ogling him instead. He paused for a moment before saying to Jenna, 'You know, Meg said she was having a few problems with the flowers for the wedding. Would you mind if I recommended you to her?'

'That would be fantastic, Jackson, thank you. I haven't been going long so all positive feedback is appreciated.' Jenna smiled. 'Here's one of my business cards if you'd like to pass it on and I'll wait to hear from her.'

'I'd best leave you ladies to your lunch and make my way back. I booked the restaurant for half past seven, Rachel, so I'll pick you up at seven. Is that okay?'

'Yes, great, thank you.'

Jackson flashed me another smile before ducking his head to go back to the main shop.

Once he'd gone, I stared at Jenna, hardly able to believe my good luck in meeting him. She stared back for a moment, equally unable to believe that she might soon be planning her first wedding. Then we both squealed in delight before going back to thinking about what I should wear.

'I think you should wear a dress, if you have one. And something that will show off a bit of cleavage too,' she suggested.

I almost choked on my drink.

'I think I have a dress or two but none that I'd like to wear in public!' I sighed. I never had the money for clothes shopping after paying all my bills each month, but I did have a little put aside so maybe I should indulge myself.

'I might go for a wander round the shops on my way back home and see if there's anything that catches my eye.' I fell silent then, wanting to ask her about Sam but not knowing how to go about it.

'What's the matter? Why the miserable face all of a sudden? You must have something to wear.'

'No, it's not about clothes.' I hesitated before taking the plunge. 'Look, tell me if this is awkward but I wanted to ask you about Sam. He's been a bit off with me lately.'

'Go on,' she said, the smile fading from her face.

'I tried asking him about it on Saturday and again on Sunday, but all he said was that he didn't want me to get taken in or hurt by Jackson. I wondered if he might be a bit jealous of Jackson, actually. Then I spoke to him about doing the audition before coming down here to see you and he was blunt about it, saying he'd only gone along with doing it to please me. Do you know what it's all about? I'm obviously missing something.'

'I probably should have told you this before but I didn't know how.' She paused and studied me for a moment. My mouth went dry. 'You're the only person who doesn't realise that Sam has a thing for you. He has had for quite a few years so I'm sure he is jealous of Jackson who's succeeding where he's failed.'

My face paled and I sat down on the nearest stool.

'As for the competition,' she went on, 'you know Sam better than anyone. He's a home-loving kind of guy, he's happy being a carpenter, going where the jobs take him. He's not after fame and fortune.' She looked at me with sadness.

'I wish someone had told me,' I said, 'because I honestly had no idea. I love Sam like a brother and wouldn't want to hurt him for anything but why hasn't he told me this? It's not like he hasn't had plenty of opportunity in the past, before Jackson came along.'

My hands were clammy now with the realisation that I might have made a big mistake with Sam in the past. I wanted to tell Jenna what had happened between us that night but I didn't know how she would take it so I kept quiet.

'I don't know.' She came over to give me a hug. 'Talk to him about his feelings and about the competition. Tell him how much it means to you. That's all you can do.'

# CHAPTER 6

Jackson looked me over as I closed the door behind me, his smile broadening as he took in my outfit.

'Wow, you look stunning.'

I'd been saved in the end by a maxi dress that I'd bought in the sale late last summer. It had a lovely ethnic print, all blues, pinks and greens and an interesting neckline that showed off some cleavage without overdoing it, I hoped.

'You look pretty handsome yourself.'

My eyes wandered greedily over his soft, brown leather jacket, worn over a pale yellow button-down shirt and chinos. He was wearing his cowboy boots again but there was still no sign of a Stetson.

He took my hand and we set off together for town. We walked in silence for a while along the quiet residential street. I was enjoying the reassuring feel of our hands together. When we arrived at the quayside, we stopped to stare at the dazzling array of expensive-looking yachts moored in the harbour. The sun shone down on the still, blue water and there was hardly a cloud in the sky.

'I'm ashamed to say that I know very little about Nashville,' I said, 'apart from the music connection. Are you close to the sea there?'

'We're about eight hours from the sea in most directions,' he explained, 'so not what you'd call close, no. But I like going to the beach and I try to get there quite often. I have a beach house at Charleston, which isn't a long flight away.'

'You have two homes then, one in Nashville and one in Charleston?'

Jackson seemed to hesitate. 'Actually, I have some other homes as well. I prefer not to stay in hotels when I travel.'

'Okay, you have to tell me now,' I said, laughing. 'Exactly how many homes do you have?'

'That's not important,' he fudged. He looked distinctly uncomfortable so I decided not to push it and turned to look out at the sea again.

'That's Brownsea Island over there,' I said, pointing. 'It's a lovely place, full of wildlife and the views are stunning. I spent hours there as a kid but I haven't been for a few years. I ought to go back with my camera some time soon.'

'Maybe you could take me there, show me the sights?'

His arm was leaning against mine and the warmth of his body, through his jacket, caused a tingling sensation deep within me.

'I'd love to do that.'

When we arrived at the restaurant, a waiter led us to our table straight away. Jackson handed his jacket over before sitting down, giving me the chance to admire his arms in his short-sleeved shirt. I looked up to find that he was watching me watching him and smirking at my attention. My cheeks heated a little from being caught in the act so I smiled quickly before looking down at the menu. I chose clams followed by sea bass and Jackson went for the local oysters and plaice. While waiting for the starters, I decided to try and find out a bit more about him.

'Do you mind me asking how old you are?' I began.

'Not at all,' he said easily. 'I'll be thirty this October. How about you?'

'I turned twenty-six this March. And what do you do for a living?' I went on.

He debated for a moment before admitting, 'I'm in the music business actually, like you.'

'Ah, now I see why you know so much, but I'm hardly in the music business. I'm a singer/songwriter destined to play pub gigs for the next few years until I give up and sink into oblivion.'

I looked up at Jackson to find him frowning at me.

'What's the matter?'

His jaw clenched. 'How can you even joke that you're going to give up when you're so talented? If you do this audition, you stand a good chance of getting through to the regional final too and maybe even winning,' he argued.

'Thank you for your confidence in me but you don't know any more than I do whether I can make a go of it, do you, to be fair?'

He paused, took a deep breath and said, 'When I said I'm in the music business, I actually own an independent record label in Nashville and I've managed to sign some of the most up-and-coming artists to the label over these past few years.' He stopped to let this information sink in. I wasn't sure if he'd intended to give that much away because he was looking down at his lap now.

'And your record label has made you rich, right? So rich that you have several homes?'

'Yep,' he answered looking down at his lap again.

'And so, is your interest in me purely business-related? Is that why you're wining and dining me and encouraging us to enter the competition?' I suddenly felt very naive and worried that I'd misunderstood what was developing between us.

His head snapped back up at that criticism.

'I would like to get to know you better. But it so happens that you're a great singer/songwriter and I own a record label. Those two things could be mutually beneficial, yes.'

He stopped talking when our starters were brought to the table.

'Let's toast then to mutually beneficial relationships.' I raised my glass by way of apology. We talked about our love of food as we ate our starters, sharing tastes of each other's meals and steered clear of the serious topics we'd strayed into.

Once our main courses had arrived, Jackson tried again with a more meaningful conversation.

'I'm serious about you being talented, you know. Your own songs were really moving. They sound like they're based on personal experience, which is what country music's all about of course. So, are they, you know, based on your own experience?'

'Well, my childhood wasn't great in many ways. My dad used to drink a lot and finally, after years of putting up with it, my mum had had enough and they split up when I was fourteen. But my dad carried on drinking and eventually his body couldn't take it any more. He was only fifty when he died. I still can't understand how he could do that to himself.' I paused to consider the futility of it all. 'My mum died a year later from cancer. She knew she had it but had kept it secret from me because of what had happened to my dad. That was about four years ago but I still miss them both such a lot.'

Tears were in my eyes as I finished telling him about my family. He reached out and took my hand. I looked up at him and saw him swallow, as if my story had touched him deeply.

'And of course, I've been incredibly unlucky in love. I'm doing what I want now, no men involved,' I went on jokingly to try and change the atmosphere.

'Maybe you haven't met the right person yet,' he offered, gazing into my eyes.

'Maybe you're right. I'm a glass half-full kind of girl so I'm ever hopeful that I'll find someone I can trust.' I paused for a moment to collect myself. 'How about you? Have you been over to the UK before?'

'Yes, my mom and Tom's are sisters. We used to see each other all the time when we were little. My sister, Shelby and I spent the first few years of our lives in Bournemouth. Then when I was seven and she was three, we upped and moved to Tennessee, which was where my mom met my step-dad and we've been there ever since. But I've kept in touch with Tom over the years.'

'Wow, what made your mum move to Tennessee from Bournemouth? That's quite a leap.'

'After my dad left, things were quite bad for us. It was a constant struggle for my mom, trying to bring up two young kids on her own. When one of her cousins in the States suggested she come out to give life over there a try, I think she jumped at the chance of a fresh start.'

'What about your real dad? Have you kept in touch with him?' I asked.

'He disappeared one day, the year I turned five and never came back and I haven't seen him since. My memories of him are vague now. I've always seen Bob, my step-dad, as my real dad.'

'Have you any brothers or sisters from your mum's marriage to Bob?'

'Hell, yeah,' he laughed. 'Two brothers and two sisters. They're all quite a handful and I'm the eldest so I'm expected to be the role model, which doesn't always work out, you know.'

He winked at me then, giving me a warm feeling right at the pit of my stomach.

The waiter asked whether we would like dessert. I wasn't bothered so Jackson asked for the bill while I went off to the toilet.

I stared at myself in the mirror, wondering what on earth he could see in me now I knew his background. Our lives were very different and he would be going soon anyway. I told myself to try and enjoy it while it lasted and not to think too much about the future.

When I returned to the table, Jackson had paid the bill and I decided not to argue and thanked him as graciously as I could.

On our leisurely walk back to my cottage, I asked, 'When is Tom's wedding?'

'It's a little over two weeks away. Have you been invited?'

'Goodness, no. I don't know either of them that well.'

'Would you like to come as my date?'

I was stunned. 'I'd love that. Thank you.'

He stopped and turned towards me then but didn't say anything. Turning to face him, I looked up at him expectantly, hoping that he would kiss me because I was too shy to be the one to make the first move.

As I looked into his dark eyes, he leaned towards me, tilting his head to one side. My heart beat a little quicker in anticipation of a kiss and suddenly his warm lips were on mine, brushing them gently at first. His kiss was so inviting that I responded naturally, moving closer, taking in his wonderful manly scent. I was very aware of his hands, one resting on my hip, the other clasping the base of my neck. I slipped my arms around his waist and the kiss deepened. He traced my lips with his tongue and when I opened my mouth a little, he took the hint and started to explore further.

I closed my eyes and a moan of pleasure escaped me. He groaned too, pulling me closer. The stubble on his cheek tickled my face and I wondered what it would feel like if he was kissing other parts of my body. My face burned at the thought of it.

Perhaps sensing my increased passion, Jackson chose that moment to pull back. 'Rachel?' he said huskily.

As he stepped away, I opened my eyes, shivering from the loss of his warmth. I knew that I had never been kissed like that before. Nick, my ex-fiancé, had never managed to awaken such strong feelings in me and that realisation was both frightening and exciting.

I could see the desire in Jackson's eyes and knew that it was reflected in mine.

There was no hesitation in my heart when I asked him, 'Would you like a coffee before you go?'

He nodded, his gaze intense on my face.

When I brought out the drinks, we sat together on my cushioned bench in the back garden. I decided then to be bold and ask him about his love life.

'Do you have a girlfriend back home that I should know about?'

'I wouldn't be here with you if I did,' he said immediately. 'I was in a relationship with someone until a year ago; in fact, we were also engaged but she cheated on me.'

'I'm so sorry.'

'It has been hard for me to get over, I have to admit. You're the first person I've kissed in all that time.'

I was surprised by this confession and didn't know what to say.

'How about you, Rachel? Are you seeing anyone?'

'No, I haven't dated for a long time. I have to say, I'm a bit out of practice.'

He was silent for a moment, as though considering that information. Then he put his arm around me and pulled me against him.

'Thank you for a wonderful evening, I've really enjoyed it,' he murmured and kissed me again briefly on the lips. I had the feeling he was deliberately trying to restrain himself.

A few moments later, he stood up, drawing me up with him. We said goodnight but as I watched Jackson raise a hand in farewell and walk away down the street, I found myself wishing he had chosen to stay.

# CHAPTER 7

I'd booked a taxi late Friday afternoon for the short ride to Bournemouth International Centre where the "Open Mic" audition was taking place. The driver dropped me off at the designated entrance for performers, much less fancy than it sounded, and I went inside to look for Sam and Matt who had come in the van with all the gear.

I checked in with a woman at the registration desk and she directed me towards one of the smaller conference rooms, where I found the guys waiting for me. I was starting to feel a bit daunted by the sight of so many other acts rushing around trying to get ready for their performance tonight, so seeing Sam and Matt calmed me down and I greeted them both with a big smile.

They led the way into a soulless conference room, which was not what I was expecting, and my initial excitement faded a little. It was a medium-sized square room with a stage rigged up at one end and some tables and chairs for the judges at the other. The sides of the room were taken up with cheap-looking tables and chairs, next to bright orange curtains and separated by an overly patterned carpet. I would have to exercise amazing willpower to stop myself being distracted by all the overwhelming colour in the room.

We'd carried out our soundcheck by six o'clock, giving us time to grab something to eat. We went out to have a look around the venue and found a little café but I could only manage a coffee because of my nerves.

'How are you both feeling about the audition?' I asked once we'd found a table. They both seemed much more relaxed than I was.

'We had a great rehearsal yesterday and the setlist we've planned is just right for the audition,' Sam replied, with a small shrug.

'I've got some good news for us too,' Matt broke in. 'I had a text today from that new wine bar we signed up with. They heard about our success at The Cork and Bottle the other night and they want us to play there tomorrow night. I know it's short notice but it means that word is spreading about us.'

'Wow! That's amazing. I'm definitely up for it if you two are?' They both nodded.

'I am up for it,' said Matt, 'but Natalie's not that impressed by all these extra rehearsals and shows we're doing at the moment.' He sighed.

I frowned, thinking about Natalie but I didn't say anything, knowing that only he could deal with that problem. Everyone fell silent and I found myself wishing that Jackson was there to boost my confidence. He'd sent me a text earlier in the day to wish me luck but I would have loved him to be there with me. Thankfully, we had to be back by half past six so it wasn't long before we were in the hall outside the conference room again, getting ready to audition.

When we arrived, we found a woman from the competition organising performers with military precision. We checked with her when we were due to perform. We were act number six and as each act had to limit their performance to two minutes, we didn't have long to wait. My stomach churned at the prospect of performing in front of these industry judges and I wished that I could hear some of the acts to give me an idea of what we were up against. Instead, all I could hear was the sound of my own heartbeat thumping furiously as I became more and more apprehensive.

Our turn came round soon enough and once I was in the room walking towards the stage where my trusted guitar waited patiently for me, my spirits lifted. It took only a few minutes for each of us to get into place and when I raised my eyes in the judges' direction, I found them ready for us. I coughed nervously before introducing the band.

'Can you tell us a little bit about your experience please?' one of the male judges asked me.

'I'm Rachel and I write the songs for the most part and I sing, play guitar and play the piano as well. Sam's on guitar and Matt plays the drums. We've been playing pubs in the local area for about the last four years.'

'Great, Rachel, thanks. What are you going to play for us today?' asked the only female judge. I didn't know any of the three judges.

'We're going to play a new song I wrote recently, called "Too Late",' I replied.

'When you're ready, then, guys. Give it your best shot,' said the remaining judge.

This was it then. No turning back if Three's Company wanted to get through to the regional final and definitely everything to gain by giving it our all. I took a deep breath and began to play my guitar. For the next two minutes, we gave our performance everything we had and the judges looked like they were really getting into it from the positive-looking glances they exchanged. All too soon, we'd finished and were making our way out again. We found a table outside and collapsed into the chairs, relieved that it was all over.

'How do you think it went?' I asked, looking at Sam and then Matt for confirmation.

'I don't think we could have done a better performance than that,' Matt replied. 'If we don't get through, it's not because we're not talented. It will only be because other acts are better than us and to be honest, tonight, we were at our peak.'

'It's great to hear you say all that, thank you.' I looked at Sam to find him nodding in agreement and my heart soared. I reached out to take their hands and give them both a squeeze.

During the interval, we removed our gear from the stage to make way for the performers in the second half, and the guys began loading it into the van. I checked with one of the organisers that we were free to leave and was told we'd be informed by email of how we'd done. Now all we had to do was get through to Monday.

In the van on the way home, Sam took hold of my hand. I didn't pull away, even though I knew I should because my hand seemed to belong in his. He hadn't said anything to me about having feelings for me but that small act spoke volumes. We needed to talk about it, to clear the air but how to do that without ruining our friendship?

'Will you come in for a quick coffee?' I asked, as Matt drew the van up outside the cottage. Matt glanced nervously at his watch but followed me and Sam inside anyway.

While the kettle was boiling, I came straight to the point.

'I need to talk to you both about the "Open Mic" competition now that we've done the audition. You both know, I think, how much it means to me to pursue this and I know that neither of you wants it like I do. I don't want to push you to do something you don't want to do so I need you both to be honest with me please about what we'll do if we get through the audition.'

I stared at them both, squashed side by side on my tiny sofa. They looked awkward and didn't say anything. I made the coffees and when I returned, Matt spoke up.

'Look, Rachel, we do know how much it means to you but take me, for example, I have different priorities. I'm married with a young baby, I can't be gallivanting off to do shows all over the place. I'm worried that if we get through the audition, it's going to get serious and I didn't sign up for any of that. I just wanted to have a bit of fun, playing my drums and doing the occasional gig. I'm sorry.'

'And how about you, Sam? You said that you only agreed to do this to please me so do you feel the same as Matt?' I asked.

'I suppose I do, yes,' he said quietly. 'I know I'm not married but I want a quiet life, you know. I like gigging for fun but not for anything more serious, I'm sorry if I didn't make that clear before.'

They both looked sorry for themselves. I went out into the garden to think about what they'd said.

'Rachel, I'm sorry, I have to get back. I'll see you tomorrow at the gig.'

I didn't turn to look at Matt, I just nodded and said goodbye. I sensed Sam come up behind me and put his arm around my shoulder. I turned my face towards him, unable to stop tears from springing to my eyes. He lifted his hand and gently wiped my tears away with his thumb, only making me cry more. He wrapped his arms around me and I fell into his embrace gratefully. We stood silently together for a few moments, neither of us daring to speak. Finally, I stepped back and wiped my eyes again.

'You know this is my dream and this is probably my last chance to try and make it happen.' He nodded at me. 'That's why I want us to make the most of this competition. Perhaps we should wait and see what happens about the audition because if we don't get through, none of this matters anyway.'

'Let's do that and see where we are afterwards,' he agreed. He smiled tentatively but both of us knew that we were putting off another difficult conversation later on. I waited for him to say something to me about his feelings but to my disappointment, he said nothing, leaving shortly afterwards. What was he so afraid of?

# CHAPTER 8

After a restless night, I settled on the sofa with my guitar and started playing a few favourite songs. I moved on to a more poignant one of my own, closed my eyes and let myself become drawn into the music. All of a sudden, the sound of someone knocking at my front door startled me out of my reverie. I opened the door to see Jackson standing there, looking absolutely gorgeous in black jeans and a grey t-shirt, his wavy hair still damp from the shower.

'Jackson, hi!'

'Did I wake you up? If I did, I'm sorry.' He grinned at me but I couldn't understand what he meant at first.

Then it hit me, I was still wearing my pyjamas. Never had my camisole top and pyjama shorts seemed so revealing. My face grew suddenly hot.

'Oh my goodness, no!' I exclaimed. 'Look, come in. I'll go and get changed.' I ran upstairs as gracefully as I could, leaving him to fend for himself for a moment, and changed into some yoga pants and a more appropriate t-shirt. I pulled my hair into a ponytail and took a few calming deep breaths before going back downstairs again.

'Sorry about that,' I said when I walked back into the lounge. 'I was busy singing and time slipped away from me.' I risked a little glance at him and found him smiling reassuringly at me. 'Would you like a drink?' I asked.

When he said no, I sat down in the armchair opposite him and tucked my bare feet up underneath me.

'How did the audition go yesterday?' he asked me, giving me one of his breathtaking smiles and a glimpse of his perfect white teeth.

'It went really well. We all agreed that it was one of our best performances.'

'Do you know when you'll find out whether you got through?'

'They said they'll email us on Monday so I need to keep myself busy till then. The gig at the wine bar tonight will help with that.'

'Is that a gig you haven't told me about?' He raised his eyebrows in query and I realised I hadn't had the chance to tell him the good news about the wine bar coming to us and asking us to play, rather than the other way round.

'I hate to say I told you so,' he said, 'but it was only a matter of time before this started happening. You guys are so good that word was bound to spread quickly round town. What time is the gig tonight?'

'We're on first at eight but I'll be getting there early, as always for the soundcheck. Will you be able to come?'

'Of course, I wouldn't want to miss another chance to hear you sing.'

He stood up then and so did I, finding myself standing very close to him. The heat radiated from his body and I looked up at him, staring into his dark brown eyes, not quite knowing what was going to happen next. My body seemed to have already made up its mind, as I leaned involuntarily towards him. He reached out to steady me, placing his hands on my waist, and bent his head to whisper in my ear.

'Just so you know, I definitely preferred your pyjamas.' I could feel his smile as his lips kissed their way slowly down my neck and my knees almost gave way at his sensual exploration of my skin. He held on tight to me and as I buried my fingers deep in his hair, pulling him even closer to me, I heard him sigh with pleasure. When the kiss came at last, the softness of his lips was intoxicating and as our tongues met, the desire I was feeling intensified further. I laid my hands against his chest, enjoying the feel of his firm muscles under his shirt and his heady, male scent. Just as I was imagining what his skin would feel like if his shirt wasn't there, he broke away and we both inhaled deeply. His pupils were dilated and I guessed mine looked the same. I stared into his seductive brown eyes and waited to hear what he would say next. Instead, he took my hand and led me upstairs where my bedroom beckoned.

At the top of the stairs, Jackson moved to one side to let me lead the way. Once inside the room, I turned to face him, desperate for reassurance that we were doing the right thing.

'Jackson, I...'

He put his finger on my lips. 'Shh. Do you want this?' I nodded and suddenly his lips crushed mine in another deep kiss. His passionate embrace was all I needed to confirm that he wanted me as much as I wanted him. His fingers slipped underneath my t-shirt and his warm hands against my skin made me tremble with anticipation. I began to pull his t-shirt out from his jeans but he saved me the job by pulling it out himself and then over his head in one swift movement.

I stared at him, my breath trapped by the sight of his now bare chest covered with a sprinkling of dark, curly hair. I moved closer to him again, raising my hand to trace the muscles I'd felt there earlier and then placed a soft kiss right in the middle of his chest. A low rumble in his chest told me how much he liked it. In that moment, I knew I wanted to feel his body against mine and I couldn't wait any longer. As that thought went through my mind, he reached out to remove my top and then we rushed through our remaining clothes, both of us eager for the same sensation of skin on skin.

'You are so beautiful,' he whispered, gazing at me with what looked like admiration. He held out his hand towards me and as we lay down together on the bed, our bodies entwined and our lips joined once again. In that moment, I knew I had never wanted to make love with anyone before as much as I wanted to with him right now. His fingers and lips ignited my body with their every touch and my back arched towards him so it wasn't long before our two bodies became one. We set up a slow, sensuous rhythm between us then, caressing each other inside and out, until we both reached the brink of our release and when that moment finally came, the sweetness of it brought tears to my eyes.

We lay side by side afterwards, both of us quiet. When I looked up, Jackson was watching me as though he could read my thoughts.

'How are you feeling? No regrets, I hope?' he asked.

'Being with you was everything I'd hoped it would be and more,' I replied, taking his hand and bringing it to my lips.

'That's how I felt too.'

I smiled to myself as I remembered our lovemaking, knowing I had never felt such deep emotion with anyone else.

---

As much as I would have loved to spend the rest of the day in bed with Jackson, I had a gig to play. I had no memory from my earlier trip to the wine bar with him, of any area that could be used as a stage for bands to play on so I didn't quite know what to expect when I turned up later that afternoon. The guy behind the bar pointed me towards the back where Sam and Matt were already setting up. I could see that there was a raised area for us to play on and a small, intimate space with some tables and chairs around it. This looked good and the customers in a wine bar would be a slightly different group than we'd experienced this far.

'This is nice, isn't it?' I said in welcome, waving my hand around.

'Yeah, it's a bit different to what we're used to. The crowd will be as well, I expect.' Sam grinned at me.

I returned it a bit awkwardly, worrying that he would be able to see that I was still buzzing after making love with Jackson only a short time ago. I felt sure I must be giving off some sign about what I'd been up to but, if I was, neither Sam nor Matt seemed to notice. I carried on as normal, giving them a hand with bringing the rest of the gear in from the van and we performed a quick soundcheck before going off to get something to eat.

When we returned, the wine bar was filling up nicely and people were beginning to settle in around the stage area. By eight o'clock, every table was taken and the audience was buzzing. I couldn't see Jackson anywhere but I knew he would slip in unnoticed by the crowd. It had only been a couple of hours since I'd left him but I longed to see him again.

I'd chosen a Dolly Parton song to start with, 'Here You Come Again', knowing it would be a good choice for our usual crowd. What I wasn't sure of was how well the song would go down in this new setting and a flicker of doubt crossed my mind. As I sat down at the piano, I concentrated on putting all my energy into it, emphasising some of the funnier lines from the song and hoping that they'd respond. I reached the end and pushed back from the microphone, scanning the room to gauge the audience reaction. I was disappointed to see that a lot of people weren't even looking our way and we received only a polite ripple of applause. It could have been because we were only the support band but, instinctively, I knew that wasn't the reason.

I looked quickly at Sam and Matt to see what they were thinking. They both gave me tight smiles in response, which I took to mean that they felt as worried as I did about the seeming lack of interest. Nevertheless, I ploughed on, ever the professional, sitting down at the front of the stage with my guitar this time and strumming the opening chords of Eva Cassidy's version of 'Fields of Gold'. As I began to sing, I spotted Jackson standing up at the back with a grim look on his face. He must have been there for the last song as well and heard the medi-ocre reaction. His presence was reassuring though and when he caught my glance he gave me a crooked smile and my heart skipped a beat.

This song was probably more familiar to the audience and I noticed that people were beginning to pay attention to us now. At the end, the applause was stronger, which gave me renewed enthusiasm for singing one of my own songs. As this gig had come up at such short notice, we'd decided to play it safe and stick to songs we knew well so the first of my own songs was 'My Turn'. It meant such a lot to me and regardless of their response to it, I was determined to sing my heart out, putting all the emotion I had into every word and note. I knew I'd done it justice but would they feel the same? Luckily, our own material did the trick again and the crowd seemed more interested in us afterwards. The applause was better, with a few people standing up to encourage us further. We broke for the interval feeling a lot more confident than we had at the beginning.

Jackson came over to talk to us, giving me a soft kiss as he arrived, and I sensed Sam stiffen beside me. God, I'd had enough of that but now was not the time to mention it.

'How do you feel after the first half guys?' He looked concerned.

'I'll go and get some drinks,' Sam interrupted, 'and see if I can find Jenna.'

'She couldn't make it,' I told him. 'I'd love a drink though. Why don't you go with him, Matt?' I suggested so that I could talk to Jackson on my own. He turned to watch them go.

'Is it me or is there some tension here?' he asked, taking my hand.

'Let's not go there right now.' I sighed. 'What did you think about the first half?'

'What you did was great, as good as in your last two shows. It's just that this audience is a bit more sophisticated, I think, and they want to hear your material, they don't want covers. What are you planning for the second half?'

'Two more covers and one of my own songs.'

'Would you be up to doing one cover and two of your own songs?'

'I'd need to agree it with the guys but I'm pretty sure that would be all right.'

After a quick check with Sam and Matt, it was decided to give

Jackson's suggestion a try, although Sam didn't look all that pleased about it. There wasn't time to debate it so I started the second half with one of my favourite recent songs, 'All your Life', by The Band Perry which I hoped was a bit more up to date for this audience. It was a good choice because they looked more animated and some people were even singing along. That was a real confidence booster for me and I'm sure for the boys too. I glanced over at Jackson and he was smiling encouragingly back at me.

I went on to introduce 'Too Late' and all at once, there was a new air of anticipation in the room as they waited to hear what this next song of ours would be like. It had gone down so well on its first outing that I was hopeful of it being as popular here. Jackson nodded at me as if approving my choice. I had the feeling he liked this one himself, professionally and personally. I was pretty proud of it too and I belted it out with as much passion as I could muster. The crowd joined in and at the end, the applause made it clear how much they'd enjoyed it. Lots of people stood up and the clapping went on for several minutes. There were lots of cries for 'more' and we were happy to oblige.

We finished the set with 'Love Me', a completely different song but judging by the crowd's reception, another great success. By the end, we had turned things around and there was no doubt that Jackson had given us some good advice. As soon as we'd taken our applause and I'd spoken to a few members of the audience, I made my way over to him.

'You did a fabulous job in the second half there. You really had them on side.'

'Thanks but it was your advice that made the difference, you know.'

'Your own material is so good that you should be singing more of that now than the covers you've been doing, I think, if you don't mind me giving you my opinion.'

'Of course I don't mind, you know your stuff and I appreciate your help.'

'Can I walk you home again, if that's not getting old?' he asked.

I leaned towards him for a kiss and he responded, dipping his head to meet my lips. It was only a second though before he was wrenched away from me. I looked up in surprise, unsure of what had happened, only to find Sam standing there with a very moody look on his face. He was holding on to Jackson's arm until Jackson pulled out of his grasp and came to stand by my side.

'What the hell is going on?' I demanded.

'I might ask you the same thing,' Sam spat back at me. 'What are you doing kissing this guy you barely know?'

He took a step towards Jackson again and I instinctively stepped between them, uncertain of what Sam was about to do. Matt came forward then too, perhaps sensing the danger in the air, and he pulled Sam back but Sam's eyes never left mine. The hard look in his eyes was unsettling and I wanted him to go because his attitude had already started to get on my nerves tonight and now he had made things even worse.

'Sam, please, don't be like this,' I pleaded with him.

Abruptly, he turned on his heel and walked off with Matt trailing behind him. We'd managed to postpone talking about our relationship up to this point but I knew we couldn't leave it much longer if we were to salvage anything from our friendship, and I had the feeling that I needed to put him straight about a few things sooner rather than later.

---

Once we were outside, with Jackson holding my guitar again, I broached the subject of Sam with him as we started the walk home.

'I'm really sorry about Sam's behaviour towards you tonight. He was rude and aggressive. I've never seen him like that and it's unforgivable.'

'Don't you worry about it, it's not your fault.'

'He's worried about me, that's all, we've known each other a long time and he doesn't want me to get hurt again.'

He stopped then, touching my arm so that he could look me in the eye. As I turned to face him, I was a bit wary about what he was going to say next but I'd brought the subject up so now I'd have to deal with it.

'Does he have feelings for you? Have you two ever dated?'

'No...no,' I stuttered, wondering whether to tell him the rest. I pressed on. 'We've never dated but Jenna told me recently that Sam has had feelings for me for a while. Apparently, I'm the only person he hasn't told about that fact,' I said, closing my eyes briefly to hide my irritation.

'And how do you feel about him?' Jackson wasn't giving up easily.

I started walking again while I considered what to say. I didn't have the courage to tell him that we'd slept together after a drunken night when things had escalated beyond our control and, besides, I hadn't even talked about that night with Sam yet.

'He's been like a brother to me all my life, I know that sounds clichéd but it's true, so I care for him very much.'

I was being economical with the truth, I knew but I couldn't tell him everything that had happened between me and Sam in the past. I risked a peek at Jackson to see how he was taking all this. He looked pensive. We were almost back home by this point.

'I'm not stepping on any toes then by getting to know you better?' He looked pointedly at me, giving me the chance to explain but I shook my head, saying nothing. 'Okay, this is how I feel,' he continued. 'I know you and I come from completely different lives but we shouldn't let that get in the way of us getting to know each other better. We don't know where this might go between us but I think we could enjoy finding out, don't you?'

'I do think that but what will happen when you have to go home?'

'I hear what you're saying and obviously I don't want either of us to get hurt but we won't know if we don't try. And there's always a risk in opening up your heart to someone new. Why don't we try and take it one step at a time and enjoy ourselves along the way?'

I nodded but that worry still lingered in my mind, even though I said nothing more about it. I'd also kept the full extent of my relationship with Sam a secret from Jackson and I knew I'd have to face up to that before too long.

'Are you going to church again tomorrow?' he asked me, as we arrived at my front door.

'No, not tomorrow, I don't go every week. I'm having Sunday lunch with Jenna's family in the afternoon again, so I won't get back till later in the evening.' On an impulse, I made a new suggestion. 'Would you like to spend the day sightseeing on Monday? We could take a picnic and go over to Brownsea Island, if you'd like.'

'That sounds like a great way to spend the day. But right now, I'm thinking about how we're going to spend the rest of tonight.' His voice was husky behind me and I turned round with a gasp. The playful grin was back on his face and I couldn't get the door open quickly enough.

# CHAPTER 9

After a tense lunch at Jenna's house the day before, I was looking forward to spending today with Jackson and getting away from things for a while. Going out would also help take my mind off the audition results which should be coming through some time today. The start of the new week was a bit misty but it was meant to be another sunny day later on.

Jackson picked me up right on nine o'clock as we'd agreed in a quick chat the night before, and hoisted the bag I'd packed for our picnic easily up on to his shoulder for the walk down to the quay. I'd made sure to take my camera with me this time, in the hope of spotting a red squirrel at some point during the day. We stopped for some breakfast on the quay, by which time the weather was already brightening up.

'How was lunch at Jenna's house yesterday?' Jackson asked once we'd got settled at a table.

'Not very good actually.' I frowned as I remembered the strained atmosphere from the day before.

He raised his eyebrows, inviting me to tell him more.

'Well, Sam had apparently been called out on an emergency job so he wasn't even there and Matt's wife, Natalie, decided to have a go at me about the amount of time Matt was away from home at the moment because of all the extra rehearsals.' I sighed heavily, wondering what I had done to deserve all this trouble lately. Jackson winced in response and then reached across the table to take my hand.

'It's a good thing we're going out for the day today then, isn't it?' He smiled and gave my hand a little squeeze. 'Aren't you supposed to hear about the results of the audition as well today?'

I nodded as I swallowed a sip of coffee.

'I don't want it to take over the day. Let's forget it and focus on having a good time.'

We bought our return tickets at the kiosk on the quayside and waited for the ferry to be ready. Soon we were on our way across the harbour towards the island, the wind blowing gently in our hair. I looked across at Jackson to find him taking in the view. His handsome face was even more striking in profile and I noticed a fine stubble growing over his jaw which was especially inviting. He turned then, saw me studying him and leaned towards me for a kiss, pulling me gently towards him at the same time. With his arm round my waist and the warmth of his body next to mine, I decided that this had the makings of a perfect day.

It was only a short journey across to the island and once we'd paid our entrance fee we headed into the woods to walk across. It was only a twenty-minute walk from one side to the other but we stopped so many times along the way to look at the church, the wildlife, the lily pond, the trees, taking photos all the while, that it was almost midday when we reached the beach on the far side. We sat down to admire the view from the island back towards the town and to look at the photos I'd taken.

'This is a beautiful island,' Jackson said. 'The views are fantastic and it was wonderful to see the wildlife in the woods.'

'I'm still hopeful about seeing a red squirrel on the way back too.'

We were so hungry after our walk that we started our lunch early, tucking into the hearty picnic I'd prepared. Afterwards, I lay down on the grass to stare at the crystal blue sky and Jackson followed suit. As I lay there, I summoned up the courage to ask him the one question I didn't want to know the answer to but would have to ask anyway.

'Jackson?' I started tentatively without looking at him.

'Mm-hmmm?' he replied. I could sense that he had turned his face to look at mine.

'When are you flying back to Nashville?' I bit my lip waiting for his reply.

'On the 26th August, just after the wedding,' he said, turning on to his side and propping himself up on his elbow to see my reaction. My face fell, even though I knew it was inevitable that he would be going back. 'Let's enjoy today and not worry too far ahead as we agreed.'

He kissed me softly, stroking my hair away from my face, then lay back down without saying anything more. I knew I was starting to like him and I thought he felt the same, even after a few days, but neither of us knew what we could do about the future. His life was in Nashville and mine was here and not only that but our lives were poles apart. Jackson took my hand and squeezed it and I tried hard not to let this new information spoil the day.

When we set off again, we followed the coastal path around the south of the island, made famous by Lord Baden-Powell, and stopped to look at the monument and read the inscription. I glanced up in the stillness after I'd finished reading and found myself looking straight at a red squirrel in a nearby tree. I got my camera ready as quickly as I could and snapped off a few shots before it disappeared. Jackson looked up as I finished, completely oblivious to the squirrel's presence. I showed him the photos as proof and he pulled a funny face.

'Oh boy, I wish I'd seen that,' he said. I laughed at his face but he shrugged it off.

We were wandering back towards the ferry when Jackson asked me about my plans for my singing.

'What do you want to do with your singing? You know, let's say you guys get through the audition, win the regionals and go on to the national final. What would you like to happen next?' It was very reassuring to see that he took me seriously.

I waited a moment or two before answering and then sighed as I said, 'In my dreams, I'd like to make a go of it as a singer and songwriter because I've wasted too much time thinking I couldn't do it, that I wasn't good enough. If we get through to the final, I am going to give it everything I have.' I paused, knowing that I ought to tell him the rest. 'The thing is, Sam and Matt don't feel the same way as I do about the competition, they made that clear to me the other day.' I looked up to see Jackson's feelings about it but his face was passive, taking it all in.

'What have you decided to do?' he asked at last.

'We agreed to wait and see whether we get through to the regional final first. If we don't, none of it matters anyway but if we do, we'll have another difficult conversation to deal with.'

'Have you checked your phone to see if you've had a message yet?' he went on.

'No, I'm out with you so I haven't checked my phone.' I rolled my eyes at him but he persisted.

'You know you want to and I don't mind at all. Go on, have a look.'

I tutted at him before removing my phone from my bag and switching it on. It took a minute for it to catch up with the texts and emails received but my eyes were drawn at once to the email symbol and the number next to it. I gave it a tap to see what was there. What I read next took my breath away. 'We got through!' I cried, looking up at Jackson to see his response.

'That's fabulous, well done, I knew you'd do it,' he replied, lifting me off my feet and swinging me round in the air. As he set me down, he gave me one of his best smiles. 'When is the regional final?' he asked as I quickly sent off texts to Sam and Matt, promising to call them later.

'It's on Friday at the same place.' I could hardly keep still, I was so excited at the news.

Jackson paused for a moment before saying, 'Listen, I have to go to London on business for a few days tomorrow but I'll be back on Friday so I won't miss the regional final, that is if you'd like me to come?'

'Of course I would.' Even so, my smile faded at the thought of him going away, which I tried to hide but didn't quite succeed. I knew I would miss him but I had to admit to myself that it might allow me to get my head around all that had been happening and to try and regain a sense of normality.

We made our way back to the ferry shortly afterwards. I was still reeling from the good news as we set off for home. I couldn't stop smiling and even though we didn't speak much, I knew Jackson was pleased for me too.

'Would you like to come in for a drink?' I asked once we returned to the cottage, flashing him what I hoped was a persuasive smile.

'Sure, a cold drink would be nice.'

We went on through to the kitchen where I made two drinks and took them outside to the garden.

'What will you be doing in London?' I asked, handing him his drink and sitting next to him on the garden bench.

'I'll have a couple of face to face meetings with some of my music partners over here. It will make a change from always having to deal with them over the phone. I have a couple of potential new artists in the pipeline as well so I need to meet with their managers too. And then there'll be dinners so I'll be kept quite busy.' He took a sip of his drink and stared at me expectantly, sensing that I had more questions.

'Do you have somewhere to stay in London? I mean, one of your homes?' I tried to ask as if it was the most natural thing in the world to me to have lots of homes.

'No, I don't have a home in the UK. I'll have to slum it and stay at a luxury hotel instead.' He grinned disarmingly and my stomach performed a little somersault.

He moved up closer to me then and put his arm around me, pushing my hair gently over my shoulder.

'How about you? What will you get up to without me to keep you occupied?' he asked softly, eyes glittering.

I swallowed before whispering, 'I think I'm really going to miss you actually, it will be hard not spending time together.' He was still gazing at me with his dark brown eyes and listening carefully to what I was saying. 'Have I said too much?' I asked when he didn't reply.

He kissed me lightly on my bare shoulder, sending a ripple of desire right through my body. I put my arms round his neck and drew him in closer so our lips and tongues could meet in a fiery embrace. When we paused, his eyes were smouldering and I felt flustered by the depth of my feelings.

'Rachel, I'm feeling the same connection between us that I think you are and I've enjoyed this time with you, more than you can realise. I'll miss you too but I'll be back before you know it, you know. I have an early start in the morning so I can't stay tonight, I'm sorry.'

He stood up then to go, pulling me up for one last kiss. He smelt so divine, like he'd just stepped out of the shower, it was all I could do to keep my hands off him, but I let him go in the end and saw him to the door.

'Take care, see you on Friday.'

'Bye, see you soon, sweetheart,' he said in his honeyed voice before disappearing along the street.

I closed the door and leaned back against it, blowing out a long breath. I had no idea what to do next. I liked Jackson but the reality was that I hardly knew him. It had been a whirlwind romance so far and I'd enjoyed every bit of it, but in two short weeks he would be gone and I might never see him again. So should I continue seeing him and get my heart broken when we had to say goodbye or should I break it now by deciding not to see him any more? Neither option was appealing for obvious reasons.

I decided that it was high time I found out exactly where Nashville was and maybe, the devil in me thought, I could Google Jackson as well (hush my mind!). I knew this was probably dangerous but at least I would have a better idea of what I was dealing with.

I made myself another drink and opened up my laptop. I started with Google maps to find Nashville, Tennessee. When it came up, I was surprised to see that it was closer to the eastern coast than I'd expected and in the Deep South. I could make out Charleston in South Carolina where Jackson had said he had a beach house. I then Googled beach houses in Charleston and could not believe my eyes when I saw the cost! We were talking millions of dollars for some of them but they did look fabulous. It seemed a bit out of my comfort zone to be looking at these luxury houses but I didn't let that stop me for a minute.

Next I typed his name into the search engine and hovered over the enter button. I wasn't sure if I ought to do this but on the other hand, better to know any bad news sooner rather than later, right?

I pressed enter and went straight for images.

Before I knew it, the screen had filled up with pictures of his lovely face. About half of them were of him on his own but most of the remainder seemed to show him with one particular woman, Stephanie Shaw. When I investigated further, I confirmed her as the fiancée who had cheated on him just before their scheduled wedding day a year ago. I flicked back to read some of the articles but they were mostly from gossip magazines and not worth bothering with.

I clicked a link to find out more about his record label though, which led me to another one telling me his net worth.

My mouth fell open. Jackson was worth twenty million dollars!

# CHAPTER 10

As I came downstairs the next morning, I was already feeling miserable at the prospect of three days without Jackson. I went to pick up the post and as I turned the largest envelope over, I saw that it had "Open Mic" Competition stamped across the front. I tore it open, desperate to read the contents. Inside, I found the arrangements for the regionals taking place in Bournemouth on Friday. I was finishing reading through all the details when the phone rang, making me jump. I was quite taken aback when I heard Sam's voice at the other end.

'Hey, Rachel, how are you?' He sounded nervous, as if he knew I might be cross with him.

'I'm okay, thanks.' I sounded frosty, I knew but I couldn't help it. I *was* cross with him since the gig the other night when he'd been so rude in front of Jackson.

'I was ringing to see how you are because I missed you on Sunday.'

I softened at once because it seemed like he genuinely wanted to talk to me and also, I'd never been one to bear grudges. 'I'm good, especially now we know we've got through to the regional final. I was going to ring you actually to ask if you and Matt could fit in a rehearsal before Friday?'

'Yep, no problem. How about tomorrow?'

'That sounds good.' I paused. 'Did you manage to sort out your emergency on Sunday?' I asked suddenly remembering.

'Yes, I did, thanks.' He fell silent for a moment and I waited for him to continue. 'Listen, we need to talk, you and I but I can't do that with Matt there.'

'I agree, we do need to.' At last, he was facing up to the fact that we needed to talk this all over. 'Have you got any time this week during the day?' I asked.

'No, I'm busy on a job over in Bournemouth all week and Matt gives me a lift home when we come to you. Could we make a date for lunch on Saturday maybe?'

'Okay, let's do that if we can't meet any sooner.'

'I'll see you tomorrow for the rehearsal then. Take care, bye.'

---

Later that evening, Jenna came round for dinner and a catch-up.

'So,' she began after I'd shown her into the kitchen/diner, 'how did the picnic on Brownsea Island go on Monday?'

'We had a wonderful day and I took some fabulous photos,' I replied, as I poured us out a glass of wine each. 'We even saw a red squirrel, well, I did, Jackson missed it.' I laughed. My arrabbiata sauce was simmering nicely and looked almost done so I gave it a final stir and moved it to a lower heat.

'It sounds like you two are getting on famously. What about you and Sam? Have you managed to have a chat about things?'

'No, we couldn't meet on Saturday night because of the gig but we'll be meeting this weekend because he says he wants to talk. Even though I'm not looking forward to it, I am glad that we'll be getting things out in the open because what with that and the competition, which is also proving to be a bit of a sticking point between us, things aren't too good right now.'

'Yes, I'm picking up odd vibes from him at home at the moment. He seemed quite off when I spoke to him last night.'

'Did he tell you the good news?' I asked.

'What news is that?'

'We got through to the regional finals!'

'Wow!' she squealed. 'That is wonderful news. Well done!'

'Well, I'm really pleased about it but Sam and Matt, not so much, which is why things are difficult. That's probably why he didn't tell you about it too.'

I paused to consider that for a minute before going on. 'And now, Jackson's away for a few days on business and I feel I need a bit of time to try and get my head round some things.'

'It sounds like you might need a bit of help with that, so go on, what's up?'

My oven beeper went off, so I drained the pasta and served up dinner before telling her all my insecurities about where the relationship might or might not be going.

'Mmm, this is delicious,' she mumbled, finishing a mouthful of pasta. When she'd finished eating, she went on, 'Okay then, you like Jackson and he seems to like you, yes?'

'Yes,' I agreed.

'But you have some worries about where it will all lead and that's natural, but it shouldn't stop you from trying.'

'I know but Sam was right about one thing at least: Jackson will be gone soon and I'm already starting to feel something for him and all I can see is me getting hurt down the line if I give in to my feelings. Then there's the competition. Sam and Matt have told me that they don't really want to come with me to the nationals if we win on Friday at the regional final in Bournemouth. If we do win, what will I do? I don't know if I'm up to carrying on alone or if it's even allowed within the rules.' I groaned. 'Everything seems such a mess.'

We cleared the plates away and sank down on to the sofa. Jenna topped up our wine glasses and we were both silent for a moment as we pondered the situation.

'I understand how you feel about Jackson,' she said after a minute. 'It is a risk of course but you can't avoid that where your heart's involved. If I said to you that you could never see him again, how would you react to that?'

I grimaced, which gave her the answer.

'Exactly. My advice is to see where it goes with Jackson and deal with whatever else happens along the way, as it happens. All you're doing is worrying about what might happen. And it's the same thing with the competition. Concentrate on the regional final first. If you do win, then you'll have to think about what to do next but wait till that happens before getting in a state about it. Try taking things one step at a time.' She smiled a rueful smile. 'Did anyone ever tell you, you worry too much?' She winked at me, knowing full well that it was something she had said to me many times over the years.

'Thanks for talking it over with me, Jenna. I will try to follow your advice, I promise but I don't think the next few days are going to be easy. Anyway, changing the subject slightly, have you heard from Meg at all about the wedding flowers?'

'Yes, I have and she's coming in to talk to me tomorrow. I'm really excited about the prospect of doing her flowers. If it works out, it could lead to so much more work for us.'

'Well, you really deserve it. I know it will all go well tomorrow but you will let me know won't you?'

'Of course. I'll want to shout it from the rooftops if she gives me the job!'

We carried on talking and catching up for a while longer over coffee before, all too soon, it was time for her to go because of her early start in the morning. I saw her to the door and hugged her again before she climbed into her car and drove away. I got into bed shortly afterwards and as I drifted off, my dreams were of a tall, handsome American from Nashville.

The day of the regional final arrived and I could hardly concentrate on anything else all morning. Jackson had texted to say he would be back by lunchtime and would pop in to see me as soon as he arrived. When he finally knocked on my door at midday, I was a nervous wreck.

'Hey, Rachel, how are you?' He beamed at me but then his face fell, as he looked at me more closely. 'Are you okay?'

'Not really,' I confessed, holding open the door to let him in. We went through to the lounge and I sat down on the edge of the sofa. Jackson took a chair opposite me and waited for me to explain. 'It's just that I'm really nervous and I can't seem to control it, I don't know why. I'm not sure I can deal with this all the way through to this evening.'

'You do know that this is perfectly normal, don't you?' he asked, smiling at me. 'I know it's not pleasant but you will get through it and soon you'll be on the stage and it will all melt away.'

'Do you promise?' It felt better already, having him there to reassure me.

'I sure do.' He stood up and pulled me up to him for a hug and a long kiss. His eyes locked with mine and his strong arms enveloped me. As our lips touched, I breathed in his familiar smell and I swear that kiss brought me back to life after several days of absence. 'What time do you have to leave?'

'Sam and Matt are setting off in the van at four and our sound-check is at half past five so I planned to get a taxi from here at five. I have to try to keep going till then.'

'Would you like me to come with you in the taxi?'

'That would be great, yes, please. You should be able to get a seat as our guest too. We're allowed to bring two people and I know the guys aren't bringing anyone. I'd have loved Jenna to come but she'll be working.'

'How about I dump my bags then and we go get some lunch down on the quayside? That should while away some hours.'

---

We were back in plenty of time for me to get ready for the evening performance. I went for a simple sundress that I'd dug out from the depths of my wardrobe, teamed with my favourite pair of wedges. I was finishing drying my hair when the doorbell rang announcing Jackson's return. He gave a low whistle on the doorstep, smiling in appreciation of my appearance. I quickly popped in my hoop earrings, grabbed my bag and my guitar, following him outside to take the taxi for the short drive to Bournemouth.

By the time the driver pulled up in front of the Bournemouth International Centre fifteen minutes later, it had started to rain. We dashed inside and went in search of the guys for our soundcheck. This time, we were in the main auditorium on a much bigger stage. It was filled with all the accompanying amps and microphones and other musical instruments needed for a gig like this, so the pressure had definitely stepped up a gear.

I breathed a sigh of relief after everything went according to plan with the soundcheck. Once Jackson was in his allocated seat, I went to wait with the other performers backstage.

We were scheduled to play right before the interval, after two other similar bands. There would be three more acts in the second half and finally, the result. Everyone was very friendly but as nervous as me by the look of their faces, with the exception of Sam and Matt, who didn't seem at all worried. Perhaps that was because they didn't have so much riding on their performance. I couldn't resent them, I was just glad that they'd accompanied me this far.

We watched the other performers on a big-screen TV in the communal dressing room. The first two bands were as accomplished as us, although they mostly sang covers. We'd decided to go purely with my own songs tonight, which I hoped would make the difference.

Before I knew it, I was standing in front of the microphone once again, taking lots of deep breaths to help myself adjust to the setting before me. I could almost taste my own fear at this point. Although I was growing more comfortable with bigger audiences, this one was the biggest so far and the noise level was incredible. It was so heartening though and I took strength from the support the fans were showing, cheering and whooping our arrival.

I adjusted my guitar to make it comfortable, then checked that Sam and Matt were ready. We launched into our first song, 'Love Me', which was catchy enough to get the crowd singing along. The applause was fantastic and we had to wait quite a few minutes for it to die down after the song ended. I was grinning from ear to ear at their response.

Once things had quietened down, I put my guitar on the stand and sat down at the piano to sing 'Don't Let Me Go'. A hush fell over the audience as I began to play and, in my mind, I was in the arena on my own, singing to myself. When I sang the final note and stopped playing, I turned to the audience, eager to hear their reaction. I ought to have been used to the moment of silence that often followed the end of a great performance but as it was, a sliver of panic started in my stomach as the doubts started to form.

The almighty roar that broke out then, quelled that fear at once and I readied myself to sing the final number. I slipped my guitar strap back over my head and moved my long hair out of the way, trying to stay calm. Even if we didn't proceed to the national final, this had been such a great experience and I would never forget it. I had pursued my dream and I'd given it my best shot so there could be no regrets.

We gave 'Too Late' our all and the crowd loved it, joining in with the chorus and rising to their feet to dance as well. The applause lasted for several minutes once again and I was reluctant to leave the stage. We thanked them before going and went back to join the other performers in the dressing room where they'd been watching us on the TV.

'Well done, you guys, you were fab!' one of the other female singers congratulated us, pulling me to her for a hug and a peck on the cheek. Her band mate shook hands with Sam and Matt, clapping them on the back too.

'Your songs were fantastic, you deserve to win, guys,' one of the other solo artists praised us before heading towards the stage herself.

We watched the remaining three acts in the second half, who were all solo performers and then settled down to wait for the results. I'd expected it to take some time and for it to be a tense wait to find out what the judges had thought. In fact, they made their decision in record time and ten minutes later we were listening to the compère start his announcement.

'In third place, Deena Barker. In second place, Quiver. And in first place, following a brilliant performance tonight...' He eked it out as long as he could. 'Three's Company!' The crowd went wild and I stood there in shock, quite unable to believe that we had really won.

The moments following the announcement went by in a blur.

We went out on stage to receive the crowd's applause once again and to hear that the national final would take place the following Wednesday in London. The crowd cheered and applauded non-stop for at least five minutes. I tried to find Jackson's face in the crowd but the lights were too dazzling. We were soon back in the dressing room once again.

'Hey, Rachel, well done. I'm really glad you won.' I looked round to see Deena, one of the runners-up grinning broadly at me.

'You were brilliant too. I'm sorry you didn't get through to the final,' I replied, giving her a hug.

'No worries. It is what it is.' She shrugged. 'Good luck for Wednesday,' she called out as she left, swinging her guitar case on to her shoulder.

The band who had come second, Quiver, would also be joining us in the final. Sam and Matt both gave me a hug and went off to pack up our gear, without discussing the inevitable problems I would now face going on to the national final on my own. I didn't blame them, now was the time for celebrations, not arguments. Once they'd gone, I went in search of Jackson in the auditorium but his seat was empty. I did a quick scan of the ground floor of the arena and spotted him by the judges' table, talking to one of them there. I approached slowly, hoping they would have finished talking by the time I got there but also wondering how it was that Jackson knew the man. He must know him through the music business, I concluded. As I drew nearer, Jackson looked up, hurriedly finished his conversation and ran over to me, sweeping me up in his arms for a hug.

'Well done, I knew you could do it!' he cried and his enthusiasm was infectious. I found myself laughing and crying all at once. 'You were fabulous tonight, there was no doubt in my mind that you would win.'

'I enjoyed it so much and the crowd were amazing which really helped. I can't wait for the final now.'

We turned to go and I noticed the judge he had been talking to was still looking at us, a small frown on his face. I smiled at him to try and break his mood but he turned away, shuffling his papers.

I shrugged, putting the incident out of my mind.

'Let's go and look for a taxi, shall we?' I suggested and I looped my arm through Jackson's.

# CHAPTER 11

The next day, I arrived at our usual pub on the seafront a few minutes late to find Sam sitting outside, drinks at the ready.

'You look a bit out of breath.' He stood up to greet me and moved to kiss me on the cheek.

'I'm fine, I was taking some photos up by the park. Thanks for the drink.' I was puffing a little as I tried to catch my breath.

'Shall we order now because it's starting to get busy? I brought a menu out for us.' I chose something quickly and Sam went off to place our order.

While he was gone, I gave some thought as to how to approach things with him when he returned but I didn't come up with anything better than going with my instinct.

'What did you want to talk about?' I asked as soon as he'd sat down again. I wasn't going to make things easy for him by doing all the talking. He needed to explain himself.

'It was about the competition.'

My mouth fell open in surprise. I thought he was going to talk about his feelings for me but he was still avoiding that topic, clearly. I closed my mouth quickly and waited.

'I am proud of our success so far,' he went on, 'but honestly, I don't think we have any real chance of winning the national competition.'

'What?! How can you say that?' I couldn't stop my voice from rising in anger at his attitude. 'It doesn't matter what you think though any more, does it? You obviously aren't going to change your mind and come with me so I'm going on my own. Contrary to what you might think, I believe I have a very good chance of winning, otherwise I wouldn't bother.' I folded my arms and glared at him.

'I'm sorry. I think it's best to be honest, that's all.'

'Thank you for that vote of confidence. It's a shame you can't be honest about everything you think.'

'What's that supposed to mean?' It was his turn to glare at me.

'I think it's time we talked about you and me and *we* were honest with each other.' I looked at him pointedly and he had the grace to look a bit guilty. I took a deep breath and plunged in. 'You've been grumpy since Jackson came on the scene and last week when I asked you about it, you said that you don't want me to get hurt but that was all you said, apart from a slightly sarcastic reference to "me not getting it", which I didn't understand.'

He looked like he was going to interrupt me but I held up my hand because I didn't want to lose my courage. 'Then, during the week,' I went on, 'I met with Jenna and asked her if she knew why you were so annoyed with me and she told me that you've had a thing for me for years and that I must be the only person who doesn't know it!'

My voice had risen unwittingly towards the end of my little speech but petered out on a pathetic sob at the end. I swallowed and tried to pull myself together. 'You haven't ever given me any hint that you felt like that about me, Sam, not even after that night we spent together.' And there it was, out in the open. When he didn't react, I continued, 'Until now, when someone else is showing an interest in me and to be honest, I'm pissed off with you when you've had all the time in the world to let me know.'

I stopped and took in a deep breath. I'd been wringing my hands together and my knuckles were white so I made a conscious effort to stop doing it, staring at my hands in my lap to try and help me calm down.

The waiter arrived at the table with our food at that point, giving us both something else to focus on for a minute. Once the waiter had gone, I knew that this was Sam's moment to tell me how he felt.

'I'm sorry that I've never said anything to you before,' he said, staring down at his plate. 'I suppose I was hoping that you'd realise by the amount of time I choose to spend with you and by the obvious way I care for you. I didn't realise I needed to spell it out.'

He glanced at me just as I rolled my eyes at that last comment but he carried on anyway. 'So, yes, I've been grumpy because Jackson has turned up and done in a couple of days what I've been trying to do for the last four years! I care about you, more than you seem to realise and I would love to take things further but I have no idea whether you'd even want that from me.'

'Couldn't you have tried telling me and then listening to what I said?' I tried but failed to keep the sarcasm out of my voice.

'If you remember, you ran out on me the morning after that night, which I took to mean that maybe you regretted it so that's why I've never been brave enough to bring the subject up again.' He fell silent then, having said as much as he felt he could right now, I supposed.

I sighed, knowing that this next part would be hard.

'I've always thought, since we were kids in fact, that you cared for me like a brother. Apart from that night, which I thought *you* regretted because you never mentioned it again, I've never had any signal from you that you had more involved feelings for me. The fact that neither of us made the effort to discuss what happened that night, maybe shows that we didn't want to start a relationship of any other kind.'

'That's not what I felt,' he whispered. My head snapped up at that.

'What did you feel?' I wasn't sure I'd want to know but curiosity got the better of me.

'It was one of the best nights of my life but I truly believed you regretted it because you'd gone when I woke up.' I closed my eyes then at the pointlessness of it all. 'What about you?'

'I remember it being a good night.' I paused, embarrassed to discuss something so intimate with him. 'But more than that, I remember feeling worried that we would lose our friendship and that meant more to me than a one-night stand.'

'You don't feel for me what you already feel for Jackson, is that it?'

'I don't know how I feel about Jackson or about you.' I didn't want to hurt him by saying any more and I didn't have the courage anyway.

'Have you thought what it's going to be like when Jackson goes home? I think there's a real danger of you getting hurt.'

'Of course I have and I know it's a risk getting involved with him but as I said before, I need to take that risk with someone if I'm ever to have any chance of happiness in my future.'

He looked so crushed by that statement that tears sprang to my eyes.

'Please don't hate me,' I whispered.

He hugged me to him then. 'I could never do that,' he said fiercely in return. 'But I do wish you could feel more for me.'

He didn't say anything more and I didn't know what else I could say. We ate our food for a few minutes and I pondered what was happening between us.

'The trouble is that the competition is threatening to come between us and I don't want that, Sam. I want to share this success with you guys. I know I can do it on my own but I'd rather do it with you so that you're a part of it with me through till the end.'

He tutted slightly then before saying, 'We've been over this, I don't want to do it and Matt can't do it for obvious reasons.'

I nodded miserably, knowing there was no point in discussing it any further.

We finished our lunch very quietly, both of us subdued after our conversation, and shortly afterwards we stood up to say our goodbyes. We hugged again and I watched as he walked off in the opposite direction.

As I walked home, I went over everything that had happened. I told myself that I'd tried to be honest and not lead him along with the promise of something I couldn't deliver but I'd seen in his face how much he felt for me and, suddenly, I was confused.

As for the competition, I didn't know whether to carry on without them or to simply give up.

---

By the time I reached the cottage, I'd decided to call Jackson and ask for his advice. Before I could ring him, my phone buzzed with a text from Jenna.

*'When were you going to tell me the good news?! Congratulations, I'm really pleased for you all.'*

*'Sorry! Thank you, me too. Just a shame that Sam and Matt don't want to go on to the final with me.'*

I knew it was unfair to dump them in it with their sister but I couldn't lie about it either.

*'What?! Let me get back to you x'*

Bless her, that's what friends are for. I wasn't that optimistic about her chances of success though.

'What do you think I should do?' I asked Jackson on the phone, after explaining that Sam had confirmed they wouldn't be coming with me to the national final.

'I think you'll have to contact the organisers but you may not be able to get hold of anyone on a Saturday. I can ring around some of my contacts to see if I can organise a guitarist and drummer from session players, I'm sure that won't be a problem. The difficulty is whether the organisers will accept them joining you as a partly new band. I think you should emphasise that you wrote all the songs and the music so Sam and Matt aren't integral to the sound.'

I winced to hear him say that but I knew he was right.

'Can I leave you to make some calls then please? But don't confirm anything until you've come back to me again. And I'll send an email to the "Open Mic" people explaining the situation to see what they say. I'm not going to wait to see whether Jenna manages to sort things out. Even if she does, at least I'll know what all my options are.'

'That's a good plan. Listen, while we're talking, do you fancy going out for dinner tonight?'

'Where did you have in mind?'

'How about eating out in Bournemouth for a change?' he suggested. 'We could set off a bit earlier so that we can have a wander first, if you like.'

'That sounds like a lovely idea. What time shall we meet?'

'How about six o'clock? I'll arrange a taxi to take us there. I can fill you in later on any news about session musicians too.'

---

On the way to Bournemouth, Jackson told me he had managed to find some session musicians for me who were on standby while I made up my mind about what to do. The driver dropped us off opposite the re-modernised pier. We walked towards the seafront and we were soon strolling along the promenade, looking down at the golden sandy beach I loved so much as a child. It was still full of people taking advantage of the early evening sun.

'Do you remember all this or is it too long ago?' I asked Jackson as we strolled hand in hand.

'Are you trying to tell me I'm getting too old to remember stuff?' He teased me.

'I didn't like to say but you are approaching the big 3-0 and that seems ancient to me!'

He grabbed me round the waist then as if about to pay me back for that insult but kissed me full and deep instead, almost taking my breath away. As I pulled back, I had to grab his arm to stop myself from losing my balance.

'I'm glad to see that your advancing years have not affected your kissing ability,' I said rather huskily and my cheeks reddened a little at the lustful sound of my own voice.

He grinned at me and made sure I was steady again before letting me go.

'To answer your question, I don't remember a great deal, no, but it doesn't seem to have changed an awful lot. It seems as lovely a seaside town as it ever was.'

We wandered for a while longer before deciding that we were both hungry enough to look for somewhere to eat. We turned around and started walking back towards the pier and we managed to find another seafood place near the pier itself which had a free table.

'Are you sure you don't mind having seafood again?' Jackson asked me.

'The seaside is the best place to have it, I always think, and I love it anyway, as long as you don't mind.'

Having settled that worry, we sat down at a table outside and enjoyed the view as we waited for our drinks. The clear blue sea and the rise and fall of the waves had me mesmerised until the sound of Jackson's voice broke the spell.

'You looked like you were someplace far away then. What were you thinking about?'

'About the situation with Sam and Matt.' I sighed, remembering my conversation with Sam earlier that day. I didn't want to tell Jackson about that though. 'Thanks for sorting out the session musicians for me, I appreciate that,' I said instead. 'I still haven't heard anything back from Jenna. I would prefer to go with Sam and Matt of course but I can't force them to come with me. I'm not sure I'm up to going to Jenna's for lunch tomorrow with all this hanging over us.'

'Yeah, that could be kind of awkward. Hopefully, you'll know before you have to go tomorrow.'

We watched the sun setting as we ate, the assorted shades of orange reflecting off the water and we both tried to keep things light, to think only about the here and now.

Jackson put his arm around my shoulder as we walked back along the seafront and I leaned into him, enjoying the feeling of having his arm close against my body. After a while, we ended up by the taxi rank and set off back home. Once we were settled in, I became aware of the beginnings of a headache and I rested my head wearily against Jackson's shoulder. I must have dozed off because the next thing I knew, Jackson was gently shaking me.

'Honey, we're back at the cottage. Are you all right?'

'I've got a slight headache, that's all.' He came round to help me out of the car after paying the driver and I was grateful for his firm hold to support me.

He followed me into the cottage, guiding me towards the kitchen and then pouring me a glass of water. I swallowed down some headache tablets, hoping to stop it getting any worse.

'I'm sorry to spoil the end of a lovely evening,' I said. 'I probably just need a good night's sleep to get over this.' I pressed my fingers to my temples, trying to ease the pain. I looked up at him with regret, knowing that the evening was being cut short and that I probably wouldn't see him the next day either.

'Are you sure you'll be all right on your own?'

I swayed on my feet, feeling suddenly faint. Jackson's arms wrapped around me at once and he lifted me effortlessly towards him. The last thing I remembered was him carrying me up the stairs towards my bedroom.

# CHAPTER 12

I woke in the middle of the night with an overwhelming need to be sick. I dashed off to the bathroom and only just made it before my stomach started heaving. I washed my face in cold water afterwards and rinsed my mouth out, trying to take the awful taste away. I stumbled back to bed and took refuge under the covers, shivering with cold. I glanced at the clock on my bedside table and groaned when I saw that it was three o'clock. As I turned back round towards the bed, I thought I saw Jackson sleeping in the wicker chair in my bedroom but I dismissed it as my mind playing tricks on me. I tossed and turned for some time before falling asleep again as the sun was coming up.

I was startled awake by the phone ringing what seemed like only minutes later. I groaned as I rolled over, my stomach churning as I did.

'Hello,' I mumbled.

'Rachel, you sound awful! Are you okay?'

'Thanks for that, Jenna. No, I've been up in the night being sick and I still don't feel good. I'd better not come over for lunch today, I don't think.' I slumped back against the pillows, worn out just through speaking.

'No, sure, don't worry about that. Do you want me to come over and look after you?'

'No, no, I'll be fine. Is there any news about Sam and Matt though?'

'That's what I was ringing about. They've agreed to come with you but Natalie's not very happy about it and that might have been awkward so I wanted to warn you to watch what you said.'

'Perhaps it's best then that I won't be coming. Thank you for talking to them anyway. I'd better go, I'm feeling rough again.'

'Take care and let me know if you need anything.'

I experienced another nasty visit to the bathroom before crawling back into bed again. I wanted nothing more than to curl up in bed all day. Shortly afterwards, there was a knock at the front door. I groaned, resenting the fact that I now had to go downstairs. I grabbed my dressing gown and plodded unsteadily down the stairs.

'How are you feeling now?' Jackson's attractive face was etched with concern on my behalf.

'Not great to be honest, I just want to be in bed.' I clutched at my stomach as it made another ominous gurgling sound.

'How about you let me come back in and look after you?'

'Honestly, I don't want you to see me like this, thanks all the same.'

'I have seen you and it doesn't bother me.' He stared patiently back at me.

'What do you mean, you *have* seen me?' I frowned, struggling to concentrate on his words.

'I was here with you all last night. I've been home for a shower, that's all. Now I'm back to look after you because the thought of you being on your own when you're not well worries me.'

He raised his eyebrows at me so I held the door open and, sighing heavily, made my way back upstairs. Even in my feeble state, the fact that he had stayed with me during the worst of my sickness made me realise how much he cared for me. I climbed back into bed, listening to the sounds coming from the kitchen. I had no idea what Jackson was up to down there.

A few minutes later, he appeared at my bedroom door with a jug of water and a glass, waiting for me to invite him in. I waved him in with my hand, not having the strength to speak. I gratefully took the glass of water he held out to me and drank it all down.

'Mmm, that was good, thank you,' I said, wiping my face with the back of my hand in a way that I was sure didn't look very attractive. I lay back against the pillows, listening to my stomach growling unpleasantly. I watched as he squashed his manly body into the dainty chair at my bedside and I had to smile at the sight.

'I wonder if it was the seafood that made you sick?' he asked me. Up until then, I hadn't even considered that.

'Probably, but who knows?' I mumbled. 'You didn't eat any did you?' He shook his head and I closed my eyes. The next time I woke up, two hours had passed and I knew I needed to go to the bathroom again. I didn't have time for embarrassment, I just ran. As I leaned over, preparing for the worst, Jackson appeared next to me in time to lift my hair out of my face, giving me the greatest sense of relief that I wouldn't have to try and do that for myself this time. He was kindness itself, helping me up afterwards and offering me everything I needed to clean myself up. He took my arm and gently led me back to bed. Then he made me drink some more water.

'I'm sorry that you've seen me at my worst,' I said to him once I was settled back in bed again.

'You were pretty fierce with me last night, refusing to let me help you. Is that what you mean?'

My mouth fell open and I was lost for words for once.

By teatime, the worst seemed to be over and I was beginning to feel a bit better. I'd dozed throughout the afternoon but whenever I woke up, Jackson was there. This time, he had a book in his hands and I was glad to see that he had found something to do while I kept on dozing. I was only sick one more time and things seemed to calm down after that.

'Have you had something to eat? You must be starving.'

'Don't worry about me, I'm fine.'

'Thank you for looking after me today. It's been good having you here. And thank you for staying last night. I'm sorry if I was horrible to you.'

'I'm glad I could help you out today and that you would let me.' He smiled at me in that playful way of his, lips twitching up so enticingly and I couldn't help but smile back.

'I think I might be up for something simple to eat now and maybe we could rustle up something more substantial for you too.'

I pulled my dressing gown on once again and slipped out of bed. By the time I reached the kitchen though, I needed to sit down again and thankfully, Jackson took over, making some toast for me and some pasta and sauce for himself. I watched him as he worked and marvelled at the ease with which he moved around my humble kitchen. If I didn't already know he was a multi-millionaire, I would find it hard to believe. He turned suddenly and caught me staring at him.

'Penny for them?' he asked me.

'It's funny to see you cooking in my little kitchen.'

He sat down opposite me and pulled a face.

'I can look after myself, you know. I don't do much cooking, I have to be honest, but I quite like it when I do. Anyway, eat your toast, it'll make you stronger.' He was bossing me about but I knew he was right and I kind of liked it anyway.

'Jenna rang this morning to tell me that Sam and Matt have agreed to come with me to the national final on Wednesday after all. I think she probably gave them what for about letting me down.' I took a mouthful of toast and then chewed it very slowly.

'I'm real glad to hear that. I know you could have managed without them but I'm pleased that you don't have to.'

'I know I should be grateful that they've changed their minds but it feels awkward. I don't believe their hearts are in it really.'

'What about the organisers? Anything from them yet?' I shook my head and pondered what on earth I was going to do.

---

In no time at all, it was Wednesday morning and I was packing a bag for London. As Jackson had some business to attend to yesterday, he'd already gone up, saying he would meet me there. He'd told me that he would sort out the hotel arrangements, recommending that I stay over after the final, returning to Dorset tomorrow.

Having had the go-ahead the previous day from the organisers to continue on to the final without Sam and Matt, I felt as if a great load had been lifted from my shoulders. I still wished they were coming with me but I was happier knowing that I wasn't forcing them or causing problems in their lives. I'd talked it over with Jenna as well to get some perspective and she'd given me the benefit of her wisdom, as always.

'Even though I persuaded them to say yes,' she'd told me, 'Sam and Matt don't want to go and it would make life a lot easier for Matt especially, if they don't have to. So if Jackson has sorted out the problem of the missing band members and the organisers have agreed to it, there's nothing else stopping you now, in my view. Do this for yourself and stop thinking about Sam. Go to London and see what happens.'

I caught the train from the station a little after nine o'clock, due to arrive at Waterloo just before half past eleven. Once the train was on its way, I took the opportunity to go over my songs before the rehearsal that Jackson had organised with the session musicians later this morning. I'd decided to sing the same three songs I'd performed at the regional final, 'Love Me', 'Don't Let Me Go' and 'Too Late'. 'Too Late' was still quite a new song so I went over the chords on my manuscript paper a few times until I was sure of what I wanted to play, making revisions as I went. As a result, the time flew by and when I next looked at my watch, I was surprised to see it was nearly eleven. I quickly visited the Ladies' to check how I looked before meeting Jackson again.

The train pulled in at Waterloo bang on time and suddenly I felt nervous about seeing him in a different setting. I took a deep breath, grabbed my suitcase and walked to the nearest door.

After descending the steps, I turned towards the barrier and even at that distance, I could see Jackson's tall, handsome figure looking out for me. I caught his eye and grinned and he returned the favour with his most dashing smile. It was all I could do not to run along the platform and fall straight into his arms.

As soon as I reached him, he took my suitcase in one hand and led me gently to one side with the other and, putting the suitcase down, he pulled me towards him. I could see the longing for me in his eyes. He cupped my face gently with his hands and bent his head towards me, his eyes never leaving mine. My body melted into his and as our lips touched, the desire I felt for him sent shivers down my spine. He tasted every bit as good as I remembered and I couldn't get enough of him. My heart was beating so loudly I was sure that he could hear it too.

'It's good to see you,' he said huskily, pulling back at last and looking at me as though he'd not seen me for years.

'It feels like it's been ages, not a couple of days. I've missed you, you know.' I smiled with delight at him.

'I thought we'd go back to the hotel briefly to drop your bag off and then go straight to the studios for the rehearsal, if that's okay with you, sweetheart?'

He had no idea that I would do anything he asked of me as long as he continued to call me his sweetheart. I nodded and he took my hand as we left the station in search of a taxi.

After a short journey, we pulled up outside the hotel. It looked truly luxurious, with uniformed doormen outside waiting to tend to our every need. I seemed to remember reading something about it in a glossy magazine a while back. I hoped that I wasn't under-dressed in my simple cream blouse and tailored grey trousers. After paying the driver, Jackson came round to open my door and took my hand as I stepped out of the taxi. He carried my suitcase as we walked inside, ever the gentleman. Placing his hand on my back, he guided me straight over to a separate lift in the corner of the lobby.

'Which suite are you staying in?' I plucked up the courage to ask.

'We're in one of the penthouse suites.'

'That sounds like more luxury than I'm used to,' I replied.

'I'd like you to get used to it because you're more than worthy of it.'

We came out of the private lift straight into an internal lobby and as we entered the suite, my breath caught as I glimpsed the sweeping staircase leading to a second floor. The lounge even had a chandelier! It was sumptuous and I was overawed by the grandeur of it all. I turned to find Jackson watching my reactions and I blushed as I realised how provincial I must look.

'Sorry, I'm not used to this kind of hotel at all. It's magnificent.'

He kissed me then ever so gently and I knew that I was falling in love with this man despite all the barriers that there might be to our future together.

I went upstairs to unpack the few things I'd brought with me. The bedroom was stunning too, with an enormous bed covered by an attractive, blue silk throw. Under other circumstances, I would have loved to spend the rest of the afternoon in bed with Jackson, but I had the final to think about and it was the only thing I could concentrate on for now. Still, I hoped that we could explore it later.

I went back downstairs to join Jackson on the roof terrace. He was admiring the view of London spread out below. I put my arm around his waist and he pulled me in close to him.

'What a fabulous view! I've never seen London like this before.' I marvelled at the sight before us, pointing out the London Eye across the river and, glancing the other way, we could see St. Paul's Cathedral in the distance.

I gazed up into his eyes and saw only happiness reflected there. Time seemed to stop for a moment, the way it only does when you're falling in love, I think. I heard Jackson sigh before saying,

'Shall we get off to the studios then? I can't wait to hear you sing again.'

'That would be great. I'll feel better with the rehearsal out of the way.'

We made our way back to the lobby where the doorman called us another taxi to take us to the studios in Shoreditch. Once inside the studios, the sound engineer came out to greet us and to introduce himself.

'Hi, guys, I'm Jim and I'm at your disposal today.'

He took me through to meet the session guys then. Ed, the guitarist and Max, the drummer were clearly very experienced and picked up on what I was trying to achieve very quickly. It wasn't long before we'd gone through all three songs and with a few tweaks, we were pretty close to what Three's Company would normally play. I didn't keep them any longer than I had to because we had to be at the West London venue by half past five again for the soundcheck.

Once we were on our way back to the hotel, I decided to ask Jackson what he thought my chances were.

'When I met with Sam the other day, he told me he didn't think I had any hope of winning tonight. Is that what you think?'

'Hell, no! What a stupid thing for him to say, if you don't mind me saying. I wouldn't be supporting you like this if I didn't think you had as good a chance as the next performer of winning this competition tonight and everything I heard at that rehearsal only confirms for me that I'm right. Put that comment out of your head if you can.'

I sighed and leaned back against the seat of the cab. 'At least you'll be there for me and that's a comfort to know.'

He cleared his throat but didn't say anything.

I glanced round and found him looking a bit uncomfortable. 'What is it?'

'The thing is,' Jackson admitted, 'I can't come with you tonight. I have a prior commitment that I can't get out of. I'm really sorry.'

I stared at him, shocked. Suddenly, I was alone and vulnerable.

# CHAPTER 13

As soon as we arrived back at the hotel, I shut myself away in the bathroom to get ready for the final. In truth, I was close to tears because no-one I loved or cared for would be with me tonight. It took all my strength not to give in to them. Jackson's absence was the last straw and I didn't want to talk to him any more either. Just as I was learning to trust him, he'd let me down.

About an hour later, Jackson knocked softly on the door. 'Rachel?'

'Yes?' I called out in reply, not bothering to actually go to the door.

'I have to go now. I wanted to wish you good luck for tonight.'

'Thanks, bye.' I knew I was being petty, not going to the door but I didn't trust myself not to say something I'd regret later.

'I'll see you later. Take care now.'

I went through to the bedroom and sank down on to the bed as I heard the door to the suite close behind him. I had no idea how I was going to get myself together for tonight's performance.

I was still sitting there some time later when there was another knock, this time on the door to the suite. I hauled myself up and went to answer it. On opening the door, I found myself looking at a glorious bouquet of flowers. The bellboy peeked out from behind them to give me the card and I asked him to come in and put them on the table while I found him a tip. Once he'd gone, I took a look at the card.

'Wishing you all the very best of luck for tonight, Rachel. You'll be fabulous! Love Jenna, Sarah, Dave, Sam, Matt and family xx'

The tears fell then.

I knew that Jenna would have organised these flowers but it meant such a lot to see the names of my closest friends all written there like that. I pulled myself up and wiping my eyes, I went to finish getting ready.

---

An hour later, I stood on the stage at the venue for my final sound-check with Ed and Max but they were nowhere to be seen. I waited anxiously for a few minutes, looking all around the arena. As I was about to go in search of them, I spotted two men walking down from the left-hand entrance door to the stalls. It was only when they got closer that I realised that it was Sam and Matt walking towards me with big grins on their faces. My mouth dropped open in surprise but I was so pleased to see them. I gave each of them a quick hug before we all moved into our positions for the soundcheck.

Within twenty minutes, we'd finished and we were back in the waiting area with the other performers.

'What are you doing here?' I asked them as soon as we were on our own.

'We couldn't bring ourselves to leave you on your own for the final. We wanted to see it through to the end,' explained Matt.

'We knew we wouldn't forgive ourselves if we missed the final, so here we are.' Sam shrugged endearingly at me.

'I'm really glad you changed your mind,' I replied smiling at them both. 'Did you tell Ed and Max? Were they all right about it?'

'Yeah, they were cool.'

And that was that. Still, I was grateful for their change of heart and their company.

The guys went off to get a drink and I found myself alone again, trying desperately not to give in to my nerves. I noticed that the room was fairly quiet and presumed that everyone else was feeling like me. Looking around at their faces, I could see this was true. We were all nervous and wanted to do our best. The marketing people buzzed around, making sure everyone was ready and had what they needed for their performance.

The only comfort I had while waiting was my guitar, which I hadn't wanted to leave on the stage with this many people around. I found a corner, sat down and lifted it out of its case and on to my knee. I didn't want to play, I only wanted to feel it, to let it comfort me. I placed my fingers on the strings, marking out the familiar chords without actually playing and let my mind do the rest. I held my pick in my mouth, tasting the worn plastic and enjoying the sensation. I closed my eyes and let everything wash over me, calming myself before the storm.

'Excuse me, are you Rachel Hardy from Three's Company?' A brisk voice interrupted my thoughts.

My eyes snapped open and I found myself looking at one of the PR clones.

I removed the pick and confirmed my name. We went through some basic details and she told me that the final would be starting soon.

I glanced over at the big-screen TV and could see that the crowd in the auditorium was warming up nicely. Sam and Matt were working their way through the crowd towards me now and I knew it wouldn't be long before it was our turn.

'We're on last in the first half,' Sam told me.

I nodded and followed them towards the screen as we heard the first act being announced by the presenter. The band walked on and we could see them arriving on the stage in front of the audience who went wild. The camera panned around to take in the judges as well as the audience and it was then that I nearly fainted with shock.

Jackson was sitting at the judges' table. He was a judge!

That's what he meant by a prior engagement. Suddenly, everything clicked into place. He must have been scouting for talent when I first met him at the pub and he'd probably been one step ahead of us all the way. I'd taken such a sharp intake of breath that both Sam and Matt were looking at me with concern. They obviously hadn't noticed Jackson up there.

'Are you okay?' Matt asked me, taking my arm to support me. 'You've gone pale.'

I led them over to one side, trying not to draw any further attention to myself.

'I just noticed that Jackson is one of the judges and I had no idea of that until I saw him then,' I whispered.

'The lying...' Sam blew out a long breath, turning round to look at the TV again.

We all understood at once the significance of what I had seen.

'And what are you thinking of doing about that?' asked Matt hesitantly.

'What do you think I'm thinking?' I retorted. 'We all know Jackson and I know him especially well. He even told us about the competition and now we're in the final and he's judging it. It's probably as close to cheating as you can get. There is an absolute conflict of interest here. I don't think we can perform, it wouldn't be fair.'

'Let's not be hasty,' said Sam. My mouth fell open in surprise. 'Everything you're saying is true,' he continued, 'but we might as well go out and perform anyway now we're here and in the interval we can tell the organisers that we're withdrawing if you still feel that strongly.'

I looked at him, considering his advice and then walked away to think about it. As I stood gazing out the window, I struggled to contain my fury. It was just as well that Jackson wasn't there in front of me because I thought I might have punched him. I released my fists then from their clenched position.

Sam was right, I concluded. We owed it to ourselves to go out there and deliver the performance of our lives. After this was over, I would have plenty of time to tell Jackson exactly what I thought of his deception. I just had to hope that my dream wouldn't be at risk because of his lie.

---

I stood on the stage facing the arena and the biggest crowd I'd ever performed to. My body was trembling and I took a moment to try and compose myself before giving the band the nod to show that I was ready. At least I couldn't see Jackson because of all the lights. After all that had happened, I was an emotional wreck but I didn't expect to get another chance like this and I wanted to give it everything I had, for myself and for my absent family, not for anyone or anything else.

I launched into 'Love Me', feeling the guitar strings against my fingers and loving the sound that they made as I picked out the chords. Once again, the audience joined in with the chorus and I knew from that feedback that we were doing well. The applause lasted for several minutes, as I made my way over to the Kawai piano at the back of the stage. The arena became quieter as I sat down and prepared to play. This crowd was more excitable than the one at the regional final and soon there were whoops and calls of support, all of which boosted my confidence as I sang and played another one of my songs. It crossed my mind that the show was probably being recorded at that point but I didn't let it bother me.

All too soon, it was time for my final song, 'Too Late'. I had come to love this song in the short time since writing it and I hoped that this audience would love it as much as all the others had so far. As soon as we started playing, the crowd jumped to their feet, swaying to the music and then, joining in with the chorus. My heart was pounding at that moment and I knew I'd done the right thing by taking Sam's advice to go on and perform, in spite of everything Jackson had done to deceive me. The song was as popular with this crowd, who were still applauding and hooting even as we left the stage.

I thanked the guys as we came off and went to get my guitar case so I could pack up my things and go. I didn't want to stay for the results. All I wanted to do was to savour the joy of our performance, without it being sullied by accusations of cheating.

Tears came to my eyes but I swiped them away, lifting my head high. As I came out into the corridor, many more people were milling around because it was the interval and I found it hard to get through. Then, all of a sudden I was free and walking towards the down escalator, a few minutes away from the exit and my escape from this nightmare.

That's when I heard Jackson calling my name.

I stopped but didn't turn round.

'Rachel, where are you going?' he asked when he caught up with me.

I frowned at him as if he were stupid.

'Where do you think I'm going?' I hissed. 'I'm leaving. I'm not going to stick around to be accused of cheating when they all find out that I know one of the judges. I won't let you do that to me. You've betrayed me enough already.'

I moved around him to continue on towards the escalator but he reached out his hand and took hold of my arm. I looked down at his hand, unable to hide my disgust.

'Please remove your hand and let me go.' I glared at him but he didn't give up.

'Please listen to me and then if you still want to go, I'll not stand in your way.'

I stood absolutely still, my eyes locked with his until he removed his hand. 'Nothing you have to say is of interest to me any more.' I looked away but I couldn't bring my feet to move.

'I know I should have told you I was one of the judges but I knew you wouldn't have taken part in the competition if I had. And you were so talented, I couldn't bear for you not to audition. I knew you could get through to the final.'

'So you led me along anyway with no concern at all for my feelings?'

'Things spun out of my control! We started seeing each other and having...feelings for each other and there was never a good time to come clean. I don't want to spoil this for you when you've made it this far, that wouldn't make any sense at all so tell me what you think I should do and I'll do it. Please, Rachel. You have a great chance here and I don't want you to miss it because of me.'

'You mean I had a great chance and you've ruined it.' A single tear escaped and rolled down my cheek. 'We're involved and you're one of the judges, for goodness' sake! How can I possibly get out of that with my dignity intact? If you tell them we're involved, they'll probably disqualify me. If you don't tell them, then we're cheating and I can't live with that. Either way, you will have caused me great shame and embarrassment because you put me in this position. I've asked Sam and Matt to tell them we're withdrawing to save myself from that.'

'Um, well, I spoke to them before I found you and I asked them to hold off for the moment when I realised that you'd left and why.' I opened my mouth to speak but he held up his hand. 'Listen, this is my mess, I know and I want to put it right. I think there is another option: I could withdraw from the final judging, saying I have a conflict of interest because I know one of the performers. I haven't been involved with any of the regional finals so it is possible that I wouldn't have known about that conflict until today. I don't want to jeopardise your chances so if I simply pull out of the judging, I won't and you'll be able to have a fair crack at winning. You're so honest and I respect that. Please let me do this for you.'

I bowed my head and my shoulders sagged. I was really tired by everything but I could see that this was a way out and I needed to make a decision soon. Reluctantly, I turned around and started walking back to the dressing room, feeling Jackson right behind me.

---

As the second half of the show began, I noticed that Jackson was still on the judges' podium. I had no choice now but to trust him to keep his word and bow out when it came to the judging process. I remembered the judge he'd been talking to at the regional final and the frown the man had given me when Jackson had hugged me after our win. It all made sense now and I kicked myself for my stupidity. I watched with Sam and Matt as the other acts took their turn on the stage, enjoying the variety of talent and marvelling at the high standards in this final. I knew we couldn't have done any more but was very aware of how we compared to the other performers out there. I was sure that the judging was going to be very difficult. Whatever happened, at least I could be confident that the outcome would be a truthful one and that meant a lot to me.

Soon it was all over and I saw all the judges, except Jackson, stand up and leave the arena. He must have told them about his conflict of interest then, I decided, and I was relieved to see that. Everyone in the dressing room started wandering around wishing each other luck before the final announcement came. A bell rang somewhere to signal the judges' return to the arena. The presenter went out on to the stage again and the crowd fell quiet in anticipation.

'Before I announce the winner of the "Open Mic" competition and the runners-up, I have been asked to read out a short statement from the judges.

*One of our judges discovered tonight that he had a conflict of interest because he knows one of the acts that performed in this evening's final. He therefore withdrew from the judging process so that all the acts could be judged equally and fairly. The three judges who have come to the final decision have not been informed which act this concerns so that they too can be confident that they were treated fairly.*

There were a few wolf-whistles but nothing major and the presenter carried straight on with his announcement.

'In third place, Daniel Eaton, in second place, Three's Company. And the winner of the "Open Mic" competition is...The Cavaliers!'

The audience went crazy on hearing the winner and I had to admit that they had been really good. I was happy to have come second to such a good act and to have done so well overall. Everyone cheered as The Cavaliers went out to take their bow and to sing once again and there was lots of hugging backstage as we recovered from the tension we'd been sharing all evening.

'We did well, guys. Thank you both so much for coming to support me. It really did mean a lot, especially with everything else that has happened.'

'We're going to get straight off home again in the van. Are you sure you don't want to come with us?' Sam looked at me with concern.

'No, I still have some things I need to sort with Jackson and my stuff's at the hotel anyway. You take care and I'll see you both soon.'

As I was approaching the exit, one of the marketing people called me over again. I tried not to roll my eyes at him, wanting nothing more than to get back to normal. I'd taken a chance on success and had my moment of fame but all I wanted now was to go home.

'Hi there, Rachel, well done on your second place! I wanted to talk to you about your prize and how to claim it.' He beamed at me in a way that wasn't entirely natural.

'I didn't realise there was a prize for second place.'

'Ooh, yes and you wouldn't want to miss out on this. Here are the details. Well done again.'

He handed me a piece of paper and zoomed away to tick off the next item on his to-do list.

I looked down at the piece of paper and had to smile as I read it. My prize was to record a demo CD at the expense of The Rough Cut Record Company, owned by one Jackson Phillips.

# CHAPTER 14

We hardly talked in the cab on the way back to the hotel. I was so let down by the way Jackson had lied to me, even though he'd tried to put it right by not taking part in the judging of the competition.

I went straight upstairs to the bedroom when we returned to the suite, intending to close the door firmly behind me so that there could be no possibility of any further discussion between us. Jackson had other ideas though and followed me right up the stairs, catching the door before it had the chance to swing shut completely.

'We need to talk,' he said quietly behind me.

'I don't want to talk any more.' I couldn't bring myself to turn around and look at him, knowing that once I did, I wouldn't be able to stay angry with him for long.

'I'm deeply sorry for what I did. I only had your best interests at heart, I hope you know that.' His voice sounded closer but still I didn't turn.

'You lied and that was unforgivable.' My voice caught on a sob and I felt his hands on my arms, caressing my skin, trying to make everything better.

'Haven't you ever made a mistake like that, Rachel?' His accent was even more pronounced than usual and it was lulling me into forgiving him, even though I didn't want to.

At last I turned to face him and as I expected, his dark eyes were full of sorrow. I took a step back trying to distance myself.

'Of course I have. But I trusted you and you let me down. And that hurts so much.' I sat down on the edge of the bed and let the tears fall. He had no idea how deep-rooted my trust issues were after being abandoned before by Nick.

He knelt down in front of me, passing me a tissue to wipe my tears with.

'If I hurt you, I'm truly sorry. I certainly never meant to do that. Please can you forgive me?'

Even kneeling down, his eyes were level with mine and the power of his gaze had me trapped with nowhere to go.

'Maybe.' His lips curled into a sexy smile and as he rested his hands on my thighs, I knew that I would give in.

He leaned towards me and kissed me lightly on the lips, before sitting back on his heels, waiting for a further signal from me.

'I do understand that you had the best intentions. I'm just unhappy about the way you went about it.' He nodded, looking serious now.

I reached towards him, grabbing his jacket and pulled him back for another, deeper kiss, a kiss of forgiveness. Our tongues met and the taste of him touched all my senses. The next thing, we were lying side by side on the bed, and I remembered that earlier I'd thought I was falling in love with Jackson. I touched his lips with my fingers and he kissed them lightly before moving in closer to me.

'Can I show you how sorry I am?' He grinned wickedly and I felt the heat of my passion for him burn deep within me. As he started to undo the buttons on my blouse, I knew I could no longer resist him.

We took an early train home the following day, taking seats opposite each other. Every time I looked up, I found him looking straight back at me, waiting for me to say something about yesterday so that we could finally move on. I folded my arms and stared resolutely out the window at the passing countryside. Although we had indulged in fantastic make-up sex last night, I still felt resentful about all that had happened.

'Did they tell you what the prize was for the runner-up last night?' he asked me eventually, when we'd been travelling for a while.

'Yes, they did.'

'And?' He raised his eyebrows at me, inviting a reply but I shrugged. 'Don't you want to make a demo CD with my label?'

I didn't answer and he seemed to give up then and leave me alone.

I retreated into my own thoughts and wondered why it was that I felt guilty when I'd done nothing wrong. Today was Thursday. Tom's wedding was on Saturday and I was supposed to be going as Jackson's date. Not only that but Jackson would be leaving next Monday. I needed some time to decide what I was going to do.

When we were nearly home, I overcame my anger with him to ask the question that had been on my mind since being offered the prize.

'If we did want to go ahead and record a demo CD at your expense, and I'm not saying we do, but hypothetically, if we did want to, where would that happen? Would you book that studio we went to in London the other day, for example for us to go and do it at our convenience?' My resolve was already weakening and I'm sure he knew it.

'Actually, I've had an idea about that. It does involve you forgiving me completely though.' He smiled at me and waited.

'Don't push your luck. Get on with it.'

'Well, as you know, I'll be going home to Nashville next Monday, which doesn't leave any time for recording the demo before I go, what with Tom and Meg's wedding and all. And I'd like to be there when you do it, so I'd like to propose that you come over to Nashville to record a demo of say, three of your own songs, in our studio over there. No strings or promises attached, we could try it and see, but it would also give us the chance to carry on getting to know each other better. What do you say?'

My mouth had dropped open so I didn't have anything to say at that precise moment. He was laughing at the expression on my face so I quickly closed my mouth.

'I...I don't know what to say to that. That's a big step to take. I mean, what about my job and how would I even pay for myself to get to Nashville and to stay there indefinitely in a hotel or something?' I garbled in a rush, forgetting for the moment that I was still cross with him.

'Well, as far as your job goes, only you can make that decision. But obviously, I will pay for your flights and you'll stay with me, not in some hotel or something, as you put it.'

'I'm going to need some time to think about all of that,' I replied, although inside I was bubbling with the excitement of that prospect.

'I know. And you do understand that the offer would only be for you to come, not for Sam and Matt, don't you?'

'I suppose so, yes,' I replied, although I hadn't quite processed that until he spelt it out for me.

'Perhaps you could let me know on Saturday when we go to the wedding, that's if you'd still like to come with me?' He looked humble and full of regret, striking right at my emotions.

'Yes, okay, I'll come with you but only because I don't want to let Tom and Meg down.' I held my head up high but I noticed the way his lips twitched up, confident that he was breaking down my defences.

---

The next couple of days passed in a blur of final arrangements for the wedding. As Jenna had been asked to do Meg's flowers, I hardly saw her because she was so busy with preparations but I did text her to let her know the outcome of the competition.

I'd finally found my dream outfit in a little boutique in Bournemouth, an amazing red sweetheart off-the-shoulder dress, so I busied myself with going to collect it on the Friday morning.

Meg and Tom had asked the band to play at the wedding so we had a rehearsal early on the Friday evening. It was the first time I'd seen them since the national final and I had the feeling they assumed that now I'd tried my shot at fame and failed, everything would just go back to the way it was before. More than that, I knew they'd be expecting me to have broken up with Jackson after all that had happened so I had some explaining to do about the prize and Jackson's offer to me. Once our rehearsal was done and I'd made them a cup of coffee, I decided to broach the subject.

'I haven't had the chance to tell you both yet that there's a prize for being the runners-up in the competition as well.' They both waited patiently for me to continue. I took a deep breath. 'The prize is to record a demo CD of my songs at a professional studio, paid for by Jackson's company. The thing is, he's offered to pay for me to go out to Nashville to record it at their studio over there.' I waited for their reaction. When a minute had gone by, I couldn't wait any longer. 'What do you think then, guys? Do you think I should give it a shot?'

'I definitely think you should make a demo CD,' said Sam carefully. 'You have the talent and he obviously has the connections. As for going to Nashville, I'm not sure that's a good idea.'

'Why not?' I asked, knowing what he was going to say.

'Because you hardly know him and that's a long way to go with a stranger, especially after the stunt he pulled the other night. I can't believe you're still with him to be honest.' He paused, looking at me for an explanation.

'We made up after he apologised for deceiving me. I still feel a bit annoyed about it but I know he had our best interests at heart.'

'I presume the offer is only for you to go to Nashville, not for us?'

he asked then. I nodded. 'Can't you do it over here? In London, for example? Then we could record it with you. You surely don't need to go all the way to Nashville to record a demo CD?' He was getting irritated now.

'No, I don't have to go all the way to Nashville but that would be a dream come true for me and it might be the lucky break I need. And Jackson's not a stranger, that's not fair.'

'I think you should go, Rachel,' Matt interrupted. 'You have a real chance here and you've proved yourself through doing so well in the competition. If you stay here, I don't honestly think I could remain in the band because of the impact it's having on us as a family right now and I would always feel guilty if I dropped out and left you in the lurch. I'm pleased for you.'

He stood up then, getting ready to go, so I went to give him a hug, noticing the way Sam was glaring at him as I did.

'Thanks for those kind words, Matt. I appreciate it.'

'I'm going to go and give Natalie a call to say we're on our way. Good luck with it all, Rachel.'

'Rachel, this is madness, please don't go,' Sam began once Matt had left the room. 'You can record a CD here and I bet there'll be plenty of record labels interested in you if you send it out to them.'

'But Sam, you don't understand. I've always dreamed of going to Nashville and now I have the chance. It would be crazy to turn that down.'

'I know you have that dream but this is about more than that for me.' He paused, collecting his thoughts. 'Look, I haven't been completely honest with you, I guess. You know that I care for you but the thought of you leaving makes me realise how special you are to me and I've wasted so much time already.'

He fell silent for a moment and swallowed, and my sense of foreboding grew even stronger.

'What are you trying to say?'

'I love you, Rachel, I always have, I've just never had the confidence to tell you. I know I should have told you before now and I wish I had but despite the timing, I have to let you know how I feel. It's probably too late but if I never told you, I'd regret it for the rest of my life.'

I swallowed then, taken aback by his confession and reached out to take his hands in mine.

'Sam, I love you too but I don't know if I could love you in the same way you love me.'

He pulled me close to him and I knew that we were in a dangerous place. He leaned towards me, his curly blonde hair falling over his eyes as always and I sensed that he was going to kiss me. I knew I should pull away because I didn't want to give him false hope but I didn't want to be that brutal either. As our lips met, I closed my eyes, trying to remember how it had felt to kiss Sam before. It was a sweet kiss, gentle at first but then more probing and I couldn't help but respond. All at once, I came to my senses and pulled away.

'I...I'm sorry, I didn't mean to pressure you. Tell me honestly that you didn't feel anything and I'll walk away.'

I stared at him for a long moment, then I shook my head. I watched as his face fell.

'We should have taken our chance long before now but we didn't and I think it's too late now, I'm sorry.' I smiled at him but although he returned it, his eyes were sad. 'I think we want different things from life, you know. I want to travel, to see the world and try my luck at having a music career before I settle down, whereas you're happy being a carpenter and living at home.'

'I'm ready to settle down with you though, if you'd have me, I'd even be prepared to get a proper job.'

He laughed then and so did I, neither of us believing that for a minute.

'I don't want to tie you down, any more than I'd want you to make me give up my dream before giving it a try. I wouldn't have been able to do any of this if it weren't for you and Matt. I mean that, Sam, you've both been so great and it pains me to hurt you like this.'

Tears had sprung into my eyes and now Sam reached out to take my hand. I never imagined it would go like this when I told him about Jackson's offer.

'Look, I can't pretend that I'm not hurt but I do understand that you want to give this a try. I wish you didn't feel the need to go all the way to Nashville to do it though. All I can do is wish you good luck, I guess, and remind you that I'll always be here for you, if you need me.'

I looked up into his soulful eyes and knew that he meant it.

'The thing is, Sam, I'm going to be scared witless without you two to hold my hand!' We both laughed then and that broke the tension.

I kissed him on the cheek and watched him as he walked towards the van where Matt was patiently waiting. They came back in to collect all the gear, driving off into the night shortly afterwards.

# CHAPTER 15

Finally, Saturday, 24th August dawned bright and clear. The wedding was at eleven o'clock at Meg's parish church over in Longfleet. Tom, Jackson and I were going to travel together by taxi to the church. At ten, Jackson knocked on my door to collect me. He looked absolutely divine in his black morning suit, grey waistcoat and pink paisley tie, as I'd known he would all those weeks ago. As I turned to face him, he extended his hand towards me. It only took me a second to decide whether to take it and confirm my forgiveness by doing so.

'You look stunning, Rachel,' he whispered in my ear, his warm breath sending a wave of desire rushing through my body. I took a moment to compose myself before getting into the waiting taxi where Tom was already seated looking very nervous. I kissed his cheek and reassured him that everything would be fine. Thankfully, Jackson sat in the front, allowing me to avoid my raging feelings for at least a short while.

We were at the church in no time and the two ushers Tom had chosen to help guests find their places were already there. I noticed their buttonholes and said a silent congratulations to Jenna for having pulled it all off. One of the ushers helped me find my place to sit inside the church, along the same row as Tom and leaving a spot for Jackson next to me. Soon, other guests were arriving, including Jenna who looked lovely in a floral chiffon dress.

'Jenna, the flowers look fantastic, you should be proud of yourself,' I said in greeting as she sat down next to me.

'Thank you, I am pleased with the results I've seen so far. I'm absolutely shattered though. I don't know if I could cope with a number of weddings on the go at the same time!' She pulled a face at that idea but then glanced around, happily appraising her work.

Soon, everyone was seated and we were waiting for the bride to come. She was only a few minutes late and when she entered the church, the music played and we all stood as one to welcome her. Tom and Jackson had arrived to take their places a few minutes earlier and now we all turned to see Meg walk up the aisle with her dad at her side and her bridesmaids behind her. She looked radiant in an ivory strapless satin chiffon dress, with a beaded bodice and train. Her bouquet had a sunny yellow theme, including roses, freesias and gerberas, all bound together with a golden ribbon. It looked absolutely stunning.

Tom and Jackson moved forward for the service, with Jackson rejoining me once he'd handed over the rings. He looked relieved that he'd fulfilled that job without incident and I smiled at him in approval. The rest of the service passed smoothly, finishing with the signing of the register.

Afterwards, we followed the newly married couple and their families outside for photos. At last, Jackson and I were called for a photo together of friends of the groom. He took my hand and guided me to a good spot towards the back where we could be seen without being too obvious.

'I love a good wedding, don't you? The celebration of love and a new life together,' he said, giving my hand a little squeeze.

'Yes, it was lovely to see them so happy together.'

We didn't have the chance to say anything else because the

photographer took charge then but I had the feeling that Jackson definitely had more on his mind today.

We watched Meg and Tom depart for the reception in the elegant burgundy and black Riley hired especially for the occasion. They looked confident and happy as they drove away. Jackson and I hitched a ride with Jenna to the reception, all of us bundling into her ancient Fiat Punto. As we were a small wedding party, Meg and Tom had decided to hire out a restaurant in the Old Town for the reception. It was soon time for the speeches and Jackson chinked his glass with his knife to encourage everyone to listen. I was very eager to hear what he had to say.

'As y'all probably know, Tom and I have known each other since we were kids together and our friendship has lasted throughout those years and even across oceans and continents. He's like a brother to me and I'm really pleased that he's found the woman he wants to spend the rest of his life with in Meg. I may have only known Meg for a short while but I know in my heart that she is "the one" for him and now he's found her, I hope he hangs on to her and never lets her go. Please raise your glasses to toast the bride and groom, Meg and Tom!' The rest of his speech passed in the usual jokey manner of best men's speeches but without any awfully embarrassing revelations. Tom wasn't that kind of guy, he was simply a lovely man and Meg was very lucky.

As Jackson came to sit back down, I needed to go and get ready with the band so, once again, we didn't have a chance to talk any further.

While everyone finished eating, we did a quick soundcheck and prepared to play. I'd decided to change into a more relaxed outfit of skinny jeans tucked into my cowboy boots and a simple checked blouse over the top, and then we were ready to go.

As soon as the opening notes of our first song began, everyone seemed to turn their attention towards us. I could see their expectant faces as I started with my newest song, 'Too Late'. People began tapping their feet, others clapping their hands along to the catchy country-pop beat straight away and some even joined in with the chorus. I had a great feeling about this song. When I looked over at Jackson, raising my eyebrows at the crowd's response, he nodded in confirmation and smiled like it was a secret only we knew. We played for about half an hour in total, a mixture of my songs and some covers but it was the new material that the crowd enjoyed the most. I was amazed at how quickly they picked up the words of the songs, joining in with me time and again. They cheered and whooped at the end of every song, showing their appreciation for our sound. When we'd finished, I gave Sam and Matt a hug before they started to pack away.

'We were really good together tonight, guys. The crowd loved us,' I cried over the rising noise at the reception.

'There was a great atmosphere at this one, you're right. It must be the love all around,' Matt replied with a wink, before going off to load stuff into the van.

'Thanks for coming to play with me again, Sam. I hope we'll get the chance to do it again soon.'

'Have you made up your mind about going to Nashville then?'

'Not totally but...' He stared at me as I faltered, then gave his head a gentle shake before following after his brother.

I wasn't quite sure what to make of that reaction but I didn't intend to let it bother me. I dashed off to get changed again and then went to rejoin the party.

Jackson found me almost at once, wrapping his arms around my waist from behind and swinging me round to face him. He looked at me for a moment then leaned towards me for a long, slow kiss. I lifted my arms and looped them round his neck, bringing our bodies close.

'You guys were fantastic, you had the crowd eating out of your hand. If I were your manager, I'd suggest that "Too Late" should be the first song you release from your first album. It would be such a hit, I'm willing to bet on it.'

'Well, you should know, I guess.'

'Would you like to dance to celebrate?'

'Do you dance?'

'Only with you, sweetheart.' He led me on to the dance floor.

Meg and Tom had had their first dance and now, they were playing 'Close to You' by The Carpenters, as he took my hand and started to guide me around the room. I gazed up into his eyes and his hand squeezed mine in reassurance. I never had been much of a dancer but it was surprisingly easy when you were dancing with someone who knew how to work the floor.

'I thought your speech went well. It was interesting,' I began as a way of making conversation.

'How do you mean, interesting?' He smiled his cheeky smile at me.

'Well, I liked the bit about hanging on to that one woman if you find her and not letting her go.'

'Yep, I truly believe that. The only difficulty is in finding that one person who's meant for you, someone you can put your trust in.' I nodded in agreement.

'Too true,' I replied.

The next thing I knew, his lips were whispering in my ear again, making every one of my nerve endings stand to attention.

'Do you trust me, Rachel?' He pulled away a little to hear my answer.

I was speechless for a moment, thinking back to how I'd felt the other night but I'd moved on now so I nodded and he held me tighter still. I rested my head on his shoulder and enjoyed the feel of our bodies moving as one. As much as I hoped the song would never end, we came to a stop as the music faded.

Soon, it was time to see Meg and Tom off on their honeymoon and we followed everyone else outside to wave them goodbye. Before getting into the car, Meg turned away from the crowd, bouquet in hand, and as tradition demanded, she threw it over her head to the next bride-to-be. It was with some surprise that when I next looked down, I found that I was holding that same bouquet of flowers. Before I could say anything, Jackson had swept me up in his arms for a breathtaking kiss. I could hear people cheering in the background and my cheeks burned with embarrassment.

'Jackson, put me down. Please!'

He was laughing as he set me down but I wasn't. I didn't want to be the centre of that kind of attention.

'What's the matter?' he asked me, noticing the scowl on my face.

'I hate these silly traditions. People are staring and laughing at me.' I bowed my head.

He put his fingers beneath my chin and gently lifted my face up so I had to look at him.

'They're staring because you're beautiful,' he told me, gently stroking my face. 'And they're laughing with you because they know it's only a matter of time before you get a marriage proposal.'

I opened my mouth slightly to protest but he placed his finger to my lips, staring deep into my eyes. 'I love you, Rachel.' My eyebrows shot up and I gasped though it was only confirmation of my own feelings.

'I love you as well,' I replied without the slightest hesitation and his lips claimed mine.

---

The next day, Jackson and I walked hand in hand into town for the last time. We were both quiet on the journey along the residential streets, each lost in our own thoughts. Now that we had told each other our true feelings, everything felt so much more complicated. I knew I would have to give him an answer today about joining him in Nashville because soon he would be gone and maybe I wouldn't have this chance again.

As we approached the sea, the question weighed even more heavily on me. The waves looked choppy today which seemed appropriate for our mood.

We stopped in for a lazy lunch at one of the bustling restaurants on the quay.

'Have you made any decisions about coming over to Nashville to record your demo with me?' he finally asked me, as we were finishing our meal.

'I thought I had but now I'm nervous about making the decision because it means leaving behind everything I have in my life.'

He narrowed his eyes at me then.

'Well, that sounds like you've already made up your mind not to come,' he said, looking forlorn at that prospect.

'No, I haven't. It's a lot to think about, that's all.'

'Let's break it down then. What's the thing you're most worried about?'

'The biggest hurdle to overcome would be my job at the music service of course. The earliest I could come to Nashville would be the end of October when we have the next school holiday, if I don't want to let schools down. I could mention it now so that they're forewarned and if it all comes to nothing, it won't matter.'

'I seriously doubt that it will come to nothing, trust me.' He smiled reassuringly. 'Personally, I'd prefer you to come as soon as you can. Why don't you ask how soon they would be prepared to let you go when you go back to school?'

'What do you mean, hand in my notice before we've even recorded the demo?'

'Maybe, or if that's too big a step, how about asking for some time so that you can come over to Nashville and see how things go?' he suggested.

'I could ask, I suppose. They can only say no.' I paused to let that sink into my mind.

'What's next on your list?'

'The cottage, which is mine but there would still be bills to pay which would be difficult if I wasn't working.'

He smiled at me then, a knowing look that said he had already solved this problem.

'No, absolutely not, you are not going to pay my household bills, as well as everything else you're doing for me! That's too generous.'

He folded his arms and pouted at me and I had to laugh at his doggedness.

We paid for lunch and set off along the shoreline towards the bay. I noticed that the sea had become a bit calmer but there were a few grey clouds in the sky and I thought it might rain now. We admired the wonderful array of boats and yachts in the marina as we progressed around the bay. It had started to rain when we decided to stop for a drink at the marina's café before starting our walk back. As we sat down to drink our coffees and indulge in a slice of cake, I brought us back to our earlier conversation.

'How about this as an idea? When I go back to work, I ask for a term off, before they allocate me to students, a kind of sabbatical if you like. At the same time, I suggest to Jenna that she could live in my cottage, rent free, as long as she pays the bills during my absence. If all of that comes together...' I paused as I blew out a long breath, 'I would be free to come to Nashville and give the singer/songwriter plan a go.' Jackson leapt up and pulled me out of my seat to hug me to him.

'That sounds like a damn fine plan to me, sweetheart!' He kissed me. It started softly but soon became more demanding. We both knew it might be some time before we would see each other again.

We sat down again and I gulped in some air. This was a big step for me but I had this chance and I knew I might never get one like it again. I would be putting my future in Jackson's hands and now, it was time for me to take a leap of faith and put my trust in him. We talked the idea over some more before starting the walk back to the cottage in the drizzling rain.

By the time we returned, it was nearly six o'clock and we were tired but happy after a long day's walking and talking. Neither of us was hungry so the question came up of how to spend our last evening together. I'd been thinking about something for a while and now was my last chance to suggest it.

'I know there are other things we might want to do now,' I said with a cheeky grin. 'But I wondered if you'd like to hear any more songs that I've written,' I suggested quietly, not knowing if he could really hear me. I guess he did though because he sat up very suddenly from the position he'd been lounging in on the sofa.

'You have more songs? How could you have kept this quiet for so long?'

I grinned sheepishly and stood up to get my guitar.

'How many songs are we talking about? This is great news.'

'Well, I think I have about a dozen more I could play you now.'

He didn't say anything for a moment so I looked up to check his reaction. It was safe to say that he looked like he might explode with the excitement of this new knowledge. Finally, he found his power of speech.

'I can feel an album coming on. Play them for me please,' he begged.

And I did and it was the best concert I'd ever given, even though it was to the smallest audience.

He had nothing but positive comments to make about each and every song. Even his suggestions for improvements were constructive. He loved my music and I knew that a new phase of my life was about to begin.

That night, we made love as though we might never see each other again. For the first time in my life, I shed tears when our love-making was over.

'Sweetheart, why are you crying?' he whispered softly into the half-light of my bedroom.

'I'm not upset, it's okay,' I replied, trying to make sense of my emotions. 'It's like, like you've reached deep inside me, to a place I didn't even know was there.'

He pulled me close to him and nuzzled my hair and I wished the night would never end.

# CHAPTER 16

## NASHVILLE, TN, USA

**Jackson**

My driver, Greg, was there to greet me when I got back to Nashville International.

'Welcome back, Mr Phillips. You look well, sir.'

'I'm very well, thanks, Greg.'

The first thing that hit me as we exited the airport building was the humidity. A few weeks away had made me forget that typical aspect of a Nashville summer night. That was another thing I was going to have to get used to again, along with being on my own once more. Greg led me to where he'd parked the Lexus and took my bags from me before I climbed into the backseat of the car for the drive home.

As he drove, my mind went back to that morning when I'd kissed Rachel one last time before the cab turned up outside her cottage.

'I'll see you real soon, sweetheart,' I'd told her, praying that I would be right. I'd held her to me as she started to cry, wanting to soothe her tears away but at the same time, loving the feel of her soft body and all its curves pressed against me.

'Bye, Jackson,' she'd whispered. 'Thanks for giving me the time of my life these past few weeks.'

It had been such a wrench to leave her after the time we'd spent together, especially after we'd become so close in the last couple of days. I had enough great memories to last me a while but I wanted more and I hoped that she did too.

I leaned back in my leather seat with a sigh, wishing that Rachel was with me so I could share my life with her.

My loft was located in one of the historic neighbourhoods of downtown Nashville, not far from the Cumberland river and a short walk to our offices, and most other places I wanted to go.

The open-plan design of the living space had appealed to me at once, and with just two bedrooms and one bathroom, it was more than enough for a single man like me. I'd kept to simple furnishings because I loved the character of the place and I didn't want to cover up the hardwood floors with rugs and the like. My biggest indulgence had been the pieces of original artwork I'd purchased to decorate the walls with scenes of Nashville's musical life.

Most of all, I loved the district. It was a bit seedy for some, especially at night but when I pushed open one of the large windows in the lounge, I could feel the heat of the day on my skin and hear the noise from the street below as the city came alive. I left the window open and let the familiar smell of fried chicken waft in, making my mouth water as I thought about it.

I headed off for a shower, not feeling like I could sleep yet, despite it being after midnight Nashville time. It took only a minute for the water in the walk-in shower room to heat up, and as the powerful jets from the extra-wide shower head pounded my skin with water, I felt my tired muscles start to relax. I crawled into bed just before one o'clock and tried to picture Rachel back in Dorset. I would call her in the morning to catch up and to hear the sound of her voice. I already knew that I didn't want to be separated from her for much longer.

Just before ten o'clock the next day, I went out to speak to my assistant, Annie.

'Is everyone okay for this meeting?'

'Yes, they're all waiting for you in the meeting room, Jackson.'

'Would you like to order in some lunch for us today so that we can catch up, if today's good for you?'

'Of course, I'll get right on it. I hope the meeting goes well.'

'Thanks, Annie, and thanks for setting it up.'

I almost saw Annie as equal to my mom in the office and she'd been a good friend to me over the years, especially when everything had fallen apart after Stephanie.

When I entered the meeting room, my creative Vice-Presidents were ready and waiting for me. I gave them a big smile and thanked them for coming. They all turned to me expectantly.

'It's great to see you after a month away but I've called you together now to tell you about a bit of a development. When I was away, I met an amazing new singer/songwriter via the "Open Mic" competition I was involved in. Her name's Rachel Hardy, she's twenty-six and she has a whole heap of fantastic songs already written and she plays guitar and keyboard. She won our prize to record a demo CD of her songs and I've offered her the chance to come over here to record it. Hopefully, she'll be here within the next few days but in the meantime, I'd like you to listen to the rough recording of her performance from the competition final last week and give me your thoughts.'

Taking a deep breath, I walked back along the corridor to my office, rubbing my now slightly clammy hands together. It meant such a lot to me for them to want the label to sign Rachel like I did. Of course, it was my company and I didn't need to consult anyone but that wasn't my style. Some of my employees had been with me since the label had started eight years ago and I took a lot of pride in knowing that they respected me.

I'd been working at my desk, going through all the paperwork that had mounted up in my absence and checking my emails, when my cell buzzed as it received a text from Rachel.

*'I can't believe I missed your call. Are you free now? Would be good to talk to you xx'*

I called her straight back and she answered on the first ring.

'Hey, sweetheart. How are you?'

'Better already just hearing your voice. Is it good to be back home?'

'In some ways, except that I miss you. I hope you can make it over here soon.'

'Well, I went to meet the head of the music service this morning, that's where I was when you called earlier. Unfortunately, he wasn't at all receptive to the idea of me taking some time off. In the end, he said that if I wanted to go, I'd have to resign and he would release me from my contract.'

'Man, talk about an ultimatum.' I rubbed my hand against the back of my neck and blew out a long breath. 'What do you think you're going to do?'

'Either I stay and accept his terms or I hand in my notice. I don't want to let them down, of course but I would obviously like to come out to Nashville. I did wonder whether there might be someone I know who could cover my lessons so that I could hand in my notice but that would be a big step for me.'

'I'm sorry that you're faced with this choice now. You know that I'll support you if you decide you do want to take me up on my offer.'

'I know and I appreciate your offer of support but I don't want to be totally dependent on you.'

'How about Jenna, did you put your idea to her about staying in the cottage if you came to Nashville?' I said, trying to change the subject slightly.

'Yes. She'd love to be nearer the shop so that would be one problem solved.' She paused and I jumped in to give her some good news.

'I've left my team listening to the recording of your performance at the final. They should be getting back to me with their thoughts soon.'

'That sounds great,' she replied. 'I wish I could be there with you now but hopefully, it won't be too much longer.'

'I sure hope so, sweetheart. Take care and bye for now.'

I felt for her as I put the phone down, knowing that she wanted to do the right thing for herself, as well as for her employer.

---

Not long after saying goodbye to Rachel, I sat back down at the conference table, eager to get my team's feedback.

'What did y'all think?' I said brightly, trying not to betray my feelings.

'I thought she had a distinctive voice and she's an accomplished musician with her own individual sound, which could be interesting for our market,' said Todd, my A&R guy. 'She's clearly a talented songwriter too if these are all her own songs. I'd definitely like to see her in person.'

The others all chipped in then with similar positive comments.

'We'd really need her to come here for a while so we could get a better idea of how to market her sound if she's British. I'm not quite sure how that would work, you know? It would obviously help if we could get to know her better,' said Will, my head of Marketing.

'When will she be here?' asked Todd.

'That's a problem at the moment because she's a singing teacher and has obligations so I'll keep you informed of the situation. Thank you everyone for your feedback and confirmation that I still have the magic touch for spotting a good artist when I hear one!'

By the time the meeting was over, it was time for lunch but I wanted to let Rachel know how things had gone. I sat down and dialled her home number once again, eager to give her the news.

'I have some great news,' I began.

'That sounds exciting,' she replied in her lovely English accent. It still turned me on to hear the sound of her voice.

'Well, my Vice-Presidents all loved the recording I played them of your performance from the final. They said you have a rich, individual sound and you're obviously a talented singer and songwriter and they can't wait to meet you! How about that? It's not just me who thinks you're great you see, sweetheart.'

'Wow, that sounds brilliant, although they probably went along with you, seeing as you're the boss,' she argued.

'No, I purposely let my VPs make up their own minds. Most of them have been with me since I started the label so I really trust their opinion.'

'I know nothing of this kind of business. I guess I'm going to have to get used to being a little overwhelmed by all these changes.'

'Hey, that's what I'm here for. I'll look out for you and guide you every step of the way, I promise.'

'Well, let's hope I hear soon about my job. Will I speak to you tomorrow?' She sounded so sweet and tentative.

'You bet. Shall I try and call around lunchtime again?'

'Yep, that sounds good.'

'I'm having dinner at my parents' house tonight and I'm going to tell them all about you as well,' I told her.

'Now you're making me really nervous.' She laughed and we said our goodbyes.

# CHAPTER 17

My family home was out in Bellevue, on the outskirts of the city and I still experienced a familiar, happy pull every time I approached the house along the gravel driveway. With Greg driving me, I could take the time to really appreciate the view of the antebellum-style house as I approached, with its red brick façade and pillars either side of the entrance. I walked up the steps to the green front door and let myself in. I called out to tell everyone I was home and in no time, my mom, Michelle, my step-dad, Bob and my younger sister, Maggie were all around me, hugging me and welcoming me back.

'Jackson, you look really well, there's something to be said for that sea air. What did you think of Dorset, going back after all this time?' asked my mom. 'I wish we could have gone with you. Still, summer school was great fun this year.'

We wandered into the kitchen as we talked and my stomach rumbled from the wonderful smells of my mom's cooking. Over dinner, I told them all about Dorset and about the wedding, answering all their questions as patiently as I could. When there was finally a lull in the conversation, I took a deep breath before plunging in with the most important news.

'I met someone while I was there. Her name is Rachel.'

They all looked up, my mom and sister gasping in surprise, while my dad just looked happy for me.

'Oh my goodness!' Maggie squealed before bombarding me with a hundred questions. 'How did you meet? How old is she? What does she look like? What does she do? When's she coming over?'

Dad held up a hand to quiet her.

'Let Jackson tell us in his own good time, Maggie. Don't crowd him. It's probably been hard enough telling us that bit.' My dad smiled kindly at me.

Over dinner, I told them everything about how we'd met and how talented a singer and songwriter she was. I told them about the demo and how we were trying to get her over to Nashville to record it as soon as possible. After we'd all helped clear away, Maggie went off to her room saying she needed to study, but perhaps sensing that I needed some time alone with Mom and Dad.

'Jackson, is it serious with you and Rachel?' my mom asked.

'I think it could be. We tried to keep it simple and to have fun without getting involved but since I came back, I've hated being without her.' I scrunched my face up for a moment.

'Try not to get too frustrated about it,' my mom reassured me. 'From what you say, she's doing everything she can to get here, which means she cares for you too because that's a hell of a commitment to come all the way to Nashville. What do her family think?'

'Her parents have both passed and she has no other family. She has some really solid friends and they've looked out for her but in a way, I think she feels she has nothing to lose by giving things in Nashville a try.'

'Well, let's keep our fingers crossed that she gets here soon. I can't wait to meet her. Sorry to ask but does she know about what happened with Stephanie?'

'Yes, I told her that but I haven't told her about what happened to me afterwards. I haven't had the courage because her dad was a drinker and died from it. I didn't know where to start with that explanation.' I looked at my mom for reassurance.

'You need to tell her at some point, Jackson, it's better not to have any secrets.'

My dad nodded in agreement.

'Yeah, I've not been doing too well on the secrets front.' I told them about the competition then and how angry Rachel had been with me for keeping my involvement with it a secret.

'Well, you did the right thing then. Don't beat yourself up about Stephanie, son. You had a tough time and you got through it the only way you knew how. Now it's over and you never have to see Stephanie again. You've moved on with your life and that took a lot of courage.'

'Thanks, Dad. I know you're both right but I still don't relish that conversation.'

We chatted for a while longer about their news. My parents were both lecturers at the university and so they had just come to the end of the long holiday and were now getting back into the swing of the new semester. Maggie attended Vanderbilt as well now. She'd only just started and was bound to have lots to tell me so I excused myself and went off to find her. I tried her room, knocking gently as I arrived.

'Hey, Maggie, how's college?' She pulled me in for a chat.

'It's great, Jackson. I haven't had many classes yet but I'm really enjoying concentrating on the one thing I love, writing.' She beamed a big smile at me. 'I'm really pleased about your news too, it's lovely to see you looking so happy and so well again. We were all really worried about you before you went away. You were working too hard and didn't seem to have any life outside that at all. I can already see the good effect that knowing Rachel has had on you.'

'Hey, when did my little sister get so wise all of a sudden?' I teased her. 'I do feel happier, Maggie.' I gave her a quick kiss and a hug and promised to see her again soon.

As I put the phone down after speaking to Rachel the next morning, I had to stifle a yawn. I went over to stretch out on the sofa in my office, planning to read through some of my paperwork, and closed the door on my way. Next thing I knew, my sister, Alex was gently shaking me awake, saying it was twelve thirty and time for the lunch we'd planned. I sat up quickly, annoyed at myself for sleeping so long.

'Jet-lag still getting to you, huh?' she asked.

'Yeah, I woke up at five this morning. Hang on while I go to the bathroom to freshen up a little.'

I did feel better for a bit more sleep and was looking forward to my lunch with her. We strolled down to our favourite midtown café and ordered a couple of club sandwiches and some drinks before settling in to catch up. As we began to chat, my shoulders relaxed and the tension began to ease away from me. I was very close to Alex. I think it helped that we both worked in the music business and we were very like each other in many ways. I told her all about meeting Rachel and how much I'd enjoyed getting away from everything for a while.

'You really needed it, you were working yourself to death before you went so it probably came at the right time for you. Rachel sounds lovely, I can't wait to meet her. When's she coming?'

'Soon I hope, it's all a bit up in the air at the moment because of her job. Anyhow, I played Rachel's performance from the final to my VPs yesterday and they loved it. Ideally, I want Rough Cut to sign her but, and this is where you come in, I want her to know that she has a choice, that she doesn't have to sign with us if she doesn't think that's the best deal for her and for that, she'll need a manager.'

'And you're thinking that I could be her manager?' Alex asked with a slight frown.

'Yes, I think that would make a lot of sense.'

'I think I should hear her sing first of all and then we'll need to meet as soon as she comes over. These things can't just be decided, we might not even get on for any number of reasons.'

'I think that's unlikely but I take your point. All I'm asking is that you'll keep an open mind for me. Do you want to stop in for a copy of her performance on the way back then?'

'Yep, that sounds like a good idea and I'll call you with my thoughts later today. Listen, I'm really glad that things are going so well for you both but don't rush it, you know. Give yourself some time to get used to being in a relationship again without any strings,' she advised.

'But I really like her, Alex, and I don't want to lose her because of my past. She already means a lot to me.' I frowned again, miserable at not being with Rachel.

Alex patted me on the arm. 'Take it easy, that's all I'm saying.' She of all people, knew how badly I'd been hurt before.

When I arrived at work the next day, I felt relaxed and happy for the first time in ages. I'd started working a more sensible day, much to Annie's surprise, leaving at six o'clock last night and not arriving till nine this morning. I'd even gone for a run yesterday evening, which was something I used to do all the time before Stephanie had set out to ruin my life. Meeting Rachel had made me realise that I'd let too many things go since then, and now I wanted to get back on track and put what had happened with Stephanie behind me once and for all. I was confident that Rachel would be able to come to Nashville and we might even know for sure today.

At ten, Todd appeared at the door of my office for the meeting that Annie had set up between us. He'd obviously been busy in my absence, listening to lots of demo CDs and attending a number of singer/songwriter and "Open Mic" nights at different venues to see who was new on the music scene. He'd picked out three new acts that he was interested in and we spent some time discussing their relative pros and cons and how they would fit together with our other artists.

We also talked about the individual financial implications of taking on each of these artists, what the costs of development, marketing and sales might be and when we could expect to recoup our costs.

I asked Todd to bring the three CDs along to the meeting this afternoon so the whole team could listen to them together and discuss where we thought we could go with them. I moved on then to talk about Rachel.

'I suppose realistically, we're looking at the same level of analysis for Rachel, aren't we, if we're to keep this strictly business?' I asked Todd.

'Jackson, I hope I'm not speaking out of turn,' he replied. 'But are you and Rachel an item? You seem to speak very fondly of her.'

For a moment, I wondered how much to reveal but I decided it was best to be honest all round. 'Yep, I think you could say that we are.' I smiled broadly and he did too.

'Well then, yes, we are really, except that you have a bit more personally invested in Rachel's success.' He smiled ruefully. 'You know that we'll give her the same level of attention as any other new act so she wouldn't lose out,' he reassured me.

'I just want her to get here and then you guys can all meet her and make your own minds up and we can get her out on the circuit.'

By the time we'd finished, it was midday. I invited Todd to walk with me to the deli on the corner to pick up a sandwich and we wandered out into the sunshine. When we got back, we went out to the roof garden to eat lunch and catch up. I'd just sat down when I saw Annie weaving her way towards me looking intent on something.

As she drew closer, I could see she was holding my cell.

'Jackson, I've brought you your cell because it buzzed with a text while you were out. When I glanced at it, I could see it was from Rachel. I hope you don't mind. I thought it might be important.'

'Thanks, Annie, I appreciate that.' I took the phone from her. When I opened the message, it said,

*'I have news. Please call me as soon as you can.'*

I stood up, gathered my lunch and apologised to Todd for abandoning him, then strode back to my office. Rachel answered straight away and I could sense her excitement.

'Hi, sweetheart, what's the news?' I hardly dared to breathe, waiting for her answer.

'They've agreed to let a friend of mine replace me. She was looking for a job anyway so I've handed in my notice and now I'm free to go!'

'Oh, that's fantastic news. I'm proud of you for deciding to take that leap. I won't let you down, I promise.'

'Thank you, I know. I'm really excited now, I can't wait to see you more than anything else. So tell me, what do I need to do?'

'Okay, well, first of all, I'm going to ask Annie, my assistant, to wire you the money you'll need for the plane ticket and other expenses. You'll need that before you can do anything. Is your passport all up to date?'

'Yes, my passport's valid for a few years yet, I'm sure but I'll check it. What about a visa, do I need one?'

'No, there's a Visa Waiver Program now. Anyway, I'll get Annie to contact you with all the relevant details if you give me your email. Then it's just a question of you getting packed up and coming over. This is awesome. We'll be seeing each other in a few days now. I'll ring you in the morning again and we can see where things are at that point, okay, sweetheart? Hey and thank you for calling and letting me know.'

'I can't wait. Speak to you tomorrow.'

The next couple of days were long, hot and drawn out, with me whiling away the hours until Rachel's arrival, which was going to be on Sunday. I spent Saturday with my folks, finally returning home around midnight, conscious of the fact that over in Dorset, Rachel would soon be setting off for Nashville. As I listened to the distant sound of the live music from the honky-tonk bars on Lower Broadway through my open window, my excitement grew. I would be able to show her the real Nashville very soon and I knew she would love it.

# CHAPTER 18

The next day was another long, drawn out affair, during which I became more and more impatient to see Rachel and yet the hours seemed to be twice as long as normal. I tried all my usual distraction techniques, going for a run, having a tidy up around the condo (already as tidy as it could possibly be), making a few calls, having a long lunch but it was still only three o'clock by the time I'd finished. I finally decided to slump on the sofa and watch a bit of TV and promptly fell asleep in front of a movie. When I woke up, it was nearly six so at least that had killed a few hours. It wasn't long now till Rachel would be landing in Fort Worth and so I sent her a text asking her to call me when she arrived.

'Hi Jackson, it's me,' her tired but still lovely voice said a short while later.

'Sweetheart, hi, how are you, apart from dog-tired?'

'Yeah, that's a good description. I am really tired but I don't think I could sleep, do you know what I mean?'

'It's crazy isn't it? I felt the same. Have you had something to eat?'

'I'll try and get something while I'm here perhaps. How are you doing? It must have been a long day for you and you still have ages to wait until I get there.'

'You are well worth the wait. I'm trying to pace myself so that I don't go mad before you get here.' I laughed and so did she and it sounded wonderful.

'I must tell you that I could seriously get used to travelling first class. What an eye opener! I do feel a bit like an impostor though.' She chuckled.

'As I've told you a million times, you deserve it as much as the next person and I'm glad you like it.' I smiled. She was like a kid in a sweet shop.

'You'll be coming to meet me at the airport then?' she asked.

'Of course, I wouldn't miss it. I'll be the one with the red carnation,' I joked.

'Ooh, cheesy, it'll be just like in the movies and will you be holding up a card with my name on it, for good measure?'

'Hmmm, I hadn't thought of that, I'll see what I can do. I will sweep you away in a luxury vehicle as well, ma'am.' I exaggerated my accent just to make her laugh.

'You really know how to spoil a girl.' She sighed and my heart skipped a beat.

'That's one of the things I'm looking forward to doing over the coming weeks,' I said and this time, my voice sounded a bit husky.

'Well, that sounds just what I'm after, thank you. I probably ought to go and look for something to eat now, my stomach did just rumble,' she said a bit reluctantly, 'and I'll see you very soon.' It was her turn to sound excited by that prospect.

'Okay, sweetheart, take care and remember that it won't be long now,' I said.

'Yes, see you soon. Bye for now.' She blew me a very sexy kiss down the phone. Phew! That had me heated up in all the right places. I decided to go and have a shower and get changed so I looked my best when she arrived.

A couple of hours later, the concierge called to let me know that

Greg was waiting for me in the lobby so I grabbed my things and set off to meet him for the short ride to the airport.

By the time we arrived, Rachel's plane would be landing and I would be ready and waiting for her as soon as she came through. There were a lot of people waiting for loved ones in the arrivals hall and soon passengers started to appear.

I rubbed my hands over my face, worrying that things might be a bit awkward between us at first. I knew this was silly because everything had been exactly the same when we'd spoken on the phone, I was just jittery with anticipation.

Then, all of a sudden, there she was, her long chestnut hair framing her pretty face, which was looking desperately for me. When our eyes met, hers lit up with pleasure and I imagined that mine did the same.

She walked as quickly as she could towards me, flinging her cases at my feet and throwing her arms around my neck. Our lips met and the kiss we shared was like coming home. It was a long time before we stopped to draw breath and I only pulled back a little, not wanting to let her go for one second. She smelled so inviting and the feel of her skin against mine filled me with desire.

'Hey, Rachel,' I whispered, 'I sure am glad to see you.' I smiled at her lovely face.

'Back at you, Jackson. I've missed you, I don't think I was aware how much until I saw you then.' We shared another kiss, our bodies drawn irresistibly to each other. I buried my fingers in her long, wavy hair and felt her sigh. I knew at that moment that all I wanted to do was to get her in my bed and show her all the love I had for her.

'C'mon, let's get you home,' I said, breaking the connection for the time being. 'I see you can travel lightly!'

I teased her and she gave me a look that said she could probably meet any challenge I might throw at her. I picked up her bags in one hand and took hers in the other and we set off for the car.

'I can't get over how humid it is here, even this late at night,' she said as we walked.

'I know, baby, it takes some getting used to. It even surprised me when I came back but I think I've adjusted now.'

I stowed her luggage in the trunk after opening the rear passenger door for her. When I jumped in, I pulled her close to me as we set off for the condo.

'Who's that?' she whispered, nodding at Greg.

'Rachel, meet Greg, my regular driver.'

'Pleased to meet you, ma'am. I hope you'll enjoy your stay in Nashville.' Greg smiled at Rachel in the rear-view mirror.

'Pleased to meet you too, Greg,' she replied a little shyly before nestling back against me. I sighed as we relaxed back into the seat for the journey home.

As we got out of the car, Rachel stood transfixed, staring at the affectionately named 'Batman' building, an icon of the Nashville skyline.

'What is that building? It looks like...like...'

'Like Batman?' I offered, amused at the look of confusion on her face.

'Exactly,' she said, still unable to look away from the view of the city at night.

I chuckled.

'That's what everyone calls it, sweetheart.' I took her hand and watched as she tried to absorb it all.

'And something smells delicious. What is it?'

'That, sugar, is good ol' southern fried chicken. We will definitely make sure you get to try some while you're here.'

---

'Wow, what a fantastic sight!' she said, going straight to the terrace for the night-time view of downtown Nashville's skyscrapers, from above this time. 'I love that Batman building. The spires look so cool lit up like that!'

I set her bags down and followed her out there, slipping my arm around her waist.

'Yeah, the view was one of the things I liked most about this place. I love being in the heart of the city, with the mix of old architecture and modern skyscrapers side by side.' I pointed out the Cumberland river to her and the famous Shelby Street bridge.

She turned then to look at me and, as I looked down into her eyes, the strength of her love for me made me catch my breath.

'Jackson, I...' she began but then faltered.

'What is it?' I asked, drawing her to me and tracing her lower lip with my fingertips. I could hear concern in her voice.

'Are you sure you still feel the same way for me as you said you did in Dorset?'

I leaned down and kissed her softly on her full lips, breathing in her now familiar floral scent. 'I love you, as much as I did before, if that's what you're asking me,' I said, gazing down into her eyes. 'You're gorgeous and it's all I can do to restrain myself right now. But we can take our time and let you get settled in first.' I smiled, trying to lighten the mood a little.

She nodded, a faint blush creeping up her cheeks.

I grabbed her hand then and took her on a whistle-stop tour of my loft, finally bringing her to my bedroom. I put her bag down on the floor and turned to face her.

'Would you like something to eat or drink or do you think you'll be able to sleep?' I asked her.

'I'm not really hungry right now but I don't want to sleep either.' She pulled at her lower lip with her teeth and raised her eyebrows at me.

I took a step towards her. 'What do you have in mind then, Miss Hardy?' I hoped that I had picked up her signals correctly.

'I think it's time we both showed a bit less restraint,' she said, with a grin.

I swept her up in my arms then, tasting her lips again before laying her gently on the bed. She looked adorable with her hair fanned out on the pillows around her, staring up at me and I wanted only to make her mine once more, to share with her the passion I'd been holding in while we'd been apart.

---

'How about having something to eat now?' I asked again, some time later, propping myself up so I could see her more clearly.

'I wouldn't mind something because I didn't eat at the stopover in the end. But you must be tired. You'll have to get up tomorrow won't you?'

'I had a snooze in front of the TV earlier, so I'm not too sleepy and I can go in whenever I want. I am the boss, you know.' I put on what I imagined to be a typical boss face, knowing I was nothing of the sort.

She laughed then and smacked my arm playfully. I swung out of bed, pulling on my boxers and went into the kitchen, with Rachel following a minute later, dressed in one of my t-shirts. I fixed some salad for her and poured out some sparkling water. I nibbled at some chips while she tucked in.

'Can I ask you something?' she said after a quiet moment.

'Sure, although this sounds a bit ominous,' I replied.

'Are you teetotal?' she asked. 'I'm only asking because I've never seen you drink alcohol.'

'Yes, I am and I have been for the best part of a year now,' I replied after the slightest pause.

'Does that have anything to do with your break-up with Stephanie?' she asked intuitively.

'Unfortunately, yes it does.' I sighed, running my hands through my hair.

'You don't have to tell me about it now, if it makes you feel awkward. It's just something I've wondered about.'

'You never make me feel awkward and you have a right to know about my past.' I paused again for a moment, gathering myself before

I went on. 'I loved Stephanie and I'd expected us to settle down and make a life together, you know. She was so glamorous and self-confident, she completely took me in. I'd moved into her apartment after a few months but I'd left something at home that day so I went back to get it in the afternoon, only to find the two of them having sex in our bed.' Rachel winced as I described that awful moment.

'I'm still ashamed of how I acted then. I was so angry I completely lost it and started hitting this guy until she managed to pull me off him. I know I said some terrible things to her and then I ran and kept on going to get as far away from them as possible. I remember sitting on a park bench in the evening finally and breaking down. Everything we'd planned had been shattered in an instant and I couldn't imagine how I would rebuild my life.' I grasped Rachel's hand and she squeezed mine in reassurance.

'I ended up in a bar then and drank myself into oblivion. Fortunately, someone there recognised me and helped me call my sister Alex. She came and took me home with her. But that was only the beginning. I kept on drinking solidly for the next three months, trying to forget what she'd done to me. My family worked so hard to care for me through that dark time and there must have been many times when they thought I would never come through.

Then one day, I woke up with yet another terrible headache and furry mouth and I decided that she wasn't worth all this. If anything, I'd had a lucky escape and now it was up to me to get on with the rest of my life. So I broke all ties with her, I went out and bought this place and I cleaned up, deciding to try never to drink again. That's when I took Greg on as my driver too and I've stuck to that promise to this day. I haven't seen Stephanie again since and I hope I never do see her again because I'm not sure I could trust myself to be a gentleman in her presence.'

Rachel's eyes hadn't once wavered as I was telling her my story. If anything, she seemed stronger with each word, as though her respect for me was growing as she listened. As I finished, she stood up and came round the breakfast bar towards me.

'You are one hell of a good man, you know, and I'm lucky to have met you when I did. I'm sorry that she hurt you but you should be proud of yourself for getting through that nightmare. Thank you for being honest with me.' She kissed me, looping her arms around my neck.

'I don't know what I did to deserve you, but whatever it was, I'm sure glad I did it.' I beamed at her. 'I have to be honest and tell you that I don't know what I'd do if I did see her again. I worry that it would send me straight back to drinking.'

'Is it likely that you'll see her again?'

'I think she left town after what happened. She hated the bad press she was getting because they found out she cheated on me. I don't have any idea where she went though.'

'All we can do is deal with that if it comes up but it doesn't sound like it will. As long as you're honest about your feelings, it'll be okay.'

---

As I came downstairs into the lounge the next morning, I saw Rachel sitting on the terrace. She looked stunning, with her chestnut hair cascading down her back and all her luscious curves outlined by her silk gown.

I stood for several minutes, drinking in her loveliness and remembering how good her skin felt to the touch. My body was already responding to that memory when she turned to look at me, obviously sensing I was there. I looked down sheepishly, caught in the act of staring but when I dared to look up again, she was smiling brightly back at me.

I walked towards her.

'Hey, good morning, sleepyhead,' she said, taking my hand and bringing it to her lips.

'What time did you wake up?'

'Five o'clock or some other ungodly hour. I've been sitting here quietly, watching the sun come up and waiting for you to surface. Shouldn't you, you know, be at work now?'

'No, I've sent a text to Annie to say I'm working at home, at least for this morning. They're slowly getting used to me not being such a workaholic since I met you.'

'Since you met me?' Her eyes widened. 'What do you mean?'

'Well, after Stephanie, I threw myself into my work, living and breathing it to try and help myself forget all the pain. And I kind of expected the same of everyone else, which I'm not proud of. But since I came back last week, I've started to rediscover my true self a little. I think that's down to meeting you.' I smiled. 'I hope you're going to help me continue that trend over these coming weeks, sweetheart.'

'It would be my pleasure.'

She came over to me and kissed me. From that point on, I was lost in her and I knew it was only a matter of time before we would end up back in the bedroom so that I could show her what I was feeling.

I suggested that we go out for lunch once we were finally dressed so that Rachel could start to get a bit more of a feel for Nashville. I decided to keep it simple for her first day and so we wandered round to my favourite sandwich shop on Union Street. It was midday by the time we got there and already feeling pretty humid but the line outside wasn't too bad and once we sat down inside, it was fun advising Rachel about what to have.

'What do you recommend? It all looks and smells great but there's so much choice!' Her eyes widened as the table next to us received their order, including the most enormous sandwiches. She laughed along with them at their surprise.

'Yeah, you're right but I've tried most things over the years. I'd definitely recommend one of the hot sandwiches but honestly, it's all good. You must try and leave some room for a brownie, they really are to die for.'

Our server came shortly after and, with her friendly encouragement, Rachel finally went for the Angus Po'Boy and I had my regular, Wicked Chicken for the spicy chipotle and green chilli sauce. We ordered a couple of lemonades too and sat back to people watch for a minute while we waited for our orders to come.

As always, the restaurant was bustling with both tourists and regulars but no-one seemed to mind being packed in because the food was so delicious. I watched Rachel's face as she took in all the cowboy hats in the room, smiling as her eyes lit up at the sight. Music was never far from her mind though.

'What have you planned for me, musically, I mean, over the next few weeks?' Rachel asked, breaking us out of our reverie. She had a glint in her eye as she posed the question. I smiled before replying, knowing exactly what her double meaning was but then focussed on the real question.

'I thought that it would be good for you to come in with me to the office tomorrow and sing a few of your songs for us live so that they can see what you're like in real life, if you'd be up for that?'

'That sounds like a good idea,' she agreed but she was twisting her hands together.

I reached over and took one of hers in mine.

'Hey, you don't need to worry about anything. I'll be there to look out for you and they're all nice people, honestly. I'd also like to invite my sister, Alex, if that's okay? She's a music manager and I've already given her the CD of your performance at the final, which she told me she thought was fantastic, by the way.'

'Hang on, why do I need a manager when I have you?' she queried.

I took a deep breath before answering.

'You don't have to answer to me about anything. This has to be your journey and if you have your own manager, you'll be taking independent advice, and don't think that because Alex is my sister, she'll do what I say. Nothing could be further from the truth, which is why I spoke to her because I know she'll look out for your best interests. She's had several years of experience already, despite only being twenty-four.'

'Okay,' she said reluctantly. 'Well, I'd like to meet Alex of course but I'm not sure that I need independent advice like you're suggesting. I haven't even recorded the demo CD yet.'

'Listen, sweetheart, I want you to do what's right for you. You won't offend me by signing with someone else if that's what you finally decide down the line, you know.'

'Jackson! How can you even think that I'd do that? I'm shocked by that idea, I really am. I know I'd be upset if you did that to me. Anyway, you're getting way ahead of things.'

'What can I say? This is business, you don't owe me anything but it is a good idea to think ahead so we're prepared.'

She pursed her lips and folded her arms, letting her body tell me that she didn't like that idea one little bit. The look she gave me made it very clear that she had her own opinion about how she wanted things to go. Her determination made me smile, even if it meant we wouldn't always agree on everything.

'Why are you smiling at me?' she demanded.

'It's just that you're so sexy when you're cross with me.' I grinned at her, knowing I'd caught her off-guard.

Then our food came, taking our attention away from the discussion for a moment at least. It was delicious as always and for a while we simply indulged our taste buds. When we both paused to let our food go down, she went straight back to the point.

'I know you want to look out for me but I think this impartiality is misguided. *You* found me and *you* made this all happen for me and I want you to be by my side as I go through this whole thing.'

'I will be by your side, I'm not suggesting otherwise.' I paused. 'Look, let's not get bogged down by this, please. How about we take it slow and see what happens and deal with things as they come up?'

She nodded but I could see that I'd unsettled her and that was the last thing I'd meant to do.

# CHAPTER 19

It was mid-afternoon by the time we returned and Rachel went straight off to unpack her stuff while I checked in with the office to arrange things for tomorrow and to deal with some emails. I found it hard to concentrate after our disagreement. I wanted only to do what was right for Rachel but she hadn't taken it that way. I would have to tread carefully not to throw her off balance again.

After an hour of being apart, I went to look for her, hoping that she'd had enough time on her own to process our earlier conversation by now. I went into the bedroom only to find her fast asleep in semi-darkness, with the blinds closed. I knew I should wake her because it would be better for her to sleep at night but I couldn't resist watching her sleep for a few minutes longer. I held my breath as I watched the gentle rise and fall of her chest and I noticed the contrast of her flushed cheeks against the cream pillowcase. I sat down on the bed next to her and reached out to caress her cheek, making her sigh.

'Sweetheart, time to wake up,' I whispered, and I kissed her lips softly before sitting back again.

She stirred and squinted at me, then sat up suddenly, her face close to mine.

'How long have I been asleep?' she asked, moving away a little.

'Only an hour, I think. Shhh, it's okay,' I reassured her. 'I didn't think it would be good for you to sleep too long.'

'I think I'll have a quick shower to wake myself up.'

She headed off to the bathroom before I could say anything further and I went back out to the lounge, wishing I'd climbed into bed with her instead of waking her up. I found myself thinking of all the contours of her body while she was in the shower, which only made my frustration grow but I didn't think she was in the right mood for me to join her in there yet.

A short while later, she reappeared, with her hair damp from the shower and her skin smelling even sweeter, if that was possible. She'd changed into fresh clothes as well and looked more relaxed. She wasn't smiling at me though.

'Are you still mad at me?' I asked.

'A little,' she said honestly, 'but I do understand your reasons, I don't agree with you, that's all.' She smiled a crooked smile. 'The important thing is that we keep talking about it all, okay?' she asked.

'Of course we will,' I agreed and I went towards her and took her in my arms. 'I wondered if you might like to go over to my parents' house tonight so I can introduce y'all? My mom is dying to meet you! What do you think?'

'Yes, that would be nice, I think.' She was biting her lip though as if she wasn't sure.

'It won't be formal or anything, my folks aren't like that, honestly.' I kissed her again, craving a taste of her. 'Shall we head over there about six?'

We made our way downstairs soon afterwards to meet Greg again for the short ride to my parents' house. I pointed out some landmarks to Rachel on the way, wanting to share all the things I loved about my home town. As we approached Centennial Park, I waited to see her reaction to our very own Greek temple in Tennessee.

'Goodness, what is that amazing building in the park? It looks like it should be in Athens, not Nashville!'

I told her about our Parthenon replica then and how it had been built for the Centennial celebrations. We could see that the park was full of people out for a stroll as always.

'The Parthenon seems a bit out of place here, I know, but the park is lovely. We spent hours there as kids.'

We rounded the corner and I showed her Vanderbilt University where my parents worked and Maggie, my sister, was a student.

My parents came out to meet us as we pulled up to the house.

'It's lovely to meet you, Rachel,' my mom said as soon as we got out of the car. My mom kissed Rachel on both cheeks after I introduced her, and my dad, ever the gentleman, took her hand and brought it to his lips.

'You're every bit as beautiful as Jackson said you were, Rachel.'

I rolled my eyes at him and Rachel blushed. We all laughed together, breaking the ice.

My mom took Rachel's arm and led her into the house, talking all the way. I shook Dad's hand, punching him playfully on the arm as well, after his showy display. Maggie joined us shortly afterwards, unable to contain her curiosity and we sat down to a simple pasta supper.

'So, Rachel,' my mom began, 'you're from Poole, Jackson tells me.'

'That's right, I've lived there all my life. I know you lived in Bournemouth when Jackson was young. Is that where you're from originally?'

'Yes, I was born and brought up there but I lived in a number of places around Dorset, including Poole for a short while, before Jackson was born. I haven't been back since I met Bob over here. I probably ought to do that sooner rather than later.'

'Rachel is an excellent guide to all the sights,' I mentioned, with a chuckle.

'I'd love to show you round sometime, Mrs Phillips,' said Rachel.

'Honey, you must call me Shelley, everyone does, except my students of course.' She laughed heartily.

'What do you lecture in, Shelley?' Rachel continued.

'French and European Studies. I took my first degree in the UK at Southampton and then completed my PhD here at Emory, over in Atlanta, after meeting Bob.'

The conversation continued without a pause, with Rachel filling them in with details about herself as we went along.

'What's Dorset like, Rachel? Is it near London?' asked Maggie, making everyone laugh.

'It's a good couple of hours away, Maggie, near the sea,' Rachel explained.

Maggie's face fell and I could see that she was mentally removing it from her list of places to visit even as we were speaking.

'It was lovely to meet you, Rachel,' said Maggie, as she kissed her goodbye. 'I sure hope we'll see you again soon.'

'Well, how about we get everyone together for a cookout this Sunday afternoon?' offered my dad.

'That sounds like a great idea, Dad,' I replied and it was agreed.

In the car on the way back home, Rachel snuggled up to me, and before too long, I sensed the change in her body and knew that she had fallen asleep. I couldn't bring myself to wake her when we arrived so I simply scooped her into my arms and carried her into the building. I was aware of every curve of her body as she wrapped herself around me, and when I laid her on the bed a few minutes later, I was consumed with desire for her once more. I lay awake for ages afterwards, listening to the sound of her breathing and waiting for the physical ache I had for her to subside.

---

Thanks to my noisy alarm, we both woke at seven the next day.

'Hey, sweetheart.' Rachel greeted me with a kiss on the back of my neck, pressing her body up against me and reminding me of the desire I'd felt last night.

I turned round to look at her, putting my hands lightly on either side of her waist.

'Hey, beautiful,' I replied, savouring every detail of her face.

'I don't remember going to bed last night and I still have my clothes on. How did that happen?' She gazed at me, waiting for me to explain, which I did.

'You looked so lovely when I laid you on the bed, it was really hard to restrain myself.'

'And do you still have those feelings now?' she asked, giving me a very seductive smile.

I reached out to unbutton her blouse in answer to her question and she arched her neck towards me for a kiss.

We still made it to the office for nine o'clock after a leisurely walk in. Annie was already at her desk when we arrived and stood up to greet us. She smiled broadly at Rachel and I felt her relax with the warmth of Annie's welcome.

'Rachel, it's such a pleasure to meet you. I'm Annie, Jackson's assistant and dogsbody.' She grinned, making Rachel laugh by return.

'Well, I suppose someone had to have that job,' she replied good-humouredly.

'If there's anything you need, let me know,' Annie went on.

'Thank you, that's really kind.'

I showed Rachel into my office.

'Wow, Annie's a real catch, isn't she?' Rachel said as we went in.

'She sure is. I like to think of her as my office mom, always looking out for my best interests and a great friend to boot,' I said.

We sat down on the sofa and I quickly ran through the plan for the day.

'I've scheduled your live performance for ten o'clock which will give you a chance to meet the VPs and Alex. After that, around eleven, I've set up a meeting for you with Todd and Alex to discuss potential "Open Mic"/live performances in Nashville in the coming week, followed by lunch with Alex to discuss things so far. Then you and I can meet back at the office after you've had lunch to discuss progress.'

'That sounds good,' she said. 'Would I be able to go somewhere with a guitar or keyboard to have a quick run-through now?'

'Of course, sweetheart. Let's go to the studio and I'll show you where everything is. Jed, our engineer, may well be in by now to give you a hand settling in.'

We took the stairs to the lower floor and walked along to the studio. I saw Rachel glance at some of the staff as we walked along and some of them returned her look with a smile. As we walked along the downstairs corridor, she stopped in front of one of the framed posters on the wall. It was a colourful print of a guitar against the Nashville skyline.

'That's an amazing print. I love the guitar and I think I'd know those buildings anywhere now.'

I laughed and we continued on our way.

'Hey, Jed, are you in yet?' I called out when we went into the studio.

'Yup, I'm here,' his deep voice replied.

'Jed, I've brought Rachel down to get settled in before she sings for us later.'

'Hey, Rachel, nice to meet you,' he drawled, appearing from his office and putting his hand out. His massive hand dwarfed hers, I noticed, and she looked quite enchanted by his bear-like appearance.

I coughed lightly to get her attention and narrowed my eyes at her when she looked my way.

'I can trust you to look after Rachel, can't I?' I joked with Jed while staring fixedly at Rachel.

He laughed and she cleared her throat nervously in an effort to regain her focus.

'Of course, what can you mean?' Jed replied with a twinkle in his eye.

Rachel seemed to recover some composure then. Jed definitely had a way with women but I didn't want him to work his magic on this particular woman.

'Okay then, well, I'll leave you to it. Jed, please make sure Rachel has everything she needs to perform. I'll be back at ten o'clock with the VPs and Alex, okay?'

'Yep, sure thing, Jackson, see you then.' He went off to look at his gear.

'Jed will sort you out. Don't hesitate to ask him for anything, all right sweetheart?'

'Okay.' She swallowed, looking nervous.

I gave her a hug and a light kiss before going back up to my office.

---

It wasn't long before I was winding my way back downstairs again to the studio, along with the VPs. Alex had already gone ahead to introduce herself and to check Rachel was ready.

We had some chairs set up around small tables in the studio area, making it like a café so it wasn't too daunting for performers and we all sat down in pairs around them. Rachel was sat on a high stool with her guitar in hand, tuning up as we arrived and she looked every inch the professional.

I remembered seeing her at that first gig and understanding that the music had the power to compose her in a way that nothing else could. Luckily, this was happening for her today too. She swept her hair over her shoulder, placed her pick in her mouth and focussed on tuning to her satisfaction.

She looked so stunning, I found it hard to concentrate on the job in hand but I willed myself to look away and take a deep breath. I noticed Alex giving me a look and I managed a tense smile in her direction.

'Hi, I'm Rachel Hardy, it's good to meet you all. Thank you for giving me the opportunity to sing for you today. As a warm-up, I'm going to start by singing one of my favourite songs, Lee Ann Womack's "I Hope You Dance".'

This song was also one of my favourites but we had no idea that we both liked it so much. I'd never heard Rachel sing it before and I realised I was holding my breath in anticipation of her performance. Well, I wasn't disappointed, she really knew how to do it justice. Damn, she was good.

I had a quick look round the others to see if I could gauge their mood. They were all smiling, if that was anything to go by. The applause was strong after her first cover and she looked buoyed up by that. Todd leaned towards me.

'She's even better live, Jackson.'

I blew out my breath then and tried to relax a little.

She moved on to sing some of her own songs, starting with 'My Turn', followed by 'Don't Let Me Go' and finishing with 'Too Late', which was the one I thought we could release straight away as a single.

At the end, we all stood to give rapturous applause because she'd been fantastic, there was no doubt about it and I could see that everyone was genuinely impressed, with a few people nodding in my direction. Rachel looked over at me then for confirmation and I winked at her to prove how well she'd done. She was beaming.

'You were right, Jackson. Rachel is an amazing singer,' Alex said to me when she joined me.

'I know and she wrote those songs herself. She is going to fit right in here in Nashville.' It was still true that for the Nashville music scene, it's all about the songs and the stories they tell, and Alex knew that as well as I did.

Everyone wanted to have a quick chat with Rachel before going so it took a while to get her on my own but when I did, I folded her into my arms and swept her off her feet. She giggled with delight mixed with a bit of relief, I think. When I put her down, we kissed and her excitement was infectious.

'That was the best feeling. I know I sang well and I really felt I did myself proud and when the applause came, it felt so good, you know?'

'I know, baby and you deserved every minute. Everyone was so impressed. It was great for them to be able to hear you sing live, rather than on a less than perfect recording.'

'Is there time for me to have a drink before my next meeting, do you think?'

I chuckled at her earnest face.

'You don't need to get permission, you're a free woman, honey!' I put on my best southern accent to tease her.

She flounced off up the stairs then, turning to give me a very sultry look over her shoulder and I chased her up the remaining stairs to the top. We were both a little breathless when we emerged into the main office and stopped suddenly, both doing our best to look calm. I glanced at her and she looked guiltily at me, pulling a face and making me laugh.

There was no doubt about it, Rachel Hardy was doing my damaged heart the power of good.

# CHAPTER 20

While Rachel was out at lunch with Alex, I walked down to Todd's office to ask how their meeting had gone. He invited me in and I took a seat across the desk from him so he could fill me in on all the details.

'Well, after Rachel's brilliant performance, it was easy to see where she would fit in for some live shows. We agreed to try for some "Open Mic" nights starting at The Bluebird Café next Monday, Douglas Corner on Tuesday and perhaps The Listening Room Café the following week. This would really get the community talking about her and promote some interest generally in the industry as well. We should get that demo CD recorded as soon as possible as well.'

'Yeah, that sounds good. This may well generate some interest among other record labels, which I think will be healthy too.'

'What do you mean, Jackson? Are you saying that you want other labels to be interested in Rachel, too? Doesn't that fly in the face of what we're trying to do?' Todd looked perplexed.

'Yes, I know it sounds crazy but I don't want Rachel to feel obliged to sign with my label out of loyalty to me. That's why I asked Alex to think about representing her. My theory is that if several labels are interested, she can then take a view about what's best for her, with Alex's help. That may well mean signing with us but it may not and I'm ready to accept that. Does that make sense?'

'Well, I understand where you're coming from, you don't want to railroad her, I get that. Have you told Rachel?' I nodded. 'And what did she have to say about your idea?' he asked.

'She didn't like it one bit,' I confessed. 'She said that she would be hurt if things were the other way round and I chose to go with someone else. I tried to explain my thinking to her, as I've done to you but she still wasn't convinced.'

Todd blew out a breath and continued to look confused.

'I do think that perhaps this is more about you seeking some kind of confirmation that she wants to be with you for the right reasons, rather than allowing her to make an independent choice of who she wants to sign with,' Todd told me gently.

'You mean that I'm afraid because of what happened with Stephanie?'

Todd nodded and shot me an embarrassed look.

'Okay, I hear you,' I said. 'I should be getting back now but I appreciate your honesty with me, Todd.'

I continued to ponder Todd's comments as I wandered back to my own office, worrying about whether I was doing the right thing with regard to Rachel's representation. In my heart, I wanted Rough Cut to sign her of course but I didn't want her to feel obliged to sign with us. I hoped that Alex would give her impartial advice so that she could make the best decision for herself.

As I neared the office, I saw Annie hovering by her desk looking concerned.

'Hey, Annie, what's up?' I asked, feeling worried myself by the unfamiliar look etched on her face.

She followed me into the office and closed the door.

'You received a phone call from Stephanie just now,' she said with a frown.

'What? What did she say?' I asked, feeling my heart pumping as I sat down heavily behind my desk.

'I think she thought I was lying when I said you weren't here so she was rude, of course.' She waved her hand as if dismissing Stephanie's rudeness. 'She asked again to speak to you several times before telling me to make sure to pass on the message that she'd called. She left her number.' She held out a note to me, which I stared at but didn't take.

'I don't ever want to talk to her again so I don't need that number, Annie.' I passed a hand over my face before banging my fist on the desk. 'Damn her. What the hell is she doing calling me again after all this time?'

'I'll get rid of this number then, shall I?' Annie asked me and I nodded. 'What do you want me to say if she calls again? I'm certain that she will.'

'If I am here the next time, you should put her through. But only so I can tell her that I don't ever want to speak to her again.'

---

I tried to put Stephanie's call out of my mind by working through lunch. Then, at two o'clock on the dot, Alex and Rachel appeared at the door of my office, looking ever so slightly conspiratorial and my mind switched immediately to them.

'Ladies, do come in and sit down,' I offered, in my best southern gentleman drawl. 'Did you have a good lunch?' I asked.

'Yes, it was lovely, thank you,' Rachel replied very politely.

'And did you make any decisions at all?' I went on, glancing from Rachel to Alex and then back again.

'Why, yes, Jackson, we did,' said Alex. 'I'm not sure whether you'll like our decision though.'

'Uh-oh,' I said out loud. 'Come on then, spill the beans. What did y'all conclude?'

'That Rachel should sign with Rough Cut and stop all this

fannying around, if you'll pardon my expression.' She gave me a look that said she was prepared for a fight if that's what I wanted.

I took a moment before replying and found them both staring at me intently when I looked up again.

'If we're being strictly truthful here, Rough Cut hasn't offered you a deal yet,' I said and I sat back in my chair in a victory stance.

'No, that's true,' Alex batted back, 'so we'll be on our way, shall we?' She motioned towards Rachel to stand up, which she did.

My jaw dropped at the way these two women were handling me. I threw my hands up in defeat and managed a smile.

'Okay, I know when I'm beat. I want Rachel to sign with us, you know I do. But are you sure that this is what you want to do?' I asked, looking directly at her this time.

She came towards me then but said to Alex, 'Would you mind giving us a minute please?'

As Alex left the room, Rachel came and took my hand, leading me over to the sofa. I waited for her to gather herself and explain her feelings to me.

'I need to sign with a label that will look out for my best interests. In the normal course of things, that would be really hard to find, wouldn't it?'

I nodded, swallowing nervously at the same time.

'But in this case,' she continued, 'I know that Rough Cut will look out for my best interests, above and beyond the normal call of duty because you own the company and not only that, but we're together so that's a double whammy. And there you have it. I don't want to sign with anyone else. I want you to look out for me and not just at work.' She raised her eyebrows a little and smiled which I found heart-warming.

'God, I love you so much, Rachel Hardy.' I leaned in for a kiss.

'I love you too, Jackson Phillips.'

I could feel her smile as she kissed me back to confirm it.

A short while later, Alex returned, and we quickly filled her in on the point we'd reached in our discussions. She jumped up and down on the spot, clapping her hands with glee. Then she gave Rachel a hug and put her hand out to shake mine before laughing and pulling me in for a hug too.

'Way to go, Rachel,' she said. 'Now all we need is a contract to pore over, Jackson.'

'I know and I'll get straight on it as soon as I get some peace from all this harassment I've been experiencing this afternoon.' I grinned.

The afternoon whizzed by and soon six o'clock rolled round so I went in search of Rachel. I found her down in the studio practising some other songs I hadn't heard before. I was able to stand listening to her without her realising I was there. The song seemed to be called 'Driving Me Crazy' and had a really good up-tempo beat to it.

I coughed lightly as the song came to an end.

She swivelled in surprise to see who had been watching her. When she saw it was me, her face lit up. That special look she gave me would never grow old.

I crossed the floor towards her, and embraced her with a deep, passionate kiss that left us both breathless.

'Hey, baby, time to go home,' I whispered.

'That sounds like a great idea.'

The rest of the week passed quickly, with Rachel spending every spare moment rehearsing and recording tracks for her demo CD and me trying to finalise the details of her contract with us. It had been a busy but satisfying week and I had already suggested to her that we spend Saturday sightseeing like proper tourists in and around Nashville.

So we were up pretty early on Saturday morning to make the most of the day. I'd decided that our first stop should be The Country Music Hall of Fame and Museum, and because I knew Rachel would love it, I'd thought ahead and bought us Platinum Package tickets earlier in the week. This would allow us to take in the fantastic RCA Studio Tour as well which was worth the entrance fee alone.

We arrived at the museum a little after it opened at nine, planning to have a look around there first before our Studio Tour. We spent quite a while outside looking at the magnificent modern building, with all its musical references, most notably the windows designed to look like the keys of a piano. Rachel took a whole host of photos from different angles but, in the end, I managed to persuade her to go in so we could see some of the museum. She absolutely fell in love with the history and all the different collections, taking in every last item in the Taylor Swift 'Speak Now' exhibit on show at the time and marvelling at all the different artefacts.

We broke off to do the RCA Studio Tour then, taking the old-fashioned shuttle bus over there, with its life-size photo of Dolly Parton on the side of it. Watching Rachel's reaction to everything was such a pleasure because she wanted to drink it all in and remember it forever.

'I can't quite believe we're standing in the place where stars like Elvis and Dolly recorded some of their greatest hits,' she marvelled.

When she sat down at the piano and played a couple of chords from her own songs, I saw the look on her face as though she was being transported back in time to the days when some of those country music greats had sat there before her. She was a bit overwhelmed by it all then and had to pause to catch her breath.

When we got back to the main museum, we had lunch in the restaurant, taking advantage of their outdoor courtyard before heading back inside again for another hour to see some more exhibits before we left. Although we'd had a good look at each floor, as well as studying some of the hundreds of plaques for Hall of Fame inductees, I thought that we would need to go again soon for Rachel to see anything else she might have missed. We finally wandered back into the afternoon sunshine, tired out but happy.

'Are you up for a bit more sightseeing or was that enough for one day?' I asked her, smiling at the excitement on her face.

FROM HERE TO YOU 161

'Oh, Jackson, I enjoyed that such a lot, I really wasn't expecting it to be that wonderful. I'd love to walk for a while and have a look at anything else we see on the way if you're still okay?'

I put my arm round her shoulder and said, 'As long as I'm with you, watching your lovely face, I'll go anywhere you like, baby.'

We walked down towards the Cumberland river and caught the Music City Trolley Hop tour to save our feet for a while and to allow us to do more sightseeing more quickly. We took in the iconic red-brick Ryman Auditorium, known as 'the mother church of country music' from the days when it was a gospel tabernacle, Bicentennial Park, and the Centennial Park and the Parthenon again before finally jumping off at the Frist Center Art Museum. We went inside for a coffee and dessert then to talk over our day.

'I can't believe how much there is to see here.' Rachel was still full of wonder, as she stirred her sugar into her café latte.

'You're right and we only scratched the surface today. I had the feeling that you could have stayed at the Country Hall of Fame all day, so we'll have to go back there.'

'That's a definite date. Thank you for a lovely day today, you're a pretty good tour guide, you know.' She smiled and drank some coffee.

'Changing the subject slightly, what shall we do for dinner tonight?' I asked her.

'How about we stay in and cook something? We haven't used the kitchen together yet. I love to cook and your kitchen looks like it needs some TLC.'

'That's fine by me. We'll stop at a market on the way home and pick up whatever you need.'

***

We sat out on the terrace to eat the delicious meal that Rachel had cooked, with a little bit of help from me. I heard Rachel's intake of breath a couple of times, as though she wanted to say something to me but didn't quite know how to start. I glanced over at her to see her biting her lip.

'You sound like you've got something on your mind. What is it?' I reached out my hand to stroke her arm.

'It's just that...' She looked at me, changed position in her chair and began again. 'I feel a bit nervous about how quickly everything is happening between us. It all feels a bit too good to be true. Did you really mean it when you said you loved me?' She glanced anxiously in my direction and then away.

'I did mean it, Rachel, I wouldn't say something like that lightly.'

She nodded, looking back at me again, before covering my hand with hers. I had the feeling that I'd passed a test but I wasn't entirely sure which one.

# CHAPTER 21

I left Rachel to lie in the next day while I went for a run, leaving a note to tell her where I'd gone. I hadn't been all week but I had remembered one of my old routes through Centennial Park when we went past it again yesterday and so decided to take myself that way. I needed some time to think about the conversation we'd had the night before too. I knew she was a bit hesitant about moving too quickly in our relationship and I could only guess at the reasons for that because she hadn't volunteered that information as yet. I didn't want to put her under any more pressure by asking her about it but I did want her to understand that I cared and that she could trust me. What I wasn't sure of was how to do that well enough for her to believe me. By the time I came back an hour later, she was still in bed, obviously not yet caught up with her lack of sleep. I busied myself making us some breakfast and she wandered into the kitchen a few minutes later.

'Hey, sleepyhead, how are you today?' I kissed her gently on the nose.

'I feel awful for sleeping in so late.' She groaned, putting her arms around me.

The warmth of her body against mine made me want to groan

too. Her body was so tempting, I had to stop myself from ravishing it at every opportunity.

'Don't feel guilty, you needed to catch up. I've been for a run and prepared us some breakfast so let's just enjoy it.' I moved carefully away from the temptation of her body and sat down at the table.

An hour later, Greg pulled up in front of my parents' house. Rachel picked up the bouquet of flowers she had bought for my mom the previous day and we got out of the car. I took Rachel's hand and this time, we went straight into the garden, knowing that everyone would be gathered there for the cookout. As we walked through the wrought-iron gate, Mom glanced up and called out to us.

'Hey, it's lovely to see you both again so soon.' She reached out to Rachel first and took the flowers she offered before enveloping Rachel in a great big hug. 'Thank you for these pretty flowers. What a kind thought!'

'We wanted to thank you and Bob for putting in all this work for us today.'

'It's been our pleasure. Jackson, give your mother a kiss. You look more handsome every time I see you,' she gushed in the way that mothers do.

'Aw, Mom, don't embarrass me!' I blushed ever so slightly at her comment.

'Just speaking the truth, there's surely nothing wrong with that, is there, Rachel?'

'No, ma'am,' Rachel replied, putting on her best Tennessee accent.

We left Mom as she went to find a vase for the flowers and walked towards Bob, who was already cooking food on the brick-built BBQ. Maggie was sitting on one of the garden benches, chatting away to someone I didn't recognise.

'Hey, Dad, how's the BBQ going?'

'So far, so good, Jackson. Hello, Rachel, you look lovely. I won't kiss you right now 'cos I'm a little greasy. I'll catch up with y'all for a proper hug later.'

'Do you need a hand with anything, Dad?' I asked, knowing he was going to say no.

'No, no, I'm fine,' he confirmed and I laughed.

'Look, we'll go over and catch up with Maggie but promise me you'll holler if you want me to help, okay?'

'Sure thing, Jackson,' and he turned back to his grilled meats like they were his babies.

I leaned towards Maggie to kiss her cheek and then I looked pointedly at her male companion. She laughed then at my big brother act.

'Rachel, Jackson, this is Ted, he's on my course at college.'

We both nodded at Ted and sat down on a nearby bench to enjoy the warmth of the sun. We chatted amiably for a while but when Ted went off to find the bathroom I jumped in quickly to quiz Maggie.

'Are you two dating?' I asked bluntly.

'We're just friends, Jackson. Relax, will you?' replied Maggie, rolling her eyes. Then turning to Rachel, she said, 'God, is he always this demanding? How do you put up with it?'

'I wouldn't call it demanding, maybe being a little over-protective, that's all.' Rachel smiled knowingly at me.

'I don't need you to protect me, Jackson, thank you.' Maggie stood up and flounced off.

I looked at Rachel and she raised her eyebrows at me.

'Am I over-protective?' I asked, a bit shame-faced.

'I guess you could say that but from my perspective, as your girl-friend, I like that. It's just that Maggie may not like it because she's your sister and so she has a different view, of course.'

'Just so we're clear though,' I replied, leaning in towards her, 'you are much more than my girlfriend.'

'How's that?' she asked, looking at me quizzically. 'I mean, we're not engaged or married, so the most you could describe me as is your partner. But I think that would imply that we were living together?'

She glanced at me from beneath her eyelashes.

'And that's what we're doing, isn't it? Living together?' I batted straight back at her.

'Yes, but I don't know if I like the sound of "partner". I'd rather be your girlfriend, if that's what's on offer.'

'I'm ready to offer you more whenever you're ready for more,' I whispered into her ear.

She turned towards me, placing one hand lightly on my chest.

'What kind of "more" do you mean?'

'I love you and you feel the same for me and I know I want us to be together all the time and, in my book, that means only one thing longer term.' I stuttered a little over my words, wanting to say everything I'd been thinking about earlier that day properly.

At that exact moment, Alex tapped me on the shoulder and said hello. I looked up, glad to see her but a bit frustrated at the interruption to my conversation with Rachel. I was only a bit surprised to see Todd hovering behind Alex but was momentarily rendered speechless. I'd kind of guessed that they might be dating from their reaction to each other around the office but it was still a bit of a shock. Rachel stepped in to cover my confusion.

'Alex, Todd, how lovely to see you both.' She stood up to kiss them.

They sat down and Todd put his arm around the back of the bench very casually. Rachel put her hand on my leg to calm me so I didn't put my foot in it with another of my sisters. I covered her hand with mine and gave it a little squeeze. She glanced at me and I could see what I thought was love shining in her eyes.

I desperately wanted to know how she felt, having bared my soul to her about where I wanted our relationship to go.

With Rachel's help, I relaxed a little and stopped being so overbearing. It turned out to be a really lovely evening, with great food and great company and pleasantly warm weather. I was really happy for Alex and Todd, they were a good couple and I told Alex that as soon as I could.

'Thanks for that, Jackson. I appreciate your support because I know you and Todd are friends and I don't want to come between you. But it does feel good with him and I hope it's going to go somewhere.'

'Hey, kiddo, I'd be pleased as punch if you two stayed the course, you being two of my favourite people.'

We went in search of our other halves then and I found Rachel talking to my mom and dad, admiring some pretty yellow roses in the flower bed.

'So, Jackson, Rachel tells me she's going to try for The Bluebird tomorrow night. That is really exciting! Why don't Bob and I come along to the next one after that? I can't wait to hear her sing.'

'That would be great, Mom. Is that all right with you, sweetheart?' I had slipped my arm around Rachel's waist when I approached and I pulled her closer now.

'Of course,' she replied, 'that would be great.'

A short while later, we were getting into the car for Greg to take us home. We were both very quiet on the way back. I didn't quite know how to get us back to the mood of our earlier conversation, and from the tightness of her shoulders I could tell she felt the same.

All too soon, we were back at the condo and we still hadn't managed to revisit the conversation. I couldn't let us go to sleep on that though so I took a deep breath and turned to face her at the same time as she turned to me. I grinned stupidly and she laughed.

'I had a great time with you this weekend. In fact, I've been having nothing but great times since I first met you and I want that to continue.'

'I feel exactly the same. I definitely want our relationship to develop into something more but things are moving fast for me in so many ways at the moment. Can't we keep going as we are for a while longer, getting to know each other and enjoying each other's company before we commit to anything more?' She spoke gently but I was still surprised by that.

It sounded like she was afraid of commitment with me and I

didn't know why. If anyone should be nervous of making another commitment, surely it should be me? What wasn't she telling me?

'Okay, sure,' I agreed and I turned away from her, desperate to hide my disappointment. I undressed quickly and climbed into bed.

'Goodnight then,' she said and I replied but I didn't turn round to face her. I heard her sigh before she rolled over and turned out her light.

That definitely wasn't the way I'd expected the day to end.

---

I was woken the next morning by the sound of Rachel cooking in the kitchen. I lay there listening for a moment. As I started to wake up, memories from our conversation the night before came flooding back and I couldn't stop the hurt I'd felt then from resurfacing. I closed my eyes for a moment and sighed. I didn't want to rush her into anything she wasn't ready for but I did want some sign of commitment from her. I sighed as I slipped out of bed and wandered into the kitchen.

'Hey,' she said softly, smiling when she saw I was up. 'How are you today?'

'How honest do you want me to be?' I replied before I could stop myself.

Her smile faded then and her face mirrored mine.

'Your face is telling quite a good story at the moment.' She pursed her lips and turned away.

'You hurt me last night,' I went on regardless, 'because you don't sound like you want to commit to our relationship as much as I do, which was unexpected.' I needed her to know what I was feeling, even if she didn't like it.

She suddenly threw down the tea towel she'd been holding and came round the breakfast bar to confront me.

'How can you say to me that you doubt my commitment to you when I have travelled thousands of miles to be with you and all but abandoned my old life to pursue my dream?' I could see her clenching her fists at her sides. 'I haven't told someone I loved them for a really long time and I don't think I've ever experienced what I'm feeling now for anyone else before. I do want to be with you and I'm really excited by the prospect of sharing these new experiences in my life with you. I don't think I could have conveyed that any more clearly than I have to you!'

'So why won't you commit to anything more right now?' I asked pointedly.

'I tried to explain last night and I realise that maybe I didn't do it very well.' She paused and swept her long, wavy hair over one shoulder and began to examine it. 'I'm frightened,' she whispered, refusing to look me in the eye. I took her hands in mine then and pulled her to me for a hug.

'What are you frightened of, baby?' I asked.

She pulled back a little to talk again.

'I'm frightened of pursuing my dream of being a singer and failing. I'm frightened of giving myself to you and leaving everything I know behind and it not working out between us. I still feel so out of my depth in your world and I don't even know the half of it after such a short time. It all feels so overwhelming.' She started to cry.

'Oh, please don't cry, sweetheart,' I told her gently.

I wiped her tears away with my thumb and then led her to the sofa so she was sitting next to me. 'I understand all your fears and how mind-blowing this must all feel for you. I'm sorry that I hadn't thought about that myself. But can I ask you why you think it won't work out between us? Have I given you any reason to think that?'

'No, of course not,' she sniffled. 'But my experience with men hasn't been good in the past and I don't know why you'd stick with me when you can have your pick of hundreds of women out there.'

'You're the only woman out there that I'm interested in. I don't care about your background. You belong in this world as much as I do. Please don't put yourself down like that. I love you for who you are and I want to be with you. Can you tell me what happened in the past to make you doubt yourself like this?'

I offered her a tissue so she could wipe her eyes.

She took it gratefully and waited for a minute to compose herself before speaking.

'When I first went to college, I fell in love with someone on my course. His name was Nick. We did everything together.' She paused for a moment, looking like she was remembering that time in her life.

'After a year had passed, he asked me to marry him and I said yes without a moment's hesitation. We decided to wait until we'd both finished college but it felt good knowing that he was committed to me. I can't believe how easily I gave him my trust.'

A wave of bitterness crossed her face, something I'd never seen there before. I reached out to hold her hand.

'Then, gradually, I saw less and less of him as he gave me one excuse after another for not spending time with me. One day, he came round to see me and told me that when his finals were over, he wanted to go on a long holiday before settling down. I got all excited and asked him where we might go on our limited budget. But when I looked at him again, he said that he was going on his own, that we could pick up our plans when he got back but somehow I knew he was lying.'

I watched another tear roll down her face.

'I asked him what had changed his mind about being with me but he refused to own up. He went off to Europe shortly after that and I haven't seen him since. He contacted me a few times but then he stopped. I knew by then anyway but I was still so hurt, so let down and I felt stupid to have trusted all his empty promises about our future together.' She paused to let her words sink in.

'Is that how you feel about me too? That I'm making empty promises?'

'I honestly don't feel that about you but I'm scared of giving myself completely again in case everything comes crashing down around me another time. I don't think I could take it. After Nick left, I felt really vulnerable, especially when my dad died, followed so soon after by my mum and I made some mistakes with...well, with relationships that I'm not proud of and I don't ever want to do that again.'

'Listen, Rachel, I've been hurt too and let down to the point that I never thought I would trust anyone again and I've made some mistakes along the way too so I understand how you feel. I also know that I've never felt the way I feel about you with anyone before. I want to do whatever it takes to show you that you can trust me and if that means going slowly, I can do that. I'd do anything for you.'

I leaned over and kissed her gently on the lips.

She put her arms around my neck and returned the kiss so tenderly that I knew we were okay but I also understood in that moment, that it was going to take some time for her to truly trust me.

# CHAPTER 22

Rachel went straight down to the studio when we got to the office the next day, to rehearse with Jed for the "Open Mic" at The Bluebird. Of course, there was no guarantee that she would be picked to play tonight given that it was such a small venue but we would give it our best shot because it was *the* place for all new singers to try for first. I kept myself busy in the office for most of the day, although I did go out to purchase a little surprise for Rachel in the morning while she was rehearsing.

At four o'clock, I went downstairs to collect her so that she could go home and get changed in enough time to get in the line ready to sign up at The Bluebird at half past five. She was packing away her guitar when I got there and she looked quite nervous when she saw me approaching.

'Are you okay, sweetheart?' I asked.

'I'm just hoping that I do get in tonight. It would be a dream come true for me to play at The Bluebird and I'll feel awful if I don't make it.'

I took her hand, gave it a quick squeeze and then led her back up the stairs and outside, where Greg was waiting in the car, patiently reading *The Tennessean*. We were back at the condo in no time and I sat out on the terrace while Rachel got ready.

When she reappeared, she looked fabulous, in skinny jeans and a simple blouse, and her hair still slightly damp from the shower.

I shook my head a little to make myself refocus.

'You look amazing.' I kissed her to show my appreciation. 'What shoes were you going to wear?' I asked her.

'Oh, I don't know, my old boots, I guess,' she said absently as she fiddled with her earrings.

'Hold on a second.' I went to my bedroom and returned with a box, which I presented to her with a flourish.

'What's this?' she asked surprised.

'Only one way to find out,' I replied, smiling in anticipation.

She pulled the lid off the box, her eyes widening as she saw what was inside. 'Oh my goodness, a real pair of cowboy boots and they're red! They're gorgeous, I love them, thank you.'

She gave me a thank you kiss, then bent to slip the boots on. Now she looked every inch a country star and I was already so proud of her.

'Ready to go, baby?'

We drew up at The Bluebird shortly afterwards and there were already lots of other people outside.

'It's not quite what I was expecting,' she confessed. 'It's quite unassuming for an iconic music venue, isn't it?'

'I know it looks a bit non-descript out here in this shopping mall but it'll be worth it when you get in, you'll see.'

Rachel joined the line with her guitar and waited for signing-up time. I hung around outside while Greg went in to check that Todd had managed to get us seats if Rachel was successful. He reappeared a few minutes later, confirming that Todd and Alex were sat at a table inside waiting for me.

Soon enough, sign-up time began and the line inched closer. There were lots of people in front of Rachel so it was going to be a nerve-wracking wait to see if she would be picked to perform tonight.

The line was now much shorter and soon Rachel was signing up and the wait was over. Now we just had to hope that her name would be drawn.

We waited nervously as they started to pick out names and announce performers for tonight's session. Ten lucky people had already been selected and Rachel was starting to look disappointed. She looked over at me for support and I smiled encouragingly. Then, all of a sudden, it was her turn and we both whooped with joy. I ran over to give her a quick kiss and wish her luck and then she disappeared inside the building to get ready for her performance.

I dashed round to the front entrance, past the neon sign of the bluebird and inside to take my seat with the others before the start. I sat down on the familiar wooden chair, glancing at the fairy lights strung all around the room, lighting up the photos of famous country musicians on the walls. I blew out a breath I didn't even realise I'd been holding. Alex took my hand and gave it a squeeze and Todd clapped me on the back. I took a sip of my drink before sitting back and waiting for the show to start.

There was a good variety of talent on at The Bluebird that evening.

'I really liked that last artist, Todd. She had a nice mix of folk with a country twang, I thought.'

'Hmm.' He nodded but was deep in thought, no doubt weighing up where we would place someone like that in our list.

I always loved watching musicians playing 'in the round' with the audience so close to the music. People said that it was at The Bluebird that the tradition of having the stage in the middle of the audience had originated and it was special to Nashville.

When Rachel's turn came, I couldn't help but notice a slight change in the audience as she introduced herself. Her accent piqued their interest and she looked comfortable up on stage, even though the audience was so close, they were almost sharing the microphone with her.

She'd decided to start with 'Too Late' which was a good choice for this crowd. It wasn't long before they were singing and clapping along to the chorus and when she finished, there was great applause for her. Todd snapped a couple of quick photos of her as she stood smiling at the crowd.

'Man, she's great,' the guy next to me told me.

I gave him a big smile by return, pleased to hear such good feed-back on Rachel's behalf.

I could see how pleased she was and she chatted a little about their reaction before introducing her second and final song of the evening. Performers were only allowed to play two songs on "Open Mic" night so I was curious about which song would be her next choice.

As she played the opening bars of 'My Turn' on her guitar, I knew that was the right choice and I smiled with pleasure at the crowd's response once again. She looked over at me then and I winked and nodded before she poured her heart and soul into the rest of the song, exposing her innermost feelings and showing the audi-ence her true talent.

The applause at the end of her set lasted for several minutes and I knew that she had passed The Bluebird test. It took a while for her to leave the stage but eventually she had to and she disappeared into the darkness behind.

In the interval, she came round to find us and although I saw her come in, I didn't get to talk to her for some time because so many other people wanted to tell her how great her performance had been. She looked real happy with all the wonderful comments from the crowd and by the time she reached me, I only had time for a quick hug before we had to sit down for the second half again. Time flew though and we were soon discussing how well her set had gone with Todd and Alex.

'You were fantastic out there, Rachel. You looked like you were born to be singing on a stage,' Todd marvelled.

'The crowd loved you and it looked like you had lots of positive comments from people too on your way in,' said Alex.

'Yes, they were all lovely. I can hardly believe it and it felt absolutely brilliant to be up there, on that stage especially and for the crowd to like it so much. Wow!' Her eyes were shining with the thrill of it all.

'That was a wonderful début,' I told her, 'and I predict that there will be a lot of interest in you tomorrow. Shall we go and get something to eat now? I couldn't eat anything earlier, I was too wound up!' She nodded, still breathless with excitement.

We said goodbye to Alex and Todd and asked Greg to take us back into town. After saying goodbye to him, we stopped in at a little Italian restaurant on Church Street to share a quick pizza and to wind down after the gig.

'How are you feeling now about how it went tonight?' I asked as we tucked in to our pepperoni pizza.

'I'm still on such a high, I don't know if I'll ever come down! My adrenaline has been pumping since we first got there to sign me up but it was such a great evening, wasn't it?'

'It sure was and I hope that it boosted your confidence. You really are a great singer and songwriter and now you know that it's not just me and my employees who think so.'

'I have to be honest, I can hardly wait to do another show now,' she exclaimed.

---

After another fabulous "Open Mic" session at the Douglas Corner Café the following night during which Rachel performed two more songs to another packed audience that included my mom, dad and Maggie, I knew it was time for me to sort out her contract.

As she finished singing the second of her two songs, a slower more poignant one about her parents called 'Don't Let Me Go', you could have heard a pin drop among the audience. When I turned to look at my family to see their reactions, their eyes were full of tears from the touching song but also from their pleasure at Rachel's obvious talent.

'Hey, son,' my dad said when he'd gathered himself together. 'She's damn good. I think she's going to go far.'

'Rachel, you made us all want to dance with the first song and cry with the second! You were wonderful, sweetheart.' My mom embraced her and kissed her on the cheek.

Before dropping us home, Alex made it perfectly clear what her expectations were as Rachel's manager.

'I'll come into the office tomorrow morning,' she said once we'd set off, 'because I want to find out why you still haven't had your contract yet.' Alex raised her eyebrows at me and I gave her a knowing smile by return.

---

I shut the door behind us as we went into my office the next morning.

'Come and sit with me on the couch, there's something I want to show you,' I told Rachel.

I handed her a large envelope.

'Go on, open it,' I said when she hesitated.

She opened it and read the title out loud, 'Contract between The Rough Cut Record Company and Miss Rachel Hardy.' I heard her sharp intake of breath.

'This is what you and Annie have been up to while I've been rehearsing, huh? This is amazing. And it's...it's massive,' she stuttered, leafing through all the pages.

'A lot of it's standard legal stuff but you'll need to look over it with Alex. You may even want a lawyer to look at it for you too.'

'Why, are you trying to take advantage of me?' Her eyes twinkled at me.

'I like the sound of that.' I grinned back at her. 'But I haven't tried to do that in this contract, no.' I put my arm around her and drew her to me for an embrace.

'Thank you, I couldn't have done any of this without you,' she whispered softly, her warm, hazelnut eyes glowing with excitement.

I bent my head down so my lips could meet hers, but when she pressed her body against mine, the kiss became deeper and when we finally broke apart after several minutes, I was breathless and she was too. We held on to each other to steady ourselves and I heard her laugh softly.

Shortly afterwards, there was a knock on the door and Alex and Todd appeared from behind it. They both smiled broadly when they saw us together.

'Hi, you two, you look good today.' Alex looked from Rachel to me and back again, as if trying to figure out what our secret was.

'Thanks, yep, we're both good today,' Rachel said, smiling and taking my hand. She waved the contract at Alex.

'Ah, I see you've given Rachel the contract at last. Have you had a chance to look through it real carefully yet, Rachel?' she asked.

'No, I think I'm going to give it to you to do that for me instead because it really looks quite boring,' she whispered the last part.

'Hush your mouth!' I cried in mock shock. 'That is a seriously important document for you to look over, boring or not, so make sure you do, please.'

'Okay, bossy,' she said, grinning at me and rolling her eyes, before going off to lunch with Alex.

I was finishing off some paperwork when my laptop pinged to tell me I'd received an email. I glanced over at it, switching to see who the message was from and my heart almost stopped at the sight of Stephanie's name at the top of the list. The title of the message was a simple 'Hello!'

*'As you won't answer my calls, I'm sending you an email instead. I only want to say hello, Jackson and to see how things are with you now that some time has passed. I regret what happened between us so much and would love to meet you in person to say how sorry I am. I'm travelling on business with my daddy at the moment but could be back*

*in Nashville real soon, if you'd say the word. So, how about it? Let's get together, even if it's only for old times' sake. Love Stephanie x'*

I could hear her spoilt little rich girl voice as I read every word and I knew without any doubt in my mind that she had some ulterior motive for getting in touch with me that had nothing to do with her apologising for what happened between us. I realised that Annie must have been blocking her calls to me, which I couldn't blame her for, and in all honesty I didn't want to speak to her or see her. On impulse, I deleted the message and made a mental note to talk to Annie about the calls later when she returned from lunch.

After lunch with Alex, Rachel asked if she could talk to me about the contract some more.

'Do you have some questions?' I asked her.

'I'm concerned that you've been too generous, from what Alex has told me.' She frowned at me. 'A royalty rate for a new artist is normally around 10%, as you know, and yet you've offered me 17% and on top of that, you're giving me an advance of $150,000 against sales from my first album, which is also way above average.' Her hands went to her hips and my eyes followed. 'Alex also tells me that the manager's cut you're offering her is below the usual but she did say this was normal because she hadn't discovered me. So my question is: are you sure you aren't being blinded by your feelings for me?' she asked shrewdly.

'Hey, you sound like an old pro already!'

She slapped my arm gently.

'I don't want you to give me preferential treatment, that's all and I don't want you to lose money on me either.'

'There's no need for you to worry,' I reassured her. 'I have every confidence that I will get back a great return on you. You're very talented and I have high expectations. As you said, Alex knows that's a good rate for an unknown and she knows that I discovered you so that's the deal.'

'No, she wasn't complaining, she was very fair and honest in her appraisal of the contract. She's going to show it to her usual lawyer, in case you are trying to take advantage of me.'

She batted her long eyelashes at me then and I swear I could have made mad, passionate love to her right there and then in my office and she looked like she might be up for that too. Instead, I took a calming breath and put my hand on her arm to still her.

'I have twelve months from now to make my first album, is that right?' she asked me, turning serious again.

'Yes, that's fairly standard and then you're expected to be gigging and promoting yourself while making that album.'

'Well, I think I already have enough songs for an album so spending the next year drawing attention to those songs sounds good to me.'

'Shall we go out to celebrate tonight? It's not every day you get a recording contract, is it?' I asked her, sitting down on the edge of the desk and pulling her towards me.

'That sounds like a great idea. Where did you have in mind?' She fell into me, wrapping her arms around me for another breathtaking kiss so I had no chance of answering that question for quite some time.

---

After work the next day, Rachel and I took a cab to the movie theatre over near the university for six o'clock to meet up with Alex and Todd. They'd already bought tickets for the movie for all four of us so we went straight on in. We were going to see a love story set in Italy, a film I'd never heard of but I didn't really care, as long as I was sitting next to Rachel, feeling the warmth of her hand in mine.

Halfway through the film, she pulled her hand away and when I looked over at her, I could see she was crying. She wiped away her tears, before offering me a wobbly smile. I took her hand in mine and she held on to it for the rest of the film.

I held her tightly to me as we left the theatre, with her emotions decidedly the worse for wear.

'Did you enjoy the film?' I asked.

'I loved it, it was really sad but so romantic at the end.'

I had to smile at the way that she loved the romance, even though it made her cry.

We settled on a cosy Italian restaurant for dinner, agreeing that it was the right choice after seeing an Italian film and it was only a short walk away. Inside, the restaurant was packed with local families and so we knew the food must be good. After we'd been eating for a little while, Todd brought up the subject of one of our other artists who was based in New York.

'Jay has been pressing me to ask if you could pop up there for a couple of days to sort things out face to face,' he told me.

I sighed as all eyes turned to me.

'I guess a couple of days away wouldn't be too bad. How would you feel about me being away, Rachel?'

Her face fell at once but then she tried to hide her emotions so as not to upset me, I guessed, but I already had my answer.

'Sweetheart, I know the timing could be better. But listen, I wouldn't need to go till Tuesday and I'd be back by Thursday so I'd only be gone for a short while.' I took her hand to soften the blow.

'I understand you have to go, I'll miss you, that's all, especially as I don't know many people.'

She looked forlorn and Alex and Todd looked uncomfortable. I wished Todd hadn't brought it up now.

'Why don't you go together?' Alex suggested. 'Rachel can always pick up on any press interviews when she gets back.'

'Of course, how stupid of me,' I said. 'Would you like to come with me, Rachel?'

'To New York? I'd love to,' she said and smiled.

'That's settled then.'

# CHAPTER 23

We pulled up outside my apartment building in Lower Manhattan about twenty minutes after leaving the airport. Rachel got out and stood on the sidewalk while I paid the cab driver. I grabbed our bags from the trunk and took her hand. She stared up at the building.

'This is...awesome! There's no other word for it.'

'C'mon, let's get you inside. I think you might be even more amazed.'

As we walked into the apartment, Rachel let out a gasp of surprise. The main reason I'd bought it was for its great view of the Hudson river, and Rachel's reaction was exactly the one I'd had the first time I walked in. We dropped our bags and walked out on to the terrace to take in the fabulous view in all its wonder. The view of Jersey City across the water and the late summer sun reflecting off the buildings there never failed to draw me in. It was still quite warm in New York but a lot less humid than at home. I put my arm around Rachel's shoulder and pulled her close to me.

'I can't tell you how much it means to me that I can share these things I love with you and that you feel the same as I do. For me, that's all I need to know that we're meant to be together.'

Her body relaxed into mine and I sighed, feeling happier than I had for a long time. We stood together for a few more moments and then, reluctantly, I pulled away.

'Sweetheart, I have to get to this meeting, I'm sorry. I thought we could perhaps share a cab to the nearest stop for the Hop On Hop Off tour so that I know you're safely there and then I'll go on to my meeting from there. Is that all right with you?'

'Absolutely. I need five minutes to get ready, okay?'

We went back down to the street and hailed a cab ten minutes later. I dropped Rachel off at her stop and then carried on to my meeting. For me, the afternoon passed very slowly because all I wanted to do was to get back to her but I tried very hard to focus on the business I'd come for. It seemed to me that it had all been exaggerated out of proportion, but sometimes my presence lent some sway and it didn't take long to sort matters out.

I chatted afterwards with Jay, our rep in New York.

'I think that went well, Jay, don't you? They seemed happier at the end anyway.'

'Yes, I agree. It's like you always say, sometimes they just want to meet the boss and hear him say the words. I did want to talk to you about something else though.'

'Okay, shoot.'

'Well, I hope that I haven't acted out of turn here but I agreed on your behalf for you to attend a charity dinner tomorrow night in aid of Phoenix House. The thing is, I only asked for one ticket because I thought you'd be coming on your own but I'm sure we can get you another ticket for you to take er...I'm sorry I don't know her name.'

'Her name's Rachel.' I sighed. This was definitely a dinner I would want to attend under normal circumstances. I just had to hope that Rachel would understand. 'It's fine, Jay. Please could you look into getting me another ticket and in the meantime, I'll discuss it with her.'

I said goodbye to him and sent a text to Rachel to find out how she was getting on. She replied straight away.

*'Ready to come home whenever you'll be there. I'll get a cab. Can you text me the address?'*

I texted back the address and set off for 'home', loving the way that Rachel made any place we were together our 'home'.

---

Later that evening, we were enjoying a meal in the heart of Chinatown, trying out soup dumplings for the first time.

'I'm sure this is dribbling down my face,' Rachel complained and I looked up from my own struggle to dab her chin with my napkin, smiling at her discomfort.

We shared our news from the day, while tucking into some pan fried noodles and finally I got round to telling Rachel about the charity dinner the following evening. She looked disappointed but understanding all at once.

'I'm sorry, I know there's a million other things you would've loved to do. But listen, we can come back whenever you like, I promise and, next time, I'll make sure I don't have any business or any engagements to carry out.'

'Don't worry, I know this is only a flying visit but I'll hold you to that promise.' Then she gasped. 'I don't have anything suitable to wear to a charity dinner and I don't want to spend tomorrow shopping for clothes.' She frowned then with concern.

'I'm sure we can contact a personal shopper at one of the big stores and get them to send some things over for you to try on for tomorrow evening. They'll know the right sort of thing.'

'How about you?' she asked. 'What will you wear?'

'I'll wear a tux. I have several here to choose from.' She was staring at me, with her eyes narrowed. 'What, Rachel?' I laughed.

'Well, I can't wait for tomorrow night now. I'm just imagining how gorgeous you'll look in a tux.'

Our knees brushed under the table and all of a sudden, desire overcame me and I couldn't wait to get back home again. I glanced up at Rachel to see her standing up, getting ready to leave. We caught a cab back to the apartment and it was all we could do to keep our hands to ourselves during the short journey back. No sooner had we closed the door, than we abandoned ourselves to our feelings, hardly able to keep our clothes on for a minute longer. We stumbled through to my bedroom, where our lips met with renewed passion, our bodies entwined and our love for each other revealed itself without any inhibitions.

As we lay in each other's arms afterwards, I knew that I didn't want to be without her in my life. I hoped she knew how much I cared for her now and that this was only the beginning of a long future together too.

'Rachel?'

'Mmm?' I brushed my fingers through her hair, watching as her eyelids drooped.

'I love you, you know.'

'I love you too.' I could hear her smile in the darkness and I held her closer to me then as we both fell asleep.

I sent a quick text to Alex early the next morning, asking her who she would recommend for personal shopping in New York. I rang Neiman Marcus a little bit later on her advice and Rachel spoke to a personal shopper there for about five minutes, explaining her requirements. The shopper agreed to send over half a dozen outfits, with shoes, by five o'clock.

Having sorted all that out, we set off for a full day of sightseeing. I planned to make sure that we did as much as we could in the day that we had available, starting with the Empire State Building. Although we had to wait in line for about half an hour, it was worth it when we reached the observatory on the 86th floor. The views of New York were fabulous whichever direction you looked in.

'This is my favourite view,' I told Rachel. 'There's Fifth Avenue leading past the Flatiron Building all the way down to the 9/11 Memorial and the sea beyond.'

Rachel took what seemed like hundreds of photos from all different angles. I explained to her that the building was open till the early hours of the morning and we made a plan to come back at night-time next time.

Next, Rachel wanted to go and see the Statue of Liberty so we took the ferry from Battery Park to Liberty Island. We spent a good couple of hours exploring the statue and the museum but decided to pass on the trip to Ellis Island this time. We picked up a couple of chicken wraps to go from the café and ate them while waiting for the ferry back to Manhattan.

On our return, we decided to go and visit the 9/11 Memorial to pay our respects. Although once again we had to wait a while in the line, we were not prepared for how moving an experience it would be. The pools and the waterfalls created such a calm atmosphere but reading the names of all the people who had died upset both of us, even more than we'd imagined it would. We went for a coffee after-wards at a nearby café to catch our breath.

'It's been a great day, with some highs and lows, I guess. Is there anything else you'd like to see before we head back to get ready for tonight?' I asked her.

'Do you know, I'd really like to see Central Park, even if only for a little while so I can say I've been there?' She smiled her special smile at me that usually made me do anything she asked. We took another cab after we'd finished our drinks and set off north again towards the park. We'd been really lucky with the September weather and the park looked wonderful as we strolled through the small part of it we could do that day. The leaves on the trees were already starting to change colour, signalling the start of fall and it was heavenly to see folks enjoying the park as much as we were.

'So, what do you think of New York?' I asked as we walked hand in hand.

'I love it, of course and I can't wait to come back again.' She sighed with contentment.

'I'm glad we managed to spend this time together. I've really enjoyed today especially.' I lifted her hand to mine and kissed it and she leaned into me for a hug.

Our final cab of the day dropped us home just before five o'clock. I'd received a text from Jay, confirming that he'd secured an extra ticket for Rachel for the evening. She'd wandered into the bedroom with the outfits sent over by Neiman Marcus when we'd arrived and I heard her cooing over them as she took each one out of the wrapper. After a while, I noticed that she'd gone quiet and I called out to her.

'Hey, Rachel, are you still all right in there?'

'Yes, I think I am.'

I stood up and walked towards the bedroom.

'What do you mean, you think you are?' I asked curiously.

'No, don't come in!' She shut the door against me. 'I don't mean to be rude but I only want you to see me when I'm all ready, sweetheart.'

I stopped in my tracks and went back to the lounge, leaving her to it. Shortly afterwards, I heard her go in the shower and I made my way to the other bathroom to start getting myself ready. I didn't take quite so long so I was back in the lounge at half past six and sat down to read some newspapers on my laptop while I waited. About fifteen minutes later, I heard the door from the bedroom open and I looked up in anticipation. When Rachel did finally appear in front of me, nothing could have prepared me for the heavenly vision that I saw. The dress she'd chosen was stunning: a one-shoulder gown, with a striped lace bodice and a bow on the left shoulder. The skirt was black and satiny looking and flared at the knee, with a mini train at the back. She looked completely transformed and I was speechless as I took in all the different elements. She'd piled her hair up and there were little tendrils framing her face. She lifted up her dress then to show me the black strappy sandals she was wearing which finished off her outfit perfectly. I walked towards her and took her hands in mine, leaning into kiss her softly on the cheek.

'You look absolutely fabulous. You're the most wonderful vision I've ever seen,' I said breathlessly.

She looked so happy, she was fit to burst. I pulled myself together and cleared my throat.

'I have something else for you, too.'

She looked at me quizzically then as I went off to get my gift from the bedroom. I returned with a Tiffany bag and I heard her sharp intake of breath.

'You didn't need to get me anything else. This is a Carolina Herrera dress and I'm wearing Manolo Blahniks on my feet. Never in my life did I dream that I would be spoilt like this. To give me anything else would be too much, Jackson.'

'But Rachel,' I protested, 'it gives me such pleasure to spoil you and you deserve that more than anyone I know. Here.' I passed her the bag, hoping that she would like my purchase.

When she opened the gift box, her face lit up and she looked at me in surprise before looking back at the eighteen carat white gold heart-shaped pendant filled with round diamonds I'd bought for her to wear.

'This is far too generous of you but thank you, I love it. Would you put it on for me please?'

I went towards her and took the necklace in my hand, undid the clasp and refastened it around her neck. I kissed her neck before turning her round to face me.

'Shall we go, sweetheart?'

She took my hand, her face shining with happiness for the evening ahead.

# CHAPTER 24

The cab pulled up outside the Plaza Hotel a few minutes after seven. I went round to Rachel's door to help her out of the car and we climbed the stairs to the entrance gracefully together and then turned back to smile for the photographers. We both paused before going in, taking a deep breath at the same time and smiling at each other as a confidence boost. Once inside, a waiter offered us cocktails. I opted for the non-alcoholic one of course and Rachel decided on a champagne cocktail.

'Dutch courage,' she said, raising her glass towards me.

'Don't be worried, you look amazing and I'm here to look after you.' I grinned at her, taking her hand in mine.

We wandered around the anteroom, greeting a few people I knew and relaxing gradually into the setting. Soon, we were being called in for dinner and I took Rachel's hand again, looping it through my arm to walk her in.

As I glanced down at her, something caught my eye in the background. I looked over to see a couple arguing heatedly under their breath. I was about to look away again, not wanting to stare, when my insides went cold with dread. It surely couldn't be her but the longer

I watched, the more I knew for certain that I was looking at Stephanie, my cheating ex-fiancée. Her long, blonde hair was straighter and shorter than I remembered. She also looked like she might have lost some weight, making her already slender frame seem gaunt now. Her usually flawless style now seemed askew as she argued with her companion.

Rachel had already turned when she heard my sudden intake of breath. She glanced behind her to see what had upset me. She turned back to me, with a slight frown on her face and gently urged me onwards because people were waiting behind us to go in.

'Who was that woman? You look like you've seen a ghost,' she muttered under her breath as we walked in. I didn't answer immediately because I was still in shock. She continued to frown at me in concern.

'It was her, Stephanie. It's the first time I've seen her since we split up.'

'Oh, God, no!' She only loosened her grip on my arm as we arrived at our table.

I sat down heavily and tried to recover myself. I hadn't thought for one minute that I would see her here. Still, I knew she had family here so it might make sense that she'd gone to New York or perhaps this was where her business trip with her father had taken her. I just wasn't ready to talk to her. In this setting, I was afraid that I might over-react and embarrass myself or worse still, embarrass Rachel.

'Look at me, sweetheart, please.' I turned towards her and shook my head a little to clear it of my thoughts and help me focus on the present. 'Would you rather leave now? I don't mind,' she offered.

'No, no, I'll be all right, really, it's thrown me a little, is all.' I tried to smile but it may have come out as a grimace. 'There is no way we're leaving anyway, not because of her.' I couldn't tell Rachel that Stephanie had been trying to contact me. I hoped that she wouldn't see me among all the other people there.

Our starters arrived shortly afterwards and we used them to keep me focussed on the here and now. One or two of the other guests tried to engage me in conversation but I found it difficult to concentrate for longer than a few minutes. After the main meal, there was a speech from the charity organisers, which, thankfully, was quite short. Then Rachel excused herself to go to the bathroom and anxiety threatened to overwhelm me all over again, as I glanced nervously around me all the while for signs of Stephanie approaching. As soon as we had eaten dessert, I took a final glance around the room.

'I think it's best that we get out of here now. C'mon, sweetheart. We've both had enough for one night.'

I stood up, taking Rachel's hand.

We made our way as calmly as possible towards the exit. Just when we thought we were home and dry, we saw Stephanie emerging from the stairwell and looking straight at us. I turned and squared up to her then. I wasn't going to stand for any of her nonsense.

She sidled up to us, her face and hair looking a mess, as though she'd been crying and, quite clearly, she'd drunk too much as well. I couldn't believe that they hadn't asked her to leave.

'Jackson,' she whined. 'It's really good to see you.' Her whole demeanour oozed danger, and fear started to spread through my body. My hands were clammy so I let go of Rachel's.

'I'd have to disagree with that statement, Stephanie. Nothing about this feels good to me.' I spoke quietly, trying to keep calm.

'Jackson, don't be mean, I've had such a bad evening and I know you could make it all better. And it's such good luck that I've seen you when you haven't been returning my calls or emails.' She fluttered her eyelashes at me in the most unattractive way and I suddenly thought I might be sick.

I took a step back from her, pulling Rachel with me. When I risked a quick look at Rachel, I saw that she had gone very pale and she was staring at Stephanie with dismay. I could only assume that was a reaction to the news about her trying to contact me. My heart sank.

'Stephanie, let me make this very clear,' I went on, trying to put an end to this meeting. 'Everything there once was between us is now well and truly over. I've moved on from the mess you made of my life and I don't ever want to spend time with you again. do you hear me?' I waited, hoping that I'd said enough to make her go away. I wasn't sure how much longer I could keep this strong-guy pretence up.

'Okay, Mr High and Mighty,' she sneered at us. 'I've moved on from *the mess you made of my life* too.' She mimicked my words in a squeaky high-pitched voice and I felt nothing but hatred for her in that moment. 'I can have a real man any time I want. I don't have to go scraping the barrel like you obviously have with your new plaything. Anyway, she's welcome to you, you're not worth it. It won't be long till she finds out how weak and pathetic you really are.' She'd switched back to her alter ego in a second and the look she gave Rachel was poisonous.

I gripped Rachel's hand once again.

'Stay away from me and my family, Stephanie.' I glared at her for a moment and then I turned abruptly, taking Rachel with me, and left the hotel.

We stood outside for a minute, allowing me to catch my breath. Then we hailed a cab and set off home. Neither of us spoke on the way back, we were both too shell-shocked to say anything after Stephanie's verbal attack. By the time we arrived back at the apartment, my shock had turned to anger and I knew that I would not be a good person to be around right now.

I turned to Rachel and said, 'Honey, you go on up. I need to be on my own to let off some steam for a while, I'll be back soon.'

'I really don't think it's a good idea for you to be on your own right now. Whatever you're feeling, come in and talk to me about it. We can handle it together,' she protested.

I wavered for only a second.

'No, this is something I need to do on my own.'

I gave her the keys, trying to give her hand a squeeze for reassurance as well but she snatched it away and climbed out of the cab without saying another word. I watched her go in, knowing that this was probably not the best decision. I didn't want her to see how angry I was or how vulnerable I felt after seeing Stephanie again. She had a way of taunting me that I couldn't seem to handle, making me frustrated at my weakness before her and yet furious all at the same time.

Of course, then I had to decide where to go to vent my frustration. The cab dropped me off a few minutes later at a bar nearby. I went on in, sat down and waited for the bartender to come over. When he asked for my order, I paused. I wrestled with my demons and wanted desperately to resist them but all I could think about was drowning my sorrows in alcohol. I looked up and asked for a beer. Then I sat there looking at the bottle for what seemed like the longest time, trying to persuade myself of the right thing to do. Eventually, I gave in and took a sip. The next thing I knew, I had downed several bottles, as well as working my way through half a bottle of bourbon.

My cell vibrated with a text at that point. It was from Rachel and she was furious.

*'Jackson, where the hell are you? I am worried sick. Please let me know you're okay. Better still come back home.'*

By this time, it was two in the morning and something in her message appealed to my inner common sense and I staggered up from the bar, unused to the effect of the alcohol after so long without it, and made my way outside to find a cab.

When I let myself into the apartment a short while later, I found Rachel in her pyjamas, sitting on the couch waiting for me. She jumped up, looking like she would run to me but when she saw the state of me, she stopped short.

'You've been drinking,' she stated as a matter of fact.

'Yes, ma'am, I have.' I grinned a little sheepishly, with the idiot humour of the drunk.

'Sit down there and don't move,' she ordered. She came back with some water and some headache tablets and made me take them and then drink all the water. She helped me to get into bed and the minute my head hit the pillow I fell straight into a deep sleep.

I woke in the middle of the night certain that I needed to be sick. Luckily, I made it to the bathroom in time. After emptying my insides, I felt better. I washed my face, rinsed out my mouth and returned to the bedroom, going via the kitchen to get some more water. There was no sign of Rachel in the bed and it didn't look like there had been all night.

I went to check the other room then and was saddened to find her asleep in there. I turned as quietly as I could to head back to my bedroom. Once I was back in bed, the enormity of my actions weighed down on me and it wasn't long before despair at my stupidity set in. Rachel probably wouldn't forgive me for breaking her trust like this. I tossed and turned for the rest of the night, finally getting up at eight o'clock when I heard her stirring.

I went out to the lounge to find her already dressed and finishing off her last bit of packing.

'Hey, Rachel,' I ventured, desperate to explain myself.

She turned to look at me and I could see that she'd been crying at some point. I went towards her automatically but she backed a step away and I stopped, chilled by her reaction.

'I figured that we need to be at the airport by nine o'clock for a midday flight so you'll need to get a move on to get yourself ready,' she said, focussing on practicalities.

'Please, I'm sorry,' I whispered.

'So am I. More than you can know.' With that, she turned away from me and went back to the other room.

The rest of the day was unbearable, with us hardly exchanging a dozen words. I wanted to put things right but she wouldn't talk to me. I hoped that she might have thawed by the time we got back to Nashville but as soon as we walked into the condo, she went and retrieved her other larger suitcase and started filling it with all her things. I couldn't take the tension between us any longer.

'What are you doing?' I demanded.

'I'm moving out of here to a hotel. I can't be with you right now.'

'Why do you want to do that? That's only going to make it harder for us to talk and sort this mess out. Please don't go,' I begged her. I waited a moment for her reply, as she considered how best to tell me what she wanted to say.

'I'm going because I need some time to process the change that came over you last night,' she said quietly, breaking my heart with every word. 'You told me that I could trust you and that you'd always talk to me, be honest with me. But at the first sign of real trouble, you turned to alcohol instead of me. My dad used to drink whenever things got tough, rather than talking things over with someone who loved him. That's what hurt me the most, that you wouldn't talk to me. I need to decide how I feel about that before anything else. You also need time to think about the "mess" you've created.' She grabbed both her cases and walked towards the door.

'Where are you going to stay?' I asked.

'I've booked a room at The Hermitage for now. I'll call you tomorrow.'

'What about the gig tonight?'

'I've cancelled it. I can't really face that now.'

And then she was gone.

I fell on to the couch and put my head in my hands, wishing I could take back the last twenty-four hours.

---

I didn't know what to do with myself once she'd gone. I kept going over and over it all in my head but coming up with no solutions. I had let her down and she had every right to be mad at me. Not only that but now she had cancelled her gig as well which meant that everyone would be wondering what had happened and I would have to be the one to tell them. Sure enough, my phone started going crazy with texts and calls shortly after that but I left them all while I went to have a shower and to try and get my head together. This time though, nothing seemed to help.

I finally decided to look at my cell around four o'clock and was staggered to see texts and calls from Alex, Todd, my parents, Annie and even Maggie. I decided to call Alex first because she would want to know about the show.

'Alex, hi, it's me.'

'Okay, this had better be good. What the hell happened between you two that caused Rachel to cancel the gig?'

'We bumped into Stephanie in New York and I went on a minor bender, coming home drunk in the early hours of the morning. Is that bad enough for you?'

'Oh my God, Jackson. Seeing Stephanie must have been bad. What was she like?'

'I'm sorry to say it but she was a complete bitch. It really threw me and I was really angry. But now Rachel has left and I can't believe what an idiot I've been.'

'She's left? What do you mean?' she gasped.

'Not left, left but moved out of the condo to The Hermitage while she thinks things through. She said she'd call me tomorrow.'

'Okay, well, you just have to hope that tomorrow you can put things right. Look, your behaviour was wrong of course but you're only human and it was completely understandable in the circumstances. Rachel loves you, she'll come round.'

'I don't know, Alex. She was more upset by the fact that I didn't want to talk to her. Instead, I went and got drunk on my own and I think she feels let down because of that more than anything else.'

'Well, let's hope she feels better about it all tomorrow. Call me and let me know, okay? You're not going to drink any more are you?'

'No, I think I've done enough damage.'

We said our goodbyes and then I rang my mom and had the same conversation with her.

'Mom, I'm just so ashamed of my weakness. I'm better than that, I know I am.'

'Yes, you are but we can all be weak and at least you can see that you've made a mistake here. Maybe tomorrow, you and Rachel can talk this all through. She needs some time, honey.'

I couldn't face anyone else but I did want to text Rachel before going to bed for an early night.

*'I'm sorry for being such a fool. I know I've hurt you and I never meant to do that. I hope you'll believe me and that we'll be able to talk more tomorrow. I love you x'*

I turned off my cell and climbed into bed, hoping that sleep would help me escape my self-inflicted misery.

# CHAPTER 25
## DORSET

**Rachel**

I was exhausted by the time I arrived in London and filled with sadness after leaving Nashville so abruptly.

The taxi had just pulled up outside the hotel in Nashville when my phone had buzzed as it received a text. I'd expected it to be from Jackson, pleading with me to come back so I'd taken a deep breath before looking at it. I was completely unprepared for the name I'd seen on the screen. It was from Jenna and as I read it I knew I would have to go straight home to Dorset.

*'Rachel, I'm sorry to be the one to tell you but Sam's in hospital. He's critical. Please can you come home?'*

'I'm sorry,' I'd said to the taxi driver, 'but there's been a change of plan. Please could you take me to the airport?'

'Sure thing, ma'am.' He'd pulled off once again into the traffic.

During the journey, I'd gone over again and again how everything had seemed so perfect between me and Jackson, and now it all seemed lost. I completely understood his anger and his vulnerability around alcohol but I didn't understand him abandoning me like that.

Hell, I'd been as shocked as he was by the way that Stephanie had behaved but he hadn't spared a thought for me.

Now here I was, back in London and freezing because I'd left in such a hurry and hadn't given any thought to what the weather would be like back in the UK. The flimsy cardigan I was wearing was no protection against the light drizzle that was falling as I arrived but I had no choice but to keep going until I got to the hospital. I still hadn't managed to charge my phone and I was starting to worry now because I knew that Jackson and Jenna would be trying to get hold of me and I couldn't let them know I was okay.

My final taxi ride of the day dropped me outside the hospital just after half past six. I gave them Sam's name at the reception desk and then followed their directions to intensive care. I found Jenna in the family waiting room, pacing the room nervously and looking exhausted.

'Rachel, thank goodness you're here safely,' Jenna cried when she saw me. 'I've been trying to get hold of you and was worried sick when I couldn't.'

'My phone battery died,' I said as I threw my arms around her for a big hug.

We held on to each other like that for a long time, giving each other strength. Eventually, we pulled apart and I sat down so she could fill me in on what had been happening.

'Mum and Dad are both in with Sam at the moment. He's still being sedated for the time being to give his body a chance to recover from the shock of the fall at the building site and for them to assess how bad the damage is. We know that he's broken a few bones so he's going to be in here for a while.'

'How did it happen though, Jenna and what was he doing on a building site? That's not his usual kind of job, that's what I don't understand.'

'His carpentry jobs had slowed and someone offered him a few weeks work, just general labouring, and I think he felt he had to take it. He's been quite low since you left and he wanted something to take his mind off things.'

My face fell as I listened. I knew she wasn't blaming me for him taking the job but I still felt guilty.

'Anyway, he was working on the roof,' she continued, 'and as he was walking along the scaffolding, he tripped and fell down to the next level, about six feet below. He landed face down, breaking his left leg and probably quite a few ribs. They've been able to set his leg without surgery and that's good at least. His face is quite torn up too but what they're most worried about are his lungs.' Tears were in her eyes as she finished and she wrapped her arms around herself, no doubt trying to push away her worries.

'I'm sorry this has happened, Jenna. How are your mum and dad holding up?'

'They're okay. It's just that we've been trying to make sure that there's always someone here and it's hard going, what with me working and Matt having to worry about his family as well.'

'Whose turn is it to stay now?' I asked.

'I'd just swapped shifts with them when you arrived. I'd best say goodbye to Mum and Dad before going home,' she said. 'You could come home with me and get changed and perhaps catch up on some sleep and then we could come back and relieve them later,' she suggested.

'That sounds like a good plan to me,' I said.

She disappeared out of the room, leaving me alone to collect my thoughts.

When Jenna returned, she asked if I'd like to see Sam before we left.

'I would like to but I didn't know if I would be allowed, not being direct family.'

'You're family to us and that's all that matters. Why don't you go in for a minute?'

She showed me to Sam's room and I went in, exchanging hugs and kisses with his mum and dad as we swapped over.

I sat down on the chair at the side of Sam's bed, taking hold of his hand very gently. He looked very pale compared to his normal tanned skin and he had bandages and tubes everywhere. I talked to him for a few minutes, telling him my news, until the constant bleep of the machines in the room became too much for me.

'I love you, Sam. Please get well.' I stood up then and kissed his damaged face. I left a minute later, afraid to say any more in case I broke down in tears.

'We'll see you again later,' Sam's mum, Sarah, told me and I kissed her goodbye before setting off home with Jenna.

---

It felt odd to be going back to my old cottage after a few weeks away and even though it was still full of my things, it felt like it belonged to Jenna now. I unpacked my stuff in the spare room, making my priority to plug in my phone to charge while Jenna made us both a cup of tea. As soon as it had been plugged in for a while, I was able to send a quick text off to Jackson.

'Hi, Jackson, my phone battery died. I know you must have been trying to get hold of me. I've had to come back to Dorset. Sam's in hospital, in critical condition. I'll call you later.'

Jenna was waiting for me in the living room when I returned.

'How has it all gone over in Nashville? I kept meaning to ring you but it's been so busy lately,' she said.

I told her the whole story then of my short time in Nashville, from my musical success and signing to the label to the developing but complicated relationship between Jackson and me. I finished by telling her what had happened in New York and how I'd moved out.

'I love him, Jenna, but it has been quite overwhelming all this change, you know, and now I feel let down that at the first sign of trouble, he shut me out.' I shrugged with the disappointment of it all.

'What are you going to do now? Is it over in your mind?'

'No, no but I can't see how to move forward with him at this point.'

We continued talking over a quick supper, planning to go back to the hospital shortly afterwards. I was so tired that Jenna told me to get off to bed for a nap. I woke up with a start just before midnight. The house was eerily silent. When I went downstairs, I found a note from Jenna, telling me she'd gone back to the hospital and would see me in the morning. I was alone and I knew I'd been putting off calling Jackson so I had no other option but to get on with it now.

'God, I've been really worried about you, especially when the hotel told me you hadn't even checked in!' I heard him release a sigh of relief and I felt bad for not contacting him sooner.

'I'm sorry, but I had no way to charge my phone until I got back to the cottage after visiting Sam in hospital. I really didn't mean to worry you.'

He was silent for a moment at the other end of the line and I didn't know what to make of that.

'And how is Sam? Is he still critical?'

'Yes, he's sedated and they're waiting for him to wake up on his own so they can see the full extent of his accident and decide how to treat it.'

There was another pause. We both had such a lot to say but neither of us knew where to start.

'Rachel, I...I'm so sorry about the other night. I was stupid and I know I've hurt you and let you down. Can you forgive me?'

'I know you're sorry but you're right, I do feel let down at the moment. I can't talk with you about it over the phone and I can't answer your question right now. I need some time to think things through before we talk about it.'

'Will you come back though or can I come over? I can't bear not being able to see you or talk to you. I want to make this right.'

'Can you give me a couple of days and then I'll know more about what's happening here and where that leaves me?'

'You don't want to speak to me for a couple of days?'

He sounded broken and I immediately felt guilty.

'It's not that I don't want to talk to you. It's just that I have to think about Sam now.'

'So Sam's well-being is more important than our future together? Is that what you're saying?' He sounded angry now.

'I don't have time for this. I'll call as soon as I can. Take care of yourself, bye.' I managed to stop myself slamming the phone down on him but only just.

After speaking to Jackson, I'd fallen asleep again for a couple of hours and when I woke on Saturday morning, it was with a heavy heart. I was worried about Sam of course, but I felt awful about the way I'd treated Jackson too. The timing of all this was terrible and even though there was nothing I could do about it, I still felt bad.

Jenna was in the kitchen making breakfast when I went downstairs.

'Hey, Jenna, I'm sorry about last night. I really wanted to come back with you but I was more tired than I realised.'

'Don't worry about it,' she replied. 'I only relieved my mum and dad for a couple of hours so they could go home for a shower and a change of clothes. They were back in no time and insisted on me coming home again. I want to get back as soon as I can this morning though.'

So we set off for the hospital straight after breakfast, wanting to find out the latest about Sam and also to give Sarah and Dave a break. They were both wearing big smiles when we arrived which cheered us up immediately.

'What's happened, Mum?' asked Jenna.

'Your brother's woken up, love.'

We could see the relief in her eyes and we all relaxed with that great news.

'Oh, that's wonderful.' Tears sprang to my eyes as I reached out to give her a hug.

'The doctors said that they'd come round again this afternoon to give a full diagnosis so that gives Dad and I a chance to catch up on some sleep and we'll see you both back here later. Is that okay, girls?'

'Of course it is, Mum. Is Sam awake now? Can we go in?' asked Jenna.

Her mum nodded and smiled, looking exhausted but clearly more reassured about Sam's condition. We said goodbye to them both and Jenna went in to see her brother.

I took a seat in the waiting room and no sooner had I sat down than my thoughts turned to Jackson once again. On my own, the doubts crept in. Wasn't I doing exactly the same as him by running away instead of staying to talk? I couldn't believe what a mess we'd made of things in so little time. I knew I'd had a good reason for leaving Nashville, but in my heart I knew it had also been a convenient way of leaving everything behind, rather than dealing with what had happened.

I managed to pop in briefly as well to talk to Sam later that morning after Jenna had been in. He seemed in good spirits but obviously very tired and shaken by his ordeal. We all waited anxiously together in the afternoon for the doctors' verdict.

'It's good news, everyone,' Sarah reported. 'Sam's fall wasn't too severe, thank goodness. He only has the broken bones we knew about and his lungs are okay. He should be able to come home in a few days but he won't be mobile for quite a few weeks.' She smiled and her face lit up with a whole host of emotions, revealing how she'd felt over these past few days. 'He wants us all to come in and see him. The doctors said it would be all right.'

'Hey, Sam, how are you?' asked Jenna, approaching the bed first as we all went in.

'Well, I've been better,' he replied with a roll of his eyes. 'But it's the shock of it all that's hit me the most.' He glanced around the room at everyone, sharing a rueful smile. His eyes came back to me, as if noticing I was there for the first time.

'Hey, Rachel, it's good to see you.' He reached his hand out to me. I went forward at once to take it.

'Listen, why don't we wait outside for a minute to give you and Rachel a chance to catch up?' said Sarah, nodding at the other members of the family.

Sam watched them as they left the room, before turning back to look at me. His handsome face crinkled into a smile.

'If I'd only known that this was all I had to do to get you to stay...' Sam laughed and then grimaced from the pain.

'That serves you right,' I replied, sitting down carefully on the bed. 'How are you feeling, seriously?'

'I'm okay, I'm trying to deal with it all bit by bit and not get too carried away with what ifs. Do you know what I mean? When I first had the accident, it was so overwhelming and when they were bringing me to the hospital in the ambulance, I couldn't stop myself from thinking the worst but now that a couple of days have passed while I've been sedated, I'm feeling calmer, especially now it's only about broken bones which will heal in time.' He paused before going on. 'I've missed you, you know.' His clear, blue eyes looked so sad that for a moment, I didn't know what to say.

'I've missed you all too,' I said, including the whole family rather than just Sam, although I knew that wasn't what he wanted to hear.

'And how are things with you? How did it all go over there?' he asked.

I looked up at him then, trying to gauge whether he really wanted to know and he smiled as if to reassure me.

'It's been great in Nashville, the music's going really well and I just agreed to sign to Jackson's label but I haven't signed the contract yet.'

'Wow, that's amazing news, Rachel. Well done!'

I'd expected things to be a bit awkward between us, given the feelings he'd previously expressed for me, but there was no resentment there, only happiness for me.

'And how's Jackson?' he went on.

'Umm, not great actually. We had a row the other day and I moved out of his place. I was on my way to a hotel when I got Jenna's text about you.' I looked up at him, not sure what emotion I would see on his face but, once again, he surprised me with a look of sympathy.

'Oh, Rachel, I'm sorry.'

I couldn't tell how he felt about Jackson but his feelings for me were clearly just as strong.

'Anyway, you don't want to know about all that.' I coughed nervously to try and change the subject.

'Will you be staying here then?' he asked me, taking my hand in his.

'I don't know what I'm going to do, Sam, to be honest.'

I leaned towards him and rested my forehead on his and he put his arm gently around my shoulders.

We sat like that for a moment before I pulled back and stood up.

'I'll be back to see you tomorrow,' I said as I turned for the door, giving him a last smile and seeing his face light up in return.

# CHAPTER 26

I decided to call Jackson when we returned to the cottage, knowing that I needed to put his mind at rest on a number of fronts.

'Hi, Jackson. How are you?'

'I'm okay, you?' It was lovely to hear his voice but I felt nervous about how the conversation was going to go because of what I wanted to say to him.

'I'm missing you, to be honest but I'm also glad to have had some time to think.'

'How's Sam doing?' His tone was firm and unemotional, which I supposed I deserved after the way I'd spoken to him earlier.

'He's awake and off the critical list now. He should be home soon but he'll be in recovery for a while.'

'Are you going to come back to Nashville then, now that Sam's on the mend?'

'Not for the time being, no. I need some more time here.'

'I see. Well, actually, no, I don't see. I made a mistake and we need to talk about it, face to face, not keep running away from it.' I was surprised by his irritation.

'I think I know that better than anyone but now that I'm here, it's helping me to put things in perspective which I was finding difficult when I was with you, not just about our relationship but about my future. I need to decide what I really want.'

He blew out a long breath. 'This is all news to me and not what I was expecting you to say.'

'I know and I'm sorry but…if you truly love me, then you need to leave me alone, please.'

'I do love you but you're making me nervous about what's going to happen next for us.'

'I'm sorry but I need to think about you, about my career, about Sam…' I sighed as my sentence trailed off.

'Hang on, what does Sam have to do with anything? He wasn't in the picture before.' He sounded really spooked.

'Look, you knew that Sam had feelings for me before, and since coming home I've realised how much I missed him so I need some time to think about all that.'

'About whether to choose him or me you mean?'

'No, look…I don't know…Can we not do this over the phone, please? I'll call again soon.'

After that, we brought the conversation to an end pretty quickly. I knew I had to be honest if there was to be any future for us but I couldn't blame him for not liking what I'd said and I regretted even having mentioned Sam.

I went downstairs to find Jenna and discuss what we were doing for dinner to try and take my mind off things.

'I'm starving, I don't know about you,' I declared on walking into the kitchen, where I found her rooting through the cupboards.

'Yes, me too. I was looking to see what we had to eat and, sadly, the answer is not a lot. Shall we get a takeaway or go out?'

'I'd be happy with a takeaway if you would, how about a pizza?'

'Great. I think I've even got a bottle of red somewhere, and by the look on your face, you need a glass of wine. I'll go and look for it and you order the pizza, okay?'

Our pepperoni pizza arrived by bike just as Jenna was pouring me a second glass of red. We divided it up and sat down to eat. I was surprised by my sudden appetite.

'Will you be going back to Nashville soon, now that Sam's getting better?' Jenna asked, catching me off guard.

I paused dramatically, as I was about to take a bite of pizza, aware of her waiting expectantly for my answer.

'I haven't really decided yet. I do need to clear the air with Jackson after what happened and I have a contract to sign too.' I'd only told her that we'd had an argument, not the full extent of it and I knew she was leaving it up to me to tell her when I was ready.

'Your music must have gone down really well over there. I'm so pleased for you,' she said.

'Yeah, although I've only actually played a couple of "Open Mic" nights so far but they did go really well and I can't wait to play some more.'

'And what's Nashville like?' she asked.

'I love it, you know, even more than I'd hoped I would. I love the feel of the place, the food, the people, the music everywhere. Jackson's family have welcomed me so warmly too and that's been a relief because I was quite nervous about meeting them all. The people at the record label have been really positive as well and I felt that I fit right in there. Now, I'm one step away from signing a recording contract. It all seems quite incredible still.'

'Do you think I might be able to come and visit you while you're there if you do go back?' she asked hesitantly.

'That would be wonderful, Jenna. Would you be all right to take the time off though?'

'Yes, a few days would probably be okay, as long as I plan it with Mary.'

We both went quiet for a bit as we finished our pizza and I pondered what I would do next. She topped up our wine glasses and turned to face me.

'So do you think you can sort things out with Jackson? I don't mean to pry but if you want to talk about it with me, you can.'

'I honestly don't know. Now that I'm here, I really miss him but I've also realised how much I miss home and all of you. And then there's Sam.' She raised her eyebrows. 'Before I left, he told me he loved me and begged me to stay but I knew I needed to go, Jenna. I needed to know if I could make it over there and I knew that Sam wasn't interested in that, despite what he might feel for me. Then yesterday, I could see that he still felt the same for me and he said that he'd really missed me. So now I'm really confused.'

'Do you have feelings for Sam?' she asked.

'I thought I only cared for him like a brother but when he kissed me, I did feel something.'

'He kissed you!'

'That wasn't all we did either.' I flushed under her surprised look. 'But that was ages ago, Jenna, a drunken one-night stand. For my part, I worried then that if we'd continued with a relationship, we would have lost our friendship and I didn't want to take that risk. After you told me that he had feelings for me, he eventually told me that he would have liked it to go further. That's when he kissed me before I left for Nashville.' I took a gulp of wine.

'God, I had no idea. It sounds to me like you have a huge dilemma on your hands and I can't advise you what you should do for the best but you will need to be careful, otherwise someone is going to get hurt.'

---

I started the next day feeling confused after my conversation with Jackson the day before. Now that Sam was out of danger, I did feel ready to think about going back to Nashville. Being in Dorset again and so far away from Jackson had made me realise how much I missed him so maybe it was the kick I needed to stop me dithering. I loved him and he loved me. The question I had to deal with was whether I loved him as he was or if his faults were too much for me to get past.

There was also the question of me and Sam to deal with so, later that morning, I gathered up my keys and set off for the hospital. The bus dropped me outside about half an hour later and a noisy grumble in my stomach reminded me that I hadn't eaten anything yet. Still, food would have to wait for now. I made it up to Sam's floor quite quickly, checked in with the nurse at the desk and went along to his room. I peeked in first through the window and seeing that he was on his own, I knocked gently before going on in.

'Hey, Rachel. I'm glad to see you, I'm so bored.' He groaned.

'Well, you sound much more like your normal self so you must be feeling better.'

'Yeah, I am but I want to go home, not be stuck in here. Come and talk to me please!' I smiled and walked around the bed, taking a seat in the chair alongside.

'I need to talk to you about us, Sam,' I said, putting my bag on the floor and looking him clearly in the eye.

'I didn't think there was an "us" or am I wrong?'

He said it kindly but I knew I must sound confused.

'When Jenna let me know you were in hospital, I was out of my mind with worry and then, after I spoke to you yesterday and you said you'd missed me, I realised that I'd really missed you too and it got me wondering about my real feelings for you. And now I don't know what to think or what to do about anything.' I felt the tears prickle at the back of my eyes and struggled to keep them at bay.

He reached out across the bed to take my hand and I let him. Before I knew it, I was crying and he'd stretched his arms out towards me. I moved to sit next to him on the bed and he put his arms around me as best he could.

'Do you want to talk about what happened between you and Jackson?'

'Sam, I'd love to talk to you about it but it wouldn't be fair on you to do that,' I managed to stutter out between sobs. 'Nor would it be fair on Jackson to tell you what we argued about, would it?'

I buried my head in his chest, unable to say any more. After a few minutes, we drew apart and he gave me a scratchy hospital tissue to dry my eyes. When I looked at him, his eyes were sad but also full of an unmistakable love for me, which made me feel even more wretched. I sank back on to the chair beside the bed, trying to put some distance between us.

'I don't want to put you on the spot. I care for you and I want you to be happy. Just tell me that Jackson's not hurting you or anything terrible like that.'

'God, no, it's nothing like that. He does love me, Sam, and I...I think I love him. We just have an obstacle to get over and I have to give us the chance to try and do that. I don't know if we can but we owe it to ourselves to try.' I smiled tearfully.

'Does that mean you're going straight back to Nashville? Because I don't think you should.'

'Why not? I need to talk to Jackson and sort things out with him. I have the contract to sign as well.' I sniffed as I thought about everything.

'Look, I can take care of you, perhaps better than Jackson can. I've known you a lot longer and I think I know what you need. I wouldn't ever hurt you either. I love you and I want to be with you. I know that means giving up on the Nashville dream maybe, but it doesn't have to mean giving up on your career dream altogether. We could still make it happen for you here.'

'Are you saying that you'd support me in that dream now?'

He nodded, a determined look in his eyes. 'I understood after you went how much it means to you and if I want to be with you, I know that you'll need me to back you all the way. I know you have a lot to think about but I want you to know that you can trust me to take care of you. You do know you can call me at any time, don't you?'

Although I nodded, I was frightened by this new information and the impact it had on my situation.

I stood up and leaned over the bed once more to kiss him goodbye before walking to the door.

---

'Jackson! What on earth are you doing here? How did you...? I only just...' I shook my head a little, trying to clear my confusion at seeing Jackson in front of me. It didn't make any sense.

'What the hell is he doing here?' I heard Sam complain behind me.

I glanced over at him, pleading at him with my eyes not to make a scene. He threw his hands up in despair and I let the door close behind me, as I went out to talk to Jackson.

'Can I talk to you, Rachel, please?'

I was still unable to comprehend how he'd got here so quickly when I'd only been speaking to him yesterday evening and he'd been in Nashville then. Obviously, he must have thought it was important to see me face to face and my heart skipped a beat at the thought that I meant so much to him that he'd come all this way. I led Jackson to the waiting room, which I was thankful to see was empty, and sat down opposite him, waiting to hear his explanation.

'You must have left pretty soon after we spoke to get here so quickly,' I said.

'Yes, I suppose I didn't waste any time,' he agreed. 'I could hardly believe what you were saying to me about Sam and I knew I didn't want to be apart from you a moment longer.' He looked down at his hands to compose himself before continuing. 'Rachel, I love you such a lot and I don't want to lose you but I know I've been stupid about how I dealt with seeing Stephanie again and I can only hope that you'll forgive me that in time.'

He swallowed before continuing. 'The most important thing for me at the moment is not seeing you throw your talent away because of a moment of madness on my part. I want you to follow your dream and make a go of your music career regardless of what happens between you and me. So I'm here to ask you to come back with me to Nashville to sign the contract and to do what you were meant to do with your life, to sing. I promise that I'll leave you alone, even though it will be the hardest thing I'll ever have to do, but if that's the deal, then I'll take it.'

I stood up and went over to the window to look at the street below, struggling to take in everything Jackson was saying to me. If he meant what he said, his love for me was even greater than I'd realised. What he wanted more than anything was for me to be happy, even at the expense of his own happiness. As I turned back round to look at him, the tears were threatening to spill over.

'I can't believe you would do that for me when it would hurt you so much.'

'I'd do anything for you, I mean it and I'm only too happy to put you first.'

He stood up, his broad frame expanding to fill the space, and he took a step towards me. He looked so pained, it was all I could do not to throw myself into his arms. Instead, I reached out my hand and he took it, raising it to his lips. I had to wipe away my tears then, so reluctantly I let go of his hand.

It was time for me to make a decision now. I was still reeling from Sam's sudden change of heart about supporting my dream of pursuing a music career but in my heart, I didn't really believe he meant what he'd said, not when he'd been so against me pursuing my dream of going to Nashville before.

Now I had all the facts and I knew I was ready.

'Okay.' I cleared my throat before going on. 'I will come back with you but I do have some conditions.' The smile on his face fell a little in anticipation of what I was about to say. 'Firstly, we must keep it strictly business and secondly, I want to stay in a hotel when we get back. Is that acceptable to you?'

He didn't reply straight away as he considered what I'd said. Then a look of such regret and sadness washed across his face that I was left feeling terrible.

'I wish you didn't feel that way but I guess I understand why you do. So you really are going to come back with me?' he asked, looking uncertain.

I nodded. 'I have to go and tell Sam what I've decided and then we can go.'

# CHAPTER 27

**Rachel**

It had been an emotional morning, having to leave Jenna, and as the taxi weaved its way through the morning traffic towards the airport, I remembered our tearful goodbye.

'I really hope you can come and stay with me over there. Let me know how things progress, won't you?' I'd said to her, giving her a big hug.

'I will and I hope things go all right with you and Jackson. Take care.'

I'd still been raw from saying goodbye to Sam the day before and now I felt wrung out. I knew of course that Sam would be upset that I wasn't taking him up on his offer but going back to Nashville with Jackson instead, and as I'd walked back into his room I knew that there would probably be no going back from this point. I couldn't see him forgiving me now. He looked up as I came into the room but there was no smile for me this time which meant he'd already worked out that I was leaving.

'I wanted to see you again before I left, to try and explain my decision.' I stood before him, wringing my hands.

'You don't owe me an explanation.' His voice was clipped and I could see the tension on his face as he wrestled with his emotions. 'But now you're here, I would like to know if you're sure you've made up your mind about going back with Jackson?'

'I think I have, yes. We've agreed to keep things strictly business for now so I'm going back to sign my contract and to get on with my music career.'

'But are you still together, the two of you?' he asked.

'I...I don't really know how to answer that and it's probably best that I don't.' I saw irritation pass across his handsome features.

'What I said to you meant nothing then? You know when I told you I loved you and I want to look after you, none of that made any difference?'

'Sam, please don't do this. Of course it means something to me but I want to try and make a go of my music career in Nashville and maybe I have to accept that I can't do that and have a relationship as well.' He let his head fall back against the pillows.

'I don't get why you have to go to Nashville when I can help you make a success of your music career right here.'

'It's what I want, Sam, and for the first time in my life, I'm going to put myself first and go after it. I'll be in touch with you again soon. Take care of yourself and concentrate on getting better.' I leaned forward to give him a kiss on the cheek but he didn't respond and his body remained stiff.

The rest of the journey back to Nashville was fairly quiet, with Jackson and I finding little to say to each other after all that had happened. Despite all my efforts to try and forget about my complicated love life for a while, it was the only thing on my mind. I fretted constantly about whether I'd made the right decisions about my future. I wanted to pursue my musical career as much as ever but it would be a hollow success if I had no-one to share it with.

## **Jackson**

I was desperate to ask Rachel how her goodbye with Sam had gone at the hospital yesterday but knew that she probably wouldn't have told me anyway so I left well alone. I couldn't stop thinking about what might have happened between them. If I were Sam, I know I'd have been begging her to stay but thank goodness she had already decided to come back with me, even if it wasn't going to be on the same terms. I just had to hope that she would come round again in time.

While Rachel was saying her goodbyes to Jenna, I had been in touch with Annie to make arrangements for Rachel to stay at The Hermitage and even though I knew it would annoy her, I'd asked Annie to book her into a suite. She hated me paying for things as it was, so when I went the extra mile and indulged her even more, she only seemed to be more cross with me. I saw it as spoiling her whereas she seemed to think I was being over-indulgent and that somehow she didn't deserve these little luxuries that I could easily afford. Annie had texted me to confirm that she had booked the suite and to tell me that The Hermitage wanted to check whether I had any special requests for the suite to make Rachel's stay there more comfortable. I gave Annie the go-ahead to contact them and go with what she thought would be best.

Greg picked us up from the airport but even his jolly manner couldn't cheer us up.

'Is it straight back to the condo, sir?' he asked as we settled into the back seat of the car, this time at opposite ends of the seat.

'No, Greg, sorry. Could you go via The Hermitage please?' I looked at him in the rear-view mirror, catching the almost imperceptible raise of his eyebrows.

We drew up outside the luxury hotel not long afterwards. Its many windows bathed the car with light as I jumped out to help Rachel with her bags.

'Thanks,' she said as I passed her the last of her two bags. 'We do still have a lot to talk about so I'd prefer to stay here until we've done that, okay?' She was at her most assertive right now, putting me on the back foot, which wasn't a place I liked being in.

'Will you come into the office tomorrow?'

'I don't know yet. I need to get myself sorted first.' My heart sank. This was going to be a lot harder than I'd thought.

She turned to go inside then and I watched as the doorman greeted her and called a bellboy to take her bags.

## Rachel

By the time I went into the hotel I was dead on my feet so when the receptionist told me that I was staying in one of their executive suites, I didn't have the strength to argue. I sighed, knowing that Jackson had organised this further extravagance but I couldn't be cross with him when it was really just what I needed.

I thanked the receptionist and turned to follow the bellboy up to my suite. My eyes were immediately drawn to the bedroom, where I could see a four-poster bed adorned with masses of fluffy pillows and a very inviting looking duvet. Once the bellboy had gone, it was all I could do to change into my pyjamas before falling into the welcoming arms of the bed and letting sleep claim me.

I was disorientated at first when I woke in the morning, forgetting for a moment that I'd checked into the hotel. Then it all came back to me and all of a sudden, loneliness enveloped me once again. Here I was in a foreign country, with no real friends to speak of and the man I loved had already abandoned me at the first sign of difficulty. What's more, I had left behind a perfectly good man who had never hurt me. Was I mad? I dragged myself up out of bed and had a shower to try and wake up. I switched my phone on, even though it was early, and was surprised to see a message from Alex.

'Hey, Rachel, Jackson told me you were back. So sorry to hear about what happened with Stephanie. If you need to talk, I'm here for you. Take care and stay in touch.'

Her kind words touched me so I replied straight away and asked her to join me for breakfast at the hotel if she was free. I was about to go downstairs to the dining room when my phone pinged with another text, this time from Jackson checking how I was today. Well, he'd have to wait till after breakfast. Alex joined me a few minutes later, giving me a quick hug and a kiss before sitting down opposite me.

'How are you, Rachel? You look wrung out,' she said gently.

'I am wrung out after leaving home again and the long journey here and now it's dawned on me that Jackson and I finally have to sort out all this mess. I do feel better now that there's been some space between us and I've had some time to think. I was surprised when he followed me home to the UK and impressed by his offer to put his feelings for me to one side.'

'Jackson definitely missed you but he knows you needed time to sort out your feelings as well. I was surprised that he could be so impulsive and jump on a plane just like that. I think it shows how much he cares for you, if you don't mind me saying. Anyway, I'm sorry about your friend, Sam. How is he now?'

'He's definitely on the mend, thanks for asking.'

'I think when Jackson couldn't get hold of you at first, he thought that you'd decided to go back home because of what happened that night, you know.'

'Well, he would only have had himself to blame,' I argued heatedly. 'At the first sign of trouble, he decided to go out and get drunk rather than talking to me and sorting things out and I'm finding it really hard to forgive him for that. He doesn't seem to understand that I was hurt by Stephanie as well. She was absolutely vile to me and she ruined what was meant to be a lovely evening.'

'Tell me something. Do you still love Jackson?' she asked plainly.

'I love him more than anything but this is a big hurdle to overcome.' I'd blurted all that out without even thinking and I'd only said what I knew to be true in my heart.

'If you love him and I know he loves you just as much, then you will overcome it,' she said gently. 'C'mon, let's eat now to take our minds off all this and then I want to schedule in another gig as soon as possible.'

---

## Jackson

I'd sent Rachel a text as soon as I got up the next day, hoping to speak to her before I came into work but she hadn't replied. I knew she would get in touch when she was ready but I wished she understood how it was killing me trying to be patient.

I'd hardly arrived at the office when Annie called me to say that Rachel was on the line for me.

'Hi, how are you today? Did you sleep well?'

'I'm fine, thanks and yes, I did sleep pretty well. Thank you for booking the executive suite for me, I really needed that, even though I know it's terribly expensive.' There was a slight pause and then she went on, 'Would you like to have dinner tonight at my hotel, say about seven o'clock? It would give us time to talk.'

'I would love that. Where shall I meet you?' I replied.

'I'll be in the foyer. Umm, I won't be coming into the office today, if that's okay so I hope you have a good day and I'll see you later.'

I was pleased to hear from her and to know that she still wanted to talk to me. I hoped that she wasn't going to tell me it was all over. I tried to be optimistic instead and went home promptly at the end of the day to get ready for dinner.

I walked from my loft to the hotel, figuring it would help me clear my head, as well as calm my nerves. On entering the hotel, I saw Rachel at once and watched her for a minute before she noticed me. She was captivating and my arms ached to hold her again. She stood up, smiled tentatively and walked towards me.

'Hey, how are you?' I asked nervously.

'I'm good, thanks, how about you?'

She seemed to see right inside me so there was no point in pretending I was fine.

'I'm nervous, to tell the truth,' I said honestly. Then she took my hand and said,

'C'mon, let's go and eat.'

I started to feel better from the minute she took my hand in hers.

# CHAPTER 28

**Rachel**

When Alex had asked me at breakfast if I still loved Jackson, my heart seemed to know the answer before my head did. It was only when I'd seen him at the hospital once again that I'd realised how much I'd missed him since leaving Nashville. Although I cared for Sam, he didn't have the power to make my heart beat faster like Jackson did.

On top of that, Jackson wanted what was best for me and now, all I wanted was to sort this out between us as soon as possible so that we could move on. I'd told him we would keep things strictly business when I returned, but I couldn't keep it up. He looked so nervous when I saw him in the lobby that I took his hand, which seemed to immediately relax him.

We sat down on opposite sides of the table in the candle-lit restaurant and looked at the menus for a few minutes. When we'd placed our orders and got some drinks, I looked over at Jackson to see him staring at me expectantly.

'Why are you nervous about meeting me?' I asked gently.

'Because I don't know if you're going to tell me that it's all over between us and that you can't forgive my stupidity.'

'I don't want things to be over between us but we do need to talk about what happened and, more importantly, how you chose to handle it, I think.'

'I know what upset you most was that I chose not to talk to you, not so much that I went out and got drunk.'

'Yes, although I'd rather you didn't go out and get blind drunk every time you see Stephanie. But you didn't even stop to think that I might have been upset too, that I might have needed to talk it all over with you. We could have talked to each other and shared our feelings but instead, at the first sign of trouble, you ran away from me.'

'Haven't you done that to some extent as well?' Jackson asked hesitantly.

'Yes, you're right. I ran away too, although I did have to go and see Sam, but once he was out of danger, I knew I'd been running from dealing with our troubles.'

Our food arrived then, causing a break in our conversation. As soon as we were on our own again, Jackson asked:

'So why did you come back?'

'I was so surprised when you came after me but more than that, I was touched when you said you were prepared to put my happiness before yours. That was really selfless of you and it made me see how much you care for me. It also helped me to focus my own feelings. In the end, I guess it was your love for me that persuaded me to come back and that's why I texted you today about meeting tonight. There's no point in dragging this out any longer. We need to deal with it and move on, otherwise we'll both just carry on being miserable.'

'I'm sorry for not staying with you and talking about how I was feeling. I didn't want you to see how angry I was. I felt ashamed of myself for that and then for getting drunk and letting you down.'

'But I love you, with all your flaws included and I was angry with Stephanie too. I completely understand that.' I took his hands in mine. 'I need you to promise me that we'll always deal with things together and not shut each other out, otherwise I can't do this any more. If you want me to commit myself to you, you have to be totally honest with me. If you want to be angry, tell me. If you're tempted to drink, tell me. I want to help you when you're feeling vulnerable but I can't deal with you shutting me out.' I was almost in tears by the time I'd finished.

'I love you, I really do and I promise I won't shut you out again from how I'm feeling.'

I breathed a sigh of relief and smiled at him.

'We also need to talk about Stephanie and what you'll do if she tries to contact you or you see her again,' I said.

'Do you really think she'd try and see me again after what I said to her?' he asked me.

'She seemed like a really mean-spirited woman to me and she was obviously jealous of us being together. I wouldn't put it past her to try and wheedle her way into your affections again.'

'I'm clearly being naïve here because I can't believe she'd be so stupid as to try anything else. But I'll go with you on it because it's better for us to be prepared for her turning up again, especially now she knows I've moved on with you. What can we do though?' He looked really concerned about this possibility.

'Well, we can't stop her turning up but we do need to manage how you react to that. I thought you handled yourself well in front of her, it was just afterwards that was difficult so that's where we'll work together if there's a next time, all right?'

'Okay.' He paused. 'Will you be staying here now or will you be coming back with me?'

'I don't know. It's been quite nice having my own suite to do what I like in.' I grinned wickedly at him. 'I can invite whoever I like up to my space.' Under the table, I slid my bare foot up his leg to show him what I meant. I saw his eyes darken with hunger for me after all the time apart.

I signed the bill after that and we hurried upstairs to my suite.

Once the door was closed, Jackson took me in his arms and gave me a long, slow kiss, leaving me breathless and filled with longing when he pulled away. He reached out towards me, starting to undress me slowly, tantalisingly slowly, and I had to stop myself from helping him. Then he was stroking my skin and his touch was at once soft and passionate. I began to remove his clothes as we kissed again and soon we were lying together, our bodies entangled and growing hotter by the minute. Making love with Jackson brought me back to life and I knew I didn't ever want us to be apart again.

## Jackson

When I woke the next morning, Rachel was still fast asleep so I was able to watch her. I knew how lucky I was that she'd been prepared to forgive me so quickly after what had happened and I'd already promised myself that I would never do something as stupid again. I wanted to spend the rest of my life with this woman and I didn't want anything or anyone to get in the way of that plan. She stirred so I turned on my side to face her.

'Hey, beautiful,' I said as she opened her eyes.

She smiled at my words.

'Hey, it's great to wake up with you in my bed for a change.' She chuckled at the idea.

I gave her a hug and a kiss on the cheek before slapping her behind playfully and jumping out of bed to get in the shower.

'Hey, that hurt,' she cried as I disappeared into the bathroom.

Twenty minutes later, I reappeared to see her eating room service breakfast. She beckoned me to join her, as she swallowed a mouthful of croissant.

'Mmm, I'm starving, I can't think why.' I grinned, picking up a croissant and putting it on my plate. 'Would you mind if I went into the office today? There's some things I need to finish up,' I asked.

'Not at all. I have some things I need to do as well. I can come and meet you at the office after that, if you like,' she said mysteriously.

'Now you have my interest piqued. Are you going to tell me what you're up to?'

'No, sir, I am not,' she replied, teasing me before she sloped off to the shower.

By the time she'd finished, I was ready to get off to work.

'Well, I guess I'll be off and I'll see you later, sweetheart, unless you're going to tell me what you're doing?' I tried again to get her to reveal what she was planning.

'Good try, but no, that's a fail.' She kissed me lightly on the lips, guided me towards the door and with a final wave at me, she closed the door behind me.

I made my way towards the elevator with a very satisfied smile on my face.

---

## **Rachel**

I leaned against the door for a moment after Jackson had gone, savouring the time we'd spent together since making up last night. Then I went to pack. By the time I'd finished, it was ten o'clock so I went down to the reception to check out and caught a cab back to the apartment. It was strange being there without Jackson because it wasn't my home, I suppose. That made me wonder what it would be like to choose a home together. I stood for a moment then, daydreaming about a longer-term future for us.

It was late morning by the time I finally arrived at the office. Annie greeted me with a great big smile, as usual.

'Rachel, I'm glad to see you,' she said kindly.

I guess she knew what had happened and was happy that we'd managed to sort it out.

'It's good to see you too, Annie, thank you. Is Jackson in his office?'

'He is, yes, he's doing some paperwork, go on in.'

I knocked lightly and opened the door. Jackson's face lit up at once with obvious relief.

'Did you think I wouldn't come?' I guessed.

'I was worried, yes but I'm really glad you're here now. Alex popped in just now looking for you. She wants to talk to you about the contract, I think.'

'I'll go and find her. She'll probably be with Todd, won't she?'

I wandered down the corridor to Todd's office and knocked tentatively.

'Come in,' he called.

When Alex saw me, she smiled and gave me a hug. Todd looked really pleased to see me as well.

'How are things with you two now, if that's not a rude question?'

'Things are good again now we've talked. I've moved all my stuff back to the apartment but he doesn't know yet so keep it quiet, won't you?'

'Of course we will and, Rachel, thanks for not giving up on Jackson. He loves you and I think you've been incredibly good for him, you know. He needs you in his life to take him forward into the future and away from that scheming cheat of a woman!'

'What could she be scheming to do next do you think?'

'Well, I don't know what exactly but I don't think we've seen the last of her, especially now she knows that you and Jackson are together.'

'Anyway, Jackson said you wanted to talk to me about the contract.'

'Yes, have you signed it yet?'

'No, I still haven't signed it yet but I can do it now.'

'No, no, my lawyer friend has some minor concerns so we'll need to hold on for a few more days but we should be able to get it signed soon.'

## Jackson

As the end of the day drew near, I started to wonder whether Rachel might decide to come home with me. I hadn't asked because I didn't want to keep on about it. I packed up my things and we went out together to the street and started walking in the direction of the apartment. When we got there, I turned to look at her.

'Would you like to come in for a while?' I asked.

'I think I'd better,' she replied.

I was about to ask another question when she put her finger sensuously to my lips, took my hand and led me inside the building. As I unlocked the door, my eyes fell on her two suitcases and I whirled round and took her in my arms.

'How did they get here?' I asked breathlessly.

'That's what I did this morning before coming into the office. I wanted to surprise you this afternoon.'

'Oh, sweetheart, I'm so glad you've come back. It was horrible here without you.' I kissed her with so much force then, we lost our balance and tumbled on to the couch. One thing led to another and soon we were basking in the aftermath of our lovemaking, back in my bed once again.

'Jackson, this morning, I found myself thinking about what it would be like to choose a home together.'

I stilled next to her at this new revelation.

'And what did you conclude?' I teased her because I thought I already knew what she was going to say.

'I concluded that it would be rather nice to choose a new home together and that I could see a future for us where we would do just that.'

I pulled her into my arms then and hugged her tight.

'Rachel Hardy, I love you!' I almost yelled at her.

'Hey, I'm not deaf you know.' She was laughing and everything seemed good again in the world.

Later on, I decided to bring up the subject of my birthday.

'Hey, it's my birthday next weekend and I'd like to take you to my beach house near Charleston for the weekend. Would that be okay?'

'Of course it would, that sounds lovely and if that's what you want to do for your birthday, then that's what we'll do. What about your family, do you usually see them?'

'Yes, I do and I thought we could maybe see them on the Friday evening and then fly down to Charleston early on Saturday, maybe coming back on Monday morning?'

'It will be wonderful to be near the sea again, even if it's a different sea!'

# CHAPTER 29

**<u>Rachel</u>**

Later that evening, I made a point of calling Jenna to bring her up to speed on what had been happening to me since my return.

'Hi, Jenna, how are you?'

'I'm fine, Rachel. How are things with you? Did you manage to sort everything out with Jackson?'

'Yes, we talked things over and I've moved back into his condo now. I didn't want to keep dragging things out and making our lives miserable. So we've moved on now and I think I should be signing my new contract next week.'

'That's brilliant news. Have you decided about the longer term yet, like with your job, I mean?'

'No, but I can't imagine going back to that now, to be honest. My life is starting to be more here. Next weekend, we're going to Jackson's beach house in Charleston to celebrate his birthday. Can you believe it? I keep having to pinch myself to prove it's real!'

'I'm so happy for you but I do miss you. You're so far away.' She sounded really glum.

'Hey, I miss you too, Jenna. There have been so many moments when I wished you were here to keep me company. But we talked about you coming to visit didn't we? Any news on that front?'

'You know I'd love to but I am worried about leaving Mary on her own at the shop, even though I know she could manage it. The business is going really well at the moment. I'm not sure I could drop everything and go.'

We paused for a moment while we both absorbed this fact.

'We were only talking about a few days though. Surely Mary could manage that, with some help from your mum, say?'

'Yeah, maybe. Sam's out of hospital now too so that's made life a bit easier for everyone.' I could almost hear her mind working.

'I'm glad to hear that about Sam. Well, how about you give it some thought and we'll speak again within the next couple of days to see what you've decided?'

'I will. I could really do with a break. Although it's been lovely living in my own place, it is quite lonely at times. I don't suppose Jackson has a friend you could recommend?' She laughed and I knew that it would do her a power of good to escape.

We hung up a short while later and I couldn't help but feel excited about the prospect of my best friend coming to visit.

---

### Jackson

Rachel had been booked for a short slot on a radio show mid-morning on Saturday. It wasn't far to Music Row, where the radio station was located but it made sense to go by cab so that she arrived looking as good as she had when we'd left. She'd taken even longer getting ready but it was worth it when she came out.

'You look gorgeous. You do know it's a radio interview, right?' I winked at her and she patted my arm, knowing I was trying to help her relax.

Alex met us at the station to add to Rachel's moral support and about half past ten, they took her off to prep her for the sorts of questions the presenter would be likely to ask and then suddenly, she was in the studio getting ready to go on air.

'We're joined today by Rachel Hardy, a talented new singer/songwriter all the way from the UK. Welcome, Rachel.' The presenter's accent was even more of a drawl than mine, which I hoped she wouldn't find too off-putting.

'Thank you, it's a pleasure to be here,' she replied.

I could tell from her body language that she was trying to relax but at the same time, she didn't want to be caught off guard by an awkward question.

'Tell me, how did you make it here, all the way from a little seaside town in Dorset? It's a place I suspect that not many of our listeners will have heard of before.'

'I was really lucky in that Jackson Phillips was over in the UK for his cousin's wedding and he heard me singing at a gig, encouraged me to enter the "Open Mic" competition and I went on to the national final. Then he offered to help me cut a demo CD and the next thing I knew, I was out here, singing at The Bluebird Café!' She laughed and the presenter joined in with her.

'And Rachel, is it true that you and Mr Phillips are romantically involved as well? That had to help, didn't it?' His gaze never left her as he waited to hear what she would say in reply.

I sucked in my breath, wondering how Rachel would deal with it. She couldn't even look to me for support.

'I'm here in Nashville because of my songwriting and singing talents mainly. Mr Phillips has certainly been very generous and supportive but he wouldn't have done any of that for me, if I hadn't had the talent to start with. Maybe you should come along to my next gig and find out for yourself.' She laughed and he joined in again with her but he knew she had won that round.

The interview went on for another few minutes and then he shook her hand and it was all over. She rushed back to us and we both smiled at her. I swept her up into my arms.

'You were so cool, sweetheart, you handled him brilliantly. Well done.'

---

We decided to have a lazy day on Sunday, enjoying spending time together. I went out to get a newspaper and some croissants first thing but that was it. It was as we were leafing through the sections of the paper that I came across a photo and article that made my blood run cold.

'Listen to this, Rachel:

*Nashville socialite, Stephanie Shaw, has returned home, like the prodigal daughter. She was last seen here when her engagement to respected independent record label owner, Jackson Phillips, came to an abrupt end after she was caught cheating on him. Snapped here at a charity ball last night, she looked like she was back for good.*

I looked up at her and found her staring back at me carefully.

'Alex told me she was a schemer and that she expected we would see her again before too long, after seeing her in New York. Now we have to be ready for her when we do see her.'

'Yep, I feel so annoyed, I guess. I don't want her here but I have no control over her, do I?' I fell silent but it had unnerved me and I didn't relish the prospect of seeing her again one little bit.

---

## Rachel

Alex was already at the office on Monday by the time we arrived and she whisked me off to a meeting room as soon as she saw me, bringing coffee with her that she had picked up on the way.

'Let's get straight down to it, shall we?' she said all business-like, the minute we sat down. 'Don't look so worried, Rachel, it's all good.'

I breathed a sigh of relief because I'd been concerned about how we would deal with any big problems.

'So, largely speaking,' she continued, 'he had no major concerns. There are a couple of minor points which I'd like to go over with you and then, if you're happy, we can go ahead and sign!'

It took only half an hour to discuss the finer details and we were done.

'I can't believe I'm on the brink of doing this, Alex. It's all nerve-wracking for me, to be honest,' I confessed.

'Well, you obviously have the talent, there's no doubt about that but it does also commit you to Jackson for the next year. Is that what's worrying you?' Her voice had become very quiet and I tried to frame my words carefully.

'I love Jackson very much and I know I want to be with him. It's just that for me, this is a complete change of life, moving country, leaving my close friends and my old life behind and trying my hand at something I'd only ever imagined myself doing in my wildest dreams. And on top of that, it's about starting a new life with someone I hardly know really and putting my trust in him completely. I'm not saying I don't want to do all of that but I'd be lying if I said I wasn't frightened by the prospect of all that change at once.'

'Have you told Jackson all this?' she asked me gently.

'I've tried to tell him but he thinks I'm afraid of commitment and when I try to explain, it all comes out wrong. I asked him to give us time to enjoy our relationship for a while before we take things to the next level but I think he saw that as a kind of rejection when we talked about it once before.' I sighed deeply.

'Well, look, there's no rush to sign this if you want to take some time to think about things,' she reassured me.

I took the contract from her again and signed it with a flourish before putting it back in the envelope. In my heart, I knew that was what I wanted to do.

'You know you've been a good friend to me, Alex, thank you.' I smiled at her and she returned it. 'I can't ask you not to talk to Jackson about what we've discussed. That wouldn't be fair as you're his sister.

But will you be careful about what you say to him? I don't want to hurt his feelings.'

'Rachel, I won't break your confidence. I know he's my brother but you're my friend as well, which puts me in an impossible situation. But I care about you too.'

She stood up then and gave me a hug, before adding, 'You'll get there, you know. You and Jackson are good together and I think you'll work it out between you. If you want my advice, try saying to him exactly what you said to me and I think he'll understand.'

'Okay, I'll give it a go this weekend, maybe. Talking of which, I still need to talk to you about his birthday present and now I have the means to pay for it as well!'

---

### Jackson

Rachel gave me back the signed contract as soon as she came out of her meeting with Alex.

'Rachel, this is fantastic! You won't regret this, I promise. We'll tell everyone at the weekend and celebrate your new contract then as well.' I pulled her to me and kissed her, knowing what a big step this was for her. As I stared into her eyes, I didn't feel any concern from her. 'Are you okay?' I asked.

She nodded and kissed me again.

The rest of the week passed quickly, and soon it was Friday afternoon and Rachel and I were getting ready to leave for my birthday weekend. I knew that she had been plotting something with the rest of the family but I was trying not to be apprehensive about it.

We got home to the condo at half past four and packed our bags for a weekend at the beach. Rachel was being very coy about her packing and I suspected she was hiding things she had bought for me in her bag. I was like a little kid all of a sudden about the prospect of sharing my birthday with this wonderful woman who had just stepped into my life out of the blue. I was certain that she would love the beach house in Charleston and, what's more, I had a little surprise of my own for her.

Greg picked us up at five and we set off to my parents' house, except that a few minutes later, I noticed we weren't going in the right direction.

'Er, Greg, where are you going? This isn't the way to my parents' house.'

'Hey, relax, everything is in hand,' Rachel said. 'Try to go with the flow, sweetheart.'

She laid her hand on my thigh in an effort to still me but her touch only served to ignite me further. I took some deep breaths and reassured myself that she wouldn't let them arrange anything I wouldn't like. Shortly afterwards, we turned up at the airport and I started to get nervous all over again. Greg bid us farewell and we were suddenly standing in the departures terminal, ready to go somewhere unknown.

'Honey, I can't stand it any more! Please tell me where we're going,' I begged.

'Okay,' she said, smiling. She took my face gently in her hands. 'I thought it might be nice for everyone to come to your house in Charleston and for us to celebrate together there tonight. I hope that was a good idea? I did check it with your mum first and she said she thought it would be all right. She's been there all day getting things ready with your dad.' She paused, biting her lip nervously, waiting for my approval.

I breathed out in relief.

'That is a brilliant idea, I couldn't have come up with something better myself. Thank you.' I kissed her gratefully for thinking so carefully about what to do.

'Everyone's coming in tonight but going home after breakfast tomorrow, leaving us on our own after that, like we planned.'

'Oh, sweetheart, this is going to be the best birthday ever. I can't wait to show you the beach house. When's our flight?'

'Well, that's the other piece of news. We arranged for a private jet to ferry everyone back and forth so we can go when everyone's here,' she smiled hesitantly.

'Wow, you sure know how to surprise a man!' I pulled her in for another kiss.

When we boarded the plane, I was even more surprised to see Alex, Todd, Shelby and her husband Josh already on board, together with Maggie and her friend, Ted. I smiled broadly at them all. It was six o'clock by the time we set off and after a very smooth flight, we were touching down in Charleston at half past seven. The weather was more balmy than Nashville when we stepped off the plane and the gentle breeze was very welcoming. I looked over at Rachel and took her hand as we walked across the tarmac and through the airport to find our waiting car. The journey from the airport to the house was short but exciting, as we crossed the two rivers and islands separating us from our destination. As we crossed over the final bridge on to Sullivan's Island and could finally see the sea all around us, I sensed everyone's mood lift, especially Rachel's.

# CHAPTER 30

## Rachel

Jackson's house was in an area of Charleston called Sullivan's Island. As the people carrier drew up outside, it was starting to get dark and the fairy lights scattered all around the outside of the pale blue coloured house made it even more enchanting. I drew in a sharp breath of delight and excitement, glancing over at Jackson as I did. He squeezed my hand, pleased at my reaction to his incredible beach-front home. It was a truly magnificent house, with steps leading to a first-floor verandah and a second floor with another verandah above that. We wandered across the lawn, past a number of palm trees and up the steps to the entrance. Inside, the house was even lovelier, with warm antique pine flooring and mahogany doors, giving the place a really cosy feel. I fell in love with it at once. I whirled around and found Jackson waiting right behind me.

'I love this house, it's absolutely beautiful and you've furnished it so well. I really do love it.' I was excited but I couldn't help myself.

'I'm glad you like it and it feels good bringing you here at last. Now, come and see the rest.' He put his arm around my shoulder and hugged me as we went towards the kitchen to find everyone.

Soon we were all hugging and kissing our hellos and marvelling at the wonderful job Jackson's parents had made of the food. The granite counters were heaving with the wonderful buffet spread of all kinds of salads and cooked meats and fish. We all helped ourselves to a plateful of food and then went upstairs to sit on the enormous verandah or porch, as I was learning everyone else called it. There were numerous rocking chairs and wicker chairs to choose from and, together with the twinkling fairy lights and the ocean view, it was a simply magical atmosphere. Bob came round offering everyone a cup of fruit punch that he'd made earlier, and soon we were all relaxing and enjoying each other's company.

We'd hardly sat down before another car pulled up on the driveway. Out tumbled two boisterous young men, calling out as they glanced up and saw us all.

'Rachel, meet my younger brothers, Jamie and Ben,' Jackson informed me.

These were the last two members of Jackson's family I had to meet. They came bounding up the stairs and were with us in a matter of minutes, staring at me with interest. Jackson performed the introductions but I was suddenly shy, like I was meeting everyone for the first time again.

'Rachel, we've heard such a lot about you and it's an absolute pleasure to meet you at long last,' charmed Jamie.

I said hello and smiled at their boundless energy. They both embraced Jackson in a man-hug before sitting down and tucking into their food.

## Jackson

It had been a lovely evening with my family and I'd really enjoyed the surprise trip by private jet and the get-together here in Charleston. It felt good to have introduced everyone to Rachel now as well and I was so pleased that she seemed to really love the house. I was looking forward to showing her round, once everyone had gone home. I was hoping that all my surprises were done now but after dinner, everyone started talking about birthday presents. Even though I'd told them all not to bother, they had anyway and that did make me feel good, if undeserving.

'You guys, I did tell you not to get me anything, you know!' I complained half-heartedly.

'Where's the fun in that, Jackson?' Ben called out, grinning. 'Here, open this one first, it's from me and Jamie.'

He handed me a large gift, which was all soft and squishy. I opened it slowly just to wind them up. When I could see what it was, I let out a low whistle.

'Oh, now that really is a perfect gift. I'm going to try it on now.' I stood up to try on the soft, black suede bomber jacket they'd bought for me and it fitted perfectly.

I glanced over at Rachel for her seal of approval and she gave me a big thumbs up. I think I saw another look in her eyes too and I returned her gaze, finally giving her a cheeky wink.

'Thank you, you guys, I really appreciate this.'

Next up was a gift from my mom and dad, a handsome leather satchel, very understated, in my style and something I would use a lot for work. Then Shelby and Josh gave me a platinum line Mont Blanc fountain pen, engraved with my initials.

Finally, Maggie, Alex and Rachel gave me a joint present from all of them. I had no ideas about this one. When I opened the box, I laughed. It was a brand new iPad, nestling inside a soft, black leather case.

'Wow, ladies, you do know how to spoil a man. I might need some help to get it set up.'

'No problem, that's where younger sisters come into their own,' laughed Maggie.

I stood up to go round to them all and thank them for their presents, finishing with a special kiss for Rachel.

'Put her down, Jackson, for goodness' sake,' teased Jamie.

Just when I thought all the excitement was over, my mom and dad went inside for something else and reappeared holding an impressive-looking birthday cake, covered in what looked like hundreds of candles but was in fact only thirty. They all sang me Happy Birthday while my dad videoed my embarrassment and they insisted on me blowing out the candles while making a wish.

'Okay, I'll indulge you but only to make you all stop harassing me!' I groaned.

I glanced over at Rachel as I made my wish and was rewarded with a little smile, tugging at the corners of her luscious lips. Then she mouthed 'I love you' at me and I think I actually blushed.

---

## Rachel

After all the excitement of the presents and the cake, we sat and chatted while watching the magnificent sunset over the marina together. It had been a truly perfect evening. I suddenly realised that we hadn't told everyone about me signing with Jackson's label so I leaned over to whisper in his ear. He jumped up then to make the announcement.

'Hey, y'all, I completely forgot to tell you that we have other exciting news as well. This is business news really, I suppose, but it's just that we signed a new artist this week and I'm really looking forward to working with her.'

He smiled knowingly around the people there and when they realised he was talking about me, everyone leapt up and came either to me or to Jackson to give their congratulations. By the time that was over, we were all exhausted and ready for our beds.

Fortunately, there were four bedrooms, which sorted out Jackson's parents, Shelby and Josh, Alex and Maggie, and finally, Jackson and I. Todd and the other guys shacked up in sleeping bags in the main living room. They didn't seem to be overly worried about sleeping on the floor. I guess they were just used to it.

After saying goodnight to everyone, Jackson led me to the master bedroom. It was another amazing room, with windows on three sides and painted in a delicate shade of mint green. I could hardly wait to see the sun come up in this room. The wrought-iron bed was very romantic, and when I sat down on it I almost melted into the duvet floating on top of it. Jackson joined me and we lay back on the bed facing each other.

'How have you enjoyed your birthday so far?' I asked him.

'It's been the best birthday ever, I'd say. And when you say "so far" that seems to suggest there's more to come.' He looked at me hungrily and I laughed at his obvious need for me.

'Well, yes, I hear you loud and clear on that front but I do have another gift for you that I wanted to give you on our own.'

Jackson sat up then and turned to pull me up into his arms.

'You're the best birthday present I could have. You didn't need to get me anything else, baby.'

'I think you'll really like this one though,' I whispered, looking deep into his eyes.

He swallowed and I could see I had his interest aroused, among other things. I stood up and went to my bag to retrieve my final gift. I returned with a distinctive Tiffany gift bag. His eyes went wide when he saw it.

'It's my turn to give you something special now,' I told him and passed him the bag.

He looked inside at the small box lying there. He took it out and opened it very slowly to reveal a sterling silver knot ring. His eyes met mine and he looked unsure for a moment.

'This is to tell you that I really do love you and that I want to be with you. Just because I asked you to take things slowly doesn't mean that I'm any less committed to you. This ring is to say that I'm yours for the long term.'

'I...I don't know what to say,' he stuttered. 'Except that this means so much to me and if it's possible for me to love you even more than I already do, then I do. Which finger shall I put it on?' he asked hesitantly.

I took it from him and slipped it on to the fourth finger of his right hand. He swept me into his arms then and we made love as though we were doing so for the first time, discovering each other all over again.

'You make me so happy,' I whispered just before we fell asleep.

'Ditto.' I heard his soft reply in the darkness.

---

## Jackson

In the morning, I left Rachel sleeping and crept off quietly downstairs to the kitchen. It was a tradition in our family for the guys to get up early the next day and cook breakfast for all the ladies. As I walked in, I could see my dad lightly whisking eggs that he'd turn into delicious scrambled eggs with salmon and chives later on. After greeting him, I set about preparing a pancake batter. Josh joined us shortly afterwards, having been reminded the night before by my dad and he started cutting up some fruit. Soon, Todd, Ted, Jamie and Ben were also with us, woken no doubt by all the wonderful cooking smells.

'Can one of you boys take care of the bacon for me please?' asked my dad. 'And someone else needs to prepare the salmon too.'

He gave the orders out and everyone jumped to attention. We finished by putting on some fresh coffee and filling jugs with juice. Just when we thought we'd have to go and call the girls, by some miracle, otherwise known as my mom, they appeared. Rachel came directly over to me, surreptitiously checking that I was wearing my ring before giving me a sweet good morning kiss.

'Hey there, baby, I hope you're hungry!'

'I am, actually. This is really lovely of you to do this for us.'

We gathered around the large kitchen table to tuck in to our sumptuous breakfast.

'What time will y'all be having to leave to catch your flight back?' I asked.

'Can't wait to get rid of us, hey?' teased Maggie. I poked my tongue out at her.

'I'd like to know what our plans are going to be for the day, that's all. I've had a wonderful time getting together with all of you, which I hope you know. We really should make the effort to do this more often.'

'I couldn't agree more, Jackson, honey,' my mom concurred. 'Anyways, to answer your question, the jet will be available to take us back from noon so really, we need to get there around then or shortly after, I think.'

'Okay, that sounds good. We have some more time together this morning then.'

While everyone was clearing up after breakfast, my dad drew me to one side.

'Son, I hate to bring this up while we're all having such a lovely time but did you see that Stephanie's back in town?'

'I did see it in the paper, Dad, yeah.' I didn't really want to think about this now but I knew my dad was just looking out for me.

'And how do you feel about it?'

'To be honest, I'm worried that she's up to something but I'm powerless to do anything to stop her scheming.' I blew out a long breath. I saw Rachel glance over at me and a look of concern passed across her beautiful face.

'Does Rachel know about her being back?' my dad asked, looking in her direction.

'Yes, I told her straight away.'

'Good. Well, I guess all you can do is hope she leaves you alone now.' He didn't look convinced and I didn't feel it either.

I wandered back to Rachel and the rest of the family, eager to put Stephanie as far from my mind as possible.

'Is that a new ring you're wearing, Jackson?' Alex shrewdly

pointed out for everyone's benefit. She smiled knowingly and I realised she'd probably helped Rachel decide on what to buy me.

'I think you know the answer to that one,' I replied. 'Rachel gave it to me last night.'

All the women came over to look at the ring and oohed and aahed about it being stunning. I smiled at Rachel through it all, remembering the words she'd said when she gave it to me. I felt on top of the world, knowing that she felt that way about me and I was more hopeful now that she would like my gift as much as I'd liked hers.

# CHAPTER 31

**<u>Rachel</u>**

As we waved goodbye to the family, Jackson grabbed my hand and pulled me to him.

'It's time for the tour of the house!'

I laughed and followed him happily as he led me round the first floor, taking in the library (a library in your own home, how cool!), the great room as Jackson called it, furnished with lots of soft leather sofas to cuddle up on and a fireplace for those cold winter nights, and there was also a dining room and an office. We went on upstairs to check out the other bedrooms and the numerous bathrooms (how many did one man need?) and we ended up on the second floor porch looking at the fabulous view of the ocean.

Jackson put his arm round my shoulder and hugged me to him. 'What do you think of the house, then?' he asked.

'I love it. You've made it into a wonderful home and it's great to be here. I'd love to go and get some photos on the beach. Could we go and do that now?'

'Of course we can. Let's grab our things and head out. We can stop somewhere for a seafood lunch as well, if you'd like to.'

'Mmm, you're making me hungry, already.'

We wandered barefoot along the beach for the next hour and I took hundreds of photos of the sea, the marina and the view back towards town. When I thought he wasn't looking, I snapped a few of Jackson as well. He looked so happy and carefree and I managed to take some wonderful photos of him as a result. We had lunch at a lovely restaurant, sitting on their patio looking out to the sea. It was idyllic. After lunch, we walked lazily home again along the beach, watching the families with small children playing together in the sand. I sighed.

'Hey, that was a big sigh. What's up?' Jackson asked, stopping me so he could look at my face.

'I was just thinking that that could be us one day in the not-too-distant future.' I paused to consider what he thought about that.

'With kids, you mean?' he asked.

'Yep, I'd love to have a family one day.' I waited to hear what he would say about the subject, aware that I was holding my breath.

Then he reached out and pulled me to him.

'I can't imagine anything more wonderful than making babies together with you.' He smiled at me and I was glad that we were on the same page about that.

'Do you know something else I've always wanted?' I said, changing the subject ever so slightly. He looked at me intently once more, keen to hear this new revelation. 'I've always wanted a dog!' I burst out laughing at the surprise on his face.

'Well, that definitely wasn't what I thought you were going to say!'

'It's seeing all these people on the beach, walking their dogs. It's made me remember how much I love watching people do that. They always seem so happy together and I could never have a dog as a child because we were all out all day. I'd love to be able to do that in the near future. Do you like dogs?'

'Yes, but it would have to be a proper dog, not a yappy sort of dog that you can carry in a handbag, if you know what I mean.'

'So you wouldn't want to carry a dog in a handbag, huh?' I grinned at him. 'What's the matter, don't you like handbags?' I ran away from him then and he chased after me along the beach.

The wind blew through my hair as I ran but I'd forgotten that Jackson was a practised runner and he caught up with me in no time, grabbing me around the waist and swinging me round to face him.

'You can't get away from me that easily, you know,' he said almost breathlessly. He kissed me deeply, so that I almost swooned right there but luckily we were just about home.

We ran the rest of the way and, once indoors, it was only a matter of time before we were in bed again, having strewn our clothes all over the house in our desperation to show each other how we felt.

## Jackson

I was nervous about when to show Rachel my surprise because I didn't have any idea what her reaction would be and I didn't want anything to spoil this wonderful weekend we were having. Lying in my arms now, snoozing after our lovemaking, she was the closest to an angel I'd ever seen and I loved her so much. She stirred then and turned to look at me, smiling lazily at our decadence.

'Hey, gorgeous,' she said.

'Back at you, sweetheart.' I kissed her gently on the lips.

'Are you all right? You looked deep in thought about something when I opened my eyes.'

'I'm fine but I was deep in thought about something, you're right.' I closed my eyes briefly, steeling myself for this. 'I bought something for you too and I want to give it to you now but I don't know how you'll feel about it.'

She sat up then and the sheet dropped to her waist. God, she was beautiful. When I raised my eyes to her face again, she was smirking at me as she pulled the sheet back up again.

'Well, you'll have to concentrate on the matter in hand first before you can do anything.'

She was trying to put me at ease so I stood up and went to get yet another gift bag from my drawer. When I returned with it, her eyes were wide with surprise.

'You're not supposed to be buying presents for me, it's your birthday!' she scolded.

'Open it, please.'

She took the Tiffany bag from me, muttering about how we ought to get shares in the company, and looked inside excitedly. Then she gasped and looked up at me.

'That looks like a ring box,' she said.

I bit my lip nervously and said nothing while she took it out and slowly opened it. Then she sat back and laughed joyously.

'It's almost identical to the one I chose for you.'

I nodded. It was a sterling silver triple band ring, meant to show that our love was going to last forever.

'I wanted to tell you how precious you are to me and that I'm in this relationship for the long term too. Last night, you almost stole the words I've been rehearsing this past week right out of my mouth. We could have practised together if we'd known,' I chuckled. 'Do you like it though and is it okay for me to give you a ring like this?' I worried, still nervous because I hadn't let her say anything yet.

She moved towards me and came to sit in my lap, bringing the box with her.

'I love this ring because I know exactly the reason you bought it for me and it is more than all right for you to give it to me. In fact, it's fantastic! Will you put it on for me?'

I slipped the ring on to the fourth finger of her right hand so that we were matching and then I kissed her. We made slow, deep love after that, bringing the day to a beautiful close.

## Rachel

Sunday passed too quickly and before we knew it, it was Monday and time to go back to reality. We were planning to be back at the airport for midday as the others had been on Saturday so we only had a few short hours left before we would have to be on our way. We sat down to breakfast on the porch for one last time and I couldn't help feeling glum about the prospect of going. Jackson picked up on my mood at once.

'You okay? You seem kind of down.'

'Yeah, I don't want this lovely weekend to end that's all. It's been good to spend all this time together with nothing else getting in the way.'

'I know, I've really enjoyed it too but we can come back whenever we like, it's not far and maybe we should make more of an effort to do that regularly, you know.'

He smiled at me and I loved him so much for understanding me.

We were back in Nashville by mid-afternoon and Jackson went off to do some work in his office while I unpacked. I decided that I needed to speak to Jenna again to see if she was going to come and visit as I'd suggested. I had such a lot to tell her.

'Hey, Jenna, it's me. I'm sorry it's late but I wanted to hear your voice.'

'It's never too late for you to call me, don't be silly. How did this weekend go? What was the house like?'

I told her everything about the weekend, finishing with the part where Jackson gave me an almost identical ring to the one I'd given him.

'Wow! It sounds to me like you two are engaged in all but name and fingers!'

'I guess you could say that, yes. Do you think we're both afraid of commitment?'

'Not at all, I think you're both totally committed to each other but you're scared to say it in the traditional way as if there's no way back from that in your minds. Does that make sense?'

'Yes, I think you've gone straight to the point. I do want to be engaged but I don't want to get hurt again, you know, and I'm sure that Jackson feels the same.'

'Well, sooner or later, you're going to have to decide whether you're both prepared to take that risk because it is a risk to love someone but it's not without rewards.'

'Oh, Jenna, tell me that you're coming to visit soon! I need you here to help me with all this.'

'I can come, yes, but only for a week, I think. I can't leave Mary in charge of everything for longer than that and Mum's tied up with other stuff obviously right now. I was thinking about coming over next weekend, what do you say?'

I squealed in delight, unable to contain my excitement. I promised to call her the next day to talk further about the details and rang off, going in search of Jackson to tell him the good news.

---

## Jackson

As soon as I heard Rachel saying goodbye, I quickly returned to my desk, hoping she wouldn't guess that I'd accidentally overheard her conversation. I'd come looking for her, missing her after only a short time apart, and had almost walked in just as she was telling Jenna about our exchange of rings this past weekend. I knew I shouldn't have listened in but I couldn't help myself. It was definitely how I felt too but I needed to work out when would be the best time to admit this to Rachel and to persuade her that we should go ahead and take this risk on each other. It was crazy the way we felt this but couldn't say it to one another.

'I just came off the phone with Jenna and she's thinking about coming here to stay for a week this coming weekend!'

She looked so excited, it was catching.

'Oh baby, that's great news. We need to get thinking about

arrangements for her, if you think she'll be okay with us helping her out.'

'Do you mean paying for her ticket and other stuff?'

'Yep, that's what I was thinking but I don't want to overstep the mark. You know her better than I do, of course.'

'I do but you're right that she would find it difficult to pay for her ticket. And where's she going to stay? Would you be happy with her staying here or would you prefer her to stay in a hotel? Come to think of it, she might prefer to stay in a hotel!' She ran her hands through her hair in concern.

'Hey, sweetheart, don't sweat it. Just ask her if she would mind us paying for her ticket and whether she'd prefer to stay with us or in a hotel. We could pay for the hotel of course.'

She looked at me for a long moment then and finally smiled.

'What is it, baby? What are you thinking about?' I asked, intrigued by her look.

'I just noticed how you're talking about *us* paying for her ticket and *us* paying for her hotel, like we're a proper couple, sharing everything, including our money, like you're saying what's yours is mine. And that feels kind of nice, like we really do belong together already.'

'Well, I think we do and what's mine *is* yours, forever.' I paused for a moment, then I continued. 'I have a confession to make. I came looking for you just now and accidentally overheard some of your conversation with Jenna.' I tried to look suitably guilty.

'You did?' Her beautiful hazel eyes went wide with surprise. 'And what did you hear?' she whispered.

'I heard you telling her about our exchange of rings.' I heard her sudden intake of breath and I instinctively closed the gap between us. 'And my next confession is that I had a different plan originally for what I was going to do and say when I gave you that ring.'

'You did?' she said again.

I went down on one knee then and took her hands in mine. 'What was it you were going to say?' she said so softly, I could barely hear her.

'Rachel, will you marry me?' I replied.

Her left hand flew to her mouth and her eyes filled with tears.

'That's what you were going to say?' she managed to choke out. 'Why didn't you say it then?'

'I didn't think you were ready and I didn't want to rush you. But after hearing your conversation with Jenna, I think I was wrong and that maybe we both just need to have faith in each other. So, will you marry me?' I looked up at her tenderly, waiting for her to reply.

She lowered her left hand by way of an answer and removed her ring from her right hand and gave it to me. I took a moment to catch on to what she wanted me to do, then I slipped the ring on to her wedding finger and I kissed her hand.

She pulled me up then and we kissed deeply.

'I haven't heard your proper answer yet, you know.' I smiled down at her.

'Nothing would make me happier than to be married to you for the rest of my life.'

She confirmed what I'd been waiting to hear and, with a whoop, I swept her into my arms and whirled her round the room.

'Thank you for making me so happy,' I cried.

When we came to a stop, she took my right hand in hers and removed my ring, slipping it on to my wedding finger.

'Now we're promised to each other forever.'

# CHAPTER 32

### Rachel

I could not believe all that had happened between us over the last few days and now we were engaged! To be married! We had overcome quite a few hurdles to get this far and this seemed to be the next step for us.

'I think this calls for a celebration! Let's go out to eat tonight, what do you think?' I asked.

'I think that's a great idea. How would you feel about asking the family along too?'

'That would be lovely. I'll call Alex.' Jackson said he would call his mum, which would include Maggie as well.

We went into separate rooms to make our calls and when we returned about ten minutes later, Jackson had managed to get his mum to call Shelby as well.

'Did you tell them what the occasion was?' I asked.

'No, I managed to get away without revealing that. How about you?'

'No, I kept it close to my chest,' I confirmed.

'Well, that sounds like a nice place to be,' Jackson quipped flirtatiously.

'Mmm, so that's the kind of mood you're in, is it?' I queried, tilting my head to one side, quizzically.

'You know me, I can always be in that mood but I'm trying really hard to focus here, honest.' He held up both hands in surrender.

I kissed both his palms in response before bringing us back to the conversation.

'What about Jamie and Ben? Could we get them to come? Is it too far for them to come back?'

'I've already dealt with that one, baby.'

'You have?' I asked, not understanding how he could have dealt with it already.

'They hadn't left my folks' house yet, so no problem.'

I took a step towards Jackson, wanting to feel his arms around me once again. 'So we're all sorted for another family celebration,' I whispered against Jackson's chest.

'Yep, all sorted and if you keep whispering against my chest like that, I don't think I'll be able to control myself any longer.'

'How do you mean?' I continued, whispering against his muscular chest as I'd been doing before.

He suddenly swept me up into his arms and carried me through to the bedroom.

---

## Jackson

A few hours later, we were walking into The Hermitage hotel, towards the Capitol Grille restaurant, where the whole family had gathered. We kissed and hugged and deflected their questions as smoothly as we could, making our way to our table quickly. Once we were sat down, I was able to take charge.

'Thank you all for coming at such short notice. I know that we've only just said goodbye and now Rachel and I are asking you to get together again.' I paused to smile at Rachel.

Then we both held up our left hands for them to study. It took only a moment for Jamie to realise.

'Wait a minute! You both have rings and they're on your left hands now, are you two engaged?'

We both grinned and nodded. Suddenly, there were whoops of joy all round, followed by backslapping and lots of hugs and kisses. Eventually, we all sat down again and I coughed politely to get everyone's attention so that I could speak.

'I asked Rachel to marry me earlier today and she said yes. We know that this is all we want for our future and we want to share our good news and fortune with all those we love.'

I glanced contentedly round the table at my family and friends and then back again at Rachel, as we all tucked into our meals. Rachel was glowing with happiness and had never looked lovelier to me.

'Have you set a date for the wedding then, Jackson?' asked Alex who was sat on my left.

'No, no, we haven't got that far yet. But I guess that will be next on the agenda,' I replied, looking over at Rachel for confirmation. She nodded looking a little bit worried.

'Hey, what is it, baby?' I asked her.

'Well, we'll have to think about the logistics of including everyone here and everyone in Dorset in our celebrations. I've only just thought about that and it's not going to be easy, is it?' Her brow creased a little.

'What about having two weddings then, one here and one there?' suggested Alex. 'Mom and Dad could come to both,' she continued.

'What do you think about that idea, Rachel? It sounds like it could work to me.' I looked at her again to try and gauge her thinking.

'Yes, I think that could work. We'll have to give it some more thought.'

'Don't worry about it now, let's enjoy tonight.' I smiled at her.

We finished our meals, chatting all the while and we were just pondering whether to have dessert when a dramatic hush fell over the table. I turned to see what had brought this on and looked straight up into Stephanie's eyes.

'Well, what do we have here? A Phillips family celebration with a few hangers-on, I see.' Her sarcastic voice cut through the air as she leered at everyone. She looked drunk again.

I tried to stand up to confront her but I simply didn't have the strength.

I was surprised to see Rachel already on her feet.

---

## Rachel

'You're right, Stephanie, this is a Phillips family celebration but you seem to be the only hanger-on in sight.'

She leered at me, swaying dangerously close.

I took a small step back before continuing. 'Jackson and I are celebrating our engagement tonight. I've chosen to be part of this wonderful, loving family and they've welcomed me with no hesitation.' I looked round briefly at them all, noting how surprised they looked by this turn of events. 'That could have been you, Stephanie, but you rejected their love.' She rolled her eyes at that. 'That was your mistake, which you seem to recognise now but it's too late for you to come back. You need to move on, like Jackson has, and find your future because it isn't here. Your future is somewhere else.'

I hadn't broken eye contact with Stephanie as I came to the end of my speech so I hadn't noticed that Jackson had stood up next to me while I was speaking and that his mum had joined me on the other side.

Stephanie swallowed hard, looking like she was about to launch a counter-attack but after glancing over at Jackson's mum and then at Jackson himself, she seemed to think better of it.

'Well, you folks go ahead and enjoy the rest of your evening,' she muttered, her words slurring and, turning on her heel, she started to walk away, wobbling ever so slightly as she did. As she reached the door, she looked back one last time before saying, 'Oh and don't worry, Jackson, your secrets are safe with me.'

Then she slipped through the door and disappeared. I saw Jackson wipe his hands on his jeans, and I noticed everyone exchange a look of concern.

I fell back into my seat at the table, feeling exhausted with the effort of standing up to Stephanie like that. I never would have thought I had it in me to do that and in front of so many people but it had been my gut reaction. I didn't want this cloud hanging over us any more and it was time someone told her straight. I didn't want to crush her but I did want to make the message loud and clear and it seemed that I'd succeeded.

Jackson's mum knelt down next to me.

'Rachel, I'm really proud of you for doing that and I'm so happy that you're joining our family. I couldn't have wished for a better daughter-in-law.' She squeezed my hand and kissed me on the cheek. Jackson helped her back up and sat back down next to me. He leaned forward and kissed me gently on the lips, holding my face in his hands. He gave me a reassuring smile.

'I love you, Rachel. I can't wait to make you my wife.'

I didn't smile back at him though. I was wondering about Stephanie's last comment. Did Jackson have secrets he was keeping? And if he did, why? I had no choice but to push my concerns away for the time being.

The rest of the meal went smoothly with desserts and coffees following along. I gave some more thought to Alex's suggestion of two weddings and the more I thought about it, the more I liked it. It would be lovely to get married in Nashville so everyone here could attend but it would be complicated to get everyone over from Dorset as well, and anyway, I wanted to get married at St James' so I would feel like my parents were there too and, more to the point, Jenna would kill me if she couldn't do the flowers! I would have plenty to talk to Jenna about then when she came to visit next weekend. I was looking forward to seeing her and I gave a little smile in anticipation.

'Penny for them?' Jackson was looking at me intently with his deep, brown eyes. I wanted so badly to ask him what Stephanie had meant but I was frightened.

Taking a deep breath, I talked about our wedding plans instead.

'Oh, I was mulling over the idea of two weddings and asking Jenna to do my flowers. You know, most men find the idea of one wedding hard enough to deal with and here you are possibly agreeing to two!'

'I would do anything for you, you know that. And if that means two weddings, who am I to argue?' I kissed him gratefully then.

'Thank you.'

'What for?'

'Just for being so wonderful mainly but for understanding that I need to include everyone back home as well.'

'Well, of course you do but I think this could work really well. And if Mom and Dad are at both weddings, that will join the circle once again from Nashville back to Dorset. I think it will be quite fitting. Why don't we mention it to Mom now?'

So we turned to Jackson's mum, Shelley, and put the idea to her. To say she was delighted was an understatement. She threw her arms around us both with obvious pleasure.

Soon the evening was over and Jackson and I were wandering slowly back to the condo.

'Are you going to tell me what she meant?' I asked after a few minutes calming myself. I stopped and turned.

'In all honesty, I have no idea what she meant. I promise you that I'm not keeping any secrets from you.'

'Why do you think she said that then?'

'I don't know but it's got me worried about what she might be scheming to do next.'

I took his hand to show that I had accepted his answer. But I knew instinctively that he was right about Stephanie. The doubt which had sowed its seed at the back of my mind when she'd said those words, began to grow.

---

## Jackson

I was still reeling from seeing Stephanie again at the restaurant when Rachel asked me about her parting shot. I wasn't keeping any secrets from Rachel but I could see the suspicion in her eyes, which was exactly what Stephanie had planned. Damn that woman! Would I never be free of her?

I felt powerless and I hated being in that position. Stephanie was up to something but I had no idea what. This was the last thing we needed now when we'd only really just got back together. Not only that but I wanted the focus to be on our future, not on my past.

---

We were into the office bright and early the next day because Rachel wanted to get down to starting work on her new EP which was what her demo CD had turned into and, by extension, her album. We were also planning a special gig for her at the end of the week, as well as some more press interviews so we were going to be kept real busy.

Annie was sorting out Jenna's travel arrangements so that she could be with us by the weekend. I knew that Rachel wanted to tell Jenna all about our plans for the two weddings and we'd both agreed that we would press ahead with them as soon as possible, hopefully before Christmas.

Meanwhile, I started to contact some real estate agents so that Rachel and I could start looking for a house together to kick off our married life. I'd just finished making a batch of phone calls when I heard Rachel's cell phone ping with a text. Realising she'd left it on my desk while she was in the studio, I pulled it towards me to see who the message was from. It said it was from Jenna and I decided to take it downstairs so she could read it straight away.

Rachel read the text out to me as she read it herself:

*'Hey, Rachel, any news on flights? Everything is in place at this end so I can come as soon as you're ready for me!'*

She clapped her hands together in excitement and then ran towards the stairs. 'I'm going to ask Annie to arrange a flight for Jenna tomorrow if possible!'

---

## Rachel

Annie managed to book Jenna a flight for the following day, arriving late at night like I had. I sent her a text to confirm the details and to ask where she'd like to stay.

*'Thanks for arranging ticket. Can't wait to see you! Happy to stay at condo if that's not awkward but a hotel's fine too :) See you at the airport tomorrow!!! Xxx'*

I couldn't wait to tell Jenna that Jackson had asked me to marry him and that we were planning two weddings as well. I wanted her to do the flowers for both if possible so we'd have plenty to talk about in terms of practical arrangements.

We set off for the airport the following night about ten, driven by Greg as usual.

'Have you had any ideas about what you'd like to do with Jenna while she's here?'

'I thought we could do some sightseeing, I want her to come to my gig on Friday, of course, and she'll be able to meet some of your family then too, as well as maybe seeing them at the weekend. What do you think?'

'That sounds good to me. Why don't you do some sightseeing tomorrow and then come into the office for some rehearsal time on Friday. I'll be able to keep Jenna company if you need me to. Then perhaps we could do something all together on Saturday and see the family again on Sunday.'

'Yes, that all sounds good. I can't wait to tell her our news as well and to make some plans with her for the weddings.'

Jackson took my hand, raised it to his lips and kissed it.

In no time at all, we were at the airport and standing by the arrivals gate, looking for Jenna.

'Should we go and check the arrivals board?' I asked Jackson anxiously, after we'd been waiting for about half an hour with no sign of her.

'Yeah, maybe we should, sweetheart.'

He took my hand and we wandered over to the nearest board, only to find that her flight had been delayed.

I felt my shoulders sag in disappointment.

'Hey, it's only another half hour delay, why don't we go and grab a coffee while we wait?'

He was trying to keep my spirits up but I wanted her to be there and to know she was safe.

We sat down at the nearest café, waiting for our coffees to cool.

'Shall we go and check the board again?' I asked for about the tenth time, standing up and smoothing down my skirt. Luckily, it said Jenna's flight had now landed so we made our way back to the arrivals gate and a few minutes later, there she was, pulling her suit-case along behind her while busily scanning all the people looking for us.

'Jenna, over here,' I called and waved and her face lit up. I ran towards her and gave her a great big hug. Jackson leaned over and kissed her on the cheek in welcome and we set off to look for Greg and make our way home.

# CHAPTER 33

**Jackson**

I could hardly get a word in edgewise as we travelled home, for all the talking the girls were doing on the way. Rachel explained that we'd be delighted for Jenna to stay with us and that we were heading back to the condo now. Then they were chatting about news from Dorset and about all their plans for the coming week and before we knew it, we were being dropped off by Greg and heading inside. I said goodnight to Jenna and left Rachel to get her settled in. They must have chatted for a long time because I had no memory of Rachel joining me in bed when I woke up the next morning. She stirred a little when I got up to get ready for work but she didn't wake up. When I went through to the lounge, Jenna was already awake.

'Morning, Jenna, did the jet-lag get you up this early?'

'Yes, it did, unfortunately.' She pulled a face for a moment but was instantly smiling again.

'I'm heading off to work but you girls should take it easy for today and get reacquainted.'

'That will be lovely, as long as Rachel doesn't lie in too long!' She laughed then and I was struck by her easy-going nature.

'Have you two known each other a long time?' I asked, realising I didn't really know much about how they'd met.

'Since we were at high school.' She nodded. 'We've been through a lot together. I'm glad that she's met you, Jackson, it's wonderful to see her so happy.'

'Rachel has made me happy too. In fact, I don't think I've felt happier than this, ever.'

Rachel appeared then, looking absolutely gorgeous. She came straight over and kissed me good morning, as if to confirm the point I was just making.

'Are you two talking about me? My ears are burning.' She grinned at both of us.

'Yes,' admitted Jenna, 'but in a good way. I'm glad to see the pair of you so happy. I would love to have some of what you two have between you so, any tips, please send them my way!'

'We have some news for you, actually.' Rachel held up her left hand for Jenna to see and I did the same.

We were both smiling like lovesick teenagers by this point.

'Oh my goodness,' Jenna squealed as the penny dropped. 'You're engaged?' She jumped up and ran over to hug each of us in turn.

'When did this happen and why haven't you told me?'

'Just after I spoke to you about it but I wanted to tell you face to face and see this reaction!'

'Sorry to interrupt you, ladies but I'd best be going. Have a nice day catching up and I'll call you later, Rachel, okay?' I kissed her, feeling her body respond to mine then, reluctantly, I pulled away to leave.

---

## Rachel

By the time we'd had breakfast, I'd filled Jenna in on all, well not quite all, but most of the details of our weekend in Charleston. I told her about the engagement celebration we'd had with Jackson's family as well.

'Then, you'll never guess who decided to show up to try and spoil things?'

'No, she didn't? Stephanie, I presume.'

'Yep, and what's more, I stood up to her and even though I was shaking on the inside, I felt strong on the outside, strong enough to tell her to get lost, anyway! By the time I'd finished, I had Jackson on one side of me and his mum on the other, like bodyguards ready to protect me. I really do hope that's the last we'll see of her but I have a feeling it won't be. Her last words to Jackson were that his secrets were safe with her.' I pulled a face as I remembered it.

'And what did she mean by that? Did you ask Jackson?'

'I did and he said he had no secrets from me and had no idea what she was talking about.'

'Well, it sounds like you left her in no doubt about the fact that she didn't belong there. As you say, hopefully that's the end of it but if it isn't, you'll be ready for her.' After a slight pause, she continued, 'How are you going to organise the wedding? We'll all want to come too, you know, and that could start to get expensive.'

'We've decided to have two weddings! One here and one at home, in Dorset.' I paused then, realising that I was referring to Dorset as home again. I mean, it was my home for nearly thirty years but things had moved on and I was going to have to think differently from now on. I bit my lip and tears sprang to my eyes. I tried to swipe them away but Jenna noticed at once.

'Hey, what brought that on? What's the matter?'

'Oh, I don't know, I'm being silly, I guess. It's just that Dorset is still the place I think of as home but it's not going to be my home any more, is it? Every time I think about it, I get upset because I want my home to be where Jackson is but I also have my memories from the past twenty-odd years of my life in the UK. It's going to be hard to move on from that and start afresh over here, without you and your family and everything I've ever known around me.'

'It's natural that you'd feel scared as well as excited by that prospect but you will be able to come back to Dorset and see us, won't you? You'd better, anyway.' She laughed and I smiled, feeling reassured.

'How's Sam doing?' I asked her, desperate to know but hardly daring to ask.

She blew out a breath before replying. 'Physically, he's well on the mend but...' She paused, looking hesitant.

'What?' I whispered, guessing what she was going to say.

'Well, he's hurting in his heart. I had a long chat with him about his feelings for you. Don't worry, nothing you wouldn't want me to know. Look, he asked me to give you this letter actually.' She dug in her bag for a moment and pulled out a slightly crumpled envelope with my name on it. She looked so torn between her love for her brother and her friendship with me that I didn't know what to say.

I took the letter from her, trying not to cry. 'I didn't mean to hurt him, you know,' I managed to say after a minute.

'I know. He needs some time to get over it but he will in the end.'

'C'mon, let's get dressed,' I said, trying to lift the atmosphere. 'Why don't we go out for a nice lunch and maybe, if you're not too tired, we could do a little mild sightseeing after that. What do you think?'

She nodded and we went off to our separate rooms to get ready.

I closed the door of the bedroom behind me and sank on to the bed. I stared at the letter for a long minute, not sure if I was brave enough to open it but knowing that I had to read what Sam wanted to say.

*Dear Rachel,*

*I'm sorry if this seems a bit strange but I didn't want to say all this in a text or email and I haven't got the courage to call you yet. I heard from Jenna that you and Jackson are back together and from what she said, I think it sounds like you've committed to each other for the long term. I have to be honest and tell you that I'd been finding it hard to accept that you don't love me the way I love you but when I heard this news, it was the push I needed to move on. I want you to know that I wish you every happiness in your life but a part of my heart will always belong to you. I hope you know that I'll always be here for you, as a friend, if nothing else. Take care and good luck with everything.*

*Love Sam x*

I looked up as I finished reading, hardly able to see for the tears streaming down my face. Sam was such a good man and a great friend to me too and I felt such sadness that we wouldn't ever be together in the way that he wanted. I knew I'd made the right decision for me but it still hurt to know I'd caused him such pain. I reached for a tissue to wipe my eyes and then folded the letter up very carefully and put it in my bag, resolving to call him at the first opportunity.

---

## Jackson

I'd set to work as soon as I arrived at the office and had managed to get quite a lot done. Just before lunch, there was a knock on the door.

'Come in,' I called out and I stood up to greet whoever was there. 'Hey, Will, what's up?'

Will, my VP for Marketing, looked uncomfortable with whatever he was about to say.

'I think you'd better sit down, you're not going to like the news I have to tell you.'

'What's this all about?' I frowned at him but sat down as asked.

Will went on, 'I just heard that *Gossip* magazine, which is published online, is going to be running an interview with Stephanie in next week's issue and in it, she says some pretty scathing things about you and Rachel.'

'What the hell?' I stood up again, immediately angry and turned to look out the window to hide my frustration. 'Do you know what she says about us?' I said quietly a couple of minutes later.

'Yes. Do you want me to read it to you?' He waited for my nod before continuing. 'There are two main things she says. Firstly, she says that the real reason you dumped her is not because she cheated on you but because she wanted a family and you told her you didn't want to have children. She goes on to say that she needed a real man, blah, blah, blah. Obviously, she's trying to win back some sympathy for the way that she behaved by making up another lie. Secondly, she says that Rachel's nothing but a gold-digger and that she's wormed her way into your affections to get at your money and that you've been fool enough to fall for it.'

He fell silent and waited for my reaction.

I let out the most almighty roar of anger at this new betrayal by the woman I'd come to hate.

Annie appeared at my door at once. I signalled that I was okay and she disappeared again but she didn't look like she believed it.

'Is there anything we can do to stop them publishing this, Will? I don't give a damn what she says about me but I do care about Rachel and I don't want them saying this sort of stuff.'

'We should check with our lawyers about libel but if it isn't, I don't think there's anything we can do. You'll have to keep your head up and try and rise above what she's said about you. It might be an idea to issue an official statement about your engagement to Rachel, or perhaps to organise an interview for you both in one of the more respected newspapers or magazines to set the record straight. What do you think?'

'I need to speak to Rachel and then I'll come back to you. Thanks for letting me know. It can't have been easy for you, telling me all that.' I smiled tightly.

'I'm sorry I had to be the bearer of that news,' Will said, looking miserable. 'Let me know what you want me to do and I'll get on to it at once.'

I sat down heavily at my desk and put my head in my hands. Would we never be rid of this woman? I heard the door open and looked up to see Annie there, looking really concerned.

'What on earth has happened?' she asked.

I gave her the main points and she sank down into the chair opposite me then, unable to believe how spiteful Stephanie was being.

'What are you going to do?' she asked.

'I'm going to have to tell Rachel, of course, which I'm not looking forward to one bit. Will has come up with quite a good idea that Rachel and I should give an interview to set the record straight in one of the better magazines. I'm going to head off home now.'

'I'm sorry, Jackson. I think that's a good idea on Will's part but see what Rachel thinks first, as you said.'

'You do think I should tell her then?' I asked.

'Oh definitely. She needs to know before it's published for everyone to see.'

After Annie left, I thought about how I would break this news to Rachel, especially as I was so damn mad about it all. I needed a run to get my head straight really. An idea formed in my mind about how I might tackle things. I picked up the phone to Annie and asked to be put through to Will again.

'Hey, Will, I was wondering whether you're busy tonight?'

'No, I haven't got anything special on. Why?'

'I'll tell you on our way out. I'll be with you any minute, I just have to send Rachel a text.'

*'Something came up again with Stephanie. Will's coming home with me to sort out how to deal with it. I need to go for a run first so he'll fill you in then. I thought we could all go out for dinner later maybe x'*

---

## Rachel

After listening to Will's account of what had happened and his suggestion of how we should deal with it, I was stunned into silence. I could not believe the animosity that this woman had towards me but worse than that was what she was saying about her relationship with

Jackson. She clearly had a different view about Jackson's feelings with regard to starting a family.

I felt like I was being kept out of the loop and as my mind whirred I began to feel very angry with Jackson. I had trusted him with my heart and, once more, it seemed like he had kept things from me. I stood up and walked over to the window, clenching and unclenching my fists as I paced up and down the length of the glass, impatient for him to come back from his run and explain himself. I knew that I couldn't talk to him with Jenna and Will there though.

'Will, Jenna, I need some time alone with Jackson, I think. Would you mind going on to the restaurant without us?' I felt guilty about sending Jenna away with Will when I'd only just introduced them but I knew he'd look after her.

'If you're sure,' Jenna replied and then turned to check that Will was okay with the idea.

He nodded and she went to get her coat.

'Try and keep calm, Rachel, and let Jackson explain first,' she said when she came back, taking my hands in hers.

I nodded but I couldn't speak. It was taking everything I had to keep myself together for speaking to Jackson.

When he returned, I was torn between relief at seeing him back safe and looking much calmer, and anger at this new turn of events, which was making me doubt him once again. I kept my arms tightly folded and waited for him to come into the lounge.

'Hey, baby. Where's Will and Jenna?' he asked, looking around as he towelled himself dry after his run.

'I sent them on to the restaurant so that we could talk,' I said quietly.

'Okay, that was probably a good plan. What did you think of Will's idea then about us doing an interview with another magazine to try and set the record straight?'

'It would be difficult for me to set the record straight seeing as I don't actually know what the record is, do I?'

'What do you mean?' His handsome face was etched with worry now as he started to understand that I was angry.

'Why did Stephanie say that she didn't cheat on you when that's what you've told me all along? Is it true that you told her you didn't want children? Again, that's not what you've been telling me.'

He swallowed but didn't speak for a moment.

I didn't know if he was preparing another lie or if he was about to tell me the truth at last.

'I did tell her I didn't want children, yes,' he whispered finally.

My mouth dropped open.

'What? You said she cheated on you and that's why you dumped her.'

'She did cheat on me, she's lying when she says she didn't and in the aftermath, we both said some terrible things to each other, including me telling her that I didn't want to have children but I meant with her, not with someone else. I do want to have children with you. I wasn't lying about that.' When I didn't reply, he carried on. 'Haven't you ever done or said something in the heat of the moment which you regretted later, Rachel?'

And all of a sudden, I remembered that I'd done just that. With Sam and I'd never told Jackson about it. It was all before I met him of course, which was how I'd rationalised not telling him whenever I wondered whether I should. I tried hard not to let it show in my face but I couldn't quite manage it.

'What is it?' he asked me.

'Jackson, I...I haven't been totally honest with you either.' I watched as his face fell, and worried whether to go ahead but it was too late to back out now.

'What haven't you been honest about?' He'd gone pale as he waited for me to answer.

I could feel myself shaking but I tried to pull myself together to tell him.

'Before I met you, I had a one-night stand with Sam but I

regretted it instantly because I knew I didn't want that kind of relationship with him.'

'And why didn't you tell me this before, when I asked you if you'd ever dated each other?'

'I hardly knew you then but I should have told you when we came back to Nashville together. We both promised to be completely honest with each other then but neither of us have been. For my part, there never seemed to be a good time to tell you when it wouldn't hurt you and perhaps ruin everything we had together.' I fiddled with my engagement ring, unable to look him in the eye.

'And that's how I felt about Stephanie. My relationship with her was over long before we met, as I told you, and I haven't lied about what happened. It's just that now she's trying to stir up trouble and we can't let her do that, not if we want our relationship to survive.'

'Even if we can get past the things we've kept from each other, if the press go ahead and publish that interview with her, my career will be in pieces before it even gets started, along with your reputation.'

He stood up then and came towards me, arms outstretched and I instinctively walked towards them.

'I wish you'd told me about you and Sam but I knew the minute we came back to Nashville that you'd forgiven me and that we were going to be together so I'm happy to leave the past where it belongs. How about you?'

'I can forgive you too but what are we going to do about Stephanie?'

His big arms enveloped me and we hugged silently for a few minutes, both of us glad that everything was now out in the open.

'At first, I thought Will's suggestion sounded like a good plan but when I was out running, I wasn't so sure. I don't feel it's going to be that easy to make her go away, you know. What about you, how do you feel about it?'

'Well, she's going to say some pretty unpleasant things about us but if we rise to her bait, trying to defend ourselves, we may only make things worse. I hate attention from the press at the best of times.'

'I know, and if we don't say anything, it sounds like she's telling the truth and what's more, we'd be letting her get away with it.' He paused for a moment, groaning at the seemingly hopeless situation we now found ourselves in. 'Look, let's go and catch up with Will and Jenna and see what they think.'

# CHAPTER 34

**Jackson**

We arrived at the restaurant a few minutes later and found the two of them sitting at a quiet table in a corner, nursing some drinks and deep in conversation. I took a moment to absorb the scene and smiled a brief smile before joining Rachel at the table. Once we'd said our hellos and then placed our order for food and more drinks, I spoke up.

'First of all, I'd like to apologise to you, Jenna for having this horrible mess take over your stay with us and I'd like to welcome you to Nashville properly with a toast.'

We all clinked glasses.

'Thanks, Jackson but please don't worry about it on my account. I'm your friend and it pains me as much as it does the both of you. What I want to know is what are we going to do about it?' She gave us all a look that showed she meant business and we all laughed, glad of the icebreaker.

'Jackson and I were just saying that we're worried that we might be playing into her hands if we rise to the bait but if we don't say anything, then she'll think she can do and say what she likes.' Rachel looked really miserable about the dilemma we were in through no fault of our own. I took her hand.

'You've got an important gig tomorrow night, Rachel, haven't you?' Will asked her.

'Yes, why?' she replied.

'Well, I was wondering if you could use that as a platform to present your side of the story without going to the extra trouble of an interview which might look like you were trying too hard.'

'That sounds like quite a good idea, Will, thank you. What do you think, Jackson?'

'Yeah, that might work. We couldn't tackle everything but we could deal with some of the things she's going to raise. I guess we'd have to leave people to make up their own minds after that. Okay, how about we leave it there for tonight and try and enjoy the rest of our evening?'

The next day flew by in a whirl of rehearsals and preparations for Rachel's show that evening so there was no time to worry about Stephanie. This was to be a charity dinner and show performed by Rachel and had been set up by my parents on behalf of the university. It was by invitation only and we were expecting about two hundred people to attend. I knew that Rachel was nervous but I also had every confidence in her. After spending the morning rehearsing, she appeared in my office just before lunch.

'Hey, sweetheart, how's it going? You look exhausted.' I went over to her and drew her into my arms, losing myself in her hazel eyes.

'It's gone well, I think but I'm dead on my feet, to be honest. Where's Jenna, is she okay?' She pulled back slightly, looking guilty at the thought of having left her friend on her own all morning.

'She's more than okay. She spent some time with me but when Will came and asked her if she'd like to go on a tour of the office, she jumped at the chance.' I gave a little smile and Rachel raised her eyebrows slightly.

'Do you think...? Do they...?'

'Yes I do and yes they do!'

We both laughed.

'Well, I'm pleased about that. Is Will coming tonight?'

'He is and so is almost everyone else from the office. It's going to be a great night. I heard that there's a great new singer performing as well.'

'I'm very nervous. It will be such an important audience, although I know I've performed in front of larger ones before but I know and care about a lot of these people and I'm scared of mucking it all up.'

I tipped her chin up so that she could see my face.

'You are not going to *muck* up, you will be fantastic as always. I believe in you and so does everyone else at the label. Our family and friends will be there and we'll all be rooting for you so try not to worry. Is there anything else you need me to help you with before tonight?'

'No, I think I'm all right. I'd like to get some lunch and then probably get off home mid-afternoon to get ready, if that's okay?'

'Let's go and find Jenna then and see if we can tempt her away from Will.'

We wandered down the corridor towards Will's office but when we got there, it was empty.

'Perhaps they're still doing the tour?' Rachel commented. We turned around to see if we could see them across the open-plan office and saw Annie speeding across from my office.

'Jackson, there you are, I've been looking for you to give you this message. Will and Jenna have gone for lunch at the deli and said for you two to join them if you wish when you're ready.'

'Thanks, Annie. What would you like to do, Rachel? Shall we join them or leave them to it and lunch on our own?' I touched her gently in the small of her back and was rewarded with an unexpectedly sultry look in return.

'If you touch me there, I will not be responsible for my actions,' she whispered seductively in my ear. My eyes lit up at her flirting but I had to drop my hand, given our location.

'I guess I'll have to take a rain check on that wonderful offer.' I smiled and touched her cheek.

'In answer to your question then, how about we go somewhere and eat on our own, and leave Will and Jenna to get better acquainted?'

'That sounds like a great idea.'

---

### Rachel

By five o'clock, we were on our way to the country club where the dinner was being held. It was over near the university and quite close to Jackson's parents' house so Greg was taking us there. Will had offered to pick Jenna up and take her there so Jackson and I were alone in the back of the car.

'Are you going to introduce me tonight then?'

'I want to introduce you anyway, sweetheart, but I don't know how much to say about the other stuff. People might think it odd before there's even been any sign of an article, do you know what I mean?'

I nodded and sighed.

'Maybe it's best to try not to get drawn in to all this bitching with Stephanie because we could end up getting more hurt by her. Perhaps if we try to ignore it and rise above it by proving that we're not like her, she'll get bored and move on.'

Jackson nodded but neither of us seemed any more convinced.

There were lots of people milling around when we arrived but I was able to find Jed quite quickly and carry out my soundcheck without any hitches. Jackson was listening and gave me the thumbs up. We'd chosen the six songs on my setlist together and I was confident that we'd made a good choice. Our next stop was to find Bob and Shelley to say hello before people started arriving in earnest. They were out in the foyer, greeting guests as they arrived for drinks.

Dinner was at seven so it was a good time to mingle and meet new people.

'Rachel, you look lovely, dear and I love those cowboy boots. Have you done your soundcheck? Was everything okay?'

'Thank you. Yes, I have and it was fine. Thank you again for doing this for me, Shelley, it's a great opportunity.'

'Sweetheart, you have nothing to thank me for. You earned it. Just try and enjoy yourself, you look nervous.'

She gave me a hug and then Jackson took me round to introduce me to some of the music industry people who were attending. We bumped into Will and Jenna on the verandah and I took a moment to check how things were going, pulling her off to one side, leaving Will to talk to Jackson for a minute.

'How are you two getting along?'

'We're having a lovely time, Rachel. I can't believe how much I like him even though we've only just met. He's such a wonderful person.' Her eyes glowed with the enjoyment of a new romance and I was happy for her.

'How about you? Are you feeling nervous about tonight?'

'A bit, yes. It's just that it's a really important crowd this evening and I could do without this whole thing with Stephanie hanging over us.' I swallowed but tried to smile.

'Is everything okay between you and Jackson after all that came out yesterday?' I nodded in reply and she took my hands in hers and gave them a little squeeze to try and reassure me and then we went back to join the guys.

It was soon time for dinner but I hardly ate a thing. Bob gave a short speech, telling everyone about the charity he and Shelley were involved with and thanking them for their generous donations to their cause. Before he went to sit back down, he introduced Jackson who went on to the stage where my small band of session musicians were settling into place. He looked calm and gorgeous, all at the same time and I took a deep breath as he started to speak.

'I'd like to take a few minutes of your time to introduce Rachel

Hardy who will be singing for you tonight. I first met Rachel in the UK, only a couple of months ago and I was so impressed by her singing and songwriting talents that I persuaded her to come out here to Nashville to pursue her dream. She performed in a couple of "Open Mic" nights when she first arrived and these were all a great success. Shortly afterwards, I signed her to my record label and she's already started work on her first album.' He paused and smiled as the audience gave a round of applause.

'Rachel and I have come to know each other real well over these past couple of months and it wasn't long before we both realised that we were meant to be together, which is why I recently asked her to be my wife. Luckily for me, she said yes! Ladies and gentlemen, please give a warm welcome to Rachel Hardy.'

I stood up amidst the rapturous applause and made my way to the stage, holding my head up high.

---

## Jackson

Rachel looked absolutely beautiful as she stood up to make her way to the stage. As I'd thought, the minute she was there and the intro to her first song was playing, she became calm and focussed solely on the music. She was singing only her own songs tonight at my suggestion because she'd made it now and needed to show the audience what a good songwriter she was. She sang her first three songs, 'My Turn', 'Don't Let Me Go' and 'Too Late', stopping only to tell the audience the names of the songs and to introduce the band members. Then there was a short interval. She was congratulated by lots of people on her way back to our table and she was smiling confidently by the time she returned.

I took her into my arms for a hug and whispered into her ear, 'Baby, you were sensational. Well done!' I kissed her gently and felt her body lean into mine with relief at her success.

We only had time for a quick drink before the second half.

She kicked off with 'Driving Me Crazy' which really got the audience going and then she paused to say a few words.

'I'd like to thank you all for the great welcome you've given me tonight, you've been a fabulous audience. I'd also like to thank Bob and Shelley for this opportunity to perform in front of you, I really appreciate it. Most of all, I'd like to thank Jackson for turning my life upside down and for showing me that dreams can come true.' And she blew me a kiss from the stage.

I hardly heard the applause because I was so taken aback by the declaration of love she'd just made in front of all these people. Someone slapped me on the back, bringing me back to reality and I gave a little smile to Rachel as she began her next song on the guitar. It was one I remembered hearing her sing in her little cottage all that time ago, 'Without You'.

*'Before we met, I felt so alone,*
*I didn't even realise just how much,*
*I yearned for someone who would love me,*
*And fulfil me with their every touch.*
*Now we're together and so much has changed,*
*I was one and have become two,*
*I can't begin to imagine, I wouldn't even dare,*
*To consider living without you, without you.'*

It was another wonderful song and Rachel gave it everything so the audience was hanging on every word and every note. I was so proud of her talent and I knew this audience was on her side and would spread the word about her to all their friends and family.

She had come to her final song now and I could feel an anticipation in the audience as they waited to hear what it would be. She coughed gently to get everyone's attention.

'This is my last song of the evening and it's called "Empty

Promises". Thank you.' She glanced quickly over at me and then went to sit down at the piano.

I remembered when we'd talked about empty promises and I hadn't heard this one before. I felt a tiny flutter in my stomach.

*'I want you to love me like there's no tomorrow,*
*Just in case you're a dream and gone when I awake,*
*Can I trust you or are you just making empty promises?*
*Are you here to stay or am I making another mistake?*
*Tell me that you love me again, it won't ever get old,*
*Make sure that you mean it, please don't let me down,*
*My fragile heart is easily broken and I*
*Don't want to be your clown.'*

She had a way with words that went straight to my heart and all I wanted to do was show her how much I loved her and wanted to be with her forever. At the end of the song, I jumped to my feet along with the rest of the audience to give her a standing ovation. We were stood there for several minutes and then someone called for an encore. Rachel responded at once, turning to the band to confirm what she would sing. I knew she would have prepared for this, just in case.

'Well, this has been an amazing evening, here in Nashville, with y'all!' Everyone laughed with her, as she tried out the accent. 'Here's a Dolly Parton classic which seems a good one to finish on.' She went straight into 'Here You Come Again' to lots of whooping and some hat throwing and everyone was singing along and, in that moment, I knew that Rachel Hardy had well and truly made it.

**Rachel**

We didn't talk much in the car on the way home. I didn't think there were any words for the excitement I felt after the show or for all the emotions I was feeling. I held Jackson's hand tightly to show him I needed some time and I think he sensed that. When I'd come down from the stage, he'd been right there to take me in his arms and kiss me so intensely that I knew he'd understood what I'd been trying to tell him in my newest song and that he just wanted to reassure me.

Once we were inside the condo, we kissed again, more passionately this time and we kept on kissing all the way to the bedroom, closing the door behind us to save Jenna from any embarrassment later, and we made love like never before. As we lay there afterwards, gradually recovering from the strength of our desire for one another, I managed to put how I was feeling into words.

'I love you. We feel so right together and I want us to be together forever, as soon as possible. Can we set dates for our weddings?'

'Sure we can, baby.' Jackson propped himself up on one arm to look me in the eyes. 'I hope you know that I feel the same and that I'll never make you an empty promise for as long as I live. I want to be with you because you make me whole and I've never felt as good as I have since I met you. I love you and I always will.'

'I was wondering about setting a date for the weekend of Thanksgiving or do you think that's too soon?' I bit my lip as I pondered this thought, seemingly rendering Jackson completely weak out of need for me once again. So it was some time later when he was able to answer my question.

'Thanksgiving is a wonderful idea. That would be a fantastic family celebration for that weekend. I'd like to keep it to close family and friends if you're okay with that and we could maybe hold the wedding at my parents' house because there's plenty of room. What do you think?'

'Oh, yes, that would be lovely and everyone would feel at ease but I don't want your mum getting stressed by any of the arrangements. It would have to be on the condition that she let us organise people to do everything. Do you agree?'

'I do, honey. I have another idea too which I'd like to run past you.' I looked at him eagerly, loving the direction this conversation was taking.

'Well, you know how we said that we'd have a second wedding in Dorset? How about if we do that as the start of our honeymoon and then spend the rest of it visiting Europe? I've never been and there are so many wonderful places I'd love to go with you to create shared memories for the future.'

I kissed him then to show him what a great idea that was before we fell asleep in each other's arms.

# CHAPTER 35

**<u>Jackson</u>**

The next morning, everything went mad. Will called me at seven on my cell to warn me about what had happened.

'I'm sorry to call you so early, Jackson, but I thought you'd want to know that Stephanie's article has been published in *Gossip* magazine but it's even worse than we'd expected and there are comments about it all over the internet. Speculation is rife about the things she said about you, which includes an accusation that you made her have an abortion when she fell pregnant but it's Rachel that people are really going for. They really seem to believe that she's after you for your money. I'm sorry. Do you want me to come over so we can work out a plan of action?'

I was speechless for a moment, in the wake of these new revelations. I climbed out of bed and walked into the living room as I gave him my reply.

'That would be great, Will, if you don't mind. I'll see you later.'

I ran my hands through my hair, unsure once again of what to do. I'd been staring out the window for some time, watching the city wake up and trying to come up with a plan, when I felt Rachel next to me as she put her arm round my waist.

'Penny for them, sweetheart?' she whispered by way of greeting.

I looked down at her trusting face and wondered how on earth I was going to break it to her. I couldn't hide from her how I was feeling, she could see it written all over my face.

'What is it? What's wrong?'

When I told her, she sagged against me and I put my arms around her to hold her steady. I felt her breathing quicken and I stepped back so I could look at her face. Tears were streaming down it and it broke my heart to see her so upset. I gently wiped them away with my thumb and tried to pull her close to me again but this time, she resisted. I heard her sniff as she tried to pull herself together and I knew how hard she would be finding this. I needed to be strong for both of us now.

'Listen, Will's coming over to help us work out what to do. I need to have a shower and get dressed. Why don't you have some breakfast with Jenna and see what you both think?' She didn't say anything so I led her to the lounge where we found Jenna already preparing something to eat. I quickly told her what had happened, gave one final glance in Rachel's direction and went off for a shower.

By the time I returned, I was still no clearer about the best course of action to follow but I was glad to see Rachel looking calmer. Will arrived a few minutes later, telling us that there were already some paparazzi stationed outside the building. It was then that I noticed the pair of suitcases by the door. I swung round to Rachel and found her staring right back at me.

'Rachel, what...?' I began but she cut me off.

'I can't take this, Jackson, I don't know what's real any more.'

My face fell at the thought of Rachel leaving me again, I didn't want her to go but I didn't know how to persuade her to stay either.

'Is that what you really want to do, Rachel? Where will you go and what about the weddings?' I asked.

'I want to be away from all these lies and accusations. As for the weddings, well...'

She brushed past me, stopping only to pick up her suitcase before disappearing through the door. I watched in shock as Jenna approached Will, kissed him goodbye and then followed after Rachel, suitcase in hand.

---

## Rachel

As we descended in the lift and made our way to the taxi waiting for us at the back entrance, I became more and more overwhelmed by this new turn of events. I climbed into the cab and sat back in the seat, feeling as if my breath had been knocked out of me. This whole situation was so unfair and I felt like such a victim, which wasn't like me at all.

I knew that I was running away again but I needed the time and the space to think about everything. I desperately wanted to give Jackson the chance to explain but I didn't know if I could trust what he said any more. I'd been such a fool for believing that he'd told me all the secrets Stephanie was keeping and I'd gone and declared my love for him in front of all those people last night as well. That would teach me to let my guard down.

'Where to, Rachel?' I was suddenly aware of Jenna's hand on my arm but I had no idea how long we'd been sitting there. 'Do you want to go to the airport?' she continued.

I glanced in the mirror to see the cab driver looking more than a bit impatient.

'No, I don't know. Could you take us to The Hermitage hotel please?'

The cab took off but I wasn't any more sure whether this was the right thing to do or not. My mind was in such a mess. Jenna and I were both very subdued on the journey. We both received texts on the way but while Jenna busied herself sending a reply to Will's, I didn't even read mine.

'Please don't tell Will where we've gone for the moment, Jenna,' I pleaded with her when I realised that she might want to let him know that we hadn't left the country.

'That's not fair. I know you're cross with Jackson but you can't take it out on me and Will as well. Besides, you ought to speak to Jackson, you know.'

'Why should I? He's only going to lie to me again and I don't want to hear any more of that.'

'How do you know he's lying? Surely he deserves more credit than Stephanie does. He loves you, I'm sure of that and I don't think he would hurt you by lying to you about something as major as that. Trust works both ways you know.'

I stared at her for a moment, hurt that she would say that to me and I thought about saying so but then I just gave up. I had no more energy left to fight with anyone. We said no more on the journey but I did think a lot about what she'd said.

The cab dropped us off in front of the hotel and a bellboy appeared from nowhere to take our luggage inside. I'd booked us into a suite with separate rooms so that we could both have a bit of space. No sooner had I sat down in my room than she was back knocking on the door.

'Come in,' I called.

'I'm going to meet up with Will for the day. I hope you don't mind too much but I'll be going home soon and I don't want to miss out on any time I could spend with him. I thought that you could probably do with some time on your own anyway. I've asked him not to tell Jackson where you are but I can't force that point really.'

All I could do was nod weakly and she turned and closed the door behind her.

Once she'd gone, I took out my phone and saw that there were at least a dozen messages from Jackson but then nothing during the past half hour. It seemed like he'd given up too. I scrolled through the messages until I reached the last one.

'*You told me once that we should always deal with things together and not shut each other out so why won't you do that now?*'

I couldn't believe his nerve so I bashed out a reply, letting my guard down once again.

'*I also seem to remember telling you to be completely honest with me so why weren't you?*'

His reply came back immediately.

'*I am not lying to you about this and it hurts me to think that you could believe I would lie to you about something like that.*'

Tears filled my eyes as I realised that I should have talked to him before leaving and not run away again. I should have given him the chance to explain and now it was probably too late. I didn't bother to reply and neither did he. I lay down on the bed and cried myself to sleep.

---

## Jackson

Once they'd left, I sank on to the nearest sofa and put my head in my hands, trying to figure out why Rachel had reacted like that. I knew that she'd been shocked by the new revelations in the interview but surely she wouldn't believe that I had forced Stephanie to have an abortion, surely she knew that I wasn't capable of such a thing? Stephanie had never been pregnant with my child and even though it would have been the last thing I would have wanted, which was what I told her, I would never have tried to make her have an abortion if she had been pregnant. She'd tried to make me believe that she was pregnant by me of course after she'd cheated on me but it had been so long since we'd had sex that it was a laughable claim and she knew it. I'd seriously underestimated her desire for revenge because now she was using that same ridiculous claim against me, and Rachel had left me again because of it.

I took my cell out of my pocket and sent off a barrage of texts to Rachel but heard nothing back. I slumped back against the chair, defeated. It was only then that I realised that Will was still with me.

'Man, I'm sorry, you don't have to stay and see me like this,' I told him, standing up and trying to pull myself together.

'I know I don't, Jackson, but I don't want to leave you in this state either. If it helps, I've had a reply from Jenna telling me that they've gone to a hotel, not back to England.'

'Oh, that is a relief. Where are they staying?'

'She hasn't told me for the moment. I think she's finding it hard to be caught in the middle between the two of you.'

'Okay, well, thanks for telling me, I know it's awkward. You can get back to your weekend, honestly, I'll be fine.'

'Are you sure you don't want me to call anyone to come and be with you?'

'Yes, I'm sure. I can do that when I'm ready. I'll need to give some thought to what to do next so can I contact you about that later maybe?'

'Yes, of course. Ring me any time.'

Shortly after he'd gone, I received a reply from Rachel at last but it wasn't what I wanted to hear and I switched my cell off then, not wanting to discuss it any further.

I threw on my running gear and left the building by the back entrance to try and run off my latest nightmare, or at least to come up with a way of making it go away. As I pounded the streets, everything became a bit clearer. I would have to issue a statement of some kind to put straight the most toxic comments Stephanie had made but not before I contacted my legal department to get them to force the magazine to remove the article and publish a public apology to myself and Rachel. Having made a plan in my mind, I picked up my pace to get back to the condo and get to work on sorting out this mess once and for all.

## Rachel

When I woke up, I was disorientated at first, unable to remember where I was. Night had fallen and the soft bedspread underneath seemed unusually luxurious. I lay there for a moment, trying to gather my thoughts and slowly, it all came back to me. The misery of my situation threatened to stifle me and I sat up quickly, gulping for air. I ran my fingers through my hair, trying to tidy the curls a little but knowing it was a pointless task. I switched on the little bedside light and was surprised to see that it was only half past seven. My stomach rumbled then as if to confirm the time and I went out to the main living room area to look for Jenna.

The living room was empty and uninviting, causing another wobble in my emotions as I was reminded of how alone I was and felt too. I found my bag and took out my mobile. There was no message from Jackson, which made my heart sink but there was one from Alex not very long ago.

'Hi, Rachel, can you give me a call when you get this? Feeling v. worried about you x'

The message brought tears to my eyes at once and made me glad that Alex was on my side. I knew that Jenna was a bit annoyed with me but I could have done with her support earlier and instead I'd been left feeling abandoned by her. I found Alex in my phone book and pressed her number.

'Alex, hi, it's Rachel,' I began.

'Oh, thank goodness. I've been really worried. Where are you?'

'I'm in Nashville, staying at a hotel. I'm sorry but I can't tell you where because I know you'll want to tell Jackson.'

'Well, at least you're still here. Have you spoken to Jackson since you left?'

'No. We texted but after that, there didn't seem to be much else left to say.'

'Ah, so Jackson hasn't told you what he's been doing then?' I could hear a smile in her voice but didn't know what to make of that.

'What do you mean? What has he been doing?' I knew I was falling into her trap but I couldn't help myself.

'First of all, go and take a look at the company website. Jackson's issued a statement there and when you've read that, click on the link at the bottom of the page. Then call me back, okay?'

I hung up and then went on to the internet on my phone. I hated doing it because it was so small but I found the site and on the front page, there was a short message from Jackson, next to a gorgeous picture of him, which made my heart ache with longing.

---

### A Message from Jackson Phillips, CEO, The Rough Cut Record Company

*As some of you may know, an interview with my former fiancée, Stephanie Shaw, was published today in an online magazine. This interview contained some serious allegations against myself and Rachel Hardy, a singer/songwriter from the UK, recently signed by our label. I could not let these allegations pass me by without setting the record straight and, given their libellous nature, I have also asked my legal team to contact the magazine in question. They have now agreed to remove the article and they have also published an apology, together with a modified version of this press release.*

*However, out of concern for Rachel's blossoming career and my good reputation in this city, I want to make a few points clear for those people who wish to know the facts. I was engaged to Miss Shaw but following her infidelity, I broke off our engagement last year. Miss Shaw was never carrying my child but if she had been, I would never have tried to force her to have an abortion. One day, I do hope to start a family with the right woman.*

*When Rachel came second in the UK final of the "Open Mic" competition, I was sure that she could make it big in Nashville and following very successful performances at a few "Open Mic" nights here, we signed her to my label. Rachel performed last night at a charity dinner over in Bellevue to a crowd of over 200 people and she is now about to start work on a new EP, as well as her first album. She has a contract with our company which was professionally negotiated on her behalf by her manager and makes her financially independent. She has no need of my wealth or anyone else's, for that matter, and she would never lower herself to marry for money. Rachel is a talented artist and the success she has had so far is all of her own making.*

*I trust that this clarifies the situation and thank you for your time.*

I swiped my hand across my face to clear it of tears before clicking on the link to the magazine's website. Jackson was as good as his word: there was now no evidence of the article, just a grovelling apology from the magazine, promising to check their facts more carefully in the future. I owed Jackson an enormous apology too of course but I had no idea whether he would accept it after all that had happened between us. I sent a text to Alex, rather than calling, because I had somewhere more important to be. I stopped in front of the mirror in the hallway to check my appearance before leaving, regretting that decision immediately. I smoothed my hair down as carefully as I could before slipping on my shoes and stepping out into the corridor to walk to the lift.

---

## Jackson

The tension of the day was beginning to slip away from me now that I had put everything right. In the end, it had all been very easy because once the lawyers were involved and started talking libel and damages, the magazine backed down straight away. Will had helped me draft the press release and Jenna helped out once she returned from the hotel Rachel was staying in. I didn't embarrass her by asking where Rachel was and she didn't betray her friend either. Once they'd gone back to the office, I waited for the website to be updated and then double-checked the magazine's site as well. Then I called Alex to tell her what had happened.

'Jackson, I knew that scheming woman was up to something else but I am really proud of you for handling it all so calmly.'

'Yeah, I'm pretty proud of myself too. Now all I need is for Rachel to see what I've done and forgive me. Can you help out with letting her know about it, please?'

'Of course and I know she'll forgive you.'

'Thanks, Alex, for everything. I owe you.'

I settled down to wait for some message from Rachel that she'd seen the statements I'd put in place, keeping my cell close to hand but there was nothing. About eight, I started thinking about going out for something to eat, as it looked like I was going to be on my own after all. My mind was whirring with what might have happened when Alex called Rachel but maybe she'd gone out and Alex hadn't been able to reach her. I had to keep clinging on to the hope that everything would be sorted out between us because I had nothing else without Rachel in my life. I made my way down to the street, lost in thought about everything that had happened that day.

'Jackson!' I heard my name being called and it sounded a bit like Rachel but she sounded far away and I couldn't see her. 'Jackson!' I heard her call again and looked all around me trying to find her, frowning at the struggle I was having. Then a cab pulled up right in front of me and suddenly, there she was, leaning out of the window, looking straight at me. I opened the door to help her out and she took my hand gratefully. The cab drove away and we were left on the sidewalk staring at each other, neither one of us brave enough to speak first.

'I'm sorry I couldn't see you,' I ventured and she laughed, a sound that filled my heart with joy.

'I was calling from the window of the cab so I suppose my voice kept being carried away by the wind. It was funny watching you looking for me.' Her face lit up with a dazzling smile. We both paused again.

'I saw the statement on the website and I came to say I'm so sorry for not trusting you and for running away again earlier. I know I hurt you but please can you forgive me?' She was breathless by the time she'd finished her speech and I knew she was nervous and must have repeated it over and over to herself on the way. I brushed one of her long curls out of her face and leaned down to kiss her gently on the lips.

'Nothing would give me greater pleasure, Rachel Hardy.'

# CHAPTER 36

**Rachel**

Once Jackson and I had got back together, things settled down again pretty quickly. I made things up with Jenna and enjoyed the remaining time with her before she left to go back to Dorset. She and Will grew even closer and she was heartbroken when she had to go.

'It won't be long till you're flying back again for the wedding, Jenna. The time will pass so quickly, you'll hardly notice.' I tried hard to reassure her but her long face and tear-stained cheeks showed how sad she was and I felt sorry for them both.

I managed to summon up the courage to give Sam a call too, having let enough time go by after reading his letter.

'Sam, hi, how are you?' I screwed up my face in anticipation of him refusing to talk to me.

'Rachel, it's lovely to hear your voice. I'm fine. How are you?'

'I'm good now, after a couple of hard weeks here.' I paused and blew out a long breath. 'Thanks for your letter, it made me cry but I accept what you said. You were right about me and Jackson, we're getting married.' I heard his sharp intake of breath at the other end of the phone. 'Sam?'

'I'm still here, it was just a surprise to hear you say that, that's all. I did kind of expect it though, if I'm honest.'

'The thing is, we're going to have two weddings, one here and one in Dorset and I wanted to ask if you would come. I'll understand if you say no but...'

'I'll be there, Rachel, don't worry.'

In the month before the wedding, I made my mind up that I was going to focus on my debut album as much as possible so I hid myself away in the studio, rehearsing and trying to lay down tracks. One particular day, I was finding it hard to concentrate and I was glad to see Jackson appear mid-morning to talk to me.

'Hey sweetheart, what's up?' I asked. He looked unusually serious.

'I just watched a news update on the TV in my office which Will told me I ought to watch.' I frowned a little at this because Jackson hardly ever watched TV.

'What was it about?' I had a worrying feeling in the pit of my stomach.

'It was a report about Stephanie. She's been arrested for driving while drunk.'

My hands flew to my face. 'Oh my goodness, was anyone hurt?'

'No, no-one else was hurt but the photos of her injuries looked horrendous. Apparently, she had over twice the legal limit of alcohol in her blood so it's a miracle that she survived.'

'Where is she now?' I asked.

'She's at the hospital under the careful eye of the police. They're waiting for her dad to arrive from Texas.' He winced as he said it.

'Her dad's not going to be best pleased, I guess.'

'Hell no! He'll hate all the bad publicity.'

'I hate to admit it but I actually feel a bit sorry for her. Does that make me mad?'

'Not at all, it's what makes you special.'

He pulled me towards him for a lingering kiss then and I let myself sink into the warmth of his arms.

'How's it going for you today?' he asked after a few moments.

'Not well at all. I can't seem to concentrate today.' I pulled a face to show him my frustration.

'Do you want something to take your mind off things for a while?' He raised his eyebrows and I grinned back at him.

'What did you have in mind, Mr Phillips?' I asked, walking my fingers up his chest, until he caught my hand and kissed it.

'Come and have lunch with me and you'll find out!' he replied with a smile.

We emerged on to the street outside the office a few minutes later where Greg was waiting in the car.

'You know, I've been thinking that I should probably sell my New York apartment now,' Jackson said once we were settled in the car. 'I don't really need it any more and if I am going up there again, it will definitely be with you and there's no shortage of luxury hotels for us to stay in. What do you think?'

'I think that's a really good decision but it's up to you, it's your apartment, not mine.'

'Well, that's something else we need to talk about, worldly goods and all that. I take the view that what's mine is yours, you know that.'

'I know, it's hard for me to get used to, that's all.' I paused for a moment, trying to work out where he was taking me. 'Where are we going then? This looks like the road to your parents' house.'

'You're right, it is but we're not going there.' He smiled cryptically at me, looking like he could hardly contain his secret any longer.

Just then, Greg made a left turn and we started down a long driveway.

When the car drew up outside an impressive colonial mansion, I had to sit for a moment to catch my breath. I looked at Jackson in disbelief. The house was so stunning that I could hardly believe my eyes. It was a colonial brick building with bottle-green shutters and two magnificent pillars on either side of the entrance, rising from the ground right up to the roof. On each side of the house were two smaller wings, adding to the overall grandeur of the building. I loved it on sight and couldn't wait to see the inside.

A woman came to meet us from the car, shaking my hand and then Jackson's in greeting. She introduced herself as the realtor in charge of selling the property before taking us on a tour of the house and grounds. We didn't say much because there was such a lot to take in. I was delighted with everything I saw and I could see that Jackson was too.

'The house is laid out perfectly and there's plenty of room for a family,' she declared, smiling at me.

By this time, we were outside the back of the property. The grounds were as wonderful, with two acres all in all, including a very enticing pool area and tennis courts as well. When the tour was finished, Jackson told the estate agent how impressed he was with the property.

'How about you ma'am?' she asked me.

'I absolutely love it!'

---

## Jackson

It felt funny to be back in the condo again after living in the new house for a while. The worst thing was how cramped it felt after all the space in our new five-bedroomed mansion. Still, it had only been for last night because Rachel wanted to stick with tradition and not let me see her before the wedding. I could have stayed at my parents' house but I preferred to be on my own to collect my thoughts before today, the most important day of my life.

I was glad that we'd held our 'hen' and 'stag' nights last week, a good time before the wedding so that we could recover in plenty of time. I hadn't drunk anything of course but the guys had kept me up pretty late, visiting honky-tonk bars and the like and I'd been shattered the next day.

Now, I felt refreshed after a good night's sleep, although I'd woken up early, unable to contain my excitement any longer. I'd already checked that I had everything ready at least ten times, most importantly the rings to give to my best man, Todd. I'd also checked our plane tickets for the honeymoon and my luggage, since we would be departing straight after the reception. What Rachel didn't know was that I'd booked for us to stay overnight in New York at the Ritz-Carlton. We would be staying in a suite overlooking Central Park and flying out the following afternoon to London which would break our trip up a little.

By nine, I was all ready to go and waiting for Greg to arrive to take me over to my parents' house. The wedding was to be at eleven so I knew I was in plenty of time and I didn't want to be hanging around when I got there. I was thoughtful in the car on the way over, thinking about how far Rachel and I had come in such a short space of time and how much I'd changed under her influence. She'd sent me a text earlier that confirmed for me that she was the one and that she felt as strongly for me as I did for her.

*'Good morning, my almost husband! Hope you're okay today and looking forward to getting married as much as I am. I love you, I can hardly wait to see you later. Lots of love till then x'*

I walked into my parents' house and was relieved that things were calm, in fact it was an oasis of peace and quiet which was exactly what I needed. I found my mom and dad in the kitchen, along with various other family members and I was glad to see Todd there. I walked over and shook my dad's hand and then kissed my mom. After that, all the women wanted to kiss me and coo over my appearance until I couldn't stand it any more and, gesturing to Todd, we escaped out to the garden. It was a cool but sunny day which I was glad about for Rachel's sake. The marquee was set up in the garden and Jenna had done a fantastic job with the flowers. Since her return, she had worked with the caterers over the last couple of days to decorate the marquee and the tables with glorious purple, orange and yellow flowers in arrangements of all different sizes. The seating area in front of the marquee where the actual ceremony would take place, was also lavishly decorated with a red carpet scattered with rose petals and a single pink rose attached with a ribbon to the back of each chair. I knew that Rachel would be delighted with it all. My mom and dad had really done us proud by overseeing everything and taking the strain off us.

'Todd, I need to give you the rings so you can put them somewhere safe for later on,' I said when I'd stopped marvelling at the setting for a moment.

'Sure thing, Jackson. How are you feeling? You look very smart by the way.' He smiled and winked at me.

'Don't you start fawning over me as well. I feel great, Todd, but I can't wait to get started, you know.'

'I know, man, but try and keep calm, it's not long to go now. Let's go and sort out your buttonhole and check that everything else is in place, shall we?'

An hour later, the seats were almost full and I stood nervously waiting for Rachel to arrive. The opening strains of Etta James' 'At Last' suddenly began and I turned to gaze at Rachel as she slowly started to make her way down the aisle towards me. She looked utterly breathtaking in an ivory silk dress and matching bolero jacket. Her hair was piled in soft curls, with just a few tendrils hanging at the sides and she was wearing a simple tiara in it with a short veil hanging down behind her. I noticed that she was wearing the Tiffany pendant I had given her in New York all that time ago too. Will was beaming at her side, looking very proud in that role and I felt so lucky as I watched the pair of them walking towards me, Rachel's eyes not once leaving mine. Alex and Jenna followed right behind Rachel, both of them taking to the role of bridesmaid with ease. As Rachel and Will came alongside me, Will shook my hand and went to sit down with Jenna, and Alex took her place next to Todd. I leaned in to kiss Rachel's cheek.

'You are so beautiful and I'm very lucky.'

'Me too,' she replied.

In no time at all, Todd was stepping forward with the rings and we were exchanging our vows. We'd chosen the rings together from our favourite shop, Tiffany's, choosing one that would fit with Rachel's ring I had given her previously while I chose a simple wedding band and moved my knot ring to my right hand. When we kissed to seal our vows, I knew that this was a life-changing moment for us both.

The rest of the day flew by in a blur of greetings, celebratory drinks, speeches and food. I was glad when it was time for us to start the dancing because it seemed like the first time I'd really had Rachel to myself all day.

I took her hand in mine and held her close to me, wrapping my other arm around her waist.

'How are you feeling now, Mrs Phillips?' I asked with a grin.

'I feel wonderful and so glad that everything has gone according to plan.'

'I still can't get over how fabulous you look,' I said, gazing into her eyes.

She kissed me tenderly and laid her head on my shoulder and we stayed like that for the remainder of the dance.

It was the best day of our lives but by the end, I could hardly remember a thing. All too soon, it was time for us to go. We went to our room to get changed and it was all I could do as I helped Rachel out of her dress not to take her in my arms and make sweet love to her there and then but we had guests waiting to see us off and a plane to catch. We changed into more comfortable outfits and went back outside to find our families.

We kissed my mom and dad goodbye and there were some tears on all sides but we'd be seeing them again very soon for wedding number two. Rachel tossed her bouquet of roses and then turned to see Alex catch it. Both their faces lit up in surprise and Todd actually blushed! It had been a wonderful day and I still had another surprise for Rachel.

## Rachel

As we drove off towards the airport, I was wondering when I would stop smiling. It had been such an amazing day, one that I would remember for the rest of my life and it wasn't over yet.

'So, Jackson, are you happy?'

'Yes, Mrs Phillips, I truly am a very happy man. Hasn't it been a fantastic day?'

'It has been a perfect day, yes, in every way, thank you.' I brought his hand up to kiss it and I leaned into him.

'You made it perfect for me and I have another gift for you now, Rachel.'

I sat up in surprise.

'There can't be anything else left to give me, surely.' I smiled at him, wondering what it was going to be this time.

'You know we're on our way to the airport, right?'

'Ye-es,' I stuttered, wondering where this conversation was going.

'Well, we're not going to the UK till tomorrow. We're staying somewhere else tonight.'

'Are we? What have you got up your sleeve?' I narrowed my eyes at him but he laughed his usual sexy laugh and kept me waiting. 'C'mon, the suspense is killing me.'

'I've booked us a suite at the Ritz in New York for tonight overlooking Central Park.'

I let out a little squeal before leaning in to kiss him with all my heart.

A few hours later, we were pulling up outside the Ritz and being whisked up to our suite in a private lift. It was late by this time and we were both exhausted but once we were in bed, luxuriating in the feel of the crisp, cotton sheets, it wasn't long before our love for each other took over and we made love to seal our union once again.

'I love you, Jackson,' I whispered sleepily.

'Back at you, Mrs Phillips.'

When I woke the next day to my first full day as a married woman, I felt confused at first, having arrived so late and not had time to check out the suite. I got up promptly and, having visited the marble bathroom, I then wandered into the separate living room, where to my delight I discovered the magnificent view of Central Park below. I was even able to see it closer up with the use of a tabletop telescope so thoughtfully provided for that purpose. I was amazed at the size and the utter luxury of the suite. Even Jackson's old apartment in New York hadn't been as magnificent as this. I didn't dare think how much this had cost but I had to get used to the fact that I now had plenty of money and didn't need to worry about it. Still, that was going to take some time. Jackson joined me shortly afterwards, laughing at all my oohing and aahing but the panoramic view of the park took his breath away too.

'What time's our flight today? Will we have any time to go to the park?' I sounded like a little kid but I really wanted to go and explore even if only for a short while.

'We'll have time, baby, I made sure to book an evening flight so we're going to have a leisurely breakfast and go out some time after that, okay?'

A sumptuous breakfast was delivered minutes later so we were crossing West 59th Street into the park by eleven. We spent a lazy few hours exploring, taking in as much as we could of the south end of the park before working our way towards the John Lennon 'Strawberry Fields' memorial. After a few moments of reflection there, we went out of the park to pick up a couple of hot dogs when we got hungry so that I could say I'd had that experience. By about three, we were starting to feel the cold and so we stopped in at a café for hot chocolate and a slice of cake.

'We really do need to come back here again soon,' I sighed. 'There's so much for us to see and do still.'

'I promise we'll be back again soon, honey. For now, I want us to concentrate on starting our new life together, just you and me.'

'Yes, you're right, it's time for us to move on from our past lives and to forge a new one together. I can't wait!'

### Jackson

We arrived to a cold, rainy day in the UK and I felt our spirits sink a little as we drove from the airport south to the coast. Rachel's cottage seemed cold and forlorn when we got there, especially as there was no-one to welcome us but she switched on the heating, as well as an electric fire in the lounge and it felt cosier in no time. We snuggled up together on the sofa and the next thing we knew, we'd both fallen asleep and the sound of a key in the front door woke us up.

'Oh, look at you two, you're like an old married couple,' joked Jenna as she poked her head round the door.

Will followed her in, holding her hand and laughing at the joke.

'Hey, you guys. How are you? Sorry, we're just both so tired.' Rachel groaned, rubbing her eyes gently to help herself wake up.

'We're fine and ready for another wedding whenever you are!' Jenna sounded very bubbly, which was a bit grating when we'd only just woken up.

'What time is it anyway?' I asked.

'It's eight o'clock now. Shall we get a takeaway in rather than cooking?' she suggested.

While we ate, Jenna and Will entertained us with tales from the wedding reception party after we'd left. We didn't stay up too long, knowing that we had to get up for church the next day to hear the final reading of our wedding banns.

After a good night's sleep, we both felt better and even the weather had improved so that we could walk to the church. It was freezing inside the church though and I worried that Rachel would be cold on the next wedding day but she didn't have any concerns about it. Maybe she was just used to the colder weather. The banns were read for one last time without incident and we had a quick chat with the rector afterwards about final arrangements.

Rachel and I stopped in for some lunch in town on the way back home.

'Is there anything else we need to do before next Saturday, do you think?' I asked her as we started eating.

'I don't think so, really, it should just be a case of checking that everything's organised. Did you contact Tom and Meg?'

'Yep and that's fine, they'll both be there. I can ring the restaurant this afternoon to check that's all set up or we could pop in if you like, before we go back to the cottage?'

'I love that you're so organised.' She nodded and sighed contentedly. 'Is there anything else you'd like to do before the wedding?'

'We could explore the coast together perhaps, if we hired a car. I know the weather's not so good but the coastline will be spectacular whatever the weather, won't it?'

'That sounds wonderful. It's been a long time since I did that.'

Over the next few days, Rachel took me to lots of interesting places along the coast, starting with the iconic Corfe Castle.

'I used to love visiting this castle as a child and roaming among the ruins,' she told me as she drove, a wistful look on her face.

From her description, I thought I knew what to expect when I got there but nothing could have prepared me for the spectacular setting of the medieval castle and the breathtaking views across Purbeck from the keep. It was my first visit to a British castle and the memory would stay with me for a long time.

We continued as far as Lyme Regis, stopping off at various tourist must-sees along the way. We managed a short walk along the Heritage Coast, giving me an idea of why the coastline is so special, before we had to set off back to Poole.

'It's been good to have this time together here. I hope we can make time to do it again soon,' I said as we pulled up outside the cottage.

'I hope so too but it won't be easy to get back here that often, will it?' Rachel replied.

'I think we ought to buy a new house here as well,' I said quietly. I was sure that this was something she'd been worrying about and I wanted to set her mind at rest.

She stared at me. 'Do you mean that?'

'Of course. I know you'll want to come back regularly and see Jenna and her family.'

She threw her arms around me for a hug then and I was glad that I'd cleared that one up for the future.

<hr>

## Rachel

The day of our Dorset wedding dawned bright and clear. Jackson and Will had taken themselves off to a nearby hotel so that we would only meet at the wedding and as this was also where Jackson's mum and dad would be staying, it made sense. Jenna helped me to get ready once again and this time she would be the only bridesmaid. Jenna's dad had hired a vintage Rolls-Royce to take us all to the church and we arrived just after eleven o'clock. Jenna handed me the lovely bouquet she had created especially for me, this time a mixture of roses, peonies and gerberas in various shades of pink, before making sure my dress was straight at the back.

Sam appeared, fresh from his role as usher to escort his mum inside and gave me a quick good luck kiss before setting off just ahead of us towards the church. I noticed that he was still limping slightly as he went.

On the way, I stopped briefly at my mum and dad's graves and laid a single ivory rose there for each of them, saying a silent prayer to ask them to be watching this important moment in my life.

This time, we'd gone for traditional processional music to accompany my walk down the aisle of St James' and so it was that I walked in to the Trumpet Voluntary. Jackson looked every bit as gorgeous as he had done just over a week earlier and I thanked my lucky stars for having found such a good man and one that I now knew I could trust completely.

I could not help but beam as I walked down the aisle, I was so happy, and Jackson looked like he felt the same. It was such a good feeling knowing that we'd already done this once and the second time was an absolute bonus, especially with Jenna's dad, Dave, giving me away. We said our vows and exchanged the rings again and although it was a small wedding group, it felt every bit as poignant as it had done the first time.

As we turned to walk back down the aisle, The Band Perry song 'All Your Life' played and I smiled at Jackson and we both let out a soft 'whoop' together.

We went on to the restaurant after chatting to people outside the church for a while during the official photos. It was a wonderfully intimate meal with just Jenna's family and Will, Jackson's parents, Tom, Meg and Jackson and myself around the table. We didn't go for formal speeches this time but Jackson did stand to give a short speech when we were finishing our desserts. He thanked both sets of parents and he thanked Tom for being his best man and acting as usher, along with Sam. He then turned to Jenna.

'I'd like to finish by thanking Jenna for being such a great friend to Rachel through all these preparations for both weddings, as well as overseeing flower arrangements on two continents. I have a feeling that Jenna's business is about to take off and she might need someone to hold her hand through all that. So, just to let you know, Jenna, I've asked Will to set up a UK office for our record label in London and I wondered if you might be able to find him somewhere to stay?'

Jenna's hands had flown up to her cheeks and her mouth had fallen open in shock. She looked at Will for confirmation to find him smiling and nodding all at once. He pulled her into his arms, seemed to ask her something at which she nodded and then they kissed to a thumping round of applause from everyone else around the table. It couldn't have been a nicer ending to our day. We danced late into the night until we were so exhausted we could no longer stand up. There were two people I had to speak to though before calling it a night. First, I went in search of Jenna.

'Jenna, I just want to thank you for everything. I don't know what I would have done without you.'

'Don't be silly, it was my pleasure for my best friend.'

'And what about that with Will, huh? Are you pleased?'

'Are you kidding? I'm over the moon. Didn't you know about it then?'

'Not at all, Jackson kept that secret very close to his chest but I'm so happy for you. I expect to have lots of updates. Will you ask him to move into the cottage?'

'If that's okay?'

'Of course it is, don't you be silly, now.' We both laughed. 'Anyway,' I continued, 'I think the cottage is more yours than mine now so take care good care of it, won't you?' Her eyes filled with tears as we hugged and said goodnight. I was glad I'd been able to do that for her.

Next, I went in search of Sam, while Jackson went to see Tom and Meg off.

'Hey, Sam, I just came to say goodnight and to thank you for today. I really appreciated you coming.'

'I wouldn't have missed it for the world. I hope you'll both be happy, you deserve to be.' We hugged and said goodbye for perhaps the last time in a while.

Finally, Jackson and I went upstairs with his parents, and after thanking them too, made our way to our suite and collapsed into bed after another long, full day.

As I drifted off to sleep, I thought how far we'd come in a few short months and I fell asleep dreaming of Paris and of the new adventure we would start together the next day.

# II

# OVER YOU (SAM'S STORY)

## ABOUT THIS BOOK

**Can the magic of Cornwall help two lost souls to heal?**

Heartbroken after seeing the love of his life marry someone else, Sam Andrews wants to escape all the painful reminders of her and to try and move on. Remembering his happy family holidays surfing in Cornwall, he travels to Newquay to help him forget.

Following a tragic event at university, Jessie Pascoe has abandoned her course and returned home to her mum's B&B in Newquay. But after months of counselling, she's no closer to being healed, and she's lost her faith in ever finding her happy ending.

When Sam and Jessie meet, there's a mutual attraction, and they begin to see a chance of finding happiness together, if only they can both let go of the past. But can they risk opening their hearts to someone new and falling in love again?

**A story of heartbreak, love and healing.**

# CHAPTER 1

**<u>Sam</u>**

Rachel crossed the hotel lobby, away from Sam and towards Jackson, every step emphasising the choice she had made. Her long, dark hair cascaded down her back against the silky blue dress she had changed into after the wedding. She looked beautiful.

Sam had told her he was happy for her, of course – what else was he supposed to say on her wedding day? – but his heart would break if he had to keep up the pretence much longer. Just a few more steps and she would reach Jackson. Sam was torn between wanting her to get there and hoping she wouldn't ever leave, but he knew if she stayed he would just be deluding himself. She could never love him in the way she loved Jackson. He watched as Jackson enveloped Rachel in his arms and lowered his head to kiss her tenderly before taking her hand and walking up the stairs.

Sam willed his feet to move, but they were rooted to the ground. He longed to hold Rachel in his arms and to feel her lips against his, even though there was no chance of that ever happening again. He had to let her go. He had to let her be happy without him, but doing so was proving much harder than he'd thought.

'Can Natalie and I give you a lift home, Sam?' His brother Matt's voice finally broke the spell. Sam was vaguely aware of his sister, Jenna, hovering in the background, no doubt worrying about him as well.

'No, no thanks. I'm going to get a drink in town.' In that split second, he'd decided drowning his sorrows was what he needed right now. Sam frowned as Matt narrowed his eyes at him.

'Are you sure that's a good idea? I don't think you should be on your own.'

Sam loved his brother, but sometimes he wished he could live his life without Matt knowing exactly what he was thinking. He stopped himself from rolling his eyes at his brother's concern.

'I'm fine, I fancy a drink, that's all. I'll see you soon.'

He moved towards the entrance of the hotel, feeling Matt watching him as he left. The cold December air blowing in from the sea bit through his suit and he realised he'd probably made the wrong decision in not accepting Matt's offer of a lift. As he made his way towards the High Street, he glanced at the sparkling Christmas lights and gaudy decorations adorning the buildings of Poole's town centre. Christmas would be coming soon. It wasn't something he was looking forward to. His life had had so little purpose in it since Rachel left that final time for Nashville, choosing Jackson over him. He missed being in the band they'd built up with Matt over so many years but in his heart he knew without Rachel, they would never have been so good anyway.

He pushed open the door of one of the pubs they'd played in many times before, glad to be out of the cold at last. He approached the bar and waited for the barman to come over. There was another band playing tonight and as he listened to their sound-check, it brought all the old memories flooding back. He could hear Rachel's voice, see her fingers on her guitar strings, remember the special smile she always gave him when the audience responded to their music. The first pint of beer he drank didn't even touch the sides.

*Three weeks later*

'Bang, bang, bang!'

Sam rolled over and pulled his pillow over his head, trying to block the noise out, but the sudden movement made him feel sick and he was immediately aware of a dull throbbing at his temple. Maybe that's what the banging was, he thought, just his own pain reverberating inside his head. He opened his eyes and stared at his bedroom wall, waiting a few seconds for it to come into focus, but then the banging started up again, only this time it was louder.

'Sam! I know you're in there. Open up.'

He recognised the sound of Matt's voice and groaned. His brother just wouldn't leave him alone. All he wanted was to be left to mourn, in his own pathetic way, the loss of the only woman he'd ever loved. He'd thought having the house to himself when his parents were away on their New Year winter cruise would be the perfect opportunity for him to wallow in self-pity, but Matt obviously thought otherwise.

He heaved a sigh and pulled himself up to a sitting position on the edge of the bed. His stomach felt like it had stayed behind and he had to take a minute for everything to rearrange itself. He stood up slowly and reached out for the wall to help steady himself. He'd made it to the end of the bed when the banging started again and he thought his head might explode from the noise. He stumbled over to the sash window, pushed it up, and leaned out just far enough to see Matt below, pacing back and forth before the front door.

'Matt,' Sam called, as quietly as he could get away with. He waited till Matt looked up, frowning at him, then brought his fingers to his lips. 'Shhh. I'm coming down.'

On the way down the stairs, he wondered why Matt hadn't used his keys to get in as normal. He turned the key in the lock and opened the door, letting his brother in at last.

'Don't shout at me, man. I've got the world's worst hangover.' He walked to the kitchen in search of pain relief.

'Are you going for the world record on that? I swear you've been saying the same thing to me for the last three weeks now.'

Sam led the way into the kitchen, wondering if his older brother was ever going to let up on him. He ignored Matt's jibe, poured himself a large glass of water and took two paracetamol. 'Why didn't you use your key instead of shouting at me from the street, for God's sake?'

'You left your key in the lock so I couldn't get mine in, making this charade all your own fault.'

Matt filled the kettle with fresh water and flicked the switch to set it boiling. He put two cups down on the worktop, adding a spoonful of coffee and another of sugar to each cup. He added milk to his, but not to Sam's. Sam was about to comment but decided against it, figuring he needed the strongest cup of coffee going to help with the hangover.

'Look, Sam, Mum and Dad are going to be back soon and you can't let them walk in and see the place like this. Mum will go ballistic if she sees all this mess.'

Sam followed Matt's hand as he waved at the empty beer cans and bottles of alcohol littering the kitchen surfaces, as well as the growing piles of takeaway containers, some still containing the pizzas or curries they'd originally arrived with. His face flushed when Matt screwed up his nose in disgust.

Sam swiped his hand over his face, feeling slightly better now his headache was starting to pass. He knew Matt was right and he was ashamed of himself, as much today as he had been every other day of his parents' absence, but he felt powerless to do anything about it.

'Shouldn't you be at work, Matt, since you've got a job to go to?' He decided to go for the attack approach in the absence of any other excuse.

'Today is Saturday, Sam, and luckily for you, I've persuaded Natalie to let me come here instead of staying at home with her and the baby. You're going to have a shower and then I'm going to help you clear the place up, and we're going to talk. You can't go on like this any more.'

Sam pushed his messy blonde hair out of his eyes and stared at his brother. He knew Matt was right but how on earth was he going to stop this downward spiral he'd fallen into since Rachel had married Jackson and shown him there was absolutely no hope of a future for them together?

By the time they'd finished clearing up all the rubbish and making the house presentable again for his parents, it was time for lunch.

'I need a pint, Matt. You know, hair of the dog and all that.' Sam grabbed his coat and keys.

'Are you buying?' Matt asked with a wink.

'Of course. Least I can do after all you've done for me today.'

They walked down the road towards the seafront, turning into their favourite drinking-hole a few minutes later. While Sam bought the drinks, Matt studied the menu. In the end, he ordered the same thing they always had – ham, egg and chips – before settling down at a table in the corner by the window. From the bar, Sam looked out at the choppy, hostile waves of their patch of sea just outside Poole, thanking goodness he didn't have to be outdoors working today. He hadn't had any carpentry work for weeks now, and he wouldn't be getting any, either, if he carried on like this.

He carried the pints over to the table and, after sitting down, took a long slow gulp of his beer. He wiped his hand across his mouth, savouring the bitter flavour of the ale after a long morning of hard work. His brother did the same and then took a deep breath before he began to speak.

'You may not want my advice, but I'm going to give it to you anyway.'

Sam stared at him silently.

'What I think you need is a break away from here and all the reminders of Rachel. You know, a change of scenery and the chance to experience something completely different for a while.'

Sam threw his hands up. 'I've thought of that too but where would I go when I have almost no money? I couldn't even afford a return train ticket at the moment.' Winters were always hard in his line of business, but he knew he could have done more to find carpentry jobs to keep him going.

Their food arrived and they both tucked in with enthusiasm for a few minutes before Matt began talking again.

'I've had an idea about the transport aspect, actually.'

Sam raised his eyebrows and took another swig of beer.

'Do you remember your old motorbike? It's still in the garage at home. Dad and I could give you a hand to check it over. It can't have been that long since you rode it last, and it would be a cheap way to travel around the country, or even abroad if you felt like it.'

'It's been a good while since I drove that thing, but it should be pretty sound. I'm not sure if I'd have to get new insurance though.'

'Why don't we get it out when we get home and take a look at it? Mum and Dad will be back later and we can always ask Dad for help with anything we can't do.'

Sam had to admit Matt had given him something to think about. All of a sudden, he didn't want a second beer, preferring instead to get home to look at the bike. Excitement was bubbling away inside him for the first time in ages.

An hour later, Sam dropped his wrench on the concrete floor of the garage and blew out a frustrated sigh.

'This is beyond me, Matt. If we can't even get the engine to turn over, I have no idea how to get started. We'll have to wait for Dad to have a look at it, but even then, it may be past its best.' He wiped his hand across his forehead, leaving a smear of grease behind, and pushed himself up to standing. They both stared at the old Yamaha bike.

'It could just need a new battery, of course,' said Matt after a few moments. 'Maybe a MOT test at the garage would pick up what needs doing?'

'Yeah, maybe.' Sam felt decidedly less enthusiastic than he had when Matt had first mentioned it. He went indoors via the back door to wash his hands in the utility room sink. When Matt didn't follow him, Sam went outside again to look for him and found him talking to his mum and dad, newly returned from their holiday.

'Hello, darling.' His mum gave him a long hug and then held him at arm's length to study him more closely. 'How are you?' Only his mum could put so much meaning into those three simple words.

'I'm okay, Mum. How was your holiday?' He shrugged off her concern and went to shake his dad's hand.

'It was great but we did miss you all.' His mum gave them both a little grin.

'I was just telling Dad about my idea for the bike,' Matt said, changing the subject.

'It's going to need a lot of work before I can ride it again, Dad,' said Sam. 'Maybe too much to be worth it, to be honest.' He looked at his dad, with that look he used to give him as a child.

'Let me recharge *my* batteries tonight, son and I'll have a look at it tomorrow, okay?'

Sam nodded. 'Of course, Dad, there's no rush. You need to tell me all about your holiday first.'

'I'd better be getting home,' said Matt. 'But we'll be here for Sunday lunch, if you're up for that, Mum?'

'Of course. We'll see you all tomorrow. I want to catch up with Natalie and my beautiful grand-daughter, especially if you're all going to be out in the garage.' She rolled her eyes with a smile.

Sam pulled Matt in for a hug. 'Thanks for today, it meant a lot to me.'

When Matt pulled away, his eyes were glossy with tears, making Sam glad he'd taken the trouble to voice his thoughts to his brother.

Sam turned to follow his parents inside.

'You've done a great job tidying the place up,' his mum said. 'I guess that's why Matt came over today.'

Sam raised his hands in defeat but didn't say anything, trying not to incriminate himself. He watched as his mum went through all the downstairs rooms checking everything was as it had been before they went away. His dad had long since gone upstairs with the bags, leaving him alone to face his mum's scrutiny.

'So,' she said, as she went into the kitchen, 'how are you really? You look like you've lost some weight.'

'Matt's persuaded me I need to get away for a break.'

'That sounds like a great idea. Is that why you've been looking at the bike today?'

'Yep, but it looks like I might have to hitch a ride instead.'

'Any idea where you might go or how long for?'

'Nope.'

He broke eye contact with his mum but sensed her staring at him, and despite her good intentions, he willed her not to interfere.

---

When Sam went down for breakfast the next morning, he found his dad in the garage already.

'Morning, Dad. I hope you didn't get up especially early.' Sam knew full well his dad had probably done just that.

His dad straightened up. 'No earlier than usual, son. Anyway, the battery has charged overnight. Listen to this.' He turned the engine over, bringing a wide smile to Sam's face. His dad turned the engine off again.

'Brilliant. And how's the rest looking?'

'Not bad. There's nothing major wrong I don't think. It's just a bit out of sorts because it hasn't been used much recently. There's no rust, so I think you'd be safe to take it for a spin and see how it feels to you. It's still within its MOT for another couple of months so it should be okay, and the insurance is good for a few more months.'

Sam wheeled the bike out from the garage and rested it on the kickstand while he put on his helmet and his leather jacket.

'Thanks, Dad. I won't be long.'

His dad wiped his hands on a rag, patted Sam on the back and went inside to wash up.

Sam drove off down the road and turned the corner, hoping the bike would be good enough for him to use on a longer journey. He definitely needed to get away for a bit and it would be perfect if he could use the bike. He was aware his miserable mood had been getting the whole family down following Rachel's marriage, and a change of scene might well be what he needed to kick-start his life again.

He followed the Parkstone Road back to Poole and was pleased at the way his bike was performing. He was enjoying the warmth of the sun on his skin, as well as the thrill of the speed from his bike. He'd been thinking about where he might like to go as he drove and had pretty much made up his mind that Cornwall would be a good choice. It had also been a long time since he'd been surfing and he'd love to be able to get back into it. He was mentally calculating how much luggage he might be able to carry on his bike when he suddenly realised where he was. He slowed down and pulled into a space alongside the harbour.

Staring at the pub and recalling so many happy evenings spent there with Rachel was hard enough to handle, but when he remembered the final time they'd been there, he felt even worse. She'd accused him of being a coward for not telling her how he felt about her and she'd been right. He closed his eyes briefly, trying to stop all the memories and the crazy what-if suggestions his mind was giving him. None of it had mattered in the end. By the time he'd told her he loved her, it was too late. She'd already fallen for Jackson, and his chance had passed. He sighed and started the engine up again. He circled back out of town but not before he'd seen some more of the pubs and bars their band Three's Company had gigged at over the years and when he saw Rachel's little cottage, where his sister, Jenna, was now living with Will, her Nashville boyfriend, he thought his heart might actually break.

He zoomed off towards the road that would lead him home and on the way, he finally made up his mind to start packing as soon as he got back again. He hoped Jenna wasn't bringing Will to their family lunch that afternoon. Will was a nice enough guy, but Sam didn't think he could bear to listen to his Nashville accent or to hear them talk about how much Rachel and Jackson were enjoying their extended honeymoon in Europe.

When he reached the house, he drove onto the driveway and turned off the engine before wheeling the bike back into the garage.

He found his parents in the kitchen.

'All right, Sam?' his dad asked.

'Fine, Dad, yeah. Listen, I'm going to take off to Cornwall in a couple of days as the bike's okay. I think a change will do me good, you know?'

His mum nodded but neither of his parents said anything. Sam was grateful they were letting him make his own decisions, even though he knew they most likely had their own opinions about what he was doing.

'Do you need any washing done?' his mum asked.

'Probably, but I'm going upstairs now to sort my stuff out. I'll put a load on when I come down again.' He paused and glanced from one parent to the other. 'I'm sorry I've been so awful to live with recently. It's... been hard getting over Rachel, but now I'm ready to do something and think about something else.'

# CHAPTER 2

**<u>Jessie</u>**

Jessie stared at the rain through the window of the bus as she made her way into town. She'd been seeing her counsellor, Karen, at the centre for several months now, but she hadn't noticed any great change for the better in herself. She still found it so difficult to talk about her feelings, especially how she felt about what had happened to her, and yet over a year had passed since that awful time in her life. She wanted so desperately to move on, but she didn't know how to and talking to the counsellor wasn't making it much easier. Their progress was still very slow.

The constant beating of the rain against the dirty window only made her feel worse and the thought of actually having to get off the bus filled her with dread. When the bus reached her stop, she pulled up the hood on her coat and descended the steps quickly before walking across the pavement and taking shelter in a shop doorway. She waited for the crowd of people to get on the bus, and while they did so, she surveyed the weather situation. The rain had eased a little so she didn't need to put up an umbrella, thank goodness. She set off for the five-minute walk to the Wellbeing Centre, concentrating on putting one foot in front of the other and nothing else.

She reached the centre in no time, climbed the steps to the front door and rang the entry doorbell.

'Hi, Jessie! Ooh come in quickly out of that awful weather.' Tina, one of the support workers, was always quick with a smile and Jessie immediately felt better. The door closed behind her and she walked into the main room of the centre. There were a few people dotted about, but it was a quiet day compared to some others she'd seen when she'd come for previous appointments, and for that she was glad. She still found it awkward to mix in large groups of people. She followed Tina towards the kitchen, hoping she might be able to get a cup of tea before her meeting with Karen. She was a bit early and there was no sign of her, so she went to put the kettle on.

'Would you like a drink, Tina?' She reached for a mug from the cupboard. It had taken her ages to feel comfortable enough to come into the kitchen and help herself, let alone to ask Tina if she wanted a drink as well. She turned around to face her and saw she'd been called over by someone in the main room. At least I asked, Jessie thought to herself.

'Is there any spare in that pot?' Jessie glanced round to see Tina had returned, and this time Karen was with her.

She gave them a tentative smile. 'There's plenty,' she replied, taking two extra cups down from the cupboard. She poured out the teas and brought them over to the counter, leaving them to add their own sugar and milk.

'How are you, Jessie?' Karen asked.

'Not too bad, thanks. You?' It had also taken her a long time to get out of the habit of saying, 'I'm fine', when people asked. She still wasn't fine, but she was marginally better than she had been.

'Shall we make a start, then?' Karen asked a few minutes later. Jessie nodded and followed her upstairs to the private meeting room where they had their sessions. The musty smell of the room invaded her senses as always but faded quite quickly as she sat down in her usual comfy armchair and waited for Karen to begin.

'So how have you been feeling since we last met?' Karen gave her a gentle smile and the familiar question helped to ease Jessie back in to talking about what had happened.

'I'm definitely feeling less anxious with each passing month. But the grief is still there.' Her voice choked on the last few words and her eyes filled with tears but she managed to hold them back.

'It's okay if you want to cry, Jessie.' Karen passed her a tissue, which she took gratefully.

'I think I've realised though that I'm also struggling with the way I had to face it all on my own, you know, because he dumped me like that. And I just feel so angry about the way he treated me. But that's quite separate from my grief, and it's taken me a really long time to work out all the different things I'm feeling.'

'I think that's a really big development, Jessie. You're able to identify those separate feelings now, as well as acknowledging your grief and your anger, and that's a major step forward.'

Jessie smiled, relieved she'd been able to say all that was on her mind without crying this time.

---

## Sam

Sam drove away from his family home early on the Tuesday morning, having said a brief goodbye to his parents after sharing breakfast with them in the kitchen. He would have preferred to avoid goodbyes altogether but it wasn't possible with his parents being such early risers. More importantly, he'd wanted to say sorry again, but this time for being so anti-social for the previous couple of days. When he'd seen Jenna and Will arriving for Sunday lunch from his bedroom window, his heart had sunk and he knew he wouldn't be able to face joining them downstairs. Both Matt and Jenna had come up to try and talk him out of his funk but had failed miserably. Matt had given up much more easily than Jenna, though.

'I can't believe how rude you're being, Sam,' she'd hissed at him in his bedroom. 'Will has nothing to do with what happened between you and Rachel, and you're being so rotten to us both by treating him like this.'

Sam hadn't been able to find any justification for his behaviour so he'd stayed silent, and in the end his sister had stormed out like a mini tornado, slamming the door firmly shut behind her. He hadn't wanted to argue with Jenna – she of all people knew how hard he'd taken Rachel's rejection – but how could he tell her that Will was nothing but a harsh reminder of his failure? He wasn't sure if his sister would be able to handle that from him so he'd decided it was best to let her be angry at him for the time being. After that, he'd kept to his room where he couldn't upset anyone else.

'Take care, my sweetheart,' his mum had whispered as she pulled him to her for a hug, pressing some money into his hand at the same time.

'Mum, you don't need to do that.' He started to protest, but seeing the look in her eye he gave up, knowing she wouldn't take no for an answer, and also that he needed every penny. His small amount of savings weren't going to get him very far. He shook hands with his dad and accepted the briefest hug from him before he was on his way.

It was a cold, late-January morning and a bitter wind whipped around him as he drove towards the A35 that would take him away from Poole and on to Dorchester. He'd put on his thermals underneath his shirt and jeans – not the most attractive sight, but one that definitely made sense given the plummeting temperatures. By nine o'clock, though, the light frost had melted and he was starting to warm up a bit as the sun came out once again. The panniers on either side of his bike were both full of clothes, including a couple of pairs of boots and trainers, but apart from that Sam was travelling light. He'd stared at his guitar for a long time, trying to decide whether to take it with him or not. If he did, he knew it would remind him of Rachel but if he didn't, he would miss playing it. He decided against it in the end, not wanting any reminders of her on his break. He'd be home soon enough anyway, and he hoped he could play it again then when he was feeling stronger.

By late morning, he'd left Dorset behind and was well into Devon, heading towards Exeter and then taking the road further south towards Plymouth. With the Dartmoor National Park to his right, the tension in his broad shoulders finally began to subside and he felt like he was leaving all his troubles behind. He stopped at a pub on the edge of the park for a quick sandwich and a drink. As he sat warming himself up by the fire, he thought about where he might stay overnight. He remembered staying in Liskeard one time with the rest of the family, but although it had been a nice enough place, it hadn't felt like being on a proper holiday. It had been too similar to home. He sipped at his soft drink and tried to work out what would feel like a real holiday – somewhere where he could get right away from all the stress of the past few months. The idea of surfing returned to him from the previous day and with it a fond memory of time spent on the beaches at Newquay from dusk till dawn when he was a teenager. It had been even better than girls, he seemed to remember, and that definitely sounded like a great idea right now. He drained his glass, stood up and picked up his helmet again. As he left the pub, he finally felt his spirits beginning to lift a little.

He pushed on towards Plymouth, crossing the Tamar Bridge shortly afterwards into Cornwall itself. By this time it was raining slightly, but he knew he didn't have much further to go. He took the clear road across the country, passing first Liskeard and then Bodmin on his way to the north coast. Traffic was light, making his journey easier, and soon he was approaching Newquay itself. He drove towards the seaside town alongside a familiar-looking river. It was only a stream to start with, but by the time he crossed it a little while later it was a river proper, and it stirred long-forgotten memories of fishing with his dad when he and Matt were children. He followed the road into town, turning left when he reached the roundabout onto the road that would take him towards the iconic Fistral Beach where he'd first learned to surf. He came to a stop in the car park and clambered off his bike to look out over the cliffs and rocks at the long expanse of sandy beach. Although the weather wasn't very good, it still gave him a thrill to see the beach again and to see that it looked pretty much the same as he remembered it. As he stood and watched the swell waves breaking onto the beach, he remembered how powerful they could be and knew for sure he would need a lot of practice before he felt confident about surfing again. There was a surf school on the beach, which he didn't remember being there on his previous visit. Perhaps he might be able to afford to take some lessons before venturing out on his own.

A lone surfer was in the sea, braving the cold Atlantic Ocean and the hostile waves hurling themselves at his vulnerable body. For a moment, Sam wondered what the hell he was doing here. Then he realised he and the surfer had a lot in common. The only difference between them was the surfer kept getting up and trying to beat the waves. Sam knew that was why he'd come on this trip: to regain his ability to fight back.

He turned away from the sea, heading for the car park to start the search for a place to stay. He needed a cheap bed and breakfast, which meant he would have to avoid the main town and look just outside it. He'd driven almost all the way out of town without finding anywhere suitable, and was about to turn around to look again, when he spotted a sign advertising vacancies at a place set back from the road. He pulled in a short way after it, did a smooth U-turn and stopped again opposite the B&B to study it. The small cottage looked a bit run-down but there were signs of love around, like the pots of brightly coloured flowers on the porch, and the recently repainted fence.

Sam crossed the carriageway when it became clear and pulled into the driveway of The Double Back B&B. Up close, there were more signs of deterioration on the house. A gutter at the side of the building was coming down and the gravel driveway looked like it hadn't seen any new gravel for quite some time. He decided the owners were short of cash, perhaps, and struggling to maintain appearances, which he knew would be difficult if customers weren't coming in. He swung his leg over his bike. This place would be perfect for a few days.

He approached the entrance and pushed open the front door. A bell rang somewhere at the rear of the house. Sam listened to the clatter of dishes and then a harsh exclamation followed by a brief silence. Then suddenly, there were footsteps coming his way. A small, grey-haired woman appeared. She gave him a tired smile, which reminded him of his mother after a particularly long day. He guessed at once that the B&B had been through difficult times and that perhaps her enthusiasm for running it had long since disappeared.

'Hello, love. Looking for a room?'

'Yes. I saw the sign.' Sam gave a brief smile.

'Just for tonight?' She tilted her head to one side as if trying to get the measure of him.

'Maybe longer, I'm not sure yet.'

'Okay. Well, it's £40 a night, in cash if you have it please, and if you could fill out this form for our records as well.' She gave a tight smile.

Sam nodded his agreement and reached for his wallet. He quickly filled in the form with his name and home address and then she handed him a key.

'Breakfast is served between seven and nine o'clock, Mr. Andrews,' she said after a quick look at his form.

'I won't be down before eight, if that's of any help to you.'

'Thanks, but I usually get up early anyway. I'm Helen Pascoe, by the way. Would you like some tea?'

'Thanks, that'd be great.'

'Okay, well your room is straight up the stairs to the first floor and then through the door and on the left. I'll bring your tea up shortly.'

***

### Jessie

Jessie strained to listen to her mum's conversation with the new arrival out in the hallway. She was annoyed at the intrusion into their personal life, which made her want to bang stuff around at the same time. As a result she could barely hear what was being said over the noise she was making. She willed herself to calm down and to find it within her to be grateful. For God's sake, what was she thinking? They were desperate for the money and she had no right to be so ungracious after all her mum had done to keep the business going. The last thing she wanted to do was upset her mum, so she gritted her teeth and finished pouring the cake mix into the tins. She put them into the oven and began the task of clearing up the kitchen, catching only the odd word from the hallway. A short while later, she heard heavy footsteps climbing the stairs and knew her mother would be along shortly.

'Jessie, love, we've got a guest for tonight at least. Can you put the kettle on for some tea, please?'

'Just about to,' she replied, filling up the kettle. 'Is it only for one night?' She held her breath, waiting for her mum to reply.

'He's not sure. Anyway, thanks for putting the cake in the oven. You can take him a slice up with his tea.'

'Hang on, who said I was taking his tea up?' Jessie didn't mean to be so prickly towards her mum but talking to people she didn't know still made her anxious.

'Oh come on, Jess, help me out here. It'll do you good to talk to someone other than me.' Her mum turned to the sink to start the washing up. 'It's either that or you do the washing up.'

Jessie heard the smile in her mum's voice and decided she probably had the lesser of two evils. While the cake cooked in the oven, she prepared a lemon-flavoured butter icing to fill and ice it with. She was looking forward herself to tasting the new recipe she'd tried.

'He seems like a nice chap,' her mum said eventually, knowing Jessie was dying to know.

'Hmmph.' Jessie worried about the way her mum always assumed the best of everyone. 'He might be an axe murderer for all we know.'

'True, but his bag didn't look big enough for an axe.' Her mum laughed and the sound made Jessie smile. She joined in, letting herself relax at last. The timer on the oven beeped and Jessie removed the tins and then, having checked the sponges were ready, she ran a knife around the inside of each tin and expertly removed them to cool on a wire rack. She helped her mum to put the dishes away and then they both returned to ice the cakes together.

'I wonder what made him come here when he could have had his pick of nicer places in town,' Jessie said finally.

'We don't know, do we love? But there's no point in speculating. He came in and that's the main thing as far as we're concerned, given the state of the business these days.' She flicked the switch on the kettle to reboil it now the cake was ready and set about making tea for them all. She set out the things on a tray for Jessie to take upstairs, adding a small plate with a slice of freshly cut cake.

'What's his name?' Jessie asked. 'Just in case I need to know.'

'Mr. Andrews. Sam.'

Jessie picked up the tray and walked out of the kitchen towards the stairs. Mr. Andrews was the first guest they'd had in quite a long time. It had been getting harder and harder to attract visitors to their little B&B and with so little money coming in, it was difficult to maintain the business in the way they would have liked. The outside of the house looked shabby and unwelcoming to new visitors, and without their custom they had no money to improve its appearance.

Not for the first time, Jessie wondered how on earth her mum had managed when she'd been away at university. She felt guilty for moaning about a new customer. It was just she'd grown used to it being only her and her mum at home, and even though they needed the business, she couldn't help but resent the fact that the arrival of a customer meant they had to drop everything. She sighed as she plodded up the stairs and tried to paste on a welcoming smile, which she hoped, along with the cake, would encourage the visitor to stay for a few more days.

She balanced the tray on one hand as she opened the door at the top of the stairs, and then took a moment to compose her face appropriately before knocking on the door of room one. The door opened and she immediately lost all sense of composure. Standing before her was a young man wearing only a towel round his waist, his damp blonde hair caressing his tanned face and his piercing blue eyes taking in her appearance with as much shock as she was sure her own face was showing.

'I'm sorry to interrupt you, erm, Mr. Andrews. Mum said you might like some tea and I just baked a cake, too.' She was babbling, she knew, when all she wanted to do was get away to recover some grace before her next encounter with this... this man. She would kill her mum for calling him a chap and not telling her how utterly gorgeous he was.

'Thanks.' He took the tray from her with one hand, giving her an embarrassed smile as he held on tightly to his towel with the other. 'Sorry, I only just stepped out of the shower.' He looked a bit flustered himself.

Jessie turned to go, sure she would only embarrass herself further if she stayed. She pushed open the door leading to the stairs, desperate to get away, but risked a quick glance back before going down to the lower floor. She was disappointed to see he'd already gone.

# CHAPTER 3

**Sam**

Sam leaned against the door. The china cup wobbled on the tray as he struggled to steady his hands and his racing heart. What a beautiful girl! She'd literally taken his breath away. He was sure he must have looked like a complete idiot and worse than that, one wearing only a towel. He groaned as he remembered both his shock at seeing her and his embarrassment at being half-naked in front of her. Her long, dark hair had framed her face and she had the greenest eyes he'd ever seen. Her eyes had widened in surprise at seeing him too, he thought. He finally set the tray down on the bed and hurriedly dressed again before pouring himself a cup of tea. He took a bite from the slice of cake and found himself in heaven at the light, fluffy taste of the sponge. He'd never made a cake in his life, but he'd eaten enough of his mum's home cooking to recognise an especially well-made cake when he tasted one. He finished it in two further bites and wished there was more. He hoped he would see the girl again when he took the tray back downstairs and maybe find out her name, too.

He started to unpack his panniers having decided he would be staying for at least a few days. His stomach rumbled, despite the cake.

He must ask for a recommendation for somewhere to eat nearby when he went downstairs, as well. He stashed the panniers in a corner of the room, grabbed his helmet and room key and picked up the tray. When he reached the hallway he called out a quick hello. The older lady he'd met before appeared from the kitchen. He held the tray out towards her.

'Thanks so much for the tea and cake. The cake was lovely.'

'You're welcome, love. Are you off out now?' She gave him a broad smile, but her eyes were heavy and he wondered if he'd woken her from a nap.

'Yes, I was wondering if you could suggest somewhere nearby where I could get some dinner?'

'Oh, there's a pub on the next corner as you go out of town. You might not have seen it earlier. The Falcon it's called and they do food. My Jessie's working tonight, so you'll know someone there at least. She started half an hour ago.'

'Great, thank you, Mrs. Pascoe.'

'Please, call me Helen.' She gave him a smile and he returned it. 'You can leave your helmet down here if you like, save you carrying it. You can walk there in a couple of minutes. Have you got your key with you to get back in?'

He dug his key out of his pocket, spotting the second key hanging on it, which he now realised was for the front door. He turned to leave with a quick wave and went out to the driveway. He stood there for a minute, considering what Mrs. Pascoe had said, and then turned left towards the corner, away from the B&B. As he went in search of the pub, he thought about the new information he'd learned. The name Jessie seemed to fit the girl he'd met earlier very well. He smiled as he thought of their encounter and he even blushed slightly at the memory. He was looking forward to seeing her again, he realised and all at once his reaction to this girl overwhelmed him. First of all, she wasn't Rachel, which proved he did still have the ability to be attracted to someone other than her. Secondly, he *was* attracted to her at this very moment, at a time when he thought he would never get over Rachel – so maybe getting over Rachel would be easier than he thought. As that idea went through his mind, he checked himself. Getting over Rachel would never be as easy as that; not easy on his emotions anyway. Physical attraction was a completely different thing to his emotional response. Still, Jessie intrigued him and he knew it wasn't only on a physical level. There was something about her he liked and he wanted to find out more about her.

He pushed open the door to the pub and found himself enveloped in a warm fug – the combination of heat and smoke from the fire and the sociable atmosphere. The pub was about half full as he made his way to the bar and no-one turned round to study him, which he took as a sign they didn't mind strangers coming in to their pub. As he neared the bar, he spotted Jessie over to his right serving someone. He pulled up a stool to wait for her to be free.

'Hey, Mr. Andrews, did my mum send you here?' She looked a bit surprised by his arrival.

'She did, and it's Sam. Can I get a pint of Doom Bar please?'

She raised her eyebrows slightly, which he could only assume was because he'd chosen a local beer and maybe that had impressed her. He hoped so anyway.

'There you go.' She put the pint of beer in front of him. 'Did you want to eat something?'

'Mmm, please.' He savoured his first sip of the beer. He knew he'd have a moustache from it on his upper lip and he flicked his tongue out over it, unaware of Jessie watching the sweep of his tongue across his lip until he looked up at her and caught her staring. 'What's on the menu tonight?' he asked.

---

## Jessie

'Hey, Jessie?'

Jessie snapped back to the present with a start.

'Sorry, what?' For the life of her, she couldn't remember the question he'd asked her.

'The menu?' He smiled at her, and that was almost enough to ruin her but she managed to pull herself together, just in time.

'Here you go.' She passed him the short menu. 'Take my advice and order the burger. It's the best thing on the menu.'

'Done. One burger, please.'

She ducked into the kitchen to place his order but more than that, to take a breather. She had no idea what had come over her. Her past history with men wasn't exactly brilliant and yet here she was, flirting and falling right into that whole love trap thing. There was something about Sam Andrews that she seemed unable to resist. She pulled in a deep breath and leaned against the wall of the kitchen for a minute to recover herself.

'You okay, Jessie?' the chef asked, narrowing his eyes in her direction.

'Yep, fine. Just taking a quick breather. It's so busy out there tonight.' She held her breath, mentally berating herself for giving the chef cause to worry about her. He meant well, they all did and she was grateful for the way they looked out for her, but she wished sometimes they would just let her try and get on with her life.

She released her breath, turned on her heel and returned to the bar. She could see someone waiting to be served and went towards them, ignoring the pull in the other direction. She glanced towards Sam, though, and her heart skipped a beat to see his eyes following her every move. I need to know more about him, she said to herself. He's probably only passing through, after all, and there'll only be heartbreak ahead if I let myself get involved with him before I know what his plans are. She nodded to herself, accepting her sage advice, and went to serve the other customer with renewed clarity of mind.

As she turned away from the bar, she heard the bell ring from the kitchen to tell her Sam's meal was ready. She returned to Sam's end of the bar and put the plate down in front of him with as much of a flourish as she could muster, given that it was just a burger.

'There you go,' she said, expecting him to move to a table to eat it, but he stayed firmly in his seat. 'Would you like any sauces?' she asked, putting his cutlery next to the plate.

'No, thanks. This looks great.'

'You'd better taste it first before you decide for certain about that.' She chuckled.

He glanced up at the sound and studied her face, making her blush. He took a bite of the burger and chewed for a minute before he spoke again. 'Mmm, not bad but then I'm no chef. I loved your cake earlier, though, and I could tell it had been made by someone who knows how to bake a good cake. My mum's a real pro when it comes to cake baking.'

'Thank you,' she said simply. She loved baking and it was always good to know someone else appreciated her efforts. 'There's plenty left if you'd like some more,' she offered.

'I'd definitely like some more. Perhaps later tonight when we get back?'

She liked the sound of that 'we' and the way he seemed to suggest he might stay at the pub all evening. She watched as he made light work of the food on his plate, her eyes widening at his appetite, and then she remembered her plan to try and find out more about him.

'What brings you to Cornwall then, Sam?' she asked, trying to make it sound like an innocent enquiry and not an inquisition. He stiffened slightly at the question and she wondered whether he would be honest enough to answer. He stretched his body up straight on the stool and took in a breath.

'I needed a break from everything at home, to be honest,' he replied, looking her straight in the eye.

'And where is home?' she asked next, boosted by his candid reply.

'Just outside Poole.'

'In Dorset?'

He nodded. 'Do you know it?'

'No, not really. I know it's near Southampton, which I know quite well, but I haven't travelled much outside of Cornwall otherwise, except for the odd visit to London.' She pulled a face, trying to convey her disappointment at her lack of any spirit of adventure.

'You look disappointed about that,' Sam said. 'Are you?'

'I guess, but only because I feel I ought to have travelled, but at the same time, I've never wanted to. I just love living here so much.'

'I get that. I feel the same way about Dorset, but I used to come here as a child and I always loved it, right up into my teens. With the sea and the surfing, it made sense for me to come here for a break.'

She wanted to know why he needed a break and whether he had a girlfriend, but felt it would be rude to ask any more pointed questions. She looked up as someone called out to her from the other end of the bar and, with a quick glance at Sam, she went off to serve them.

---

## Sam

Sam took advantage of Jessie's absence to try and get a hold on what was happening between them. His track record with women wasn't exactly a good one but there was definitely something going on between them and he liked it. He wanted to know everything about her but he didn't want to frighten her off by asking too many questions all at once. He watched her quiet but friendly manner with the customers and the way they interacted with her, as if they liked her and wanted to look out for her. He wondered why they felt the need to do that.

Jessie returned a few minutes later to collect his plate, but they didn't get to talk again for a while because she was so busy. He was surprised she was the only person serving behind the bar when it was so full of customers. It was almost half past ten when she was able to chat to him again.

'Sorry if I've abandoned you a bit. Are you okay?' she asked as she tidied up around him.

'Yeah, I'm fine. Could I have another half, please?' She took his glass and poured him a fresh one. 'I wish I could have given you a hand. You were run off your feet.'

'I've never seen it so crowded in here in all the time I've worked here. There's usually someone else with me, but she's off sick at the moment.'

'Have you been working here long, then?'

'Since I...' She paused, as though wondering whether to say more. 'Since I came home from university.'

'What did you study?' Sam was genuinely interested to know what she loved doing most.

'I went to Falmouth to study illustration.' This time there'd been no pause.

'What do you most like to illustrate?'

'Cookery books, although I haven't done any yet.' She smiled and so did Sam.

'I think that would make a lot of sense for you.'

'I can't see it ever happening though, what with Mum struggling to keep the B&B afloat. I can't leave her to do all that on her own.' She sighed and went off to ring the bell to signal last orders.

When Jessie returned, Sam decided to be brave and ask one more question.

'Can I walk you home, Jessie, when you finish?' He swallowed nervously and he saw her do the same.

'Sure. I'll be about another ten minutes.' She flashed him a smile and went off to shoo people out. Sam stood to help her collect the last few glasses and put them on the bar.

'Thanks for helping me,' she said. 'You seem quite familiar with bar work. Have you done it before?'

'Oh, years ago, but I've spent a lot of time in pubs over the years, one way or another.'

Jessie laughed. Sam knew he was avoiding telling her what he really meant was he'd spent a lot of time in pubs playing in the band, but he wasn't ready to get into all that yet.

Once Jessie had loaded the dishwasher, she went to say goodnight to her boss before they started the walk back to the B&B. Sam pushed his hands into the pockets of his jeans to ward off the cold while Jessie wrapped her scarf tightly around her neck. They walked in comfortable silence along the road for a minute until Jessie spoke first.

'How long is it since you last surfed?' she asked with a grin.

'God, years. I don't know, maybe ten.'

Jessie sucked in her cheeks at that reply. 'You're going to need a bit of practice to get into the swing of it again.'

'I saw the surf school on Fistral Beach earlier today. I thought I might go and get some one-to-one time with them.'

'Good idea.'

'Do you surf, Jessie?'

'A bit. I don't mind it but I don't love it, if you know what I mean.'

They were back at the house by this time and Jessie opened the door to let them in to the silent hallway.

'Would you still like a piece of that cake?' She turned to face him in the small space and then took a step back so they weren't quite so close.

'Only if you're sure. I don't want to keep you up when you've been working all day.'

'You go on up and I'll bring it to you, if you like.'

Sam pulled a face. 'I feel bad now. I can wait till tomorrow, honestly.'

Jessie reached out towards him and put her hand on his arm, trying to show she didn't mind bringing him some cake. Her action surprised them both into silence. He took her hand gently and placed both of his around hers. For a moment, they stared at each other, as the attraction flooded between them. Eventually, Sam leaned forward and kissed her softly on the cheek. He let go of her hand and gave her a soft smile.

'Okay,' Jessie croaked, her voice catching. 'I'll make sure to save some for you to have tomorrow, then. Goodnight, Sam.'

'Goodnight, Jessie. See you tomorrow.' Sam stepped around her, not touching her again, and started up the stairs, sensing her gaze on him all the way to the top. When he reached the small landing, he turned to look at her again, giving her a little wave before disappearing through the glass door.

---

## Jessie

Jessie tossed and turned all night. She couldn't believe how bold she'd been in touching Sam, and then for him to respond was even more surprising. Her heart had been thumping when she first climbed into bed and she'd lain there for at least an hour, trying to calm down.

This emotional high was then followed swiftly by self-doubt. Had she been too forward? Well, he'd kissed her, she reasoned so she couldn't have been. Did that mean he liked her too? Well of course, you idiot, otherwise, he wouldn't have kissed you. And anyway, it was only a kiss on the cheek, it couldn't have meant anything. She thought about that over and over, convincing herself in the end that his reaction to her touch had simply been instinctive and natural. Her head felt like it was going to burst with all the thoughts going round it. When she finally got out of bed in the morning, she was so tired she wondered if she should have even bothered trying to sleep.

She showered quickly, got dressed and went downstairs to help her mum with breakfast.

'Morning, love. Did you sleep okay?' Her mum gave her a worried look. 'You look a bit rough round the edges.'

'Thanks, Mum.' She pulled a face. 'No, I hardly slept at all. Anyway, what can I do to help with breakfast?'

'We're fine. Mr. Andrews has had his and gone already. He said he was heading down to the beach to see about some surfing lessons.' She shuddered. 'Rather him than me in this weather.'

Jessie looked out the window at the neutral-coloured sky, trying to hide her disappointment from her mum's eagle eyes. She would have liked to have seen Sam this morning to try and gauge how things stood between them after last night. It had been nearly two years now since she'd felt attracted towards a man and she was out of practice at dealing with her feelings.

'What would you like for breakfast, love?'

'To be honest, I don't feel that hungry.'

'You've got to eat, Jess. What about a slice of toast?'

Her mum put a toast rack on the table and poured out a cup of tea, and Jessie found herself eating and drinking absent-mindedly while her thoughts raced.

'I've put some washing on and everything else is set for the day, so I'm going to pop into town to meet up with Val for some shopping and lunch. How about you?'

Jessie shrugged. 'I don't have anything particular I have to do.'

'Why don't you come into town with me, then? You can go for a wander and see what happens.'

'No, thanks, Mum. I'll stay here and catch up on some things. I do need to make my next appointment at the centre, so I can do that today. Don't worry, you go and have a nice lunch with Val and I'll see you later.'

The house was strangely quiet after her mum left. Jessie recognised at once the feeling of loneliness that threatened to invade her spirit. After always being with her mum, she'd found it hard to make new friends when she went to college after school to resit her exams. It had been just as difficult to adjust to being on her own when she went off to university, but she'd got used to university life in time and eventually made some good friends. Since being home though, she'd grown used to being around her mum again and she was in danger of becoming too dependent. She decided to make her phone call while she was having those thoughts, before she changed her mind. After finishing the call, she blew out a large sigh and tried to be grateful for the chance to get some illustration practice in while she was on her own.

She walked over to the window and looked out once again at the colourless January sky, willing herself to be inspired enough to illustrate something. She'd only just found the strength to start illustrating again after many months of counselling and it was still difficult to get started sometimes. Then she remembered the cake she'd made the previous day. She went to retrieve the tin from the larder in the kitchen and lifted the cake out carefully. Only one quarter had been eaten which she concluded would still make it work as an illustration. She dashed upstairs to get her camera and her sketchbook and pencil case, then carried the cake into the dining room at the rear of the house where the light was brightest. After setting it down in the middle of one of the tables, she took photos of it from every angle so she had lots of reference material for later on. Then she took out her sketchbook and pencil and set to work. The smell of the cake was distracting at first, but she soon forgot about it in her determination to capture its image as accurately as possible.

An hour or so later, she was startled out of her focus on drawing by the opening of the front door. She listened as Sam shut the door behind him and walked along the hallway. When he didn't go upstairs, she stood up and went out to talk to him.

# CHAPTER 4

**Sam**

Sam stood by the front door in the hallway, freezing after his attempt at surfing that morning. The house was eerily quiet and he jumped at the sound of Jessie's soft voice behind him.

'Hey, Sam, how did the surfing go?'

He hung up his jacket and turned round to face her. 'Not great, to be honest.' He grimaced.

'You look freezing. How about a cup of tea and that piece of cake I promised you? Mum's out in town shopping.'

He followed her into the kitchen and slumped down at the table while she busied herself putting on the kettle. He picked up the open sketchbook and studied her drawing, blowing on his hands one at a time in an effort to warm them up.

'This is brilliant, Jessie.'

She turned round and saw him looking at her illustration.

'Oh, thanks,' she said awkwardly, taking the book gently from him and closing it. He immediately regretted making her feel uncomfortable.

'I don't know anything about illustration, of course,' Sam continued, 'but it looks good to my eye.'

She blushed then, and he smiled. He accepted a cup of tea from her a moment later and promptly added two spoonfuls of sugar with just a dash of milk. He wrapped his hands around the mug, grateful for the warmth.

'I see you like a builder's cup of tea.' She laughed. 'Is that what you do for a living in Dorset?'

He was glad she wanted to know more about him, and he was happy enough to talk generally about himself.

'No, but it's close. I'm a carpenter but I do labouring work from time to time as well.'

They fell quiet for a moment and then Jessie remembered the cake. She took a cake slice from the cutlery drawer and pulled the cake towards her, cutting a slice for each of them and handing one to Sam.

'Mmm, it tastes even better today,' he commented after his first mouthful, closing his eyes at the rich, creamy taste of the sponge combined with the icing.

'So, did you have a surfing lesson this morning?' Jessie sat down next to him at the small, round table.

'No, they were a bit understaffed today, so I had a go on my own. There was a tutor out there with someone else, so I watched them to try and remind myself of what to do.' He groaned. 'What a disaster! It was so cold, even in the wetsuit I'd hired from them, and I couldn't seem to remember any of the techniques. I managed to book a lesson in a couple of days' time though so that should help.'

'How long do you think you'll be staying?'

Sam pondered his reply for a moment, unsure why she was asking and not sure whether he wanted to get into all his history yet. 'I don't know, Jessie. I needed to get away, as I told you, and I have nothing to rush back for either but I don't have an endless supply of money so... I don't know.'

'Do you mind me asking what you needed to get away from?'

Sam wiped his hand over his face.

'I'm sorry, I shouldn't have asked.' Jessie laid her hand on his arm once again, but this time by way of apology. She stood up and he looked at her.

'Don't go, Jessie, please. I want to tell you about it but I'm just finding it a bit hard to talk about, that's all.'

'Was it a girl?' she asked, sitting down again.

'Yes, her name's Rachel and I... I loved her but she didn't feel the same. She's just got married to someone else in fact, and now she's gone for real, I can't stand all the reminders of her I see everywhere I go at home.'

'You must have really loved her.'

'We'd known each other for years. She's my sister's best friend and we'd been friends for a long time.'

He thought about saying more but in the end, he wasn't ready to do that when he and Jessie had only just met.

'I'm sorry,' she said simply, when it became clear he wasn't going to reveal any more.

'So, I'm just trying to have a break and get my life together again, you know?'

'Yes, I know what you mean.' She started to clear the table and an awkward silence grew between them. He didn't know what to say to make things right again.

'I'd better go and get changed into some warmer clothes. Thanks for the tea and cake,' he said in the end.

'Sure.' She gave him an easy smile and he hoped that meant that things were still okay between them.

On an impulse he decided to say one last thing.

'Are you up to anything this afternoon?' When she shook her head, he smiled. 'Would you like to go for a ride with me on the bike and remind me of the sights?'

## Jessie

Jessie hugged on tight to Sam as they pulled away from the B&B half an hour later. She'd never ridden on a motorbike before and the feeling was both exhilarating and frightening. It felt good to be so close to Sam and she already trusted him to take care of her. It was a new sensation to travel at such speed with the wind in her face and the knowledge she wasn't in control. She leaned with Sam as he went round corners, like he'd told her to do before they'd set off, and sometimes she closed her eyes, like she did whenever she went on a rollercoaster at the fair. After a while, though, she felt herself relax and start to enjoy the journey.

They followed the road back into town but this time, instead of driving towards Fistral Beach, Jessie guided Sam towards the harbour. They turned and drove slowly, looking down on the sea below and the few people brave enough to be out walking in the cold weather. Sam drove on, twisting and turning along some of the smaller roads that led towards the next beach. Then, just after the station, Jessie tapped him on the shoulder, indicating he should turn right. When Sam came to the road leading to the miniature railway and the zoo, she pointed for him to take that route and eventually he stopped in a car park.

Sam helped Jessie off the bike and held her arm as she found her balance again.

'What did you think of the ride then?' he asked with a grin.

'I was scared stiff at first, I have to admit, but once I got used to it, it wasn't so bad.' She laughed and tried to tidy her hair.

They stashed their helmets in the panniers before setting off for the gardens which Jessie wanted to show him.

'I love it here,' she said, as soon as they entered. 'It's not the sort of place most people want to visit when they come to Newquay. They think it will be boring but I've always loved to wander among the trees and flowers. I used to come here a lot to sketch when I was younger, as well.'

'Do you still do that?'

'No, not so much. I tend to stick to drawing food these days but it was good practice when I first started sketching.'

'Would you like to find work as an illustrator? You must have had lots of experience during your degree course.'

Jessie looked down under Sam's gaze as he waited for her answer. She swallowed nervously, wondering what to say. As he'd been so honest with her, she felt she at least owed him some explanation. She met his gaze again.

'I haven't actually finished the course. I'm on a break at the moment but I don't know if I'll go back yet.'

She waited for Sam to ask his next question but he didn't say anything.

'Aren't you going to ask me why?' she asked him finally.

'I don't want to push you to answer any more than you wanted to push me. I can tell something happened and I guess you'll tell me when you're ready.'

The sense of relief she felt at his words was liberating. She didn't have to tell him all about it now – for the moment it was enough for him to know she'd left her course.

'So you know how I was saying I love these gardens?' she said, changing the subject as they walked on. 'And I really did want to show them to you. But there's another reason I've brought you here as well.'

'There is?' he asked with a grin. 'What can that be, I wonder?' They'd arrived in front of a lovely tearoom as she'd finished speaking and they both stood gazing at it, as if it were an oasis in the desert.

Jessie pushed the door open. The bell tinkled, alerting the staff to their arrival, and all at once they were enveloped by the warmth provided by a wood-burning stove in the centre of the space. They went towards the counter.

'I can recommend the hot chocolate with whipped cream, and the scones are always perfect.'

The girl behind the counter smiled at Jessie.

'Hello, I've seen you here before. Is that what you'd like to order?'

'Fine by me,' said Sam. 'It all sounds delicious.'

'You go and sit down by the stove then, and I'll bring your order over when it's ready.'

They settled in at the table and Jessie rubbed her hands together, trying to warm up. The girl brought their drinks and scones over a few moments later and they tucked in.

'You were right about these scones. They're very tasty.' Sam licked his lips to hoover up the crumbs before taking a sip of his hot chocolate.

'Watch out for that cream moustache as well,' Jessie warned him and they both laughed. She hadn't laughed so much in ages in fact, and she put that all down to Sam's easy-going manner and openness. She found herself hoping he would stay for quite a while to come.

---

## Sam

As Sam drove Jessie home from the gardens, he wondered whether he might be able to work out some way of staying down in Newquay for a bit longer, so he could get to know Jessie better. There was definitely a connection between them but he also wanted to be sure he wasn't just on the rebound from Rachel. Jessie deserved better than that and he didn't want to let her down or hurt her.

The only obstacle in his way was lack of money, but if he could get some carpentry work, those earnings would tide him over till he decided to go home. He did have a suggestion for Jessie's mum, which would allow him to earn his keep a little, but he'd only just arrived and he didn't want to overstep the mark by making suggestions too early. Not for the first time he regretted his refusal to settle down and get a steady job, or to have done something more with his life than play the guitar and take on the odd-job carpentry work he'd been doing since he left college. He snorted in disgust at himself and felt Jessie hold on tighter behind him.

He pulled back onto the driveway of the B&B a few minutes later and helped Jessie climb off the bike. She turned the sign back the other way, so it read 'Vacancies' again, in case anyone should now pull in looking for a place to stay for the night. As she turned to go in, he busied himself stowing the helmets in the panniers and then followed her inside. There was still no sign of Mrs. Pascoe, and he was grateful for a bit more time alone with Jessie. He followed her into the kitchen and waited as she busied herself putting the kettle on. He'd come to realise she made tea as a way of hiding herself away when she didn't want to talk.

'Are you okay, Jessie?' he asked when she turned round again. He reached his hands out towards her and held her gently by the arms as he bent his head a little to look in her eyes.

Her smile lit up her whole face, taking his breath away. Her green eyes were so beguiling. 'I'm fine, yes. Thanks for today. It was good to get out and even better to have someone to go out with.'

'Thanks for being my guide to all the sights I'd forgotten since my childhood.' They both laughed and then stopped suddenly. They were now standing very close to each other. Jessie looked down again and he let go of her elbow to gently tilt her chin up.

Then his lips were on hers and he put his arms around her, pulling her close. Her lips were soft and inviting, and when she moved her hands up to his back, their bodies moulded together as one and the kiss deepened. Time passed but Sam wasn't even conscious of it. He was only conscious of Jessie, her floral perfume and the way her body fitted with his.

The sound of a key in the door brought them both abruptly to their senses. They broke apart at once. Sam felt his face flush as he sat down. He tried to look as though nothing had been going on when Jessie's mum came in. Jessie had her back to the door and was gathering cups, so she could take longer to compose herself.

'Hello, love. Oh, you angel. A nice cup of tea is exactly what I need. Have you been okay? Oh sorry, Mr. Andrews, I didn't see you there. How did your surfing go?'

She walked straight back out of the kitchen without waiting for an answer. Jessie glanced at him over her shoulder, rolled her eyes and gave him a quick conspiratorial grin by which time her mum had returned, having taken her coat off, and was bustling about again.

'I've been fine, Mum, thanks. I took Sam out to see the sights of Newquay. I should say he took me out actually, because we went on his bike.'

'You did? I'm glad I didn't know about that, but at least you're both back safe and sound. And the surfing? Freezing I imagine.'

Sam could only nod and thank goodness she hadn't given him any time to speak. He was still recovering from the loveliness of the kiss he'd shared with her daughter.

---

Sam ventured out again the next morning for some more surfing prac-tice, and although he still wasn't that good, he was beginning to remember how to do it. One of the tutors even gave him some guid-ance. Once again it was cold – so cold he wondered why he was even doing this in January, for goodness' sake, but he had to admit to getting a buzz from it. And he couldn't think about anything else while he was surfing, so that was an added bonus.

He came home hoping to see Jessie again, but there was no sign of her when he returned and the house was very quiet.

When he went back to his room after a quick shower to warm himself up, there was a text message on his phone from Matt.

'*Hey, how's it going down there in the wilds of Cornwall? Would be good to hear from you even if it's only to stop everyone from asking me how you're getting on ;)*'

He smiled. He missed seeing his brother and talking to him. He called Matt straight back.

'Hi, Matt, how are you?'

'I'm good, Sam. What have you been getting up to and where are you?' He laughed and Sam was glad he'd called.

He told him about the B&B and the surfing.

'I don't know how you do it. It must be bloody freezing out there at this time of year.'

'Well, I'm wearing a wetsuit but yeah, you can't do it for too long. It'd be enough to freeze your balls off.'

'Thanks for that great image. I'm probably going to have that in my mind for the rest of the day now.' Matt paused for a moment. 'Listen, Jenna's heard from Rachel. I didn't know if you'd want to know or not, but apparently they're having a great time.'

Sam knew he should be happy for them and he wouldn't want them to be having a miserable time, but what could he say truthfully?

'I'm sorry, Sam. I didn't mean to remind you of it all. I just thought you'd want to know.'

'Listen, it's fine,' he replied, finally finding his voice again. 'I just don't know what to say that would be an honest reply. I am glad for them, of course I am, but... well, you know.'

'Yep. Well, everyone sends their love. Mum's worried about you, of course.'

'What about Jenna? Has she forgiven me for being so grumpy with Will?'

'She understands how you feel, but she's got Will to think of now as well, and she doesn't want to be forced to take sides. So it's probably going to take a while for her, to be honest.'

Sam sighed. He needed to get a grip and let it all go. 'Okay, well, I'll be in touch again soon, I promise. Give my love to Natalie and the baby.'

Sam dropped his phone onto the duvet and fell back on to the bed, staring up at the ceiling. Just as he'd been starting to get past everything, he'd been reminded of it all again. He closed his eyes as if that would shut out all the memories. Rachel would always have a special place in his heart but he knew they could never be more than friends now. And that was all he wanted – to be able to be her friend without always wondering what might have been if she'd accepted his proposal to marry him, and not Jackson.

The door downstairs slammed and he sat up, wondering if it was

Jessie returning home. He pushed himself up from the bed and went towards the door, planning to go downstairs and catch up with Jessie's news. He opened the bedroom door only to find her standing there with her hand raised, ready to knock. He would have laughed but the look on her face stopped him.

'Hey, Jessie, are you okay?'

Her hands flew to her face. 'Oh, I'm sorry, I shouldn't have disturbed you. I don't know why I knocked really. I... I just wanted some company, but you're probably busy.' She turned to go.

'It's okay. I was on my way down to talk to you, so, you know, great minds and all that.' He grinned trying to take away her embarrassment.

She gave him a wobbly smile and led the way downstairs.

# CHAPTER 5

**Jessie**

Jessie went into the kitchen and busied herself with her usual ritual of making tea while she gathered her thoughts after her latest visit to the counsellor. She was still only just beginning to move on from her sadness.

'So you went surfing again this morning, did you?' she asked as she set the cups of tea on the table and sat down.

'Yes, and it wasn't so hard today.' He smiled and took a sip of his tea, wincing slightly when he realised it was still too hot. 'How about you? What have you been up to?'

'Oh, I just had an appointment, that's all.' She wasn't brave enough to look him in the eye. She knew he would realise she was being deliberately vague.

'Do you want to talk about it?' he asked softly.

She shook her head, unable to cope with the thought of him knowing what had happened to her. 'No. I don't want to be on my own right now, that's all.'

'Well, I've just had a phone call from my brother, Matt,' Sam replied cheerily, making her look up with interest. He smiled at her and she was grateful for his understanding.

'Oh, so you have a brother. Is he younger or older?'

'Older. I have a sister too, Jenna. She's the middle one and I'm the baby.'

They both laughed at that, but her own laugh sounded hollow to her ears.

'I don't have any siblings, unfortunately. My dad left before that could happen. Anyway, why did your brother call?'

'He was checking in with me. They all want to know I'm doing okay, you know.'

'It's good you're a close family.'

'Yes, you're right. Most of the time, anyway. He also told me Jenna had heard from Rachel to say she was having a good time on her honeymoon.' He blew out a breath.

Jessie reached out and patted his hand. 'How do you feel about that?'

'Not as bad as I might have expected, actually.' He closed his eyes briefly. 'I'm sorry, I shouldn't be telling you all this.'

'Don't be silly. You can tell me what happened between you if you want to.'

He gazed at her in silence for a minute and she guessed he was trying to make up his mind whether to tell her any more. She resisted the temptation to encourage him. It had to be his decision.

'Well, we'd known each other as friends for years, as I said. In fact, we were in a band together. I was on guitar and she was the singer and songwriter. Then one drunken night, we slept together.' Sam stopped and scrubbed his hands across his stubble, remembering that night. 'For me, that was the turning point. I wanted us to be together more than anything, but stupidly, I didn't tell her that. She'd gone when I woke up the next morning. So I thought she regretted having been with me and I didn't mention it. She then thought I was full of regret too so we went back to being friends as if nothing had happened.

Then she met this American guy who whisked her off her feet. I did try to tell her how I felt, but by then it was too late for us. I wished her well of course, but after the wedding, I found it much harder than I thought it would be to move on. I've been on a bit of a bender since then and that's why my family persuaded me to get away for a bit.'

Sam heaved a big sigh and turned to look at Jessie for the first time since he'd started telling his story. She guessed he was expecting to see pity in her eyes but instead, she was angry, and his look of surprise confirmed she'd failed to hide her reaction in time. She stood up abruptly and started clearing the table. Then she stopped what she was doing all of a sudden, realising he must be feeling vulnerable now. She kept her body turned away from him, taking lots of deep breaths to try and calm herself.

'Jessie, what is it?' Sam stood up and came to her, gently turning her round to face him.

She tried to swipe the tears away before he saw them but she wasn't quick enough. He reached out with his thumb and gently wiped her face.

'I just wish I knew a single story with a happy ending.' She tried to laugh but it came out as a sob. 'All love does is cause pain and hurt, from what I've seen and experienced. My dad upped and left when I was young, with no thought for how that would break my mum's heart, let alone how it would force her to struggle to make ends meet with a young daughter. And then, all the men I've ever been out with only seem to want sex and no commitment. There's just no such thing as love, is there?' She wiped her tears away furiously with the tea towel, her eyes burning with the injustice she still felt.

Sam reached out and took a gentle hold of her arms. She looked into his eyes at last.

'It hasn't stopped me believing in love, Jessie.'

'But why?' she exclaimed. 'Why would you expose yourself to that risk again after all you've been through?'

'Because I know I have to if I want to find love, and I do want to. It's going to take me a while to get over the pain, I know that, but it's getting better with each day that passes, and one day soon, I'll be ready to try again.'

Jessie took hope from that statement. If Sam could try again after what had happened to him, then maybe she could as well.

She touched Sam's cheek with her fingers, as if she were checking he was real. He shivered slightly at her touch. She immediately withdrew her hand but he stepped closer to her and put his hands around her waist. She didn't resist this time and as he pressed his body against hers, she savoured the warmth of his breath on her skin. She turned her face up to his and lifted her arms to put her hands around his neck, bringing their bodies even closer together. Their lips were inches apart, the anticipation of kissing each other again heightening the attraction between them. Then she pulled him gently towards her and their lips met, tentatively at first. He brushed her warm lips with his and then stopped, looking deep into her eyes. She sensed his need for reassurance from her that this was still what she wanted before they went any further.

Jessie issued a soft sigh of pleasure. This time, when Sam kissed her again in response, she opened her lips to him, allowing their tongues to meet and the kiss to deepen. Sam's fingers tangled in her hair and she arched herself against him, making him groan. When they both came up for air, they were smiling at each other and then they were laughing.

'Mmm, I'd forgotten how good kissing can be,' Jessie whispered, touching her swollen lips.

'How long has it been since you kissed someone?' Sam asked, still holding her in his arms. She blinked and all at once, her shutters came down and she made to turn away from him but he pulled her back. 'I'm the last person to judge you, Jessie. Don't push me away.'

He looked at her openly.

'I'm sorry, Sam. I'm not pushing you away. I just don't know if I'm ready to tell you about it yet.' She took a step back into her own personal space and this time he let her.

'I didn't mean to rush you, Jessie. I wouldn't do that to you.' Sam smiled gently and sat down again at the table. 'Anyway, listen, I wanted to ask you about something.'

Jessie took in a deep breath and composed herself.

'Go on,' she said finally.

'Well, I was wondering if your mum might let me stay on here if I do some work around the B&B in exchange for my board. What do you think?'

Her eyes lit up. 'That's a great idea! I think Mum would be more than happy to do that but you'll have to check with her. You'd be doing us a big favour, though. I'd be really glad if you were able to stay as well.'

'You would?'

She nodded and hoped he understood how much she wanted to spend more time with him.

'There's a lot of work to do, though. Are you sure you want to be doing work when you came down here for a break?'

'I've been on a "break" from work for far too long as it is. It would do me good to be doing a bit more than surfing or sightseeing.'

'So you don't want me to show you any more sights then, is that what you're saying?' She schooled her face to look serious as she held his gaze and he groaned. She had to try really hard not to laugh, as she knew he was worrying he might have upset her. In the end, she couldn't hold it in any longer and a bubbly laugh escaped her lips.

'Hey, that's not fair. I really thought I'd upset you.' He smiled at her laughter and the way he looked at her warmed her heart.

'Where shall we go next then?'

'Maybe we could drive up the coast a bit and explore what that area has to offer?'

'I haven't been up that way for years so it would be good to see how much things have changed.'

'It's funny how you don't always take the time to explore what's on your doorstep, isn't it? I'm a bit like that with Dorset. It's right there waiting to be explored and yet I never do it.'

'It makes a difference if you have someone to show it to, though,' Jessie replied.

'Shall we make a plan to go out tomorrow, if the weather's okay?'

Jessie nodded. She wanted so much to focus on the present and on getting to know Sam better.

'We're a right pair, aren't we?' Jessie exclaimed. 'You're lost in your thoughts and so am I. Maybe it's time for both of us to try and leave the past behind?'

He stood up and came to her once again. 'Or at least to start reconciling ourselves with it and trying to move on.' He lowered his head to kiss her softly and she melted into him once more.

They stopped in at Mawgan Porth on their way north in the morning and, after some breakfast, they strolled on the beach with almost the whole expanse of sand to themselves. They continued their drive up the coast towards Padstow, another town Sam said he remembered fondly from his childhood visits. Jessie enjoyed herself immensely by showing him all the hidden nooks and crannies of the coastal village she knew so well as a native and that tourists never manage to find. They spent a wonderful day together and as they wended their way home, Jessie found herself thinking she didn't want the day to end.

'Can we stop here?' she called out suddenly. Sam pulled over a minute or two later, parking the bike expertly in a tight space. He climbed off and helped Jessie to the pavement.

'Is there something special you want to see here?' He looked around at the signs for Porth Beach.

'There is a place I'd like to show you, yes. It's somewhere I like to go to be alone with my thoughts sometimes.'

'Okay, lead the way,' Sam replied.

They walked back a little way along the road they'd just come on, taking a left turn after only a few minutes towards the hidden cove she knew was unknown to most people. Shortly after they turned off the main road, they found themselves on a narrow track leading to the beach. It was a long time since Jessie had been down here. She glanced over at Sam and when he sensed her looking at him, he gave her a warm smile before taking her hand as they walked on to the beach. She returned his smile but felt a sinking feeling in her stomach as she thought about whether to tell him her story.

They found a sheltered spot hidden behind a sand dune but where they could still see the sea. Jessie was relieved to know the beach was deserted. As she sat down next to Sam on the blanket they'd brought with them, she summoned all her courage from deep within her to tell him what had happened to her at university.

'I was ten when my dad left home and over the next few years, I saw my mum struggle to keep herself together. She loved him so much and he just disappeared without even leaving a note. We got up one morning and found all his things were gone. We waited a few weeks to see if he would come home but as the weeks turned into months, we realised it wasn't going to happen. Mum worked every spare hour to keep the B&B going so she could provide for me and I had to help whenever I could as well. By the time I was in my teens, I was ready to rebel against the injustice of it all and his betrayal.'

Jessie pulled up her knees and grabbed her legs with her hands as she relived her difficult memories. It was too late to go back now though. Sam put his arm round her and gave her shoulder an encouraging squeeze.

'In the final year of my A levels, I started staying out late in town, hanging round with boys I knew I shouldn't be with, doing things I knew I shouldn't be doing. Then I started drinking as well and eventually the police had to bring me home one night. I took one look at my poor mum's face and realised I was hurting the only person who'd ever truly loved me. When I did badly in my exams, I knew I needed to sort myself out and concentrate on my studies so I could get to university. So I took a year out and did my exams again. My mum was so proud when I finally passed. I was glad I'd stopped my rebellious phase just in time before anything serious happened to me.'

Jessie paused for a moment to look out to sea. She stole a quick glance at Sam, trying to gauge what he was thinking.

'Are you okay?' he asked. 'You don't have to tell me all this, you know.'

'I know. I've never told anyone the full extent of it all, to be honest, but I... I want to tell you.' She took his hand and held it tight. 'Towards the end of my second year at university, I met someone and we started going out together. I never thought I'd ever be able to trust a man after what my dad had done to us, but I wanted to take a risk and see what it felt like to get close to someone.

Then one night, I stayed over at his place and I only realised the following day that I'd forgotten to take my pill. By that time, it was early evening and although I took it as soon as I got home from uni, I knew I might be in danger of falling pregnant. I didn't even think about going to the doctor's to see if there were any other options. Anyway, I found out I was pregnant shortly afterwards and when I told him, he went mad, accusing me of trying to trap him and all kinds of other rubbish. I went back to my house and sat in my room and cried. In my heart, I knew I wanted the baby, but I also knew it would be hard to do it all on my own. I decided not to tell my mum, thinking she'd be cross with me, which was another mistake. I thought I'd leave it until I had to tell her.'

Sam took in a deep breath and she felt him shift around next to her. She looked briefly at him and then stared out to sea again.

'Then I lost the baby at six weeks.'

'Oh God, no.'

Jessie pulled away from him, wrapping her arms protectively around her waist.

'Mum had to come then, of course, and she took me home to look after me. It took her a long time to forgive me for not telling her what had happened, but also to forgive herself for not being there for me when I needed her most. I never did return to do my final year because after all that had happened to me by then, my heart wasn't in it. I've been at home for nearly two years now and I'm only really just starting to move on. I've been seeing a counsellor for the past year, though, and that is helping.'

She leaned towards him again and let her head fall on his shoulder. Sam put his arm round her once more, holding her tight as her tears fell and she cried out all her pain. When the worst of her tears had passed and her body had calmed, Sam spoke to her.

'I'm so sorry,' he said softly, kissing her hair. 'I know you must feel betrayed by the men you've been close to in your life. But I do want to stay here, Jessie, so we can get to know each other better.' He tilted her face up towards him so he could look in her eyes. 'Would that be okay?'

She searched his eyes for a clue to prove she should take a risk again and put her trust in him. And yet, deep down, she knew that was why she'd told him what had happened to her – because she already did trust him. Then she kissed him with such a fierce passion she needed no words to confirm her acceptance of his suggestion.

---

**Sam**

Sam heard someone go out early in the morning and he presumed it was Mrs. Pascoe going into town to visit friends again. He wasn't sure her heart was in running the B&B any more and that worried him as far as his plan to do odd jobs around the place was concerned.

He decided to get up and go and find Jessie to see what she was planning to get up to as it was a Saturday. In the shower, he thought again about what she'd told him the day before and he was overcome with sadness. No wonder she was wary about getting involved again after being dumped when she was pregnant. He couldn't imagine how she was dealing with the tragedy of losing her baby as well but he was glad she was getting counselling and that it was helping her move on. He hoped he could help her rebuild her faith in men over time, but he knew there was a lot at stake for her.

He found her outside in the garden sketching some very sorry-looking plants.

'Morning, Jessie. Crikey, it's freezing out here.'

She glanced up at him but her eyes were a bit glazed over. She must have been so immersed in her illustrating that she'd hardly heard him. He waited for her to catch up, smiling softly as he saw her come back to reality.

'Ooh, it's cold.' She shivered despite her thick jumper and coat.

'How long have you been out here?' Sam turned to go inside and was relieved to see she was following him in. For once, he led the way to the kitchen. Jessie would definitely need a cup of tea to warm her up today. He switched the kettle on as Jessie was taking off her coat, and then waited for her to appear. When she did, he pulled her into his arms to try and warm her up.

'Now that's what I call a hug,' she said as he rubbed her back gently. She looked up at him and he couldn't help but kiss her soft lips in response to her clear invitation.

Once again, the sound of a key in the front door forced them apart. Jessie's mum appeared.

'Is the kettle on? I could do with a cup of tea.' She smiled at them both before taking off her coat and going out to the hallway to hang it up. By the time she returned, Sam had retreated to the doorway and Jessie was making the tea as normal. Sam had the feeling Mrs. Pascoe knew there was something going on between him and her daughter. He wondered how she would feel about it, given everything that had happened to her and Jessie.

'Did you have a nice time with Val, Mum?' Jessie asked as she put the water on to boil once more.

'Mmm, lovely, thanks.' Jessie's back was turned. She didn't notice the slight hint of colour that rose to her mum's cheeks, but Sam did. 'How about you? What did you get up to?' her mum continued.

'I managed to do some illustrating this morning.'

Mrs. Pascoe's eyes lit up as Jessie handed her the sketchbook. Jessie obviously valued her mum's opinion.

'Goodness, you've managed to make those plants look much more interesting than they do in real life.' She carried on turning the pages. 'Oh, what's this? I haven't seen these ones you did of the cake we made the other day. They're very lifelike, Jess. It makes me want to eat a piece, it looks so good. I don't suppose there's any left now, is there?'

Jessie laughed as she reached for the tin. She glanced at Sam standing in the doorway and waved him over to the table.

'It's all right, there's probably enough for us all to have a last piece. You don't have to pretend. I know you'd like some cake too.'

Sam laughed and pulled out a chair, glad they'd drawn him in to their inner circle. Jessie's mum beamed at him.

After they'd finished off the rest of Jessie's cake and drunk their tea, Sam decided it was time to put his idea to Mrs. Pascoe.

'Mrs. Pascoe, I...'

'Oh, Sam, you must call me Helen. Mrs. Pascoe is far too formal when we're becoming friends.' Her smile was genuine and he warmed to her even more.

'Okay, Helen. I don't know if Jessie's told you, but I'm a carpenter by trade and I do odd-jobbing of all kinds, too. I'd really like to stay on here a bit longer but...' He glanced over at Jessie to find her staring at him with what looked like admiration so he pressed on with his idea. 'The thing is, I don't have much money at the moment, so I wondered if you'd let me do some odd jobs for you in exchange for allowing me to stay?'

'Ooh, now, that sounds like too good an offer to pass up. What about tools though? You can't have brought any with you on that bike of yours.'

Sam's face fell. Jessie reached out and patted him on the arm. 'It's okay, Sam, we have all the tools, just none of the skills.'

She laughed and Sam joined in. He glanced over at Helen in time to catch the knowing smile that passed across her face.

# CHAPTER 6

## Jessie

Jessie was woken early the next morning by the sound of banging. She stirred underneath the duvet, struggling to open her eyes and groaning at the incessant noise. She rubbed her eyes and listened, trying to identify the source of the sound. As she came to, she realised it was coming from inside, and then a second later, she knew Sam had already made a start on one of the jobs he'd seen needed doing around the house. She sat up in bed, smiling at his enthusiasm for his work and at the knowledge that this meant he really did want to stay for a bit longer.

After the quickest of showers, she hurried through getting dressed and was soon skipping down the stairs to see what was going on. She followed the banging until she found him. He was working on a door which he'd lifted up and rested on top of two chairs so he could plane it. It was the door to the downstairs loo, which had been sticking for some time. Jessie watched him for a few minutes until he must have sensed she was there. He turned round to look at her.

'Hey, sleep well?' His face lit up with a smile that made her knees feel slightly wobbly. As he lifted his head, his wavy blonde hair fell into his eyes, and he swiped it out of the way with the back of his hand.

'Great, thanks. You're up early, I see.' She gestured at his activity.

'I work best if I get off to an early start.' He stood up and studied her face. 'You look beautiful,' he said and smiled as she flushed at the compliment. She patted her cheeks, willing them to return to normal. She had no idea how he managed to make her so giddy. She felt like a teenager experiencing her first romance.

'You charmer, you,' she managed to say at last.

'I mean it.' Sam pulled her to him and kissed her lightly on the lips.

Jessie inhaled his masculine smell as she felt the kiss all the way through her and her body warmed at the familiar, yet almost forgotten, sensation of arousal. Instinctively, she pressed her body against his and kissed him back, parting her lips to show him the depth of her feelings. Sam stumbled back slightly, steadying himself against the door frame so he could still hold on to her.

She pushed away from him, suddenly self-conscious after being so forward, and turned to go. She sensed him watching her as she went towards the stairs to return to her room, but she didn't look round again.

She stayed in her room after that, purposely keeping out of Sam's way. Half an hour later, she breathed a sigh of relief when she heard the front door slam shut following his departure for his surfing lesson. She'd been so embarrassed afterwards by the way she'd flirted with him, she couldn't bear the thought of facing him again just yet. What had she been thinking? Well, she hadn't been thinking at all. That was the problem.

She gathered up her sketchbook and pencils before walking slowly back downstairs to the dining room to study the garden. She stood at the window, looking outside and trying to put her attraction towards Sam out of her mind. Her mum had gone out to see her friend Val again and would probably be out for most of the day. It occurred to Jessie that her mum had been seeing a lot of Val lately, more so than usual. Still, she didn't mind. She liked to be alone with her thoughts, and now Sam had gone out as well, she could forget about everything and everyone else for a while and hopefully get some more sketching done. It was a cold, crisp day but the sun was shining and she was inspired to go for a stroll around the garden again to see what might catch her eye. She pulled her coat on, along with her fingerless gloves and, camera in hand, she ventured out.

She followed the stepping stones across the dewy grass towards the picket fence which stretched across the boundary of their garden. She stood there looking at the fields that backed onto their property, remembering the many happy times she'd spent there as a child, just exploring at first and then, as she grew older, indulging her love of horses by going on hacks this way. Jessie missed horse-riding and wondered why she hadn't tried it again since coming home. She assumed the farm still had a riding school and she was suddenly consumed with a need to visit it again, if only to see the horses.

She was already halfway over the fence, courtesy of the stile between her garden and the fields, when she remembered no-one would know where she was and she was supposed to be in charge of the B&B. With a sigh, she climbed down again and returned to the house, leaving a note for her mum before dashing out to the driveway to turn the sign over so it read 'No Vacancies' again. Guilt washed over her. Neither she nor her mum had their heart in running the B&B any more, preferring to spend their time anywhere else but here. They would have to have a serious talk about their future, and soon.

Jessie retraced her steps, locking all the doors behind her, and was soon back in the field walking towards the riding school she'd loved so much in her youth.

## Sam

Sam braced himself for another onslaught from the brutal waves of the North Atlantic coast. Not for the first time, he wondered why exactly he was putting himself through this. He changed quickly in the surf school's changing room and went outside to meet his instructor for his one-to-one tuition. The only person waiting outside the building was a young woman in full wet gear bearing the logo of the school.

'You must be Sam,' she said, holding out her hand. 'I'm Amy and I'm going to be your instructor today.'

Sam's heart sank, even as he put out his hand, to hear her Australian accent. She was going to be an excellent surfer and he was sure to look like a fool.

'Nice to meet you, Amy,' he managed to stumble out.

'So, what are you looking to achieve from this lesson?'

He briefly filled her in and she began by reminding him of some of the basic techniques he might have forgotten. He followed her down to the water's edge, the surfboard the school had loaned him tucked neatly under his arm as he listened attentively to everything she said. Before they went into the water, she checked which foot he favoured putting forward. He remembered it was his left foot. Then she checked his position on the board wasn't too far forward for him to be at risk of flipping the board over once he was in the sea. Next, he showed her his paddling technique and lastly, he popped up from lying on the board to his standing position. Amy nodded with satisfaction and then, after attaching his strap to his right ankle, he strode into the water and out to the surf. After already spending some time at the beach himself, he was familiar enough with how far he needed to walk out to find where the waves were cresting and breaking.

When the water was waist-high, Sam climbed onto his board, laid himself down flat on his stomach and started to paddle towards the more turbulent, white water, where the waves were breaking.

'Okay, now you're in the right place, let's start by trying to catch the waves lying down and riding them all the way to the beach,' Amy said.

Sam thought he could do better than that but he decided to

accept her advice and see what happened. He enjoyed the feel of the board swaying as it rode the wave, moving from side to side as it progressed back towards the beach. He didn't experience anything like the usual thrill he got when surfing because he was lying down, but it was useful all the same to reacquaint himself with the feel of the board and how he would need to balance himself when he stood up. They did this a few more times until Amy declared him ready to surf properly at last.

Sam paddled out again as he had before, past where the waves were breaking.

'I want you to sit and watch a few waves first, Sam, to see how they roll in, crest and break. That way, you should start to see a pattern.'

Sam struggled not to roll his eyes at Amy. He knew where the waves rolled and he knew how to catch a wave. He just wanted to get on with it, but he remained silent and tried not to be too impatient. He watched the waves for a few minutes and began to notice them breaking in roughly the same place each time. All at once, he under-stood the point Amy was trying to make. He sat up a little on the board, watching the last wave roll onto the beach.

'Yeah. I think I get it now. I can see the waves are breaking in pretty much the same place every time. I have to admit that maybe I don't know as much about this as I thought.' Sam glanced over at Amy sheepishly, expecting to see a smug look on her face but she was smiling, not judging him.

'That's great you can see the pattern, cos I can't tell you exactly where you need to be to catch a wave. That's something you need to work out for yourself, but if you can see the pattern of where the waves are breaking, you're already halfway there. Tell me, Sam, have you been surfing on your own before our lesson today?'

'Yes, I have.' He pulled a face.

'Oh, so it was that good, huh?' She laughed and Sam joined in.

'Yeah, I was rubbish. I kept falling off long before I reached the beach.'

'Okay, so that's what I'm trying to help you with. You need to start paddling and catch the wave before it breaks and don't forget as the height of the wave grows, it moves more quickly. So to catch it, you need to be paddling as fast or faster than the wave itself. Easy, right?'

'Hmm. There's a lot more to think about than I first realised.'

Sam looked back at the waves, watching for one that was about to crest. Seeing a wave he thought would work, he pointed his board to the beach and began to paddle. When he sensed the board was gliding on the wave, he pushed himself up to his standing position in one smooth movement and swayed a little until he felt his body find its balance. With his feet planted firmly in the position Amy had taught him, he kept his legs slightly bent to help maintain his balance and realised he was on target to reach the beach. He held his breath with anticipation and when he finally managed the whole journey, he felt euphoric. He jumped off his board and turned round to watch Amy as she rode her board in to join him. She had a massive smile on her face, and when he started jumping up and down with pleasure, she burst out laughing, only just managing to stay on her board until she landed on the beach.

'That was amazing!' Sam's adrenaline was still pumping as Amy joined him. She put her hand up for him to high-five it.

'That was what I'd call textbook, mate.'

In truth, he'd only needed a little guidance to remember his techniques. Now all he needed to do was to keep it up.

They called it a day then and returned to the main building so Sam could get changed. He thanked Amy and set off for the changing room, still smiling with delight from their work together. As he changed, he finally realised he'd been so engrossed in his lesson and his sense of achievement that he hadn't thought of Rachel at all. He only wished he could afford more than the one lesson to help him continue to move on with his life.

## Jessie

Jessie trudged back home through the muddy fields, feeling more tired than she had for a long time. When she'd arrived at the stables, she'd been surprised to see what a hive of activity it was these days. She'd also been happy to find so many familiar faces still working there and it had taken her no time to get chatting to her old friends as if she'd never been away. Time flew and before she knew it, it was time to come home, but she'd arranged to return another day to draw some of the horses with the owner's blessing, and also to try her hand at riding again.

When she pushed open the back door, she called out to see if anyone else was now home. Hearing no reply, she went upstairs and into her en-suite bathroom to run herself a bath. She stripped off her damp clothes, poured in some of the expensive bath creme she'd received at Christmas and inhaled the citrus smell of the oils as the water heated up. A few minutes later, she was covered in bubbles up to her chin. She pushed herself down into the water with a sigh. As she lay there, she thought again about Sam, and how much she was starting to care for him. Maybe she should let things play out and see what happened. Sam was a nice guy and he was obviously attracted to her. She reasoned with herself it might do her good to be with someone for the pleasure of it, with no strings attached if neither of them wanted that kind of commitment. She also knew he would be gentle with her and that was exactly what she needed for this first time after the miscarriage.

She lifted one of her hands out of the water and was surprised by the already prune-like nature of her skin. She must have been in the bath for ages. She sat up and pushed herself out of the bath to standing, pulling the plug out on the way. She reached for the towel she'd left warming on the radiator and wrapped it around herself to warm her body before drying off and stepping out of the tub. She slipped her feet into her fluffy slippers, tied the bath towel around her and wrapped her hair into a turban with the hand towel. It was time for a cup of tea, she thought, before getting herself dressed again.

She opened her bedroom door and made her way down the stairs to the first floor. Her mum would probably be home soon, although Jessie had no idea of the time. When she heard the sound of cups being placed on the counter in the kitchen and the kettle being filled, she realised her mum was already home. She skipped down the last few stairs that bit more quickly, eager to tell her about her visit to the riding stables. She walked through the door of the kitchen just as Sam turned round from the sink. It was too late for her to retreat. She wasn't sure which one of them was more shocked to see the other.

'Sam!' Jessie clutched the towel around her, dreading the thought of disaster adding to her embarrassment.

'God, Jessie, I didn't think there was anyone here. I'm sorry.' He glanced down at the kettle in his hands, his face flushed. He set the kettle down on the table and stuck his hands in the pockets of his jeans, refusing to look at her.

'It's fine, I'm the one who should be sorry for giving you a fright.' Jessie could feel her face heating up too. 'Look, I'll go and get dressed and see you in a minute.' She turned, but before she could escape, she felt his hand on her arm.

'Wait, don't go.'

Her heart beat rapidly at his touch and the suggestion underlying his words. Their bodies were close but not touching. Sam reached out to caress her cheek and she leaned into him as he bent his head to kiss her.

---

## Sam

Sam felt Jessie's soft body press against his and he pulled her as close as he could, caressing all her contours as far as the towel would allow him to. He let his hand rest against the small of her back. As she tipped her head up to meet his lips once more, the towel on her head came loose and fell to the floor, releasing her long, wet hair against his face as it tumbled down her back. Abruptly, he stopped kissing her and the only sound in the kitchen was of them both trying to catch their breath. He gazed down into Jessie's darkened eyes and was surprised to see the intensity of the desire in them. For a moment, neither of them said a word. He was overwhelmed by his need for her.

Then, after scooping up the towel, he took Jessie's hand and turned towards the doorway. She followed him without the slightest hesitation as he began to walk up the stairs. They carried on up to her room at her insistence and were soon standing in front of her bed. Sam watched mesmerised as she lifted her hand to the knot in the towel to release it and let it tumble to the floor. His gaze travelled hungrily over her soft curves and he was suddenly keen to be rid of all his clothes as well. She helped him with his jumper and shortly afterwards, with the belt on his jeans. As their bodies finally came together, skin on skin, he felt her shudder and a moment later, they were side by side on the small, double bed, caressing and kissing as though they simply couldn't get enough of one another. Sam finally eased his body over hers when he knew neither of them could wait any longer. As they became one, it was as if their bodies were made for each other and they fell into an easy rhythm together, building until neither of them could take any more. After they'd finished, Sam lay down on his side next to Jessie, feeling the soft sheen of sweat on her skin and enjoying the fact that their lovemaking had caused it.

Jessie's eyes were closed.

'Hey.' He stroked her arm gently, looking right at her so she would see him when she finally decided to open her eyes. 'You okay?'

She turned her face to look at him and smiled. 'Okay doesn't even begin to cover it.' She laughed and he joined in, relieved. He was so worried about hurting her physically after all she'd been through, but he'd taken his lead from her, and the signals she'd given him all suggested she'd enjoyed their closeness as much as he had.

They both got dressed and went downstairs once more to the kitchen. When the tea was made, they sat side by side at the table, each of them deep in thought.

'What's on your mind, Jessie?' Sam asked, breaking the silence.

'I'm just wondering where all this might be going between us. I know you'll be going home soon and I don't want to get in too deep only to have to watch you leave.' She bit her lip nervously.

Sam took her hand. 'I like you a lot, Jessie. It's been a long time since I felt I could be honest enough to say that to anyone other than Rachel. You're right, though, I will have to go home eventually.'

Jessie's face fell. Sam pushed his hands through his hair in frustration, not wanting to lead her on with the promise of something he probably wouldn't be able to deliver in the long-term.

'I'm sorry, Sam, I'm getting ahead of myself but I want you to know how much I like you as well.'

Her confidence had grown, and perhaps her belief in herself as well, and that made Sam glad.

'Perhaps we can see how things go, and use the time I'm here to get to know each other better, rather than thinking too far ahead?'

'I'd like that.' She leaned over and kissed him once more.

He groaned at the softness of her lips against his.

'If you keep kissing me like that, there's going to be no holding me back, Jessie.'

They heard the key in the lock and they both sat back. Sam stood up to go, smiling at Jessie on his way. He took in the frustrated look on her face and knew they would have to pick up the conversation where they'd left off at some point again soon.

# CHAPTER 7

## Jessie

'Hello, love. Is there any more tea in that pot?'

Jessie stood up to make the tea for her mum, using the familiar routine to steady herself after the wonderful experience she'd just had with Sam.

'You don't seem to have any bags. Didn't you say you and Val were going shopping?' Jessie asked. When her mum didn't reply, she turned round to look at her, only to find her mum with a sheepish look on her face.

'Sit down, love. I want to talk to you about something.'

'That sounds ominous,' she said but sat down anyway.

'It's nothing bad. It's just that I haven't seen Val today.'

'Yeah, I thought you'd been seeing a lot of her. So didn't you fancy it today?'

'No. I wasn't actually planning to see her at all, even though I said I was. I'm sorry, I've been a bit economical with the truth.'

Jessie's eyebrows shot up at this admission. Her mum sighed and Jessie reached out to take her hand.

'I'm sure it isn't so bad, Mum, that you can't tell me about it.'

'I've met a man, Jess. His name's Geoff and we've been seeing each other for about a year now.'

'Why haven't you told me before now? That's not like you to keep things from me.' Jessie spoke softly but found it hard to hide how hurt she felt.

'I thought you had enough to deal with at the moment. And I wasn't sure whether things would develop between Geoff and me so I didn't want to jump the gun.'

Jessie reached across the table and her mum did the same, taking her hands in hers. 'I'm so pleased for you, Mum. I just would have liked to share in your happiness sooner. I couldn't be happier for you if you've found someone you like and want to be with.'

Her mum smiled back at her and her face softened. 'The thing is, Jess, I love Geoff and I think... I think we could have a future together. And that's the first time since... since, well, you know.'

Jessie stood and put her arms around her mum's tiny frame for a hug. 'I'm so happy for you, Mum, I really am. I know how hurt you were, but if you're ready to move on now, that's great.' She pulled back to look at her, only to find her with tears in her eyes. 'And when am I going to get the chance to meet the elusive Geoff and find out all about how you both met, and what your plans are for the future?' Her eyes twinkled as she tried to distract her mum.

'Whenever you want, love. Why don't I invite him round for dinner one evening? Perhaps Sam would like to come along too.'

'That... that would be nice. I'm sure he'd appreciate that.' She glanced at her mum's expression and blushed. 'You know, don't you?'

'I am your mum after all,' her mum replied.

'We're keeping things simple, Mum. I don't know how long Sam will be here and neither does he, so don't get ahead of yourself.'

'I won't, Jessie. But whatever it is between you, as long as he takes care of you and it's what you want, that's all that matters.' Her mum smiled at her. 'Sam seems like a nice boy and I think you go well together.'

Jessie was grateful for her mum's understanding, but she took a deep breath, not wanting to engage in any further debate about it right at that moment.

'Anyway, there was something I wanted to talk to you about as well,' she said, deftly changing the subject.

'What's that love?'

'It's about the B&B. Every time you go out, I either have to stay here in case any new guests should turn up or I have to put up the "No Vacancies" sign, which makes me feel terrible.'

'Oh, Jessie, I'm sorry. I've been so selfish. I've hardly given the B&B a moment's thought in my hurry to spend as much time as I can with Geoff.' Helen heaved a sigh and smoothed a silvery hair out of her eyes.

'Don't feel guilty, Mum. We've looked after this place for years, you especially, and our lives have changed now. But we do need to decide what we're both going to do in the long term.'

'Have you had any more thoughts about whether you'll return to uni?'

'I've thought about it a lot but I still haven't made a final decision. I think I'm getting my love for illustration back at last though, so maybe I am finally ready to return. If I do return to university, I'd like to rent a place on my own if possible, but that would cost a fortune. And that's as far as I've got. I could maybe save up the money from working at the pub for a bit to get me going when I first go back.'

'That would take forever, Jessie. I understand you want to be on your own though. It's just a question of how we'll manage it.'

'Well, we can keep talking it over and I'm sure we'll work something out in the end.' Jessie glanced up at her mum and could see in the look she gave her that she wasn't any more convinced of that than she was.

'The thing is, Jess, I've been thinking about this as well and I do have an idea but I'm not sure if you'll like it.'

Jessie stared at her mum, wondering what she could possibly have in mind.

### Sam

Sam stretched out on the bed, thinking about what Jessie had said to him. He didn't want their relationship to be 'friends with benefits'. He could only see trouble ahead for the two of them if things went that way, and the last thing he wanted was to hurt Jessie more than she'd been hurt already.

He hadn't planned to be away from home for more than a few days, but if he went home now, there was no way Jessie would not be hurt. As he lay there pondering his dilemma, his phone buzzed in his shirt pocket. It was another text from Matt. It caught him by surprise coming so soon after the last one.

'*Just checking you're still okay all the way down there. Wanted to let you know Rachel is stopping in here this w/e on way home from honeymoon in case you want to extend your hols.*'

Sam groaned. Thank goodness for his brother's foresight in letting him know. He didn't think he was ready to face Rachel again right now. At least he would be able to stay for a few more days and spend time with Jessie. Perhaps by then he would have worked out a plan that would work for both of them.

He made his way downstairs again, having decided to get on and do some of the other jobs that needed doing around the house. He bypassed the kitchen, heading towards the back of the house where he'd left the toolbox that morning. As he bent down to retrieve his tool belt, he noticed a small, upright piano in the corner of the dining room. The top half was covered with a throw, so he hadn't spotted it before. He wondered if Jessie was the one who played it and he resolved to ask her about it when he got the chance. He straightened up so he could make a start. He could hear Jessie and her mum talking in the kitchen but didn't catch any of the words. He was just fixing a loose piece of skirting board back to the wall when Helen appeared.

'Sam, I'm sorry to interrupt, but I wonder if you could join us in the kitchen for a minute.'

Sam couldn't hide his surprise and he was suddenly worried Helen might think he'd overstepped the mark with Jessie, given all she'd been through. He followed her along the corridor and took a seat on the other side of the kitchen table from Jessie.

'Mrs. Pascoe, if this is about me and Jessie...'

'It's Helen and no, it's not about you and Jessie, but if you want to know, I'm very happy the two of you are getting on so well.' She smiled kindly at them both and Jessie blushed bright red. Sam took Jessie's hand and laughed.

'Don't be embarrassed, Jessie. It is normal, you know,' Sam said, trying to reassure her, but she only groaned more.

'Shhh,' she told him, and he fell silent, not wanting to make her feel worse.

'I've just been telling Jessie that I've met someone. His name is Geoff and I think the time is right for us to get together properly, as a couple.'

Sam looked at Jessie, wondering why Helen was telling him this.

'The thing is, my heart hasn't been in running the B&B for a long time now and I don't think Jess wants to do it any more, either. So, I was wondering if you would help us fix it up with a view to selling it?' Helen took in a deep breath.

'Well, yes, if you're only doing what you absolutely have to in order to make it presentable for sale.'

'There is a lot that needs doing – most of the rooms need repainting, and there are some odd woodwork jobs that need doing as well, like the sticky doors and broken skirting boards you've already made a start on – but there's nothing major. I'd pay you a proper wage, of course,' she continued, 'but I'd like to get it done within a week, or two at the most. Do you think that's feasible?'

Sam nodded, but Jessie interrupted before he could speak again.

'How are we going to pay for all that though, Mum?' She cast an apologetic glance at Sam.

'I still have some savings left, Jessie, so don't worry about that. So that's settled then. We'll start tomorrow.'

———————

The following week got off to a busy start, with everyone tackling a different task from Helen's to-do list. Sam finished off fixing the loose skirting boards on the ground floor before repainting them. Meanwhile, Jessie and her mum continued with the repainting of the upstairs rooms. Sam then moved outside to start work on clearing the gutters and tidying up the back garden and the front driveway. It was tedious, back-breaking work for all of them, but by the end of the second day, when they met up for a cup of tea in the kitchen, they could see their efforts were starting to pay off.

'What shall I do tomorrow, Helen? Do you have a preference from what's left on the list?' Sam asked after swallowing a mouthful of tea.

'Well, if you've finished outside, I think it would be good for you to follow us round upstairs fixing and repainting the skirting boards in the rooms we've done.'

Sam nodded and glanced over at Jessie, who'd been very quiet since they'd come in.

'You okay, Jessie?' he asked. She didn't reply at once, seemingly lost in her own thoughts. 'Jessie?' He touched her arm lightly.

'What?' She jumped slightly before turning her green eyes on him and focusing on his face. 'Sorry, were you talking to me? I was miles away.'

'I was asking if you were okay.'

'Yes, I'm fine.' A faint blush crept up her cheeks. Sam decided not to press things in front of her mum.

'Are you working at the pub tonight?'

'Yes, do you want to come and keep me company?'

'Absolutely. My body is crying out for one of those burgers.' They laughed together and the moment of tension passed.

A couple of hours later, they walked hand in hand down to the pub and Sam tried again to find out what was on her mind.

'Is everything okay? You seemed deep in thought about something earlier, and I sensed it was something you didn't want to say in front of your mum.'

'I don't know how to tell you, Sam, without sounding all needy and complaining.' She glanced at him to find him studying her.

'Are you trying to tell me you miss my body?' He laughed and she smiled at his attempt to be arrogant, knowing he was nothing like that.

'There is that, of course,' she replied in a breathy voice, squeezing his hand. 'But...' She stopped in the middle of the pavement, looking down at the tarmac as she gathered all her courage to say what was really on her mind. 'I assume once the work is done on the B&B, you'll go home again and I know I'm going to miss you, that's all.'

Sam pulled her into his arms and kissed her lightly on the lips, feeling her body melt into his.

'I don't have to go home straight away, you know. I'm my own man. I can stay here as long as I like, or as long as you like.' He didn't tell her he wouldn't be going home until Rachel had left for definite, although that was on his mind as well.

'You will go home at some point, though, and when that time comes, I know it's going to be hard for me to say goodbye to you.'

She turned and started walking towards the pub again, leaving Sam to ponder what she'd said, as well as what she'd left unsaid. When they reached the pub, he took a seat at the bar, watching her as she greeted the customers with her usual, easy-going manner. After a few minutes, she brought him a pint of Doom Bar, setting it down in front of him with a small smile, but she didn't say anything. He was glad to see her workmate was back on duty tonight, so Jessie didn't have to manage everything on her own. Soon, his thoughts returned to their earlier conversation.

He liked Jessie and it seemed she liked him too. Once the B&B was sold, he wondered what she would do with her life. Would she go back to uni or would she move in with her mum and her new boyfriend?

'Penny for them?' Jessie asked, suddenly appearing before him once again. 'You just pulled an awful face so it must have been pretty bad.' She tilted her head to one side.

'Oh, no, I was thinking about ordering something to eat, that's all.' He laughed to cover up the lie, but when he looked up at her again, he could see she wasn't fooled.

'Another burger then?' He nodded and she walked away without another word. Sam hoped they'd get the chance to talk later after her shift. In the meantime, he needed to get clear in his mind what he wanted from her. He couldn't afford to let her down by not being honest with her. In his heart, he knew he had nothing to go home for, except his family. He had no job there, but then he didn't have one here, either. He took a sip of his beer as he considered how much he'd enjoyed fixing up the B&B for sale and keeping himself busy again. He could find odd jobs to do around this area, he was sure, if he and Jessie decided to make a go of things together, but he wasn't getting any younger, and the time for working at odd jobs had passed for him. He wanted to settle down somewhere, to know what he was doing week in, week out and who he was doing it for. He looked up to find Jessie staring at him and he smiled.

---

On the walk home, Sam tried several times to tell Jessie what he'd been thinking about earlier, but in the end, he didn't say a word. He didn't want to reveal the full extent of his feelings without her saying something first. From the way she'd been so hesitant towards him at times, she probably felt just as vulnerable as he did. They reached the B&B in no time and still neither of them had managed to express their feelings.

'Jessie, I... I...' he began at last once they were inside, but she cut him off. He readied himself for her rejection.

'Don't worry, Sam. We've had some fun, but we both knew it wouldn't last. Let's not analyse it to death and spoil what we had. I'll see you in the morning.' He read in her eyes that she was trying to be brave but her face fell as she turned away to climb the stairs.

The minute he saw her mask slip, Sam knew she really did have feelings for him. He reached out and grabbed her hand, hearing her gasp at the contact. She stopped on the second stair with her back to him.

'I thought you said you were missing my body,' he joked, trying to move them back to where they'd been in happier moments together. He stepped up behind her and pressed his body close to hers, slipping his arms around her waist. He heard her sniff then and in a second, he spun her round to face him, dismayed at the sight of the tears streaming down her face.

'I don't want meaningless sex, however much I might be missing your body.' Her voice caught on the final syllable and he pulled her into his arms, wanting to take away all her pain. 'I'm sorry if I gave you that impression.'

'I told you I wanted to get to know you better,' Sam whispered to her. 'And nothing has changed about how I feel. I'm not going to run away from you and I definitely don't want to hurt you.' She raised her head from his shoulder and he brushed away one last tear from her cheek before kissing her gently in the very same spot. Then he took her hand in his and stepped around her to continue on up the stairs to his room. When they reached the door, he held on tightly to her hand while he removed the key from his pocket and opened up.

'Are you sure about this, Sam? I know everything has moved so fast between us,' she said softly behind him as he led her into his room and closed the door. He took her face gently in his hands and kissed her firmly.

'You're right, things have moved quickly but I have never been more sure about anything.' He watched her face light up with a smile before he kissed her once again.

# CHAPTER 8

**Jessie**

When Jessie awoke, it was still dark and Sam's arms were wrapped tightly around her, as if he couldn't bear to let her go. She moved slightly, trying not to wake him, and remembered how passionate their lovemaking had been the night before. She had no doubt he was developing deeper feelings for her, just as she was for him. They would have to talk in the morning so they both knew where they stood with each other. She sighed gently and heard Sam respond in his sleep.

She went over the state of her life one more time, hoping when she'd finished, a solution to her current problems would have presented itself to her, despite nothing having changed since her last review. She still had no idea where she was going to live once the B&B was sold. She'd been thinking more and more about returning to uni, but she wanted to know what Sam's plans were before she made her mind up about that. She would only know what he wanted to do if she asked him and asking him might put their whole relationship in danger if he felt she was forcing his hand. This time, she heaved a bigger sigh and Sam stirred as he let her go and rolled on to his back.

Jessie glanced at the clock and saw it was nearly seven. She was ready to get up but she didn't want to leave Sam, so she turned around to face him. She studied his profile as he lay there sleeping next to her, admiring everything about him from his messy blonde hair to the sexy angle of his jaw, covered as it was in a light stubble.

He rolled towards her and enveloped her in a hug.

'Were you staring at me while I slept?' he whispered seductively.

'Well, I thought I was but you were awake all the time and probably lapping up the attention.' Jessie smiled and accepted his good morning kiss. She could feel his arousal pressing into her as their bodies moved closer and she smiled with delight at his obvious attraction for her. They kissed and the strength of feeling Sam put into it stretched all the way down to Jessie's toes. She pulled away after a moment, though, still distracted by all the thoughts running through her mind.

'What is it, Jessie?' he asked.

She closed her eyes briefly in an attempt to stop him seeing deep inside her soul. 'I thought you were trying to tell me something about how much you're attracted to me,' she said, desperate to avoid the subject.

'I was, and I am.' He grinned. 'But I have a feeling you have other things on your mind. You look like you've been thinking.'

Jessie glanced down, worried about how to tell him all that was on her mind. Sam reached out to touch her cheek, and she looked up at him again.

'Can I ask you a question that's been on my mind?' he said.

She nodded, her eyes widening in anticipation.

'Have you thought what you'd like to do once your mum sells the B&B?'

Jessie's body sagged with relief. Sam had been thinking about her future too. Maybe even their future.

'I have thought about it, yes, and I know I don't want to move in with Mum and Geoff. I need to start living my own life again now.'

'Okay. When you picture your own life, what do you see yourself doing?'

Jessie wanted to open up to him but she was afraid. She stared at him for a moment, suddenly wondering whether he was also showing her he was prepared to open up to her by asking these questions.

'I think I'd like to finish my degree but...' She paused and looked away from him again.

'But...' Sam lifted her chin and smiled. 'Falmouth is a long way away?'

'Yes, and...' Jessie drew in a big breath and then closed her eyes. 'I want to know what your plans are before I make up my mind. Your plans as far as I'm concerned, I mean.' She kept her eyes tight shut, waiting for him to speak, unable to contemplate how she would deal with his rejection. She couldn't believe how quickly he'd come to mean so much to her.

'Okay. My turn now,' she heard him say. She opened her eyes in surprise because he hadn't rejected her, not yet anyway. 'I've never been one for making plans in my life but I think now would be a good time to start. I feel it's time for me to settle somewhere now and to put down roots, to get a proper job so I can get my own place.'

'And I suppose it would make sense for you to do that at home in Dorset, where your family are?' Jessie asked with trepidation, biting her lip.

'It would make sense,' Sam replied, nodding.

Jessie's face fell.

'Except for one thing,' he continued.

'What's that?' she whispered.

'You wouldn't be there and that wouldn't make any sense to me at all if we want to get to know each other better.'

Jessie blew out a long breath.

'Would you come with me to Falmouth then?'

'Is that an invitation?' He reached out and touched her lip before leaning in close to her and kissing her. The kiss deepened and it was some time before Jessie finally replied to his question.

'Yes, please. Come with me.'

'Nothing would give me greater pleasure.' And he kissed her again, putting everything he had into showing her how much he was falling for her.

———

Within a few more days, the B&B was ready and Helen had estate agents coming round to value the place. Even though it wasn't in the best condition, the B&B was still in a good location, and with six letting rooms and good-sized accommodation for the owners too, the agents predicted a lot of interest. The morning after they'd put it on the market, one of the agents called to arrange a viewing. Jessie decided she needed to talk to her mum about her plans before things went any further.

They were in the kitchen having a cup of tea and Sam had gone up to his room to call home. This was as good a time as any.

'So, Mum, I've made a decision and I'm going to go back to uni to finish my illustration degree.'

She kept her eyes trained on her mum's face the whole time to see what her reaction to this news was going to be.

'Well, that's great news, love. And you're going back to Falmouth to complete the course there, are you?' Her forehead creased with a small frown.

'Yes, I think it makes sense to finish it where I started. I won't be on my own though this time.' Jessie waited for the penny to drop.

Her mum gave her a broad smile. 'Oh, Sam's going to go with you?'

Jessie nodded and accepted her mum's hug, surprised the conversation had gone so well.

'As long as you're both sure about it,' Helen went on. 'I think it's time for you to try again with someone new and just see where it goes.'

'Like you say, we're going to take our time and see where things go between us.' Her mum nodded and Jessie sensed her relief. 'And you don't mind that I won't be moving in with you and Geoff?'

'Of course not. It's time you got on with your own life. You don't want to be hanging round with us at your age. I'm pleased you and Sam are getting on so well together. I think he's going to be good for you, and you for him.'

'As the house is up for sale now, would you mind if we went to Dorset for a bit so I can meet his family? He suggested it yesterday and it sounds like a good idea.'

'That sounds like a wonderful idea to me. I'm going to move all my personal stuff to Geoff's now and just leave the furnishings that will be sold with the business.'

Sam came back into the kitchen at that point. His usually tanned face was ashen. Jessie stood up and went to him.

'Sam, what is it? You look terrible.'

Sam grasped onto Jessie's arms for support. 'It's my dad. He's had a heart attack and they want me to go home straight away.'

'Oh, Sam, I'm so sorry,' Jessie said, her eyes full of sadness for him.

'How quickly can you be ready to go, do you think?' Sam asked.

'Me?'

'Yes, I know this changes our plans slightly but I still want you to come with me. I'm not going to abandon you just because my situation has changed.'

'Sam, you need time with your family and they don't know me at all. I understand if you want to go on your own to be with them. I'll still be here when you come back.'

'No, Jessie. This is the most important time for us to be together and I want my family to meet you. Please, come with me.' He pulled her into his arms and she knew he meant it.

In the background, Helen coughed lightly to remind them she was still there.

'Is there anything I can do to help?' she asked, her eyes shining with tears.

'Oh, Mum,' Jessie cried and reached out to hug her as Sam slipped away upstairs again to begin packing up his stuff.

'Go with him, Jess, it's the right thing to do. He needs you even more at a time like this and you were going to go off for a bit together, anyway. Everything will be fine here. I've got Geoff to help me if anything crops up. Please keep in touch though, won't you?'

'I will, Mum, I promise. Will you come and help me decide what to pack? I've got a feeling I'm going to struggle to fit anything of mine into one of those panniers.'

---

## Sam

They were on the road within the hour, the two panniers filled to the brim on either side of the bike but balanced by the weight of an extra person for the return journey. Sam was desperate to get home as quickly as possible, so they'd agreed only to stop briefly when they reached the halfway point, just after Exeter. The feel of Jessie's warm body behind his comforted him and distracted him from all the anxiety he felt about his dad's condition. He just hoped they'd arrive at the hospital before his dad got any worse.

After a quick stop at a service station outside Exeter, they set off again, thankful for the increased warmth of the sun as the day progressed. It was mid-afternoon by the time they reached the hospital car park. Sam looked at the familiar building with sadness as he remembered the time he'd spent there after his accident on the building site. His mind naturally jumped to Rachel and the memory of her visits to him during that stay. He'd told her how much he loved her and wanted to be with her, but in the end she'd left with Jackson for a second time. He sighed.

Jessie tapped him on the shoulder and he climbed off, then helped her to get down safely before removing his helmet.

'Are you okay? You were deep in thought.' Her beautiful face was filled with concern and he touched her cheek briefly with his palm.

'Just remembering the last time I was here, that's all. I had an accident when I was working on a building site last year, and it was pretty bad. I was in here for quite a while with a broken leg and some broken ribs too. I don't have any fond memories of the place.'

Sam took her hand as they walked inside to look for the Coronary Care Unit. His pace picked up as they drew closer to the lift, knowing he'd wasted time dwelling on the past. Another part of him almost didn't want to get there, though, frightened by the thought of what he might see. The doors to the lift opened. They stepped out onto the fifth floor and headed for the ward. Once they'd been let in, Sam approached the desk to ask after his dad, holding on to Jessie's hand all the while.

'Mr. Andrews is in room three,' the nurse told him. 'The rest of your family are with him at the moment.'

As they approached his dad's room, Sam felt Jessie tug a little on his hand and he stopped to look at her.

'They won't be expecting me, Sam. Shouldn't you go in on your own first?' She was biting her lip anxiously.

'I don't want to leave you on your own out here but I can understand you being nervous about meeting them. You don't have anything to worry about though, honestly. Trust me?'

She nodded but didn't look convinced.

He knocked softly on the sterile-looking grey door before continuing inside with Jessie following behind him. His mum was sitting on one side of the bed, with Jenna and Matt on the other. His dad was hooked up to various beeping machines and his eyes were closed. His mum tore herself away from him and gave Sam a small smile before pushing herself to her feet with obvious effort. She came round the bed to give him a hug and as he advanced further into the room, her gaze moved to Jessie standing behind him.

'Mum, this is Jessie.'

His mum reached out to shake Jessie's hand and she tried to smile but her lip wobbled.

'Hello, I'm Sarah. I'm sorry we're meeting you like this, Jessie,' she said, trying to regain some self-control.

She sat back down and Sam took Jessie's hand again before introducing her to Jenna and Matt. Jenna turned round briefly to give them both a quick smile but she didn't say anything, reminding Sam that they hadn't parted on very good terms. He looked at Matt but his brother just shrugged. He would have to apologise to her later.

'How is he, Mum?'

'He's stable, Sam, but they're keeping him sedated for now while they carry out all their tests. We won't know any more until they've finished them.'

'Have you had anything to eat? You look like you could do with a break.' He glanced at his brother in the hope Matt would back him up. Matt gave a small shake of his head, which Sam took to mean there was no point in trying to persuade his mum to do anything that involved leaving his dad. He pulled up two chairs for him and Jessie, and soon the only sound in the room came from the endlessly beeping machines.

---

## Jessie

After about half an hour of the most tense silence she could ever remember, Jessie forced herself to stand up. She wasn't at all comfortable being there when she wasn't a family member.

'I'm going to go and get a coffee. Does anyone else want anything?' She looked around the room.

'I'll come with you.' Sam made to stand up but she put her hand on his shoulder to stop him.

'No, I'll be fine. Would you like a drink?'

He shook his head and slumped in his seat, all the fight seeming to have gone out of him.

As soon as Jessie stepped outside the room, she drew in a deep breath of air that wasn't tainted by tension or illness. She felt like such a spare part and wished she hadn't come. Still, there was no way out of it now and she wanted to support Sam, she really did. She just didn't know if her presence at this terrible time was making things worse for him.

She found the café in no time and waited in the queue to buy a cup of coffee, lost in her own thoughts. As she turned away from the till, she glanced up searching for the sugar stand and saw Matt coming towards her. He gave her a tentative smile, which she returned.

'Is everything okay?' she asked.

'Yes, I just thought you might be getting the wrong idea about us from the reception you've received. I didn't think that was fair so I've come to try and make things right. Shall we sit down for a bit?'

They sat down at the nearest clean table and Jessie wondered what to say.

'The thing is,' he began, 'Sam and Jenna had a bit of a row before he left. She hasn't completely forgiven him for what he did, so she's waiting on him to apologise.' He rolled his eyes.

Jessie smiled. 'What did they argue about?'

Matt blew out a long breath. 'I'm not sure I can say much about that. I don't know how much Sam has already told you and I don't want to put my foot in it. I just wanted you to know she hasn't got anything against you. I left him there in the hope they can sort it out while we're gone.'

'Well, thanks for coming to talk to me. It was a bit awkward in there. I told Sam I shouldn't have come with him but he wanted me to, and we had planned to come up here shortly anyway.'

'How did you two meet, then?'

Jessie filled him in, then added, 'My mum's selling off the B&B now though. She's had enough of trying to make ends meet, and also, she's met someone after years of being on her own. She's looking to settle down.'

'And you? Are you looking to settle down?'

Jessie blushed, but Matt kept looking right into her eyes. She realised just how close he was to Sam.

'I'm going to go back to university in Falmouth when the B&B is sold... and Sam's going to come with me. He's told me he's ready to put down roots somewhere and get a place of his own. Falmouth is as good a place as any, I guess. I know we haven't known each other very long but we have become very close. This will give us a chance to get to know each other even better.' She shrugged, not knowing if she'd passed the test or not.

Matt nodded but didn't say anything. Jessie finished her last mouthful of coffee and stood up, eager to get back to Sam, and away from Matt's subtle but persistent questioning.

They walked along the sterile corridors, neither of them saying a word. Jessie reached the room first and opened the door to see Sam with his arms wrapped around a woman she didn't recognise, his head resting on her shoulder. He looked up when she came in and straightened immediately, stepping away quickly from the woman who was now looking closely at her.

She came forward and put out her hand.

'You must be Jessie,' she said. 'I'm Rachel.'

Jessie shook her hand and moved nearer to Sam but she didn't touch him. He didn't reach for her either. Suddenly, Jessie was tired of being the only person who didn't know all the minute details of Sam's history. She picked up her bag and lifted her jacket from the chair.

'I'm going to go, Sam,' she said.

'What, Jessie? No, you don't need to go.'

She turned towards the door, and the others moved out of her way, all of them unable to look her in the eye.

Sam followed her out to the corridor and caught her arm.

'Please don't go. I need you with me.' The look in his eyes was sincere and he nearly broke her resolve but in the end, he didn't quite manage it.

'It hasn't felt like you needed me here since we arrived, Sam. I can't sit in that room any longer trying to deal with tensions and history I know nothing about because you haven't told me. I wanted to be here to support you after what's happened to your dad but if you want me to stay, you need to put me in the picture about everything that's gone before.'

# CHAPTER 9

**Sam**

Sam watched in desperation as Jessie turned away from him and headed towards the lifts. He pushed his hands through his hair and let out a low groan, knowing he couldn't win whatever he chose to do next.

'Jessie! Please, wait.' He ran to catch her up, arriving just as the doors to one of the lifts opened.

She stopped and looked at his face. He could sense her hurt and hated himself.

'Well?' she asked when he didn't say anything.

'I know you're right and I do want to tell you everything, but I need to let them know where I'm going and that I'll be back later, okay?' He gave her an imploring look, hoping she would accept his explanation. 'Will you wait here for me? I'll only be a moment, I promise.'

Jessie spotted a chair in the area in front of the lifts and fell into it, suddenly exhausted from everything that had happened since they first heard the news about Sam's dad. Before she knew it, Sam was back and crouching down in front of her so he could look directly into her eyes.

'Jessie, I'm so sorry about this. Why don't we go and get a coffee somewhere so we can talk this all over?'

She nodded and he stood up, extending his hand to pull her up from the chair. He held on to her hand all the way down to the ground floor and on the walk to the car park. Within ten minutes, they were sitting inside a coffee shop on the quayside, warming their hands against their hot cups and recovering from the onslaught of the wind against their faces on the short ride from the hospital. Neither of them seemed to know how to start the conversation so they sat in silence for a few minutes. Eventually, Sam put down his cup and looked over at Jessie.

'I'll start by telling you about Jenna, shall I?'

Jessie glanced at him and gave him a slight nod. She'd heard some of the story from Matt, of course, but she wanted to hear the whole thing from Sam.

'Jenna is Rachel's best friend.'

Jessie had to stop herself from rolling her eyes.

'After Rachel met Jackson here and then went back to Nashville with him, Jenna went to visit them. While she was there, she met Will and they got together. At Rachel's wedding, Jackson announced he was opening an office of his record label over here, in London, and that he'd asked Will to run it for him. So Will and Jenna have been living together here ever since.' Sam paused and looked at Jessie to see if she was still listening.

'Go on,' she said.

'Just before I left for Cornwall, they came over for Sunday lunch at our house. I'd been in a bit of a bad way since the wedding and I couldn't face them being all loved up and him particularly, being all, you know, American, and so I refused to come out of my room to see them.' He looked sheepish but he wasn't prepared for Jessie's reaction. She burst into laughter. He watched her in amazement. How could she laugh at something so pathetic?

'Tell me,' she said when she'd got herself back under control, 'what does being "all American" look like?' She smiled and Sam blushed.

'I know, it's ridiculous but I was jealous of Jackson, and of Will by extension. They'd got their girl and I hadn't so I found it hard to be around Will as well. Jenna couldn't understand that, and she was angry at me, quite rightly. I knew I needed a change of scene after that. I need to speak to her to apologise for my behaviour last time, and then everything should be okay.'

'Okay, that all chimes in with what Matt told me.'

'Did you know all that already?' He looked at her in surprise.

'Some, but not all of it, so thank you for being honest. Matt was giving me the third degree in the café, wanting to know how we'd met and whether I was ready to settle down with you. I can see now he was looking out for you, that's all.'

'And that just leaves Rachel,' Sam said, after a minute.

'I guess there's more to what happened than you've already told me.' Jessie tried to look sympathetic but she wasn't sure if she managed to pull it off. Inside she was still hurting about the way he was keeping things from her.

'You're right and I'm sorry. When I was in the hospital here, after the accident, she came to see me. She and Jackson had fallen out after only a few weeks. I told her again that I loved her, that I'd look after her and support her in her dreams to become a country singer.' Jessie's eyebrows raised at that and he realised that although he'd told her about playing guitar in the band, he hadn't revealed the extent of Rachel's ambitions and how they'd fallen out over them.

'But she turned you down and went back to Jackson, right?'

'Yep. It took me a very long time to get over her after that. But I did and I wished her well. I even went to their wedding, as you know. And I've been trying to move on ever since.'

## **Jessie**

'Is there anything else you want to know?' Sam studied her face.

Jessie was in complete turmoil and she wondered if he understood he was responsible for that.

'Yes, there is.' Jessie focused her green eyes on him, hoping to wear him down with the strength of her scrutiny. 'I want you to tell me honestly whether you still love Rachel. I don't think you're completely over her yet.'

'I think there'll always be a part of me that loves her, Jessie, but it's not about that. It's about whether I can get over my love for Rachel and move on to love someone else in the way they deserve.'

'How did you feel when you saw her at the hospital?' Jessie asked, not letting up with her questioning for even a second.

'I... I was so surprised to see her at first, I didn't know how I felt apart from that. And then she was hugging me and I was expecting it to be so difficult, you know, when she touched me.' Sam swallowed nervously. 'But it felt like I was just hugging my friend again. There was none of that old spark there.'

Jessie's eyebrows shot up.

'So...?' she whispered.

'I guess that means I have moved on and it's all because of you.' He reached across the table and took Jessie's hand at last, and she was happy to let him. She released a long breath and then smiled at him.

'I'm so relieved to hear you say that, Sam. And I think Rachel would be happy to know it too. It must have been hard on her as well, trying to deal with all this when she cares so much for you.'

Sam stared at her, his mouth dropping open.

'You are such a caring person. Not many people would care how Rachel felt in all this, you know. They'd just be consumed with jealousy.'

She shrugged. 'I have to confess to being a bit jealous, I can't lie about that, but I wouldn't want you and Rachel to lose your friendship over this. You've known each other a long time.'

'We have and I wouldn't want to lose our friendship either.' He paused briefly. 'I realised when I was telling you everything that I've never told you much about our band and my guitar playing.'

She shook her head, swishing her hair as she did so. Sam's face was a picture and she wondered what exactly was going through his mind.

'Are you okay? You're blushing.' She put her hand on his arm and he stood up, putting his hand out towards her. Whatever was on his mind, he wasn't going to tell her anything.

'Come on, time to go,' he said.

As Sam passed Jessie her helmet, she spoke again.

'Will you play your guitar for me some time?'

He leaned in and kissed her lightly.

'I'd do anything for you.'

---

When they returned to the hospital room, Matt and Rachel had gone. Jenna and Sam's mum both looked up as they came in. When Jenna smiled at them both, Sam could see her steely outer shell towards him was softening at last.

'Can we talk for a minute?' Jenna asked Sam. At his nod, she led the way out of the room and Jessie found herself alone with Sam's mum.

'Has there been any news while we've been gone?' she asked.

'No, love, they're still running their tests. It's been hours now and I don't know how much longer I can take.' Her voice cracked on the last word and she stifled a sob.

'I'm so sorry. I know it must be hard.'

Sam's mum looked at her for a long moment. She had strikingly dark hair and eyes, so different from Sam, but Jessie had sensed her kindness from the first moment of meeting her.

'I wish we could have met under nicer circumstances, I really do. I'm so pleased to see Sam moving on and to see he's met such a lovely person in you. I know we've only just met but I'm usually a good judge of character.'

Jessie blushed and looked down at her hands in her lap. When she looked up again, she was dismayed to see tears in Sarah's eyes. She stood up at once and walked round to the other side of the bed to put her arm around Sam's mum. She comforted her while she cried but didn't say anything, unsure of what would be the right thing to say, anyway. She just knew Sarah needed to let it all out and she was happy to be her shoulder for that moment. She was still holding her when the door to the room opened again, signalling Sam and Jenna's return. Sarah pulled herself together at once, reaching in her pocket for a tissue and squeezing Jessie's hand at the same time. Jessie was glad she'd been able to provide some comfort to this woman she hardly knew but was already becoming very fond of.

'Is everything all right now?' Sarah asked looking pointedly at first Sam, then Jenna. They nodded, both looking a little contrite.

'Any idea when the doctor will be back, Mum?' Sam asked.

'No, it's been hours now and I'm so desperate to know your dad's going to be okay.' She wiped her eyes again and Sam paled as he watched her struggle with her feelings.

'I'll go and see if I can find out any information,' he said and with a quick glance at Jessie, he disappeared out of the room.

They all fell silent again and Jessie worried how much longer she could put up with the incessant beeping. A minute later, the silence was broken by the door opening again. Everyone looked up at once to find the doctor ready to talk to Sarah. His awkward air suggested he had bad news to impart.

'Could I talk to you outside for a minute please, Mrs. Andrews?' he said eventually, coughing to clear his throat.

'Of course.' Sarah straightened up, head held high and walked towards the door. Jenna went to follow her out but at the last moment, she turned to Jessie.

'Come on, Jessie. Don't stay in here on your own. You should be with us while we hear the news.'

Jessie smiled gratefully at her and followed them all out to the hallway. Sam was talking to one of the nurses at the reception desk. When he saw them come out, he caught up with them, taking Jessie's hand in his as he did so. They entered the sterile family waiting room and sat down on the uncomfortable, plastic chairs, seemingly specially made for moments like this one. They all turned as one to look at the doctor.

---

## Sam

'We have now completed all our tests,' the doctor began, 'and the news is encouraging.' Sam looked at his mum and watched her blow out a long breath. He reached for her hand and she grasped it tightly. 'We can see no sign of brain damage from our tests but, and this is important, we won't know for sure until we wake Mr. Andrews up.'

'When are you going to wake my dad up, then?' Jenna was first to ask.

'We'll start the process of drawing him out of sedation tomorrow morning, but it will be a gradual process and may take a few days. I would therefore recommend you all go home tonight and get some rest. You can come back tomorrow afternoon for an update. Should there be any news before then, I will ring you of course, Mrs. Andrews.'

Sarah stared at the doctor in what looked like disbelief before saying, 'I can't just leave him here with no-one that loves him by his side.' Tears were falling down her face now and Sam enveloped her in his arms for a hug.

'Mum, this is for the best. You need a rest and it will do Dad good as well, before all that's going to happen tomorrow. We can get here at once if they need us but you do need some sleep.'

Sam's mum slumped in his arms.

'Please listen to your son, Mrs. Andrews. We'll leave your husband to rest tonight and then start the procedure in the morning.

If there are no more questions, I must get on but I will see you tomorrow.'

The doctor left the room and Jenna followed him outside. When she returned, she went to her mum too.

'Mum, we don't want to see you falling ill as well. Please listen to the doctor and come home.' She carefully put her arm round her mum's shoulders and led her out to the corridor.

'I will go home, Jenna, but I want to come back again in the morning. I can't wait until the afternoon.'

Jenna nodded and guided her towards the lifts. Sam and Jessie followed behind. When the lift arrived, they were all surprised to see Matt burst out of it, and then dismayed to see the look of worry that crossed his face at the sight of them all leaving together.

'It's okay, Matt, Dad's fine. We're going home for the night.' Sam filled him in on what had happened as they went down to the ground floor before they split up to make their way home.

Sam and Jessie arrived at the family home before the others and Sam took her to his room. He longed to spend some time with her for a bit after all that had happened. He put down the panniers in the corner by the large double-fronted bay window and watched as she walked around the room taking in all the details. She stopped in front of his guitar and reached out to gently touch the strings.

'I wish we'd talked more about your band and your guitar playing,' she said softly.

Sam frowned slightly, wondering why that would have made a difference.

Jessie went on. 'It's just that... it's...'

Sam stood up and went to her. He took her hands and bent down a little so he could look into her eyes.

'What is it, Jess? You can tell me anything.'

'It's just that before everything bad happened to me... I used to write my own songs and sing.'

Sam gasped and held her at arm's length to study her face.

'So it was you who used to play the piano at the B&B?'

'I haven't touched one for years now, let alone written any songs or done any singing. That time has come and gone for me, I think.'

Sam wrapped his arms around her and held her tight, wanting to protect her from any more terrible things happening in her life.

'Music can be very healing, they say. And though, like you, I haven't played any music for a while, I think now it might be just the thing for both of us, to help us start again.'

He kissed her softly and then they hugged again. He was sure they were going to be good for each other in the months to come, if they could only get through this crisis with his dad. As Jessie moved away to continue her unpacking, he finally admitted to himself how glad he was to have told her everything about Rachel. He hoped he was over her now and that nothing else was going to happen to test his willpower.

# CHAPTER 10

## Sam

Just as Jessie and Sam finished unpacking their things, they heard the front door open downstairs. Everyone else had arrived. Sam went down to join them, leaving Jessie to finish sorting her things out. His mum came in first, followed by Matt and then Jenna.

'Are you okay, Mum?' he asked as she came in, reaching out to her for a hug.

She didn't reply but let out a loud sob instead. Sam's heart felt like it might break for her.

'I need to get some sleep, Sam,' she said, finally pulling away from his warm embrace. He nodded and let her go. 'I'll see you all tomorrow,' she told Matt and Jenna, who nodded in agreement and watched as she walked slowly up the stairs.

'I'd better get off myself, but I'll see you all at the hospital tomorrow,' Matt said as he turned to leave.

'Me too. I haven't seen Will for days.' Jenna looked as exhausted as her mum, and Sam was worried about her.

'Can I talk to you quickly before you go?' Sam asked, after Matt had closed the door behind him.

'What is it, Sam?' She frowned at him.

'I wanted to ask you if Rachel is still here or whether she's gone now.' He blushed a little under her gaze, but he needed to know for his own peace of mind.

'I don't know, Sam. Why do you ask?' Jenna narrowed her eyes and he felt her suspicion wash over him.

'Don't look at me like that, Jenna. I'd like her to have left so Jessie and I don't have to face any more awkward situations with her, that's all.'

'Well, as I said, I don't know if she's gone. She cares about Dad and she probably wants to know he's okay before she leaves. But look, Sam, if you're truly over Rachel, and I so want to believe you are, then you've no need to feel awkward around her any more. You will see her again from time to time so you're going to have to deal with it at some point.'

'Couldn't you extend at least a little bit of sympathy my way? You've got to understand how hard this is for me!'

'I do understand that, Sam but it's not me you have to worry about now, is it?' She glanced over Sam's shoulder and he realised Jessie was there and had probably heard every word he'd said. Jenna stepped forward to kiss his cheek, then turned and quietly left the house.

Sam summoned all his courage before turning round to see Jessie staring at him from the top of the stairs.

'Jessie, look, please don't read anything into that. I just wanted to be sure Rachel had left so we could both breathe a sigh of relief.'

Jessie came down the stairs so she was standing right in front of him before she spoke again.

'As Jenna said though, if you're over Rachel, then you shouldn't feel awkward around her any more.'

'In my heart, I do believe I'm over Rachel, Jessie, but I can't help still feeling a bit awkward around her. Please, I'm trying to be honest with you. I had no idea she'd be here and this is the first time I've seen her since I met you. I'm trying very hard to cope with that.'

'I know that, Sam and I understand how hard it must be for you, but, if I can be honest with you, I don't think you're completely over her yet, and maybe all this between you and me,' she waved her hand between them, 'is just too soon.'

Sam didn't speak for a long minute. The stillness in the hallway seemed to suck all the air out of his body.

'Jessie, I don't know what to say to you to convince you that I am over her. I want to be with you. I just need you to be patient with me.'

He took her hands, willing her to believe him. The look she gave him was one of love mixed with pity, and in that moment, he knew he hadn't managed to persuade her. He let her hands drop and walked over to the big bay window in the front room. There was a taxi pulling up right outside the house. Mesmerised, he watched to see who would get out. Then the passenger door opened.

Sam swung round to face Jessie. 'Rachel's just arrived. I had no idea she was coming, I swear.'

But Jessie had already started back up the stairs. Sam dragged his hands through his hair and let out a groan. This time, he thought he might have well and truly blown everything.

---

## Jessie

Jessie returned to Sam's room with a heavy heart and began the process of gathering up the things she'd only recently unpacked. She expected Sam to come and persuade her to change her mind but when he still hadn't arrived after five minutes had passed, she realised with sickening clarity that perhaps she'd been right: he did still love Rachel as more than a friend and would rather stay downstairs and talk to her. Jessie had been a fool to ever get involved. She cast a final glance around the room before closing the door behind her.

She walked downstairs with a carrier bag full of her things, wishing she had a proper suitcase with her. As she reached the last step, Sam appeared in the hallway. She had no idea where Rachel had gone and she was damned if she was going to ask him.

He looked broken and she was filled with pity for him.

'Jessie, please don't go, I really want to be with you.' He looked at her with such emotion that she was blinded for a moment into thinking he did have feelings for her after all but he still didn't say the words she was waiting to hear. She shook her head gently to clear her mind.

'Sam, I've said everything I needed to say so there's no point in my staying here. You said you were over Rachel, but now she's here, I feel like you'd rather be with her than come and talk me out of leaving. I'm going to go and leave you to decide what you really want, without the pressure of me being here.' She paused briefly, trying to keep calm. 'Could you call me a taxi for the station please, Sam?'

His mouth dropped open. 'Didn't you hear what I said? I don't want you to go. And Rachel isn't here to see me, anyway.'

Jessie absorbed that final news in silence, realising Rachel had come to see Sarah. For a brief moment she felt guilty.

'Look, you need some space to be with your family and to think about what you want for your future. I'm going home to get on with my life and I hope you will come and join me when you've come to a decision.'

Sam turned away without another word. Jessie heard him speaking on the phone and it was all she could do not to call out to him and tell him to stop. She knew she had to go.

She passed several agonising minutes on her own in the hallway waiting for the taxi to arrive and then blew out a sigh of relief when she heard the driver blow the horn. She walked towards the door, stopping at the front room to say goodbye. Sam was standing at the window with his back to her. All the fight seemed to have gone out of him, and her heart was breaking.

'I hope your dad is okay, Sam. Take care of yourself too.' Then she was gone.

She walked along the short pathway to the pavement in front of the Victorian house. As she opened the door to the taxi to get in, she glanced back to find Rachel had come up alongside Sam at the window. When she saw Rachel look her way, she wished she'd never lingered. She turned away quickly, climbed in and asked the taxi driver to take her to the station. She didn't turn round in the car, she just kept facing forward, desperate to get away from all the drama of the past few days and back to her normal life. Sam was a long way from being over his love for Rachel and until he was, there was no room in his life for anyone else.

---

**Sam**

'Rachel, what are you doing here?' he asked, disappointment finally overwhelming him. Her timing couldn't have been worse, even though he knew she wasn't to know.

'Well, that's not the nicest welcome I've ever had.' Rachel laughed softly and he smiled in spite of everything. She'd always been able to cheer him up, even when everything seemed awful. 'I came to check on your mum, but also because I wanted to talk to you. Does your bad mood have anything to do with Jessie departing in that cab?'

He was suddenly so weary of everything that it took all his remaining energy to walk over to the sofa and slump down onto it. Rachel followed in his wake. She sat down in one of the armchairs and waited patiently for him to reply.

'Jessie thinks I'm still in love with you and she's not prepared to stay here with me while I sort myself out.'

Rachel responded with a sharp intake of breath. He looked up at her beautiful face, the one he'd loved for so long and had once ached to wake up to every morning.

'You're not still in love with me though, are you? I thought we'd talked this all through before the wedding.'

He took in a deep breath. 'No, Rachel, I'm not in love with you any more but I have to admit it was harder than I'd expected to watch the woman I once loved getting married to someone else. So in the end, I went away for a break to Cornwall. That's where I met Jessie. But now she's gone and I've made a mess of everything again.'

'Do you have feelings for her, Sam?'

'Yes, I do. I only wish I'd had the sense to reassure her of that when she most needed to hear it.'

'Well, you need to tell her you do and that you want to be with her. She seems so right for you.'

'We get on really well together and I want to spend more time with her, getting to know her better. We'd already made plans to be together down in Falmouth when she returns to university.'

'It sounds to me like you two have something good together that's worth exploring.'

'Thank you.' Sam looked at Rachel as though he were seeing her for the first time. His heart already felt lighter for being able to tell her he didn't love her any more. 'Anyway, what did you want to talk to me about, apart from helping me sort out my love life?' He gave her a big smile and sat up to pay his friend some proper attention at last.

'Sam... I'm pregnant.' She spoke so softly he hardly heard her, but when he looked up at her, he could see the doubt in her eyes. She was worried about hurting him, and was putting everyone else first, as always.

'Okay, this is the part where I'm meant to congratulate you and Jackson, isn't it?' She smiled nervously and he knew he needed to get this next bit right. 'A piece of my heart will always be yours, Rachel, but it's time for to you build your life with Jackson and your new family, safe in the knowledge that I couldn't be happier for you both.' He grinned at her and jumped up to give her a hug. 'You're going to be a mum!'

'I know, it's scary, isn't it?' As they pulled apart, she gave him a radiant smile and he was glad to see she was happy too.

'I'm sorry for all this, Rachel. I didn't mean to drag you into my troubles.'

'We're friends, right? That means we share our troubles and we help each other out, just like we've always done since we were kids.'

'Listen, they're going to bring Dad out of sedation tomorrow. Will you come to the hospital to see him again, or do you need to get back to Nashville?'

'I would definitely like to come and see him before I go. We have flights booked to Nashville in a couple of days' time. I know it's tight as to whether he'll wake up before then, but I'll come anyway. Would you... would you mind if I bring Jackson as well? He'd like to see everyone.'

'Have you kept him away because of me?' Sam groaned.

Rachel nodded. 'You all had enough going on and I sensed things were difficult for you when I saw you. I didn't want to make it worse.'

'Well, then, you'd better bring Jackson with you tomorrow.'

After Rachel left, Sam climbed the stairs with a much stronger sense of wellbeing. He popped in briefly to check on his mum, only to find her fast asleep. He headed to his own room and collapsed on the bed. Tomorrow needed to be his new start, first with Rachel and Jackson, and then, if she'd have him, with Jessie.

---

## Jessie

Jessie sat on the train, staring out the window and struggling to make sense of all that had happened in the last twenty-four hours. Having left in such a hurry, she had an awful lot of unanswered questions. She went over and over everything in her mind on the long journey home, but she was still no clearer about it all when she left the train at Newquay station. She caught a bus from the station and was soon pushing her door key into the lock, silently willing herself to find the strength to tell her mum everything that had happened without bursting into tears. The minute she opened the door, her mum came out into the hallway, took one look at her daughter and then enveloped her in a warm hug, breaking down all

Jessie's barriers and bringing on the floods of tears she couldn't hold back any longer.

Jessie told her mum everything of course over a cup of tea and an enormous piece of cake.

'Everything had been going so well between us until Sam saw Rachel again, and then suddenly, all bets were off. He'd told me he was over her and that he'd moved on, but then he told Jenna he still felt awkward around Rachel. So I had no idea what to believe in the end.'

'It sounds to me like Sam has a lot of thinking to do to get his mind straight about how he really feels. To be honest though, it's very early days for you both and there are always ups and downs at the start of any relationship as you get to know each other.' Her mum paused briefly. 'In my heart though, I don't think he was lying about how he felt for you, Jess.' She patted her hand and smiled kindly at her.

'No, I don't think so either, but I can't help him take this next step. If he wants to be with me, he has to be sure he's over Rachel, otherwise both of us will end up getting hurt.' To make everything worse, Jessie was having doubts about whether she should have stayed and persisted about talking everything through with Sam. Maybe if she'd listened to what Rachel had had to say even, she might be in a better position now.

'Jessie, I have some news,' her mum said a few moments later breaking into her reverie. Jessie looked up at her mum and knew that could only mean one thing. 'We have a buyer for the B&B and they're prepared to offer us the full price.'

'Oh, Mum, that's fantastic. That must feel like such a weight off your mind.'

'It is, love, but we're going to have our work cut out for us packing the place up over the next few weeks.'

'Well, that's good. I could do with something to keep me busy,' Jessie replied, with a smile that didn't quite reach her eyes. She stood up, stretched and then went upstairs to her room to unpack the few things she'd taken with her to Poole. With the B&B sold, she could plan for going back to university in September and getting on with the rest of her life. It looked like she was going to be on her own again and that thought was strangely not as frightening as she'd expected, even though there was a large part of her heart that still longed for the new start to be with Sam.

---

## Sam

Sam moved away from the hospital bed to let the rest of the family take their turn at giving his dad a hug. It had taken nearly two days but now their dad was back with them in the real world once more, and with no side effects, either. Sam wasn't much of a praying man, but he'd still sent a silent prayer up to the heavens to say thank you for saving his dad from an early death.

First Rachel, then Jackson moved in to his dad's bedside and then away again. Sam was relieved to have talked with them both since Jessie had left. He knew Rachel would probably have told Jackson what he'd said, but not once had Jackson ever held it against him. Jackson adored Rachel and Sam only wanted her to be happy, which she so clearly was.

He walked over to his mum and gave her a hug.

'Thanks for everything, Mum.'

'You take care, and remember, you and Jessie have all the time in the world to get to know each other, so don't rush it.'

He nodded and kissed her goodbye before picking up his guitar case and slipping quietly out of the room. He went back down to his bike where both panniers were now loaded with his stuff once again. The journey back to Newquay seemed to fly past, helped no doubt by the crisp, blue skies of February and the fact that his heart was ten times lighter than it had been on his previous journey down. This time, he didn't even stop for lunch, so strong was his desire to reach his destination.

Sam pulled on to the driveway in the early afternoon, taking in all the rubbish in the skip that had appeared since he'd left, and a selection of odd bits and pieces strewn about the gravel. The B&B had obviously sold in his absence and he knew it must be hard on Jessie and her mum to be clearing everything out. He strode to the front door and rang the bell. He was relieved when Jessie's mum answered and beamed at him, before throwing her arms round him for a hug.

'Who is it, Mum?' Jessie called from somewhere down the corridor.

Sam pressed his finger to his lips and Helen walked off towards the kitchen, still smiling at his reappearance. He put his panniers down in the hallway and made his way down the corridor towards the back of the house, ducking his head into a couple of rooms along the way as he searched for Jessie. He finally found her in the dining room, clearing out a dresser full of old napkins and coasters by the look of the stuff she was throwing into a plastic bag. The door creaked as he pushed it further open and she turned her head to see who it was. He watched as her beautiful green eyes widened and her face lit up with a warm smile.

'Sam.'

'Jessie.'

'How are you? God, sorry, how's your dad?'

He took a step towards her.

'He's much better and no lasting effects. He should be all right now. I'm not so good though.'

A frown creased her forehead.

'Y-you're not?' she stuttered.

'No. I missed you too much. I wanted to be with you again to see if we can make a fresh start together.'

'Are you sure?' She swallowed nervously and he knew she was really asking whether he'd finally moved on from Rachel.

'I'm sure. I just need to know if you'll still have me?'

She reached out her hand to him and he took it, pulling her body gently towards him so it aligned with his. She slipped her arms round his waist and he lifted his hand to stroke her hair and her cheek, as though he wanted to remind himself of what she felt like.

'I've missed you too,' she said, resting her head against his warm, broad chest.

He lifted her head gently and looked deep into her eyes.

'Can you forgive me?'

She nodded, moving her lips closer to his and closing her eyes.

His lips met hers in the sweetest kiss she'd ever experienced. It was so full of love and hope that Jessie opened her eyes to see Sam's passion for her so clearly reflected in his own. Sam broke the kiss at last and she missed the feel of his lips against hers at once.

'I care about you, Jessie and I want to be with you, wherever you are. When you left, I saw Rachel again and it was only then I realised how much my feelings for her had changed. What I feel for you is real and so very different and I'm sorry I didn't tell you all that when you asked me.'

Tears sprang to her eyes. 'I want to be with you too, Sam, and I'm so glad you found your way back to me.'

# III

# FINDING YOU (JENNA'S STORY)

## ABOUT THIS BOOK

**Can love blossom despite all the obstacles in its way?**

Jenna Andrews' delight at welcoming her boyfriend, Will back from his business trip to Nashville is short-lived when he tells her that his next stop is Paris for the next few months. What with running her busy flower shop and developing wedding business, everything is conspiring to stop them being together.

Will Thompson loves his job but hates the way it keeps taking him away from his girlfriend, Jenna. When he gets called back to Nashville again because of a family bereavement, he starts to think he and Jenna will never get to spend any time together.

As the survival of their relationship becomes more at stake, Jenna and Will finally realise they need to put it before everything else in their lives if they want to be together forever.

**Are Jenna and Will determined enough to finally get their own happily ever after?**

# CHAPTER 1

**<u>Jenna</u>**

Jenna was about to light the two votive candles on the wooden dining table as the final touch to her dinner preparations when she heard Will's key in the door. She put down the box of matches she was holding and went to welcome him home from Nashville. It had been a long three weeks without him and her heart skipped a beat at the thought of seeing him again.

He was closing the door as she emerged from the tiny dining room at the back of the house. Her face lit up at the sight of his tall frame filling the narrow hallway.

'Will, sweetheart, it's so good to see you.' She reached her arms out towards him and he dropped his bag to envelop her in his warm embrace. Stroking his dark, wavy hair, she inhaled the familiar cologne he wore.

'Oh Jenna, baby, it's so good to see you and to hear your voice.' He dipped his head and kissed her tenderly before stepping back to study her face. 'I've missed you so much.'

Just the sound of his American accent thrilled her as she took his hand and led him towards the kitchen. 'I've prepared a lovely dinner to welcome you back and you can tell me everything that's happened since you've been away. I'm dying to hear all the news.'

Will took the wine bottle she handed him and set about removing the cork while she removed dishes from the oven and started serving.

'This is amazing of you to do this for me. What have you made? It smells delicious.'

Jenna put a plate down for him and watched the smile on his face as he took in the meal she'd prepared. 'So, it's nothing fancy – just a steak and pan-fried potatoes, and there's a salad in the fridge.' She went to fetch the salad, cast her eye over the table and then finally sat down, sure everything was in its place.

Will raised his glass of red wine. 'To you, Jenna, it's so good to be home.'

She returned his smile, her heart warming as he referred to their little terraced cottage as their home. It really did feel like home with all their things around them. The cottage had been her friend Rachel's until Rachel went off to Nashville to live with her husband, Jackson. It was through Jackson that Jenna had met Will, and they'd been together ever since.

'So, tell me all your news. How was Rachel?' Jenna asked.

'She looks so well. She must be five months' pregnant now, and she's definitely blooming.'

Jenna's eyes filled with tears as she thought about her friend and how much she missed her. She wiped her eyes, reminding herself Rachel was happy, and that was all that mattered.

'I hope I get to see them before the baby comes along. I miss seeing her and chatting to her every day.'

'You could always Skype her.' Will reached out to caress her cheek.

'I know but it wouldn't be quite the same. Still, you're right. I should give it a go. Anyway, what other news is there?'

She listened as he told her about his business meetings with Jackson over in Nashville. It was the first time he'd been back to the States since taking on the job of establishing a new London office for

Jackson's record label. It had all been a great success, and it also gave Will the chance to stay in Poole with Jenna.

'Jackson's got such big plans for the company. You never know what he's going to come up with next,' he finished. 'Mmm, Jenna, this dinner is superb, thank you.'

For a moment, Jenna wondered if he was changing the subject. Was there something awkward to do with Jackson? Then she thought she must have imagined it. Will had always been so open and honest with her. It was one of the things she'd come to love him for.

'The shop is going from strength to strength now,' she told him. 'I mostly leave Mary in charge on the days she works, so I can concentrate on the wedding side of the business. We're in full swing already, even in May.'

'That's great. I'm pleased everything's going so well. You might be able to take on an assistant to help you with the wedding flowers soon, if you carry on at this rate.'

'I'm still worried about handing over all that responsibility to someone else when it's my business.'

'You have to start trusting other people if you're ever going to get any time off yourself.'

Will was right, but Jenna still didn't find it easy to let go of the reins. She was so proud of how far her little florist's shop had come in such a short time, but she wasn't sure she was ready to hand over responsibility to anyone else just yet. She finished eating and picked up her wine glass.

'Shall we go through to the front room and sit down for a while before we think about dessert?'

Will finished his last mouthful of wine. 'That would depend on what you mean by dessert,' he said with a cheeky wink, and Jenna laughed.

'Will Thompson, what can you mean?' She stood up and went towards him, longing for his touch once again. Will pushed his chair back and she sat down in his lap, lifting her arms around his neck and bringing her lips to his. This time, the kiss deepened with their mutual need to show the depth of their feelings after all the time they'd been apart. Jenna's heart was pounding when she pulled away.

'Shall we take this upstairs, sweetheart? I want us to get comfortable as soon as we can for what I have in mind.' He stood up with her in his arms and made his way towards the stairs. She could have been a feather for all the ease with which he carried her. She nestled into him, so glad to be safe in his arms once again.

***

## Will

In the early hours, Will found himself wide awake staring at the high ceiling in their bedroom. It was a combination of jet lag and worry about how to tell Jenna the bad news following his trip to Nashville. He'd been so eager to tell Jackson how successful the new branch of Rough Cut records was after such a short space of time, he hadn't thought for one minute that Jackson would respond by asking him to do the same thing somewhere else. He and Jenna had hardly seen each other over the past few months as it was. Will was always travelling to and from London during the week, and Jenna was always planning weddings or setting up the flowers for them at the weekends. Now, things could only get worse for them both.

He finally fell into a deep sleep barely a couple of hours before the grating sound of the alarm clock jolted him awake once more. He missed the comfort of Jenna's body next to his immediately. Hitting the button on the alarm before dozing back to sleep again, he listened to her getting ready in the bathroom.

'Will, it's nearly six thirty. You need to get going or you'll be late.' She stroked his face, then kissed him on the forehead. The bed dipped as she sat down next to him.

He opened his eyes to the most beautiful vision. Dark blonde curls surrounded her face and warm, chocolate brown eyes enveloped him. Will wanted to tell her the truth, but he didn't want to ruin his homecoming. He would have to tell her soon enough and deal with the fallout then.

'I... I'm going to work from home today so I can recover from the jet lag.' He glanced away, unable to look her in the eye for fear of what he might reveal.

Jenna got up with a sigh. 'That sounds like bliss, to be able to work from home. I have three meetings today about new weddings and my last one isn't till five thirty, so I'll be home late as well.'

'I'll cook something special for you tonight so at least you can relax when you come in.' He sat up, fully awake.

Jenna glanced at him in the mirror as she put in her earrings. 'That will be lovely, thank you.' She came back to give him a quick kiss before leaving. 'I'll have to get some breakfast in town. I'm already running late for my first meeting.'

'Have a good day, sweetheart.' Will stared wistfully after her as she disappeared down the stairs, hating himself for not being truthful with her.

In fact, Will had a long day ahead of him too, making travel and accommodation plans for his trip to the new location next week. He was excited to be travelling again, but his anticipation was tinged with the sadness of knowing Jenna wouldn't be able to come with him. She wouldn't want to just drop everything, he was certain of that. But with some planning, he was sure they could work something out so they could still be together as often as possible.

By late afternoon, his flight was booked and he'd managed to rent an apartment for the next couple of months via a great new online site he'd found. He'd also made some appointments to view potential business properties for the new branch of the label. He stood up and stretched before making his way to the kitchen to consider what he would make for dinner. Pulling out some courgettes from the vegetable rack, he reminded himself that no-one called them zucchini over here, and once he'd found some tomatoes as well, he was all set. He was aiming to be at his most persuasive when Jenna came home, because he wanted to plan their future together. All he needed from her was an open mind.

The front door slammed as he was opening the bottle of wine to go with the pasta dish he had made. He put the bottle down and went out to meet Jenna.

'Hey, baby, how was your day?'

She grimaced as she removed her shoes. 'Interminable.'

Will took her coat and her bag and set them down before taking her into his arms and kissing her. He was disappointed when she pulled away and walked off towards the kitchen.

'Thanks for making dinner. When will it be ready?' she asked.

'It's ready now.' He frowned a little, unsure what mood she was in.

'I'm going upstairs to get changed. I'll be back by the time you've served up.'

Will stared after her, wondering if she was just overtired after her busy day. As he turned round with the plates, she came back in again, taking a seat at the table.

'Are you okay? You seem a bit unsettled. Has something happened?'

'You tell me.' Her eyes flashed as she lifted her glass and took a sip of white wine.

'What the hell, Jenna? What's with this attitude all of a sudden? I've made dinner and I've been looking forward to spending time with you. Why are you being so difficult?' He stabbed at his pasta with his fork.

Jenna set down her cutlery and looked him straight in the eye. 'In all the time I've known you, you have never worked from home. You've travelled here and there, and never taken a day off. So I just don't accept that today you were working from home to get over your jet lag. Something doesn't sit right with that explanation and it's been niggling at me all day.' She heaved a sigh, all the fight going out of her. 'Just tell me the truth, Will.'

Will stared at her, his bowl of pasta going cold in front of him, weighing up whether to tell her now or not. His honour finally won through and he bowed his head.

'Jenna, look, I do have some news but I haven't lied to you. I haven't told you because I didn't want to spoil things when I've only just come home again.'

'Whatever it is, you'd better tell me now.'

---

## Jenna

Jenna jumped as Mary, her assistant, touched her gently on the arm. She shivered and pulled her cardigan tighter. It was always colder in the back of the shop because the flowers needed to be kept cool.

'Is everything all right, Jenna? You've been in here for ages.'

Jenna shook her head, trying to bring herself back to the present. 'Yes, sorry, I was miles away.'

'If you don't mind me saying, you've been like this all morning. Are you sure everything's okay?'

Jenna's eyes filled with tears, despite all her efforts to hold them back in front of Mary.

'Come and sit down for a minute.' Mary guided her to the little table they had squeezed into the corner of the kitchen, and then she went back to finish making the cups of tea Jenna had started on some time ago.

'I'm sorry, Mary. You don't want to hear about my troubles.'

'Why on earth would you think that? I tell you all about mine often enough. So what's happened? You haven't seemed your normal self since Will came back, if you want my honest opinion.'

Jenna's lip wobbled and she dabbed at her eyes with her now scrunched-up tissue to stop a new flood of tears falling.

'Will told me last night he's been asked to open another office for Jackson's record label – in Paris.'

'Oh my goodness, how exciting!' Mary's face lit up, just as Jenna's own would have done under any other circumstances. 'I don't understand then, Jenna. Why are you so upset?'

'Because I can't just up and leave everything behind and disappear off to Paris, can I?'

Mary's face fell. 'Oh God, sorry. How long's he going to be gone for?'

Jenna sniffed. 'A couple of months, at least. I don't know what to do. My whole life is here, Mary, so there's no way I can go with him. And to be honest, he's already made that decision for me.'

'What do you mean?'

'He didn't even offer me the chance to go with him. He just assumed I wouldn't want to give the business up, or leave my family behind.' Jenna crossed her arms remembering how hurt she'd been when he'd said that the night before.

'To be fair, he was right, wasn't he?' Mary ventured.

'Yes, but that's not the point. He should have asked me and as he didn't, I can only assume he doesn't love me as much as I love him. Maybe he doesn't even love me at all.'

'Jenna, come on, you know that's not true. He's head over heels in love with you. Anyone can see that. Maybe it's because he understands how important the business and your family are to you, and he wouldn't dream of asking you to give that up.'

Jenna bit her lip, pondering Mary's words. Maybe she'd got the wrong idea. 'He did tell me he loved me and that it was only a few short months. He even talked about us visiting each other while he was away.'

'There you go, then. He wouldn't have said all that if he didn't love you, would he?'

'But I can't take time off to visit him in the middle of the wedding season, can I?' She sat up straighter in her chair. 'We've barely seen each other at the weekends while he's been here, living with me. I don't think we'll stand a chance of keeping our relationship going if he moves to France.' She stood up and started pacing.

'You've been talking about getting an assistant to help you with the weddings for some time now.'

Jenna stopped in the middle of the room and looked straight at Mary. 'Hmm, that's what Will said, too. I've been putting it off because I find it hard to delegate responsibility to someone else. And even if I did go ahead with it, I could only afford to get someone part-time.'

'Oh.' Mary's face fell.

'What is it?' Jenna asked, confused.

'It's just I've been meaning to ask whether I could shift up to working full-time in the shop. I could do with more money myself and I'd also like the responsibility.' Mary flushed red, clearly embarrassed at putting herself forward.

'Oh Mary, I'm sorry, I had no idea. I'd love for you to work full-time in the shop, but I don't think I could stretch to a part-time wedding assistant as well.' She sighed and pulled absently on one of her curls.

Just at that moment, the bell rang in the shop. Mary went back out to serve the new customer, leaving Jenna with an even heavier load on her mind than when the day had started. She'd been thinking about expanding for some time, but she was worried about how much more it was going to cost her. Still, if she increased Mary's hours, it would free up her time to spend on more weddings, and if she could do that, she might then be able to afford an assistant. In these situations, she would normally talk to Will, but she was still upset with him over what had happened.

Once Mary had closed the shop and gone home, Jenna sat poring over spreadsheets and figures all afternoon, trying to make sense of them to see what her options were. By five o'clock, she could no longer see straight. She stood up and stretched, knowing she couldn't put off going home any longer. At least she didn't have a wedding to attend the next day, which meant she could go for Sunday lunch with her family. She missed going to see her parents, and her brother, Matt and his family. Her dad and Matt would be able to look at her accounts too, and if she was lucky, her mum might be able to tell her how the hell she would survive without Will for the months ahead.

---

## Will

Awake early once again, Will longed to snuggle up to Jenna and make things up with her, but she'd rolled away from him the previous night. He had no idea how they were going to resolve their differences. Maybe he should have asked her to come with him. He'd clearly made the wrong decision. He groaned and rolled over onto his side to face her.

Her fair skin was so free of worries when she was sleeping and her mess of curls framed her face, making her look like an angel. She was his angel and he didn't want to let her go, no matter what happened. He reached out and stroked her freckled cheek, unable to resist the magnetic pull towards her. He withdrew his hand when she opened her eyes and looked sleepily into his.

'I'm sorry, I didn't mean to wake you,' he whispered.

'Don't you want me to come to Paris with you?' she asked, making his heart ache from the sadness in her voice.

'Of course I do. I would love that. I didn't want you to feel even worse about it by asking you, because I thought you would reject the idea flat out. But I'm sorry. I didn't mean to make you think for one minute that I wouldn't want you to come with me. You mean the world to me, Jenna, and I hate that it's my fault we're going to be apart.'

She turned on her side so they were facing each other.

'I'd love to come with you but I can't, you're right. I was hurt you didn't ask me, despite it being impossible. I may have over-reacted just a tiny bit though.' The beginnings of a smile tugged at the corner of her lips, and Will took his chance to snuggle up to her.

He slipped his arm round her waist and drew her soft, inviting body closer to his.

'I'm sorry for being such a fool, Jenna. I don't want to lose you, and I know we can make this work for us. It is only just a few months, after all.'

They came together, kissing each other deeply to seal their mutual apologies. Jenna pushed her fingers into his thick, curly hair and he shivered at her touch.

'Show me how much you love me, Will,' she whispered, and he didn't need to be asked twice.

Much later, when they were both eating a late breakfast, the air grew heavy again with Will's impending departure.

'I was going to go over to Mum and Dad's for dinner this afternoon, but I guess you'll be packing for your flight?'

'I do have to pack, but it won't take me long. I don't intend to take everything with me, because I'll be home again soon, even if it's just to visit. So I could come with you, if you don't mind? I would like to see everyone before I go.'

'There's something I could do with your help with, too.'

'What's that?'

Jenna told him all about her conversation with Mary, then grabbed her laptop to show him her spreadsheets.

'I'll make some more coffee to keep you going,' she told him as he zoned in on her income and outgoings over the previous six months.

'I can't believe it's been so long since I last looked at these with you,' Will told her when she returned. He took the coffee cup she offered, meeting her gaze as she sat down at the table next to him.

'I didn't want to bother you with it all when you were so busy with your own work to do.'

He nodded, accepting her point. 'The good news is that you're doing even better than you thought. Based on your projections for a full-time salary for Mary, I think you'd be doing well enough to hire a part-time weddings assistant as well, as a result of the extra income they'd both bring in. I know you've been thinking about it for a while, but these figures speak for themselves.'

'That's great news. Thanks for checking it through with me. I guess that's going to be my first job this week – to try and find a new assistant. Once Mary's working all the time, I'll have a bit more free time to think about expanding the business.'

She smiled at him and leaned over to kiss his cheek.

'We'd better hurry if we're going to go have Sunday lunch with your folks.'

'I was going to talk to you about that.' She paused and he looked up from the computer again, turning round towards her this time. 'I can see my family any time but this is your last day and I want to spend it together, just the two of us.'

'Are you sure? That sounds wonderful, but I don't want you to miss seeing your family just because of me.'

'I'd rather be with you because I don't know how long it will be before we can see each other again. So why don't you pack your bags and then we could go out for a nice lunch in town?'

'That sounds like an awesome idea.'

Will stood up and drew Jenna into his arms, soaking in the feel of her body and the intoxicating coconut fragrance in her hair. He tried to commit it to memory so he would be able to recall it when he was away. He only hoped it wouldn't be too long before they saw each other again to lessen the blow of parting from the woman he had come to love so quickly.

# CHAPTER 2

**<u>Jenna</u>**

After a full week of moping following Will's departure, Jenna decided it was time for action. Now Mary was working full-time in the shop, Jenna had the time she needed to focus on employing a part-time assistant. Having put off her advert for so long, she'd come into work especially early ready for the new week and was determined to get on with it.

She was delighted to find Mary had already opened up before she got there. Her assistant was making light work of creating their core bouquets for the shop's stock that day.

'Morning, Mary. How was your weekend?'

'Not bad at all, thank you. How about you? You seem a bit brighter today.'

She followed Mary through to the kitchen.

'Yes, I feel it. I've been miserable for long enough. I'm going to start work on recruiting my new assistant today to take my mind off missing Will.'

'How's he getting on?' Mary passed her a mug of coffee.

'It all sounds amazing, to be honest,' Jenna said, taking the coffee with a grateful smile. 'He's got an apartment in Paris and it sounds like he's out at wonderful gourmet restaurants all the time. He is missing me, though, and he's desperate for me to come and visit him as soon as I can.' She blew on her coffee before taking a sip, her earlier high spirits already deflating.

'You'd better get started on that advert, then. The sooner you find an assistant, the better.'

Jenna set up her laptop in her tiny office behind the kitchen and left Mary to finish preparing the shop for the day. She took in a deep breath, absorbing the variety of heady fragrances from the flowers, and let it out again, relaxing into the work she was about to do. Half an hour later, she had the first draft of a new post for her website. She stood up to go and show it to Mary for her opinion.

'Okay, this all looks pretty good to me,' Mary said, casting a critical eye over Jenna's ad. 'You've asked for someone with experience of working in a busy florist's, as well as experience of preparing flowers for weddings. Those are the most important things in terms of the ability to do the job. I like the way you've said about being proactive and flexible too, and you've mentioned weekend working. So you're good to go.'

By lunch time, Jenna had put the advert up on the website and had also sent it to an online jobs portal she sometimes used, in the hope of reaching more people.

Mary popped her head round the corner of her office at exactly the right moment. 'I was going to pop out to pick up some salad for lunch, Jenna, if that's okay. Would you like me to get you something?'

'Oh yes, please, that would be great. I'll come out and watch the shop. It will be a nice change for me after staring at the computer all morning.'

Mary had just left when Jenna's phone rang. Pulling it out from her back pocket, she saw it was Will.

'Hello, sweetheart, how are you?' she said.

'I'm better for hearing your voice. How's your Monday going?'

Jenna told him all about the job advert and how hopeful she was that there would be lots of interest.

'If I can get someone in place soon, and someone with a good amount of experience, I'll be able to come out to Paris and see you in no time.'

'That would be amazing, and you're right, there will be a lot of interest in your position. Listen, I wanted to tell you I'll be in Brussels for the next couple of days and it might be difficult for you to get hold of me.'

'Brussels! Why?' Jenna's mind swam with his frequent changes of location. All of a sudden, things seemed to be out of her control once again.

'I'm going over there to meet someone who might be interested in one of the jobs at the new Paris office.'

'But shouldn't he be coming to see you?'

'It would be better for me to see *her* in her current job, to see what she does and how good she is at it.'

'Oh. I see.' Not only was Jenna struggling to keep up with Will's travels, but now he was going to be meeting up with a woman she didn't know. Probably a very beautiful woman. All her insecurities rose to the surface, along with more tears.

'Now, Jenna, don't go reading anything into this.'

'I'm not doing that at all.' She tried to sound strong and nonchalant, but her voice betrayed her, wobbling on the last few words.

'Jenna, baby, I love you and only you. Please don't be upset.'

Mary came back into the shop at that point. Jenna took a deep breath and brought the conversation to a close.

'Look, Will, I have to go but I'll speak to you soon. Take care.'

She took the salad Mary held out to her, thanked her and disappeared off to be on her own in her office again. In her heart, she knew she had nothing to worry about with Will – he would never cheat on her – but she felt vulnerable all the same. She pulled the lid off her salad and extracted the plastic fork. As she began to eat, she checked her calendar on her laptop to see which wedding she should concentrate on today. Then her email pinged with a new message.

*'Hello,*

*I saw your advert on your website. I would like to apply for the position, but I only have two years' experience, rather than the three you were asking for. I wondered if it would still be worth me applying for the job?*

*I look forward to hearing from you.*

*Greg Harris.'*

---

## Will

The Eurostar from Brussels to London St. Pancras had been trouble-free for once, and by Friday lunch time, Will had crossed the capital to catch the train from Waterloo down to Poole. He was so looking forward to surprising Jenna tonight with his arrival, and even if she was busy with weddings at the weekend, he didn't care – he'd go to her weddings with her if she would let him. All he wanted to do was to be with her and to catch up on everything that had been happening since he'd left for Paris. He wanted to show Jenna all his photos of his apartment and all the wonderful sights nearby. She'd absolutely love it, he was sure. By the time the taxi pulled up outside the cottage, he was aching to take her in his arms.

Letting himself in a minute later, he made his way into the kitchen, but there was no sign of her. He took the stairs two at a time, but Jenna wasn't anywhere upstairs either. He glanced at his watch. It was only just after five, so perhaps she was still at the shop. Dumping his bags, he set off for the town, his long legs making short work of the distance into the centre. He was so focused on getting to the shop, he didn't even indulge in his favourite past-time of studying the boats in the harbour. But when he reached the building, all the lights were off. The shop had closed for the evening. Will blew out a frustrated sigh. Now he would have to call her and spoil the surprise.

He leaned against the wall outside the shop and pressed the button on his phone. He let it ring a few times, and listened in dismay as the answerphone kicked in.

'Jenna, it's me. Where are you? Please call me back as soon as you can.'

He ran his fingers through his hair. His excitement was long gone, and he tried not to worry about where Jenna might be. He was just about to call her parents as a last resort, when his mobile rang.

'Jenna! Are you okay?'

'Yes, of course. Why wouldn't I be? You sound ever so worried.'

'Where are you? I was worried when I... I couldn't get hold of you.' He didn't quite want to give away where he was. There still might be a chance for his planned surprise to work.

'I'm meeting someone for a drink. I left the shop a bit early today because it wasn't too busy. Where are you?'

'Are you in town?'

'Yes. Will, what's going on?' Her voice was sharp and he wanted to get to her so he could explain.

'Can you bear with me and just tell me where you are?' He'd started walking along the cobbled street towards their favourite wine bar in the hope of finding her there. 'Are you at Angelo's?'

'Well, yes... Will!'

She rang off at last, her eyes sparkling with pleasure.

Will swept her into his arms and hugged her tight. Then he was kissing her and finally he put her down.

'It's such a lovely surprise to see you but I... I'm actually here interviewing someone for the wedding planner role.' She dropped her voice to a whisper. Will looked over her head to see what the interviewee looked like. He couldn't have been more surprised to see a man sitting there. Walking round Jenna, he wasted no time in introducing himself.

'Hi, I'm Will. I'm Jenna's boyfriend.'

'Hi, I'm Greg. It's a pleasure to meet you.'

'Greg was very keen in applying for the job and we decided to have an informal meeting after work to discuss what's involved. Obviously, I had no idea you were coming home.' Jenna gave him a pained look, embarrassed in front of a potential employee.

'Look, I'll go and get a drink and just sit somewhere quietly out of the way while you two have your meeting.'

Jenna nodded, but she still looked uncomfortable about it. Will ordered a large glass of red wine and took a seat at a table round the corner out of sight, to let Jenna get on with her meeting. He caught up on some emails while he was waiting and was surprised when he heard her voice getting closer a short while later. She stopped next to his table.

'Thanks so much for coming, Greg, I'll be in touch.' Jenna shook his hand, and Will stood up to do the same.

'Great to meet you, Greg.' He shook the younger man's hand firmly, and as Greg walked away, he turned to Jenna.

'I wish you'd told me you were coming, sweetheart,' she said. 'It was a bit awkward having you turn up in the middle of my interview.' She frowned at him briefly before smiling. 'I'm so glad to see you though.' She leaned forward to kiss him and he pulled her into his arms.

'I'm sorry. I just wanted to surprise you after not seeing you for so long. Look, let me get you a drink and we can catch up. White wine?'

She nodded and he shot off to the bar, returning a few minutes later to take a seat next to her.

'Cheers to a wonderful weekend.' They chinked glasses and he relaxed at last at the prospect of all the time they had ahead to spend together.

---

## Jenna

'You will try and come to see me as soon as you can, won't you?' Will asked as he was leaving on the Monday morning. A taxi was waiting to take him back to the station.

'You know I will. I just need to put my plans in place and then I'll be there.'

Just as Jenna had been getting used to Will being away, he had come back again and everything had returned to normal. Now Jenna felt even more forlorn as she waved him goodbye a second time.

Over the weekend, she'd talked to Will about Greg. She had instinctively liked him at their first meeting. Will had advised her to wait and see whether anyone else applied before making her final decision, and she knew he was right. Checking her emails first thing after getting into work, she was surprised to see another half a dozen applications. She decided then and there to make it her top priority to sort through them all that day and see if anyone else was worth calling in.

After helping Mary to get the shop set up, as she still did most mornings, she settled down with her laptop to start sifting through. A couple of hours later, she had made little progress. She groaned from the effort of studying application forms and CVs for so long. Needing fortification, she stood up and went to put the kettle on before popping into the shop to talk to Mary.

'I'm making a brew. Would you like one?'

'Have you ever known me to say no to a cup of tea?' Mary's eyebrows shot up and her eyes twinkled. She followed Jenna back into the kitchen. 'How's it going? Or shouldn't I ask?'

'The trouble is they're all pretty good. How am I going to choose between them?'

'Where's that list of criteria we drew up?' Mary was all business-like now and Jenna admired her for it.

'Here it is.' Jenna brought the list up on her laptop.

'Why don't you compare them to your list of criteria and choose the three who are closest to your requirements?'

'Hmm, I could try that, I suppose. I need to do something, other-wise I'm never going to get it finished, and I did want to get it done today.'

'When's the closing date? You might get some more in after today.'

'It closes tomorrow but I'd like to get a shortlist sorted today of the ones I've had in so far, and then it will be easier to check any last few that come in.'

An hour later, Jenna had her shortlist down to three people, including Greg. She was delighted to have finished work on it and she set about drafting an email asking them to come for an interview on Wednesday. There was no need to wait any longer, now she had an assistant in her sights.

She spent the afternoon working on her upcoming wedding arrangements, ordering in flowers and making sure she had all the trimmings to put on the finishing touches. This weekend was going to be a busy one. She was glad Will had chosen to come home at a time when she wasn't so frantic.

'I'm off now, Mary. I'm going to dinner with my parents tonight so I need to buy a few things before I get there. Will you be all right?'

'Yes, of course. Did you get your shortlist sorted?' She smiled.

Jenna thought once again how much more relaxed she felt knowing Mary was now in charge of the shop.

'I did, and there were no more applications today. Have a lovely evening and I'll see you tomorrow.'

Jenna had a definite spring in her step as she walked through town towards the stop where she would catch the bus to her parents'. She had made progress towards getting her assistant and as soon as that was done, she'd be able to go to Paris. She'd never been and it was one of her romantic dreams to be able to spend time there with the man she loved. Over the weekend, Will had waxed lyrical about his apartment and all the beautiful sights nearby, making Jenna even more envious. He was living in Montparnasse, quite near a famous cemetery, which sounded grim but fascinating. He'd told her that a few famous people were buried there. He'd also told her about visiting the beautiful Jardin du Luxembourg. She longed to go and share the pleasure of it with him.

She let herself into the tiled hallway of the Victorian house, cool after the unusually warm May sunshine, and called out to announce her arrival.

'Jenna, darling, how are you?' Her mum welcomed her with open arms when she appeared in the hallway. Her mum always embraced her as if she hadn't seen her for a hundred years, but Jenna lapped it up every time.

'Not too bad, Mum. You?'

'I'm so glad to see you, sweetheart. It does seem like ages since we've seen you, what with Will's comings and goings. How's he getting on?'

'Very well, from the sounds of it.' She followed her mum down the long corridor to the kitchen, where her dad was waiting to greet her.

'Hey! How are you? We've missed you on Sundays recently.'

'I know, Dad, it's just been crazy. You look so well, both of you. Are you still doing well, Dad?'

'I'm fine.' He rolled his eyes affectionately. 'You've all got to stop wrapping me up in cotton wool. I had a heart attack, but I've been so much better these past few months.'

'I'm glad to hear it, Dad.' She paused briefly, glancing round the kitchen. 'So, what's for dinner?' she asked. 'I'm starving.'

# CHAPTER 3

**Will**

'Hey, Will, how's it going?' Jackson's enthusiastic voice boomed across Skype, making Will smile.

'Great. How are things there?'

'The same – busy, busy – but lots of interesting things happening, as always. So tell me, how did it go in Brussels?'

'The woman I met there, Cécile, was great, but she didn't have the practical experience we're looking for. So unfortunately we're back to square one, but I have some other people to interview this coming week.'

'And how's Jenna handling you being away?'

'We're both finding it tough being apart, to be honest, but she has her business and it means a lot to her, as my job does to me. At the moment, we're compromising as best we can.'

'I know, man, and I'm sorry your job is taking you away from her. Have you managed to get back to Poole yet?'

'Yes, I've just got back from spending the weekend there, but in a way, it feels even harder now to be apart again, if that makes sense.'

'And will Jenna get the chance to come and see you at some point?'

'I hope so. She's looking for a new assistant to help her with the weddings, and Mary runs the shop now, so, in time, she should be able to get over here.'

They chatted for a few more minutes before saying goodbye. Will released a sigh and tried hard to think positively. He had a meeting booked at lunch time with several more candidates for the role of managing the new Paris branch. He pulled their details up on his laptop to run through them. He'd been lucky so far in that all the candidates he'd interviewed had spoken very good English, as the job description had required, which was just as well because his French was almost non-existent. If he was staying for longer, he would definitely be taking lessons to improve his spoken language. He'd never been in this kind of situation before and he was ashamed of his lack of knowledge.

When he was sure he was ready, Will packed up his laptop and left his apartment. As he approached the RER station a few minutes later, he thought again about how much there was to show Jenna. He wanted to explore the area further with her and hoped she'd be able to make it soon.

Twenty minutes later, he was walking along the bustling Rue de Rivoli towards the café where he had agreed to meet all the candidates that day. His walk took him past the Louvre and he mentally added the world-famous museum to his list of must-see places during his stay. At this rate, he wouldn't manage to see everything before it was time to go.

Once in the café, he settled himself at a table in a quiet corner to meet his guests. After a quick *café*, he glanced around to see his first candidate coming towards him. He'd asked them all to send their latest photo to enable him to recognise them easily.

'*Bonjour. Lucien?*'

'*Oui, bonjour, monsieur.*'

The two men shook hands and sat down. Half an hour later, after struggling to understand each other, as Lucien spoke very little English, they finally gave up and brought their meeting to a close. Will was none the wiser as to whether Lucien was up to the job, and the thought of his other meetings turning out the same filled him with dread.

After the third candidate had been and gone, Will wasn't feeling much better. Only one of them had been able to speak enough English to get through the interview, and from what he could make out, he was the least suited to the actual position. He would need to be more vigilant before inviting any other applicants.

Now he had some time for lunch, Will took out his mobile to check if he had any messages, and found one from his sister, Kim. He frowned. Kim hardly ever contacted him these days. In truth, she was his half-sister, and while his dad was alive they'd always been close, but as Will had no affection for his stepmother, they'd been in touch less and less. He clicked to see what she had to say.

'*Hey, sorry I haven't been in touch for a while. Hope you're okay. Mom very poorly now and may not last much longer. Any chance of a visit? Xx*'

Will scratched his chin, now flecked with stubble, and thought about how to reply. Kim's mother had Alzheimer's and he felt churlish in keeping up his dislike of her. He wanted to support Kim in her hour of need, if nothing else. But her request couldn't have come at a more awkward time. He would have to call her and talk to her, rather than sending an impersonal text. He sent a reply promising to call her later, and put his phone away.

Kim had been Will's rock when his father was dying and the least he could do for her was to be there for her now. He sighed as he thought about his stepmother, remembering how cruel she'd been to him when he was growing up. She'd always favoured her daughter, which should have made Will hate Kim, but if it hadn't been for Kim sticking up for him, his life would have been a whole lot worse. Now was his chance to repay that kindness.

## Jenna

Jenna's dad had retired to the front room, allowing her to chat with her mum at length about all the recent developments in her life.

'So how's Will getting on in Paris?'

'Oh, he was full of all the joys of his Parisian life when he came to visit me last weekend.' Jenna laughed and her mum joined in. 'It's so hard because I've always wanted to go to Paris, and to be there with Will would be a dream come true.'

'What's stopping you then?'

Jenna rolled her eyes. 'There's the not insignificant matter of my shop and my wedding business, both of which are expanding all the time.'

Her mum patted her hand. 'I know, sweetheart, but surely you could get away for a weekend, now you have Mary running the shop?'

'I honestly can't, Mum. It's bang in the middle of the wedding season. I have weddings most weekends, and on both days, too. It's great to be so busy, but now I have my relationship with Will to factor in as well, it's doubly difficult. I feel like I'm being pulled in so many different directions and I can't seem to do anything well.'

'Is there any news on your new assistant?'

'There is. I've drawn up a shortlist of people to interview. Now all I have to do is get on with it. The thing I've realised is that even when I do employ someone, I can't just dump them in at the deep end by taking off for Paris. I'll need to train them and be there for them until they find their feet.'

'Yes, of course. Have you explained all this to Will? How does he feel about it?'

'That's the problem. He's impatient for me to go and visit him, and I do want to, but I can't just drop everything. I have to consider my job as much as he has to consider his. In some ways, it's easier for him to come and see me, anyway.'

'Have you two talked about the future?'

Jenna frowned. 'How do you mean?'

'Are you planning to get married?'

'Oh, Mum, I don't know. We haven't talked about it. We've both been happy getting to know each other. It's only because Will has been sent off to Paris that everything has changed, but we do love each other, and that means making compromises, doesn't it?'

'It certainly does. It's what being in a relationship is all about. You're both doing all the right things but I do think you should go out to Paris very soon. Your business could survive without you for a weekend. I suppose you have to ask yourself whether you could survive without Will.'

Jenna was still thinking about her mum's last point when she went into work the next day. She was so proud of her business and she didn't want to lose it, but losing Will would be much more painful. She'd resolved overnight to get the interviewees in quickly, but she'd also come up with a new idea she wanted to talk to Mary about.

She brought it up over their morning cup of tea.

'I'm going to crack on with setting up the interviews today, but I wondered whether you would be confident enough to cover me for a weekend if I went to see Will? Once the new assistant is up to speed, I can ask them to do it, but Will's so desperate for me to go and see him I wanted to put the idea to you and see what you thought.'

Jenna held her breath and waited for Mary's reaction.

'I think I could do that. I've helped you prepare so many times and now I'm actually taking the bookings in the shop, I know what's involved.'

Jenna clapped her hands together and did a little dance on the spot, making Mary laugh.

'That's excellent, Mary. Thank you so much. You'll get the time off in lieu of course, and we can start talking about it today if you like.'

Once Mary had gone back to the shop, Jenna called Will to tell him the good news but his number went straight to his voicemail and her excitement dissipated at once. She decided against leaving a message or sending a text, preferring to wait until she could hear his voice.

The day flew by and by the time she was ready to go home, she'd managed to set up all her appointments over the next few days. By Friday, she should be in a position to choose her new assistant. Grabbing her bag from the little cupboard next to her office, she fished out her phone and smiled when she saw there was a text from Will.

'*Hey, sweetheart, sorry I missed your call. Is everything okay? Let me know when you finish work and I can call you back then.*'

Jenna sent him a quick text to reassure him everything was all right and that she was on her way home.

Twenty minutes later, as she was walking in the front door, her mobile rang.

'Will, hi,' she gushed, delighted at the thought of telling him her good news.

'Hey, how are you?'

Will sounded subdued, but she pressed on, hoping to cheer him up.

'I'm pretty good. I have some great news. First, I think I'll have a new assistant by the end of this week and second, Mary has agreed to cover me until the assistant gets up to speed so I can come and see you in Paris.'

'Oh, that's great. How soon can Mary step in?' They both laughed and Jenna relaxed. Everything was going to be okay.

---

## Will

Will could hardly believe Jenna was finally coming to see him. On the Friday evening, he went straight from work on the RER train to Charles de Gaulle airport, longing to see her as soon as she landed. By the time he arrived, it was only ten minutes before her flight was due. Jenna would have spent most of the day travelling – he knew that from experience – and he was expecting her to be tired. He'd take his cue from her about how much she wanted to do on her first evening.

When Jenna's slim figure finally came into view in the Arrivals Hall, his breath caught as he took in her beautiful face, framed by the unruly blonde hair he loved so much. When her eyes locked on him, he met her smile and his heart lifted at the sight of her.

'Jenna, sweetheart, it's so good to see you.'

'And you! It really is true that absence makes the heart grow fonder.' She kissed him softly.

Will picked up her bag and clasped her hand in his before guiding her towards the RER station.

'How was the journey? I know how long-winded it can be.'

'It's been a bit of a day, travelling from Poole to London and then out again to the airport, but it all went according to plan. And now here I am, in Paris! I can't wait to see all the sights.'

Will shared her excitement.

'I wondered if you might be too tired to go out tonight.'

'No, not at all. I'd like to go out and see at least some of the city this evening, if that's okay with you?'

'Of course. We'll go back to the apartment and drop your bag off and then go from there. What would you most like to see?'

'Obviously I want to see it all but for tonight, more than anything, I want to see Notre Dame. All those French Gothic novels I read when I was a girl have stayed with me and I'd like to see it lit up tonight if possible.'

'You always manage to surprise me. I was fully expecting you to want to see the Eiffel Tower first.' He laughed and she joined him. Will squeezed her hand and didn't let go for the whole ride home.

By early evening, they were on their way back to Notre Dame, and in no time they were exiting the Métro and walking back towards the ancient *cathédrale*. Will waited for Jenna's gasp, which he knew was sure to come as soon as she spotted the spectacular cathedral's towering façade.

'Oh, my goodness! The photos don't do it justice, Will.'

They stopped to take it all in for a moment, ignoring the tourists rushing around them to get to the cathedral and take their souvenir photos.

They finally managed to get through the crowds, but Will guided Jenna round the side of the building rather than going inside. In many ways, the building was more stunning when viewed from the rear, and he wanted her to see the gargoyles and the flying buttresses the church was so famous for. They passed through the gardens alongside the river Seine, enjoying the fragrance from the cherry blossom trees in full bloom. At the back of the church, they stopped and gazed in awe at the building in all its magnificence and Jenna finally took a photo on her phone.

'Did it meet your expectations?' Will asked, although he already knew the answer to his question.

'I've never seen another building quite like it.'

'Paris has more than its fair share of stunning buildings, but this one was a great one to start with. Do you want to go inside? The stained glass is meant to be amazing.'

'Maybe we could do that in the daytime. For now, I want to be outside for as long as we can before night falls.'

'In that case, can I tempt you with an ice cream?'

'That sounds perfect.' Jenna gave him such a bright smile. Will couldn't remember ever feeling happier.

They strolled hand in hand across the Pont Saint-Louis towards the ice cream shop Will had visited recently, at the suggestion of one of his recent interviewees. It took them a while because Jenna kept stopping every now and then to look back and stare at the cathedral from all the possible different angles.

'I have to warn you there's an almost impossible number of different flavours at this place. You'll probably find it hard to decide.'

They joined the queue of waiting customers until finally it was their turn.

'You weren't joking about the variety of flavours,' Jenna groaned.

In the end, she plumped for a combination of coconut ice cream and mango sorbet, while Will chose pistachio ice cream and a lemon sorbet. Will ordered in confident but fledgling French before passing Jenna her tub.

'*Merci, madame. Au revoir.*'

'Your French sounds amazing, Will. You've only been here a few weeks and yet it sounds so authentic.'

'It really isn't, but it is much better than it was before. I've been picking it up so quickly because I'm here all the time and it's all around me.' He went on to tell her about the interviews and how terrible he'd felt afterwards about not being able to speak the language well enough to communicate.

'I'm so impressed. I never did very well with languages at school, despite really wanting to.'

They sat down on a bench, eating their ice cream, watching the sun go down and the lights of Paris switch on. Jenna's wish to see Notre Dame lit up was granted and Will was so glad she'd been able to see it.

# CHAPTER 4

**<u>Jenna</u>**

Paris was everything Jenna had imagined it would be, from the amazing architecture to the little *places*, as well as the particular smells of *patisseries* on every corner. Will had chosen a cosy little bistro for dinner and as they raised their glasses to each other, everything seemed right in their world.

'So where would you like to go tomorrow?' Will asked, setting his glass down.

'I loved the sound of the Jardin du Luxembourg you mentioned, and even the cemetery sounds interesting.' She screwed her face up, despite all her efforts to keep an open mind.

Will laughed. 'Let's start with that, and I think you'd like going up the Montparnasse Tower as well, because you can see a quite different view of the city from there.'

'We will go to see the Eiffel Tower too, won't we?'

'Of course. I can't deprive you of the most famous Parisian landmark.'

She put her hand on top of his. 'It feels so good to be here with you at last. I'm hopeful I should be able to come regularly with Mary's help, as well as my new assistant's in time.'

'It sounds like you've got it all in hand.' Will smiled, but she noticed he wasn't looking her in the eye any more and his smile wasn't the full-on type he normally gave her.

'What is it, Will? Is there something you're not telling me?' Her stomach churned at what he might be about to say.

He didn't say anything for a minute, then he took a deep breath and looked up at her.

'I had a text from my sister this week. She said her mom is very ill now and may not have long to go.' He paused again, and Jenna knew there was more to come. 'She asked me if I would go visit.'

Jenna felt like all the air had been knocked out of her.

'Back to Nashville?'

Will nodded. 'The thing is, there's no love lost between me and my stepmom, as I've told you before, but I feel I should go back to support Kim. It's what she did for me when my dad was ill.'

'I understand,' Jenna said softly. 'When are you going to go?'

'Probably some time during the next week.'

Tears sprang to her eyes. He'd only just come back, then he'd flown off to Paris, and now he was going away again.

'I'm so sorry, Jenna. The timing is awful but it's out of my hands. I don't want it to spoil our weekend together.'

It already had spoilt Jenna's visit, but she didn't say so. She was at a loss for what to say in the circumstances that wouldn't sound mean-spirited.

'We'll just have to make the most of the time we have together, I guess.' She put a brave face on and blinked her tears away. Throughout the rest of their dinner, they talked about everything else, but they didn't come back to the topic of his leaving again.

As they left the restaurant to make their way back to Will's apartment, he put his arm round her shoulder and pulled her close.

'Let's try and enjoy the rest of the weekend and not let this get us down. I won't be gone for long and I can still Skype you like I did before, sweetheart.'

Once they reached the apartment, Jenna set about unpacking her things to try and take her mind off all that had happened. By the time she went to bed, she was exhausted and still emotional about Will's imminent departure. As she slipped under the crisp, fresh duvet, Will rolled over to face her.

'I'm sorry this means we're going to be even further apart, Jenna.' He reached out to stroke her cheek and the familiar thrill coursed through her at his touch. 'We'll be okay. We'll get through it like we've done so many times before.'

'But will we ever be together for longer than a few months at a time? I'm not sure I can keep doing this, Will.' A lonely tear rolled down her face.

He swept her into his arms.

'Our time will come, Jenna, I promise.' He released her a little so he could look at her face. 'I love you and I want to be with you. It's just hard right now, but it won't be forever. Do you believe me?'

She nodded, but her heart wasn't convinced.

He leaned closer and kissed her, reassuring her he meant what he'd said. Jenna's body relaxed and her lips parted, allowing the kiss to deepen. She ran her hands softly up his bare back, flitting over his taut muscles and enjoying the feel of his skin. He pulled her closer still and his desire for her pressed against her body. He stroked his fingers up her thigh, and when he reached the bottom of the t-shirt she wore in bed, he paused to lift it over her head.

'I will never get enough of seeing your beautiful body.'

Jenna flushed at the compliment, even though Will had told her she was beautiful before. It always sounded wonderful, no matter how many times he said it.

Will stripped off his boxers and as they became one, she remembered all the love she had for him. She could never let him go – they were meant to be together – and that meant they could weather all the storms life might throw at them.

'I love you, Will,' she cried as she reached her release in his arms. He followed her over the edge shortly afterwards, holding on tight to her as he whispered his love in return.

---

## Will

Despite Will's news over the weekend, he and Jenna had spent a wonderful time together. Every time they said goodbye, he missed her a little bit more. To distract himself, he scheduled meeting after meeting with various record company executives he had heard of by word of mouth, but in the end, he wasn't sure any of them was the right fit to be Jackson's distributor in France.

Will had found an office base and he'd also employed an executive assistant, Bruno, who spoke fluent English. While Will was away, Bruno was going to get on with finding other staff for the office, as well as sifting through candidates for the manager's position.

Will arrived back in Nashville to sultry May temperatures that he was quite out of practice at dealing with. He caught a cab over to Kim's apartment block in East Nashville, looking forward to seeing her again. He made his way up to the second floor of the dilapidated building and knocked on the door of her apartment. There was no reply. Will berated himself for not sending Kim a quick text to let her know he was coming. She was probably visiting her mother at the hospice. He took out his mobile to give her a call, but it went straight to voicemail.

'Hey, Kim. I'm here at your apartment. Are you at the hospice? I can come and meet you there if it's easier.'

He hung up and wondered what to do for the best. It was now early evening, so he decided to go and look for somewhere to eat while he waited for Kim to call him back. He found a nearby diner and settled down to wait for the burger he'd ordered. Then his mobile pinged with a text.

*'I'm at the hospice because Mom has passed away. Lots of paper-*

*work to deal with. No need for you to come. Can I meet up with you later?'*

Will called her right back.

'Hey, Kim, I'm so sorry to hear about your mom, and for not letting you know I was coming. I was planning to ask if I could stay with you, but would you prefer me to stay in a hotel?'

'I don't know, Will. I can't think straight at the moment. No, listen, I'd be glad of the company in the next few days. Where are you now? I'm nearly done so I could meet you somewhere.'

Will told her where he was and waited for her to arrive. When Kim turned up twenty minutes later, she took off her coat and slumped into her seat.

'Oh, Will, thank goodness you're here. It will be so good to have your help with the funeral and all the paperwork.'

Will didn't want to get involved with his stepmother's funeral, if he was honest. She wasn't his mother and he wasn't here for her. He didn't say anything, because Kim was only just holding everything together.

'I took the liberty of ordering us both a burger, and they've been holding them till you arrived. Is that okay?'

She waved her hand at him. 'Food is the last thing on my mind right now, but that's fine. Thanks.'

'So did it all happen today?'

'Yes. She was quite frail yesterday, but no more so than the day before that. I left her at six yesterday evening and they called this morning to say she'd passed away in her sleep. There won't be a post mortem, because the circumstances were clear. The doctor has been in and done his report, and I should be able to collect the death certificate tomorrow. Then I can arrange the funeral. You will stay, won't you?'

'I'd like to stay for the funeral, but it kind of depends when it is. I can't stay away from work for too long. I'll need to check in with Jackson tomorrow to tell him what's happening.'

'Her affairs were largely in order. We did that together before she went into the home. And she didn't have much in the way of belong-ings.' Kim sniffed and delved into her bag for a tissue.

'I'm so sorry, Kim. This is going to be a difficult time for you. I know your aunt didn't get on well with your mom, but isn't it worth giving her a call to come help you now?'

Kim shook her head, making her long, blonde hair whip across her face. 'She didn't bother to visit Mom while she was still alive, so why should I contact her now? Apart from her, there's only me. Everyone else has gone now.'

They ate their meals in awkward silence, with Will unable to comfort her when he had no fond memories of her mother to draw on himself.

They walked back to Kim's apartment and she showed him into the spare room.

'Thanks for being here, Will. I'll see you in the morning.'

Will retreated to his room and texted Jenna to tell her he'd arrived, and also what had happened. He only hoped he wouldn't have to stay too long and that he would be back in Paris within a few days. He was so tired when he got into bed, he expected to fall straight asleep, but his mind was racing with thoughts of Kim and her mother, as well as Jenna and how everything seemed to be conspiring to keep them apart. He had absolutely no idea when he was going to see her again.

---

## Jenna

After an intense few days since returning from Paris, Jenna had finally managed to find herself a new part-time assistant. She had whittled them down to just two candidates in the end – Greg was one, despite his lack of experience, and a young woman called Becky was the other. It had been so hard to choose between them, but although they both had great personalities and Becky did have a bit more experience, in the end, Greg had won her over with his enthusiasm for developing the wedding side of the business.

Greg had started on the Thursday morning, and it had only taken that first shift to show him how they ordered their flowers and also how they took delivery of them.

'It's such a relief to see you picking things up so quickly, Greg,' she told him at the end of the day.

By the time they met again on the Saturday morning for their first wedding of the weekend, Will had texted her to say he was in Nashville and that he didn't know how long he'd be staying. As she pulled up half an hour later outside yet another church for yet another wedding that wasn't hers, Jenna wondered what the point of it all was. She loved Will and he loved her, but they were still thousands of miles apart, with no prospect of seeing each other again in the immediate future.

It was eight in the morning and she and Greg were standing at the door of the beautiful old church, looking down between the pews towards the altar. They'd already delivered the wedding bouquet, corsages and buttonholes to the bride's house. Now it was time to decorate the church. Jenna needed something to take her mind off all her negative thoughts and the wedding was sure to keep her busy.

'Shall I do one side and you do the other, once you've shown me how the bride wants it?' Greg asked, breaking into Jenna's distracted thoughts.

'That sounds like a brilliant idea,' she replied with a smile. She whipped out the wedding plan she had made and demonstrated how she wanted the flowers tied to the end of the pews. Greg picked it up straight away and went and got on with it, with no further instruction needed. Jenna marvelled at her luck. The church flowers were done within the hour. Then they climbed back into the van to make their way to the nearby village hall, where the reception was taking place.

When they pulled up in the car park, Jenna saw there were a few people already about inside the recently renovated building.

'At least the hall's open, that's a good start,' she told Greg. 'I've had nightmare days before now where no-one has had the key to open the hall and it has taken most of the day to find it.'

Once inside, Jenna made a beeline for the bride's sister to tell her they were there and that the church was all ready.

'Oh that's brilliant, thank you. Ellie will be relieved. She has a thousand things on her mind this morning, as you can imagine.'

'That's one less thing for her to worry about. Are we all right to make a start here too?' Jenna turned round to survey the room, noting how it had emptied with their arrival.

'Yes, of course. I asked everyone to leave you space to work for the next hour or so. The main thing was making sure the hall was unlocked for you.'

'Excellent. Wish Ellie luck for me and I hope you all have a wonderful day. We'll slip off when we've finished here.'

While Jenna had been talking, Greg had been steadily bringing in the trays carrying the flower arrangements for the tables. Now it was just a matter of putting them in the right place.

'Where have you been all my life?' Jenna cried, making Greg laugh. 'You just might be worth your weight in gold.'

Once the tables were decorated with the fresh flower arrangements, they set about attaching the red and gold silk ribbons they had brought with them to the backs of all the chairs before interweaving tiny posies inside them.

They were done by lunch time, a first for Jenna, and she drove them back towards Poole in a happier mood than when she'd started.

'What are you up to this afternoon?' she asked Greg as they drove along the country lanes.

'Oh, a bit of freelance writing work, and maybe a bit of shopping, I expect. My boyfriend's working today so I'll just be pottering until he gets home.'

'What does he do?'

'He's a builder and they're working on a job that's run over a bit because of the weather, so the boss has offered them overtime to get the job done.'

'These building projects rarely run to plan, do they?' They laughed together and Jenna was struck once again by Greg's easy-going nature.

She dropped him off outside the shop and parked her van in the tiny car park to the rear of her parade of shops. On her walk home, the sun glinted off the sea and there were very few clouds in the sky. The warmth on her skin made her glad to be alive, and even though Will wasn't with her, she appreciated her home town. She never tired of studying the boats in the harbour, and she didn't even mind the tourists. She had made a good choice in hiring Greg. The pressure of having run the business on her own for so long was already starting to ease. With Mary and Greg working with her, she could afford to take a bit more of a back seat in future, especially if Will was going to be travelling more in the coming months. Still, she wanted to know what their future was going to look like – would they get married one day? Jenna had no idea if that was what Will wanted – marriage, a family – but if it was, they would need to settle somewhere, and sooner rather than later.

# CHAPTER 5

## Will

'Hey, Jenna, how are you?' Will had called Jenna on Skype, and his heart filled with love as her face lit up at the sight of him.

'I'm better for seeing you, even though it's not in person.' She gave a small pout but then reverted to her beaming smile. 'How about you? How's Kim holding up?'

Will sighed. 'She's keeping busy dealing with the paperwork, but in reality, I think she's only just keeping it together. These situations are hard, because there's so little I can say to make her feel better.'

'Yes, but you being there with her must be making a big difference. When's the funeral going to take place?'

Will pulled a face. 'Not for another week apparently.'

Jenna's face fell. 'Oh, that's a long time away. I'd kind of hoped you'd be back before then.'

'So did I, but I promised I'd stay till then, so I don't have a lot of choice.'

'I do understand. It's just I miss you.'

'How are things going with Greg?'

'Oh, Will, he's wonderful. If I'd known I would be able to find someone like Greg to be my assistant, I would have got round to it ages ago. He's enthusiastic and he just gets on with the job without me having to give him step-by-step instructions. It's fantastic. Coming over to see you in Paris won't be a problem at all now.'

'That's great news.' Will smiled. 'I'm going into the office this afternoon to see Jackson and bring him up-to-date with all that's been happening. And he's invited me to the house for dinner tonight, so I'll send Rachel your love.'

'Oh, I wish I could tell her myself. It's been ages since I saw her last. It was back when Dad was in the hospital and Sam was here. It seems like a lifetime ago when we were all together.'

'Why don't you come visit her over here soon? What do you think? Perhaps once Greg has had a chance to settle in a bit more.'

'That would be lovely. But you're right, Greg needs more time.' Jenna's voice sounded wistful.

Will wished he could take her in his arms and make her feel better. 'Look, I'd better go but I'll call again soon. Take care, won't you? Love you.'

She blew him a kiss before saying goodbye, making him miss her even more. Another week here without Jenna seemed like forever and although he hadn't mentioned it to her, he had the feeling Kim wasn't going to let him get away straight after the funeral either.

He packed up his laptop into his satchel and gathered his keys and phone before setting off for the short walk downtown to the office. It had been a couple of months since he was last there and he was looking forward to seeing everyone again. He'd always got on well with his work colleagues. He walked alongside the Cumberland river, enjoying the sight of the spring blossom in the trees and reminding himself of all the things he loved about Nashville. He had always loved the city, with its broad streets, the way everything was within easy reach, and the friendly community revolving around the music industry. But since both his parents were now gone, he had no real link to the place any more, not even through his job since he'd been based in Europe. His life was with Jenna, and although it was nice to visit Nashville, it no longer felt like his home. Jenna's family had made him so welcome right from the start, and that was where his heart was now.

He took the stairs into the office two at a time and appeared in front of Annie, Jackson's secretary, a couple of minutes later.

'Will! What a lovely surprise. How are you?' The older woman stood up and came round her desk to give him a hug.

'Not so bad, Annie. How about you? I hope Jackson's not been working you too hard?' He pulled back from the hug and winked at her, making her laugh.

'That man! He's always worked me too hard, but you know how much I love my work. Is he expecting you?'

'Yes. He asked me to come in as I'm over here again.'

'What brings you back so soon?'

Will told her about his stepmom and she extended her sympathy. He didn't tell her they hadn't been close – he mostly kept his private life to himself around the office – but he thanked her for her kindness. Annie picked up her phone to call Jackson, and a minute later his boss appeared.

'Will, good to see you. How's everything going?' Jackson extended his hand and Will shook it before following him into his office.

'My sister's obviously taking it all quite badly and there's another week until the funeral, which makes it even harder.'

'So you're planning to stay till then at least?'

'I did promise I would, but I'd like to get back to Paris as soon as I can after that.'

'Any developments there?'

Will told him about the property he'd found, and Bruno, the executive assistant who was busy setting up the office in his absence.

'The only problem I'm having is finding the right person to run the branch for us. There are plenty of good people, but very few of them speak fluent enough English and their skills have been a bit lacking so far.'

'After you mentioned the problems you were having before, I asked around a bit at other labels and I've had some good recommendations for people to contact. I thought you might like to make a start on those calls while you're here this afternoon.'

'Excellent. Are we still on for dinner tonight?'

'You bet. Rachel can't wait to see you. She just wishes Jenna was with you.'

'Jenna's so sad about that too. We need to get them together soon.'

---

## Jenna

As yet another weekend full of romantic weddings loomed, Jenna grew more and more despondent about the lack of romance in her own life. She had the man she wanted but she couldn't seem to spend any time with him. It was hard to shake the feeling that Will would end up staying in Nashville after his stepmom's funeral and his trip would drag on and on.

After work on Friday evening, she made her way to her parents' house for dinner, since she would be busy all day on Sunday and wouldn't be able to make it home. Over a comforting meal of barbecued sausages and potato salad, she told her mum and dad all about her woes.

'You've survived without each other before, Jenna. Surely you can hang on in there for just a couple more weeks?' her dad asked.

She glared at him. 'I'm fed up with us being apart all the time, Dad. It's not like it's been every now and then. It feels like we're apart more often than we're together.'

'You're doing all the right things. You've promoted Mary and you've employed Greg. It is only a matter of time now, isn't it?'

Her mum's words were meant to reassure her, Jenna knew, but it still all involved her not seeing Will. She blew out a long breath, trying not to get annoyed with her parents who were only trying to help.

'Anyway, I'm sorry to go on. How are things with you?'

'I'm bored and your mother's sick of the sight of me.' Her dad laughed but the sadness in his eyes showed he meant it.

'If you're feeling much better now, maybe you should start looking for a little job yourself. Nothing too strenuous, but something to get you out of the house.'

'That's exactly what I've said,' her mum chimed in. 'But we can't seem to decide what would be the right thing. And I could do with something as well, not just your dad.'

Jenna stared at her mum for a long moment.

'Are you okay, sweetheart?' Her dad patted her on the arm, breaking the spell she'd fallen under.

Jenna closed her mouth, which had dropped open in shock.

'You have both just given me the most brilliant idea,' she said finally, her voice a mere whisper.

'We have?' Her mum and dad looked at each other and back at their daughter.

'Yes! This is brilliant. You've helped me in the shop plenty of times, Mum, and Dad would only have to drive the van. Don't you see? It's the perfect solution, and I can go and see Will in Nashville.'

'I don't understand,' her mum said. 'What exactly are you saying?'

'You two need something to get you out of the house and I want to go and be with Will. I'm asking you both to cover for me and help Greg, and Mary if she needs it, so I can go to Nashville.' She clapped her hands together and gave her parents a big smile.

'But Jenna, we know nothing about what you do,' her mum exclaimed.

'What are you doing this weekend? Why don't you come and help me and Greg so you can see exactly what's involved? Please give it a chance. I could really use your help.'

'Oh, I don't know about this, Jenna. It all might be too soon for your dad.' Her mum looked anxious.

The heavy burden of guilt washed over Jenna.

'I don't want to force you if you're not ready, Dad, but you said yourself you were bored and it would only involve driving the van around. There's no heavy lifting, just a bit of to-ing and fro-ing.'

'I reckon I'd be all right doing a bit of driving, Sarah, love.'

'Why don't you give it a try this weekend and see how you feel?' Jenna crossed her fingers underneath the table. 'If you don't feel up to it after that, I'll understand.'

'Okay, if your dad's happy with it, I'll come along too. It will be nice to be with you and to see how you prepare for weddings. One thing. If we do go ahead with this plan, you will come back from Nashville, won't you? You won't be there for weeks on end?'

Jenna laughed. 'I promise I'll come back. A week with Will would keep me going for a while. Plus I could visit Rachel, which would be wonderful as I haven't seen her for so long, and I don't know if I'll be able to meet up with her again for a while.'

'Oh, did Will say how she's doing?'

'She's blooming, he said.'

'I hope you'll bring me back some photos. I do miss her.'

'I Skyped with Will the other day. Maybe we could do that all together with Rachel?'

'How does that work?' Her dad looked puzzled and Jenna laughed. Her dad didn't really get technology.

'Hang on a sec.' She went to get the laptop out of her bag, opened it up and set it on the table between her and her parents. After opening Skype, she dialled Rachel's number. She checked her watch and confirmed it was mid-afternoon over there.

'Hello stranger!' Rachel's happy face suddenly appeared, but when she saw Sarah and Dave, she promptly burst into tears. Then Jackson came into view, his initial concern replaced by an enormous smile when he saw the three of them sitting there at the other end.

'Hey, you guys. How are y'all?'

Then everyone was talking at once, Jenna's parents not quite in sync with the slight time delay of the chat on Skype. Jenna held up her hand finally and silence fell.

'We were just talking about you, and Mum said how much she missed you so I suggested we do this. It isn't quite the same as being together, but at least we get to see you.'

'Oh, it's lovely to see you all, it really is. Now, tell me all your news – but one at a time, please!'

---

## Will

'Morning, Will, it's Rachel. Sorry to call you so early, but we need to talk.'

'No problem, I'm up anyway. Is everything okay?' Despite what he'd said, Will was surprised to hear from Rachel at eight in the morning, and only a couple of days after they'd had dinner together. He stared out the window at the traffic on the highway, gridlocked even on a Saturday morning, and thanked goodness he wasn't part of it.

'I want us to come up with a plan to get Jenna over here, and soon. She called me on Skype last night with her parents, and it's clear she's missing you terribly, but she's stuck because of her business. So, what can we do to help her out?'

'She's on it, Rachel. She's got a new assistant who's working out very well and Mary's working full-time, so it won't be long now.'

'But Jenna's fed up with waiting, Will, especially when she has no idea how long you'll be here. Not only that, but I'd like to see her too.'

'I know, but what else can I do?' He tried to suppress the note of irritation which was threatening to creep into his voice. 'She needs someone to cover her weddings if she's going to take time off and she's already done all she can about that. Look, I'll give her a call and talk to her but I can't promise there's anything else we can do at the moment.'

Will rang off and blew out a long breath. He understood everything Rachel had said, and he knew she was only trying to help. But being apart was just as frustrating for him as it was for Jenna. He checked his watch. It was too late to call her now. She'd be busy with weddings, as always on a Saturday afternoon in June, and besides, he had stuff to do with Kim today.

'Hey, Will, who were you talking to so early?'

'Morning, Kim. I was talking to my friend, Rachel. I don't know if you remember her? She's my boss's wife but she's also Jenna's best friend.'

'Oh yes, Jenna. Are you still seeing her?'

Will frowned, his patience now wearing thin. 'Of course I am. What do you mean?'

'Just with you living in *Paris* now, I assumed you'd split up because she hadn't come with you.'

Will didn't like Kim's tone, but he let the jibe about Paris go. 'God, no. We're not going to let a bit of distance get in our way. We love each other.'

Now it was Kim's turn to frown. 'Hmm, it doesn't seem like she loves you that much if she hasn't followed you to Paris or here. She should be with you, if you ask me.'

Will took a deep breath to stop himself from snapping back at his sister. He hadn't asked her opinion and she was being deliberately unkind when she'd never even met Jenna. He would never want Jenna to blindly follow him anywhere. She was her own woman.

'For your information, Jenna runs a successful business and she's finding it hard to get away. But even so, she's doing all she can to get here and be with me so she can support me.'

'While we wait for her to arrive, can we talk about all the things we have to do today?'

For a moment, Will stared at Kim, seeing a selfish side of her he'd not noticed before but he let it slide. He knew she was under a lot of pressure. He shrugged and waited for her to continue.

'I want to finalise the list of people to invite to the funeral today and get those invitations sent out. After that, I'd like to go to the church to finalise the arrangements for the funeral. The pastor said he would be free to see us this afternoon.'

'I can help you this morning, but I'm busy this afternoon. You know what you're doing at the church. You don't need my help.'

'But...' Kim pouted, but Will stood firm, refusing to let her manipulate him into going.

'I have plans, Kim, and I also have work to do. Now, why don't you draw up the list and I'll write the invitations?' He took out his pen, gathered up some of the fancy invitations she'd had printed and sat down at the table, giving her no room to argue.

An hour or so later they'd finished the invitations, but the tension between the two of them was palpable. Will needed some fresh air and some time to think.

'Okay, Kim, I'm going to get off now. I'll see you later.'

'Will you be back for dinner?'

'No.'

He avoided making eye contact with her, knowing her face would be full of disapproval. He packed up his things and went to collect his bag from his room. A few minutes later, he emerged onto the street below Kim's apartment and set off for town, eager to get away and clear his mind. He didn't actually have any plans for the day – he just needed a break from Kim's smothering need to be with him all the time. Now she had extended her approach to commenting on his life and his girlfriend, he had had enough. He wondered if it might be time to move to a hotel to give them a bit of much needed distance. She wouldn't like it, but she'd have to put up with it.

He was coming up to Broadway when his phone rang.

'Hey. This is a lovely surprise.' He sat down on a bench facing the river while he waited to hear what Jenna had to say.

'Hi, sweetheart. I wanted to tell you my good news.'

'Go on, don't keep me waiting.'

Jenna laughed and he wished she was with him so he could see her beautiful face.

'You won't believe it, but I've managed to persuade my parents to cover me next weekend so I can come out to Nashville. I can probably get away on Tuesday.'

Will jumped up with excitement. 'Oh Jenna, that's great news! How did you manage that? And are they sure?'

'It's a bit of a story, but they're bored at home and I need a break, so it seemed like a win-win for all of us. I'll do some research on flights and everything tonight and I'll let you know when I'll be arriving. I can't wait to see you.'

# CHAPTER 6

**<u>Jenna</u>**

Jenna settled back into her seat on the internal flight for the final leg of her journey from Chicago to Nashville. She thought about the previous time she'd been in Nashville, only last year. She'd come to visit Rachel, who had only just moved out there, and Rachel had told her how she and Jackson were engaged. No sooner had they announced their engagement than they were on the brink of splitting up, because of nasty allegations made by Jackson's ex. Jenna wouldn't have met Will if it hadn't been for all that drama, and it had all come right in the end. Now Rachel and Jackson were married and about to become parents. She envied them their happiness. She longed to settle down with Will and start a family too. Why hadn't they ever talked about their future together? She was determined they would have that conversation before she went home again.

It seemed no time at all before the plane was landing in Nashville and Jenna was waiting in line to have her passport checked. Once she'd cleared security, she sent Will a text to say she was about to collect her luggage.

*'I'm right here, sweetheart. See you soon xx'*

She didn't have to wait long for her bag and then she was on her way to the exit as fast as her feet could carry her. In the much smaller Arrivals Hall at Nashville, she spotted Will easily, his tall frame standing out above the other people waiting. She beamed at him, desperate to get past all the other passengers and to be in his arms once again.

'Oh, Will. It seems like forever since we last saw each other,' she cried as he swept her up into his arms. Will hugged her tight to him, lifting her off the ground before setting her down and kissing her.

'I know, and it's made me realise how much I hate being apart from you.' He picked up her bag and took her hand, leading her towards the exit where they'd be able to take a cab back into town.

'Me too. I feel like we've spent more time apart recently than together, and I don't want that to continue.'

Will squeezed her hand as they continued towards the taxi rank. Once they were seated in the back of the cab and on their way, he spoke again.

'I've booked us into a hotel. Kim's guest room is a bit on the small side and I also wanted us to have some privacy while you're here.'

'That sounds great, thank you. How's everything been going? How's Kim handling it all?'

'She's been a bit odd these past few days, which I'm trying to put down to the pressure she's been under, but I'm not honestly sure that's the reason. She just wants me to stay here and look after her. She doesn't seem to realise I have my own life as well.' He sighed, glad of the chance to talk it over with Jenna.

'It will probably do you good to have a break from each other before the funeral.'

'I did agree to having lunch with her tomorrow though so you could meet each other. Is that okay?'

'Of course.' She gave him a big smile and he relaxed at once knowing he had Jenna on his side.

Once the cab had been paid off, and they were inside their hotel room, Will closed the door on the rest of the world behind them.

'I've booked this suite for a week while you're here, but I hope we might be able to travel back together,' he said.

'Really?' Jenna whirled round to face him. 'That would be wonderful.'

He took her hands in his. 'The only reason I'm still here is for the funeral. I want to be back home with you as soon as I can after that.'

'But what about Paris?'

'I'll have to go back and finish what I've started, but I'd like to come home to Poole for at least a few days first. I've been talking with Jackson about everything and he says he has some ideas for how to get things going, so maybe it won't be for too much longer.'

'And when will we be able to see Rachel and Jackson?'

'They've invited us over there tomorrow for dinner. Is that okay with you?'

'Of course. That means we can spend today together, which is exactly what I want.'

'And how would you like to spend that day together, Miss Andrews?' He wiggled his eyebrows at her and she laughed.

'I have a couple of ideas, and from the looks of it, you might have had exactly the same ones.'

Will stood, picked Jenna up and threw her over his shoulder.

'Is this what you had in mind?' He chuckled as he walked through to the enormous bedroom.

'You caveman, you.' She beat her fists lightly on his back. She was loving his dominance and couldn't wait to end up in bed to show him just how much she'd been missing him.

'Are you protesting just a bit too much?' He slid her down from his shoulder and gently placed her in the middle of the kingsize bed. As she landed, her hair fanned out across her shoulders and she puffed, out of breath from the exertion.

'I'm not protesting even one tiny little bit. Come here, Will. I've waited long enough for this.'

Her wish was his every command and when their lips met, Jenna enfolded him in her arms.

## Will

As they were waiting for the cab the next morning, Will wondered once again whether he was making a big mistake in trying to help Kim get to know Jenna. Jenna kept fiddling with the cuffs of her jacket and her necklace, so he knew she was nervous about it too. In fact, he was now dreading the whole thing.

'Hey, Jenna,' he said, reaching out and taking her hand. 'I'm sorry. I meant this to be a good thing, not a stressful one. Are you okay?'

'Yes, I'm just a bit nervous, that's all, after what you've told me about Kim.'

'Look, it's just lunch, and then we can go off on our own and do something else together, all right?'

'Sure.'

The cab picked them up a few minutes later and took them off to The Hermitage Hotel, which was where Kim had decided would be best for them to have lunch.

'Do you remember the last time we were here?' Will asked Jenna, trying to distract her.

'I do. It was when Rachel had left Jackson for that last time and she'd insisted I go with her, but you came and rescued me and took me out for the day.' She smiled at the memory. 'Rachel wasn't very pleased with me, as I remember, but it spurred her into action at least. And now look at them, married and expecting a baby.'

'Yes, it all worked out in the end, didn't it? It'll be good for you to see more of each other once the funeral is out of the way.' He winced at his words, thinking how bad that must sound.

'Don't worry about it, Will. Remember you're doing a good thing here by supporting Kim. Maybe you should remind her of that if she gets funny with us at lunch.'

They arrived at the hotel where they climbed out and stood for a moment taking in the magnificent frontage of the building. Soon they were being ushered through the doors where Kim was waiting for them in the foyer. She was dressed smartly in a cream suit and had obviously spent time on her hair and make-up. Will smiled at her as they approached. He leaned forward to kiss her on both cheeks before stepping back to slip his arm round Jenna's waist, trying to boost her confidence.

'Kim, I'd like you to meet my girlfriend, Jenna.'

Jenna went to kiss her but found Kim's hand in her way, extended for Jenna to shake. Jenna flushed at her faux pas as she shook Will's sister's hand.

'Charmed, I'm sure.' Kim dropped her hand quickly before turning to Will and proceeding to ignore his girlfriend.

Will glared at Kim and took Jenna's hand, preventing Kim from looping her arm through his as she'd become accustomed to doing.

'Shall we go in?' he said.

Kim tutted, clearly annoyed she wasn't going to be his centre of attention. She turned and stalked off towards the restaurant.

'That was a great start,' Jenna whispered under her breath.

'I don't know what's got into her, but try not to take any notice of her behaviour. I am so sorry.'

'I hope she's not going to continue like this, because I'm going to find it hard to keep holding my tongue if she does.'

By the time they reached their table, Kim had sat down on the leather bench seat. She beckoned to Will to sit down next to her. The other seat was a single chair. Will ignored her and, placing his hand on the small of Jenna's back, guided her to sit down in the seat next to Kim instead. Kim pulled a miserable face at him and he shook his head at her in warning.

After they'd ordered some drinks, Jenna turned to Kim.

'I'm sorry about your mother. This must be a very difficult time for you.'

'It is, yes. I don't know how I would have got through it all if it hadn't been for Will.'

'Yes, you're very lucky to have a supportive brother like Will. It's been good of him to come back here and help you with the funeral arrangements.'

Kim was stunned into momentary silence for once. Will stared at the two women, both of whom he cared for but in very different ways.

'Is everything organised for the funeral now?' he asked.

'Yes, I think so,' Kim replied. 'Will you come to my place and travel with me in the car to the church?'

'Yes, of course. Jenna and I will be there in plenty of time.'

'Jenna? She didn't even know my mother. No offence, but why is she coming?'

'*Jenna* is coming with me because she's my girlfriend and an important person in my life. I would like her to be by my side. It doesn't matter that she didn't know your mother. I didn't even like your mother, but I'm still going, aren't I?'

'Will!' Jenna and Kim chorused the single word together, the first thing they had agreed on.

'I'm sorry, Jenna but I've had enough of Kim being so rude to you. And trust me, Kim, if you keep on like this, I just won't come.'

Kim stood up, pushing the table away from her in her haste. She threw down her linen napkin on the table, looking at each of them in turn.

'If that's how you feel, you needn't trouble yourself to come at all.'

She stormed out of the restaurant and disappeared through the door. Silence fell over the dining area as other diners took in the unusual scene unfolding before them.

Jenna stared at Will for a moment, aghast. 'Go after her, Will,' she urged.

Will rolled his eyes, pushed his chair back from the table and took off after Kim. It was the last thing he wanted to do, but he knew Jenna was right. He couldn't leave things like this.

## Jenna

Jenna sat alone in the restaurant, embarrassed by what had happened and annoyed at herself. Kim was under a lot of pressure following the death of her mother, and Jenna should have been more understanding. She took another sip of her water and tried to avoid the anxious waiter's gaze. She didn't know if she wanted Will to persuade Kim to come back or not – either way, the aftermath was going to be uncomfortable. She released a sigh and scanned the room for him one more time. He was making his way back to the table alone.

'What happened?' she asked as he sat down heavily in the single seat once again.

'She was angry, but she was also sorry for her outburst. She couldn't face coming back in here again though, she said. Kim never was very good at apologising.'

'I'm sorry, Will. I should have been more sympathetic to her, rather than letting her goad me with her comments.'

'I don't know what's got into her. It's a difficult time, of course, but she's being so unpleasant. That's not what she's normally like. The funeral will be even more difficult now.' Will ran his hands through his hair.

'If you'd rather I didn't come to the funeral, I wouldn't mind. It might make the day easier for you.'

'I appreciate you offering, Jenna, but selfishly, I'd rather you were there with me. Listen, anyway, let's eat and let's talk about something else.'

'How are things going with the Paris office? Any news on finding someone to run it yet?'

'No, not yet, but the leads Jackson gave me look hopeful.'

They paused their conversation to give the waiter their orders, and resumed speaking once he'd left.

'Can I ask you what you're thinking of doing after Paris? I mean, has Jackson suggested where he might want you to go next?'

'No, he hasn't said anything, and I'm not sure I'd want to take another job like that. It's killing me being apart from you like this, as it is.'

'But you wouldn't want to give up your job working for Jackson, surely?'

'I've been giving the future a lot of thought since I've been away from you. And look, I'm sorry we're not having this conversation in a more romantic setting, but I want us to be together all the time, Jenna. And I need to know if you feel the same.' He took her hand and rubbed his thumb gently across her knuckles, sending a shiver down her spine.

'I want that too, Will,' she said. 'But I honestly don't know how we're going to achieve it without one of us giving something up. You love your job as much as I love mine. I couldn't ask you to give it up for me, any more than you'd ask me to give up my business.' Tears sprang to her eyes.

'Hey, sweetheart, don't get upset. We'll work it all out.' Will stood up and slid onto the bench seat next to Jenna to put his arm around her. 'We're doing all the important things at the moment. As long as we both know what we want, we just have to keep making it work. Maybe when we go home, I could work from Poole and commute back and forth each week. What do you think?'

Jenna sniffed and raised her watery eyes to his. 'Maybe that would work, but it would mean some very long days for you. We'll have to look at it when we get back, but we should also look at the long-term for my business.'

'How do you mean?' Will frowned but didn't say anything more as the waiter arrived with their meals. They waited for him to serve them and to top up their wines before they picked up their conversation.

'I'm quite interested in exploring options with my parents.' Jenna sat up straighter in her seat, regaining focus as she told Will her thoughts.

'Go on.' Will made a start on his chargrilled steak salad while she outlined the beginnings of a plan.

'I've been wondering about bringing Mum and Dad in as partners to the business. I know they're both retired, but they're also
bored, and there's a lot more life left in them yet.'

'You're right, but would they want to work with you all the time?
Once they get involved, it would be hard for them to take a back seat
again.'

'They could always be silent partners for the most part, just stepping in as and when perhaps, although I'm not sure they'd go for
that.'

'It's worth exploring it with them, but don't get your hopes up,
just in case they say no.'

They finished eating and returned to the hotel on foot to enjoy
the spring sunshine. Will led them down towards the river and Jenna
marvelled at the view of the Shelby Street bridge as they turned right
at the end of the road. She wasn't sure exactly where they were, but
she knew they were close to downtown and she loved the sound of
music all around them.

'Are you sure you wouldn't want to live here, Will? It must be
hard being away from your home town, and your friends and family.'

'It's weird. I love Nashville but there's nothing here for me, now
all my family except for Kim have gone. My job was the only thing
keeping me here and now I just want to be where you are. These last
few weeks have taught me that. So, no, I wouldn't miss living here. I'd
want to visit, sure, from time to time, to catch up with Jackson and
Rachel, and Kim, but I can manage without living here.'

'And how do you feel about Poole?'

'I'm happy there. It's where we've made our home together, and
your family have been so welcoming to me. Right now, that's all that
matters.'

# CHAPTER 7

**Will**

After the argument with Kim, Will was still tense even as he and Jenna arrived for dinner at Jackson and Rachel's colonial house out near the Bellevue area. He was glad his half-sister had shown remorse, but he was nervous about what was really going on with her. On top of that, he'd told Jenna earlier he was sure everything would work out for them, but in all reality, he couldn't see how he was going to make that happen.

Rachel and Jenna hardly stopped talking from the first moment they saw each other and Will was pleased they'd both been able to get together at long last.

'Will said you were blooming and he was absolutely right. You look amazing, Rachel,' Jenna gushed as she hugged her friend.

'Yes, I've been lucky. Hardly any morning sickness, and after that it's been mostly plain sailing.'

Will was reminded of how close Jenna and Rachel were, almost like sisters, and yet they weren't blood-related at all, whereas he was related to Kim and they always seemed to be at loggerheads.

'Hey, Will, how's everything? How's your sister doing?' Jackson shook his hand and clapped him on the back before leading him over to get a drink from the kitchen. He passed Will a beer and pulled out a bottle of water from the fridge for himself.

'To be honest, Jackson, I think the strain of it all is getting to her. We had an argument earlier today after she was rude to Jenna and although Kim's apologised, I don't think it's over.'

Jackson frowned. 'You're having a hard time one way or another, man. I'm sorry about that. She's your half-sister, right?' Will nodded. 'And there's no other family?'

'No, just us two. I think Kim's expecting me to move back here to look after her, but my life is with Jenna now. I love Nashville, but it's not home to me any more.'

Jackson's eyebrows shot up. 'Is that really how you feel?'

'I guess it is. I want to be with Jenna, wherever that might be.' He gave Jackson a slightly embarrassed smile.

'So, being in Paris isn't helping you guys out at all, is it?'

Will took a sip of his beer as he pondered how to answer the question. Jackson was his boss as well as his friend. 'Not really, but it's not forever, so we can handle it.'

'Have you thought about what you'll do after Paris?'

Will's heart sank at the question. Jackson was so shrewd and Will should have known he would have thought ahead already. 'I have given it some thought and I have to be frank with you, Jackson. I wouldn't want to go to yet another city to set up a new office. I'm not sure Jenna and I can withstand that separation again. I don't want to lose my job, but she means more to me. I'm sorry.'

'I appreciate your honesty, always have done. I'll give it some thought and see what I can come up with. Let's not worry about it any more tonight.'

They rejoined Rachel and Jenna and soon after, they moved outside so Jackson could start the barbecue. They settled around the enormous wooden table, facing the long expanse of freshly mown lawn and neatly tended flowerbeds.

'It is so good to see you both together. I've missed you guys.' Rachel beamed at them both.

'You almost sound like a true Southern belle now, Rachel, and after only a matter of months.' Will smiled at her, feeling himself finally beginning to relax.

'I'm getting that comment from a lot of people now, aren't I, Jackson?'

'You sure are, honey. You've always been my belle.' Jackson leaned over and kissed his wife, making Will envious of how simple their life seemed compared to his and Jenna's. He glanced over at Jenna to catch the wistful look on her face before she schooled herself to smile again. He reached out and took her hand and she squeezed his gently to say she understood. Will pulled her closer to him, resting his arm around her shoulders.

'So,' Rachel continued, 'how's your dad now? I hope he's taking it easy?'

'No, he's not actually, and that might be my fault.' Jenna flushed and Will sensed her guilt about asking her parents to cover for her.

'I'm sure it's not,' Rachel chided her, clearly certain her friend would never do such a thing. Jenna filled her in on how her parents had stepped in to help her with her shop and the wedding side of the business.

'It sounds like your business is doing really well, Jenna and that's all down to you. I remember all that time ago coming in and asking you to help my cousin Tom's fiancée, Meg, with her wedding flowers. And now look at you.' Jackson gave her one of his full-beam smiles and Will was grateful to him for his encouragement. Jenna was too hard on herself.

'Weddings are big business these days. If Mary's running the shop now, it sounds like you're absolutely right to develop the wedding side of the business,' Rachel added.

Jenna nodded but didn't say any more. She sipped her wine, looking as though she couldn't wait for the spotlight to move away from her. They fell silent for a moment around the table while

Jackson finished barbecuing steaks, burgers and enormous prawns and brought them over. Rachel went to the kitchen to fetch some salads and Will helped by topping up everyone's drinks.

'Let's toast to friendship,' Rachel said, and they all clinked glasses.

'And to new beginnings,' added Jenna, gesturing with her glass towards Rachel's growing bump.

'Have we told you we're having a baby girl?' Jackson announced. Will knew full well they hadn't, but he laughed at the look of fatherly pride on Jackson's face.

'Oh, how wonderful,' Jenna gasped. 'Have you chosen a name yet?'

'We've got some ideas, but we're keeping them to ourselves until the baby is born to see which one fits best.' Rachel patted her bump gently.

Everyone laughed and Will wondered what their next gathering would be like once the baby was born.

---

## Jenna

The day of the funeral dawned dark and grey, with a light drizzle falling. The sombre weather was appropriate for the event, but if Jenna hadn't already been dreading the day, the weather certainly made her feel even worse. Will was insistent she travel in the car with him and Kim, but Jenna was uncomfortable about upsetting his half-sister further. They took a taxi over to her place and Jenna was surprised to see the hearse already waiting in the car park.

'We're not late, are we?' she whispered to Will.

'Not at all. Don't worry, everything will be fine.'

Will went up to Kim's apartment and returned with her a moment later. She had obviously been waiting for them to arrive, Jenna thought, as she allowed Kim to usher her straight towards the car.

'I want to get to the church early to make sure everything is set up correctly,' Kim said after they'd got in.

The journey passed in silence after that, with only the sound of the increasingly heavy rain beating against the windscreen in the background as they progressed to the other side of Nashville, where the modern church was located. There was still nearly an hour to go before the service, but there were already people with umbrellas milling around outside when they arrived. Their bright colours were a stark contrast to the darkness of the day. Jenna went inside to take a seat in a quiet corner of the church while Will helped Kim check everything was all set up. Before long, people started coming in, and Will found Jenna again so she could greet people with him.

The service itself went smoothly until Kim stood up to say a few words about her mother. She had been crying throughout, and Jenna had given Will a concerned glance before Kim had even started talking.

'My mother was a wonderful woman, but she was also difficult to get on with.'

Jenna sensed Will's stifled groan at the beginning of this tribute. The speech ran on, and soon people in the church started shuffling on their wooden seats, conveying how awkward they, too, were finding Kim's eulogy. When Kim finally finished, she collapsed back into her seat next to Will, with her tissue in hand and very red eyes.

The pastor looked politely relieved and the rest of the service passed without incident. Kim's speech had taken so much longer than they had been expecting, there was no time to linger at the church. The service at the modern crematorium was much more efficient, which, for once, was a blessing, and then they just had the wake to get through. By the time they arrived back at the church hall, there were only a handful of people gathered.

'Where is everybody?' Kim wailed. 'Who's going to eat all this?' She gestured at the tables laden with sandwiches, salads and cold cuts. Jenna didn't know what to say.

'They must have had to go because the services have taken so long, Kim. We're due at the lawyer's office this afternoon anyway, so it's probably for the best.' Will was keeping calm despite Kim's panic.

An hour later, everyone had left. Jenna was surprised so few people stayed behind and also that none of them had any fond memories of Kim's mother to impart.

They took a cab back downtown to the lawyer's office. Jenna was glad it was nearly all over. It had been such a long day, but at least Kim had been more manageable.

Once inside the beautiful red brick building, they waited for the lawyer to be free.

'Ah, Kim, Will, good to see you both. I wish it were under better circumstances.'

'Hello, Mr. Bennett,' Will said, shaking his hand. 'This is my girl-friend, Jenna.'

Mr. Bennett shook Jenna's hand too before showing them in to his office, where they all took a seat opposite him.

'Well, Kim, your mother's general affairs were all put in order long before she went into the hospice. However, she also had some property which she had asked me to dispose of when the time came. I have now dealt with all that, and the proceeds from the sale of those properties were added to your mother's estate before she died. Your mother also asked me to update her will when it became clear she was in her final days.'

Kim let out a large sob and Will patted her hand. Jenna returned her attention to the lawyer and waited to hear what he was going to say next. Will had told her it was all a formality; as Kim was his step-mother's natural daughter, the estate would pass to her. Jenna had wondered about that. Why would Will have been invited to the meeting then?

'Mrs. Thompson left an estate totalling $336,000 and she has stipulated that the estate be shared equally between her daughter, Kim, and her stepson, Will. As the executor of her will, it will be my job to make sure her instructions are faithfully carried out.'

Kim let out the most enormous cry. Will, on the other hand, was speechless. Kim pushed Will's hand off hers and jumped to her feet, waving her arms at the lawyer.

'How can this possibly be? Will's not her son. I am her only child. The whole estate should be mine. I've been looking after her for months now, while he's been swanning off in England.'

'Please sit down, Kim. I have a letter for each of you from your mother explaining her motives and I would strongly urge you both to read these before getting upset any further.'

He held out the letters, but Kim refused to take hers, although she did sit back down. Will was still recovering from the shock of hearing the will read out. Jenna stepped in and took the letters. She held Kim's out to her, but Kim folded her arms and stuck her nose in the air. Jenna handed her letter back to Mr. Bennett and gave Will his, which he slipped inside his jacket pocket.

'Please take some time to read your letter, Will, and if you have any questions, please let me know. I will need to take your contact details over in the UK so I can make sure everything is done correctly for you to receive your inheritance.'

Kim snorted in the background.

Will got to his feet. 'Thank you, Mr. Bennett. I'll be in touch.' He and Jenna shook the lawyer's hand and they left the room, leaving Kim to her own devices while they escaped.

---

## Will

Will was quiet in the cab on the way back from the lawyer's office. His fists were clenched and his mind was awash with competing emotions. He didn't want his stepmother's money, that much he knew for sure, but more than that, he resented the way she was still manipulating him after her death, and putting him at odds with Kim in the process.

'Will, you've not said a word since we left.' Jenna's voice broke into his thoughts.

'I'm sorry. I'm trying to process what the hell just happened, and why my stepmother would go to the trouble of leaving me her money when she never had any time for me when she was alive.'

'It does seem odd. You haven't read the letter yet, but my guess is that maybe she was trying to atone for all the bad things she did to you.'

'It's too late for all that now. Anyway, I don't want her money. I will read the letter when we get back, but I honestly wonder if the only reason she left any money to me was just because she knew how much it would annoy Kim.'

'Hmm, perhaps you're right. But are you sure you don't want the money?'

'Absolutely. At least that will cheer Kim up. Do you know, Jenna?' he asked, looking her in the eye for the first time since they'd got into the cab. 'I'm just about done with being here. I'd like to go back home as soon as we can.'

Jenna patted his hand and smiled at him. 'Whatever you want, sweetheart.'

By the time they reached the hotel, it was early evening. They were both exhausted after all the events of the day. They'd left their phones behind out of respect while they attended the funeral, so Will was surprised when the receptionist called him over because she had a message for him.

'Your sister called while you were out, sir.' She handed him a piece of paper and he opened it.

*'Will, please call me when you get back to the hotel. I want to talk to you urgently about my mother's will.'*

He read it out to Jenna and she grimaced.

'She just can't let it go, can she?'

They rode up to their floor in silence while Will pondered what the hell Kim was going to say now. He needed to make it clear to her once and for all that he didn't want the money. He didn't care if she had it all.

His phone was ringing as soon as he walked into the room. When he crossed to the bedside table to retrieve it, Kim's name was flashing on the screen.

'Kim.' He didn't offer any pleasantries – he had none left to give her.

'Look, Will, we need to talk.'

'No, Kim, we don't. I don't want this money. I'm happy for you to have it all. So, that's it, end of story.' He waited to see what she would say to that but there was silence at the other end of the line. He smiled to himself. That had to be the first time Kim had been speechless in her life.

'That's all very well for you to say,' she said finally, recovering her usual poise. 'You'll need to tell the lawyer and get him to draw up documents.'

'I don't *need* to do anything, Kim. In any case, Jenna and I will be returning to the UK very soon, so I won't have time to spare on dealing with this for you. You'll have to do that yourself.'

'What? What do you mean? You can't leave the country now.'

'I can and I will. I've been here a long time already. I know this has been a hard time for you, but frankly, I've had more than enough of all this drama to last me a lifetime.'

'How can you say that to me after all I've been through?'

Her wheedling voice almost drew Will in, but he remained strong.

'I have to go now, Kim. You'll be fine, but I wish you luck all the same.'

With that, he disconnected the call and put his phone on silent.

'That sounded like a very demanding phone call,' Jenna said, coming back into the room. She was in the process of removing her make-up. When every scrap was removed, the "real" Jenna appeared beneath, and Will sighed at the sight of her.

'You are so beautiful, inside and out,' he told her, going to her and taking her in his arms.

'That wasn't the answer I was expecting, but it's still lovely to hear.'

Will pulled her closer, revelling in the glorious smell of her. 'It was difficult speaking to Kim,' he agreed. 'But I've said all I needed to say to her. From now on, it's up to her.'

'Are you going to read that letter from your stepmother now?'

Will pulled a face. 'What about organising the tickets to go home?'

'When do you want to go?'

'As soon as we can,' he replied, pulling back a little. 'Let me get my tablet and we can check availability.'

'Why don't you leave that to me while you read the letter?' Jenna took the tablet gently from his hands. Thankfully, she had bought an open-ended return, so as long as there were seats, she could go ahead and book.

Will left her to it while he went over to the window to read the letter from his stepmom.

'*Will, I know you will be surprised to learn of my decision to split my inheritance between you and Kim, but it was the only fair thing for me to do in the circumstances. I was a foolish woman in my youth, and I took things out on you that were not your fault. It's never easy step-ping into another woman's shoes, and I felt inadequate compared to your mother. I had no right to take that out on you, and I was ashamed of it right up to the end of my life. I could have made it up to you so much sooner, especially after your father's death, but I didn't know how, and I expect you would have rejected any attempt on my part. So, please accept this token as my apology. I know Kim will be upset about it but I hope in time she will understand. With love, Angela.*'

Will folded the letter carefully and put it in his laptop bag. If anything, reading the letter had made him even more determined to go home and build his future with Jenna. Nashville belonged to his past now and the sooner he left it behind, the happier he would be. He only hoped Jackson would accept that plan as far as his work was concerned and would agree to liaise with him in other ways rather than face-to-face.

# CHAPTER 8

**<u>Jenna</u>**

The flight from Charlottesville back to the UK passed slowly. Will kept his thoughts to himself, despite Jenna trying to engage him in conversation several times. In the end, she left him to it, figuring he would talk about the letter when he was ready. She was glad to be going home, to get back to a kind of normality. She was looking forward to finding out how her parents had got on and how everything was going with her business. Guilt had threatened to overwhelm her at times, because she'd been so busy in Nashville she'd hardly had a moment to check on the business and her staff. Still, she'd exchanged texts with Mary every day and she had reassured Jenna everything was fine.

She drifted off to sleep and when she woke again, it was nearly time to land. She gazed out of the window at the inevitable rainy landscape and sighed. That was one thing she definitely preferred about Nashville. She glanced over at Will to find he was just waking up too. He rubbed his eyes and blinked a few times as if he'd forgotten where he was.

'Hey, feeling better?' she asked, touching his cheek.

He reached out and took her hand. 'I guess. I'm sorry I've been so grumpy. I've been going over and over it all and I can't seem to make any progress with it.'

'Let's not talk about it any more. Let's just get home and we can sort it all out there.'

It was late afternoon by the time the taxi pulled up outside their cottage and they were both exhausted after their long journey. Once they'd dumped their bags inside, Jenna decided to call her parents to find out how everything had gone in her absence, while Will went off for a shower.

'Mum, hi, it's me. We just got back.'

'Oh, darling, so good to hear from you. How was your trip? Did the funeral go all right?'

'The funeral went as well as can be expected, and the rest of the trip was mainly good, but there's a lot to tell you. I wanted to find out how you and Dad got on working with Greg first.'

'It was wonderful, sweetheart. I enjoyed every minute. Greg is such a lovely young man and your dad thoroughly enjoyed having something to do with himself after all this time. To be honest, I think we're really going to miss it.'

'That's fantastic! I don't know whether to be pleased or upset at how dispensable I've become.' She laughed.

'Oh, Jenna, don't say that. It's not true, but we did enjoy having something to occupy our days.'

'We'll have to talk more about it, but I just wanted to check in with you both. How's Dad? Is he still doing well?'

'Yes. He feels better for being active, to be honest, so it's all good. Anyway, come to dinner the two of you and we can catch up with all your news too. Did you see Rachel? That was the one thing I did want to know.'

'We did and she was doing so well. She's still got a few months to go and she's already getting impatient.'

'Oh, bless her heart. I do miss her.'

Jenna rang off and smiled. Her parents had surprised her, but she was glad it had all gone so well for them. She went in search of Will and found him back in the bedroom, his hair damp from the shower and a towel wrapped around his waist.

'Hey, sweetheart. How are your parents?' He caught her eye in the mirror. When she didn't reply, he turned round. 'Jenna? Are you checking me out?' He grinned at her.

'You bet I am. You look good enough to eat and I am feeling quite peckish right now.'

He laughed and reached for her before tumbling with her onto the bed.

'I love you.' He kissed her deeply and when her lips parted, he groaned with pleasure.

'I know,' she replied when they broke after a long few minutes. She made light work of his towel and sat up to remove her t-shirt and bra. The touch of his hands on her skin was like balm to her soul and she moaned as he kissed the skin between her breasts.

A second later, he'd freed her from her jeans and was lying on top of her.

'You are so beautiful,' he whispered, his warm breath caressing her skin and making her shiver with desire.

She yielded herself completely to him and it wasn't long before they both reached their release, as if their pent-up desires had been held in for far too long. Will pulled her close to him as they lay back on the bed recovering from their lovemaking. She rested her palm on his chest, circling her hand gently in his fine hair.

'How are you feeling about everything now?' she asked.

'Oh, much the same even though I've had a chance to get some perspective on it now. It all feels so unreal. I can't believe my step-mother left me anything at all, and part of me automatically wants to reject the money because it would be hypocritical to take it. Then there's the fact that it would annoy the hell out of Kim if I did take it when she was clearly expecting to inherit it all. I saw a side of Kim I didn't even know existed, and I just want to steer clear of her now. I have no desire to go back to Nashville for the foreseeable future and I never thought I would say that.'

'You don't have to take the money. And that would solve the problem with Kim but as for your future relationship with her, that might take longer to work out.'

---

## Will

Will woke early the following morning and was surprised to see Jenna was still asleep. He tossed and turned for a while, desperate to fall back to sleep, but in the end, he just gave up. Inevitably, his mind filled with his worries and he became more and more frustrated the longer he went over them. He finally got up out of bed and went to get started on breakfast.

In the middle of putting the coffee on he realised he had made at least one decision: he didn't want to be apart from Jenna any more than he had to in the future. He was going to try spending the week in Paris but coming back at the weekend, as he'd suggested to her. His priority apart from that was to get the Paris office finalised as quickly as possible. After that, he wasn't sure whether he wanted to continue doing the work he had been doing. It was time for a change, but to what exactly, he had no idea.

He was just beating up some eggs when Jenna joined him in the kitchen. She slipped her arms around his waist and pressed her warm body against his back.

'Hey, if you do that, we won't get any breakfast, sweetheart.'

'We can't have that,' she purred, 'because I am starving!' She laughed and let him go.

Will reached out and pulled her to him for a kiss before she could get away.

'Okay, time to focus. Let's get these eggs scrambling. Could you take care of the toast, please?'

'I'm on it,' Jenna replied, taking two slices of bread out of the bag they'd picked up at the bakery the day before. 'Did you wake up very early?'

'Yes – earlier than you anyway.' He glanced at his watch and winced to see it was still only six thirty.

'You sound a bit brighter. Have you made some decisions?'

'Yes, one or two. The most important is that I'm going to try the idea of staying in Paris during the week so I can be with you at the weekend.' He set the plates down on the table and they both sat down.

'Are you sure you won't get fed up with doing that?'

'Yes, I'll be fine. I have a lot of flexibility around my movements, and I don't want us to be apart, that's all.'

She smiled at him and rubbed her foot against his under the table. He grinned back.

'And what else did you decide?'

'This might sound crazy, but I'm thinking about looking for a new job when I've finished setting up the Paris office.' He released a long breath, relieved to have finally told Jenna what he was thinking.

'What? Stop working for Jackson?'

'It's not that I want to stop working for Jackson, but I feel ready for something new and I want something here, so we can be together as much as possible.'

'If you're sure that's what you want, you should go for it, but don't rush into it. Oh my goodness, I'm going to have to dash, Will, time's running on. I love you and thanks for breakfast.'

She leaned over and they met for a kiss across the table.

'You go, I'll clear up, don't worry.'

'I love you,' she called, rushing off to get ready for work.

Will's flight to Paris was later that afternoon. He wasn't going to see Jenna again for a few days, and his heart was heavy by the time he landed in France.

He was heading into the office for an update on all that had happened while he'd been away, and he planned to get right down to things the next day so he didn't waste any more time.

'*Bruno, salut, c'est bon de vous revoir.*' He shook hands with his executive assistant and glanced around the office to see how things looked.

'It's good to see you, too, Will. You will be very happy with the progress we've made while you have been away.'

Will sat down at his new modern desk, smoothing his hand across the sleek, dark wood finish, and Bruno took the seat opposite, flicking through his tablet to find what he wanted to tell him.

'So, first of all, I have arranged four new appointments with candidates for office manager following the recommendations you gave me when you were away. They all speak fluent English and have very good experience matched to your criteria.'

'That is good news. When are these happening?'

'Tomorrow. I confirmed with them all today when I knew you were coming back.'

'Excellent. Anything else?'

'The office is all organised and I put all the systems in place while you were away – phones, broadband, computers, utilities, etc. It's all done and we've been working smoothly for a good few days now.'

'How about the other staff? Any issues there?' Will glanced around the office to see a few people still working. Everything seemed well established already.

'Everyone has settled in very well. I have the résumés of the people you'll be interviewing here for you.' Bruno passed him a bundle of papers. 'I've summarised the key pros and cons of each candidate to make it a bit easier for you.'

Will looked up at him. 'You've been a star, Bruno, thank you.'

Bruno smiled. 'And you, Will? How was your trip?'

He groaned. 'It was very difficult in many ways and it has made me re-evaluate what I'm doing with my life.'

'That does sound bad. I hope things will work themselves out soon for you.'

Will didn't tell Bruno of his work plans, not wanting to worry him before a manager was in place. 'I have decided I will be going home for the weekends in future, Bruno, so Fridays and Mondays will have to be a bit more flexible, but I hope we can work round that.'

'Yes, of course, that won't be a problem.' Bruno stood up to go. 'I'll see you in the morning.'

---

## Jenna

By mid-morning, Jenna had already sorted through her outstanding paperwork. Her desk had never looked so tidy. Mary had been fine without her and had managed the shop with no problems. She had also kept on top of all the shop paperwork. Jenna was pleased about that, but at the same time she felt deflated at the thought that Mary was able to manage so well on her own.

Greg and her mum had overseen four weddings while Jenna was away. Between the two of them, they had also managed pretty well, only deferring to Mary when they were really stuck. The customers hadn't noticed any difference, which was the main thing. And her dad had worked alongside both Mary, running the shop, and Greg, organising the weddings. He had brought his own special brand of customer service to the whole operation. Jenna sighed, feeling superfluous.

'Ooh, that was a big sigh. There aren't any problems, are there?' Mary came in for her morning cup of tea.

'No, that's the issue. You guys have managed so well without me and I'm feeling a bit redundant.' She tried to grin but failed.

'Oh, that's not true at all, Jenna. It's just you've trained us all so well and that means we can get on and do everything when you're not here. It's much nicer when you are here, but now you can get away once in a while too.' She flicked the switch on the kettle.

'There was one query here I was unsure about, from Lulborne House, asking me to call them.'

'Oh yes, I'd forgotten about that one. They called one day asking for you and said they needed to speak to you directly and that they could wait till you were back. I took the lady's name and phone number for you.' Mary peered over Jenna's shoulder to check.

'Yes, you did. That's fine. I'll give her a ring back in a minute.'

Mary passed her a cup of tea. 'So how's everything with you and Will? Did you manage to have a good time in Nashville, apart from the funeral?'

By the time Jenna had told her all about what had happened, they'd had to move back out to the shop to deal with customers. When things finally quietened down, Jenna returned to her office to call the lady at Lulborne House. She was quite excited to think that a stately home was contacting her, but she had no idea what they might be looking for.

'Hello, could I speak to Lucy Peterson, please? It's Jenna Andrews calling.'

'Oh hello, Jenna, this is Lucy. Thanks so much for calling me back. We're looking for a new supplier to take over all the flowers for our weddings here at the house. I've heard such good feedback about your business, I thought I would get in touch to see if we could organise a meeting.'

'My goodness, of all the things I was expecting you to say, that wasn't it. Thank you so much for thinking of us, that's a great compliment.'

Lucy laughed, a genuine, bubbly sound, and Jenna liked her immediately.

'So shall we arrange a meeting? Would you be able to come up to see me at the house one day?'

'Yes, of course. In fact, I know this is short notice but I'm free this afternoon. Would that suit you?'

'Actually, that would work for me. Just let me double-check my calendar.'

Jenna held her breath. She could hardly believe this was happening. It would be such a big contract if they were successful. She had no idea how they would manage it, but she was determined they would.

'Yes, that will be fine. Shall we say two thirty?'

'Lovely. I'll see you then. I'll bring our portfolio so you can see the sort of things we've been doing for our most recent weddings.'

'I'll look forward to it. Thanks for calling.'

Jenna rang off and it was all she could do not to squeal out loud. She ran out to the shop to find it full of customers. She pitched in to help instead, itching to tell Mary her news. The moment the last customer left the shop, she finally let rip.

'Squeee!' she cried, much to Mary's surprise.

'What is it, Jenna? Is everything okay?'

Jenna laughed at her concern before telling her all about her phone call with Lucy.

'Oh my goodness! That sounds fantastic. Greg will be happy to hear the news as well, I'm sure.'

'Right, I'm going to go and grab some lunch before I have to set off. Do you want anything?'

After lunch, she gathered her portfolio together, glad to see Greg had updated it with photos from the weddings he'd attended while she'd been away. She made a mental note to thank him when he was next in work.

Soon she was in the van driving north out of Poole before turning west in the direction of Dorchester. Her dad had also given the van a clean and a hoover, something Jenna had been meaning to do for ages. She basked in the comparative luxury of the van in its new incarnation, feeling glad to be back home again in Dorset with familiar villages and lanes around her.

Jenna finally saw the turning for the house and was soon driving along the gravel driveway which led to the splendid Georgian building. The façade never failed to impress her, no matter how many times she saw it. It reminded her of an Italian palace, and she had spent many a happy hour as a child exploring the beautiful gardens of the estate. Now she was coming for a meeting for her own business. How things had changed!

# CHAPTER 9

**Will**

Will spent the whole of the following day interviewing candidates for the role of office manager in Paris. It was gruelling, but by the end of the day, he had a favourite. Chantal had a fluent command of English and German, as well as her native French, and she had been working for a mid-level independent record label in France for the past five years. She was enthusiastic and had lots of good ideas about how to develop the office as a new organisation in the field. More than that, Will had really got on with her and liked her easy-going nature.

'I've made a decision,' Will said, as Bruno returned from showing the last candidate out towards the bank of lifts.

Bruno smiled. 'That's excellent news. I bet I can guess which one you liked the most.'

'Go on. Who do you think I went for?' Will folded his arms and leaned against his desk, confident Bruno wouldn't be able to work it out.

'I reckon your favourite would have been... Chantal!' He

chuckled as Will slumped forward, disappointed he'd been able to work it out so quickly.

'I did have the advantage of seeing the candidates' details before you and of communicating with them over the past week. I just had a feeling about Chantal from the first time I spoke to her.'

Will straightened up, remembering just how great a match Chantal had been. 'We have our manager, then. I'd like to have her come in for the day before we officially offer her the job, so we can double-check how you two work together. Would you be able to get onto that tomorrow please, Bruno? And you'll contact the other candidates, won't you?'

'Of course.'

Will left the office not long afterwards to go back to his apartment. The glorious sunshine lifted his spirits as he walked to the nearest *Métro* station, but he didn't feel like walking the romantic streets with no-one there to share them with. As he travelled home on the train a little later, his excitement about Chantal waned. His apartment would be empty when he got there, and he would have no-one to share his good news with. Specifically, Jenna wouldn't be there.

Once indoors, he called Jenna on Skype, desperate to talk to her and catch up with her news. He was relieved when she picked up straight away.

'Hey, baby, how are you?' he asked, when her gorgeous face appeared.

'I am really good. I've had a great couple of days workwise. How about you?'

'I'm good too, although I miss you. But go on, you go first. Tell me your news.'

He listened carefully while Jenna told him all about her visit to Lulborne House.

'Wow! That sounds like a great new potential business partnership.'

'I know, and I did absolutely nothing to make it happen.'

'That's not strictly true. Your reputation has preceded you and people are getting to hear about how good you are. You might not have done anything directly, but indirectly you have brought this about all on your own. So what's going to happen next?'

'Lucy wants me to go back again and talk over the final details. She's emailed me a provisional contract, and I'd like to talk it over with you at the weekend before I decide.'

'Sure, that's a good plan and thank you for waiting to talk with me about it.'

'So that's my big news. How about you?'

'I carried out the interviews today and I think I've found our new office manager. Her name's Chantal and she's going to come in to spend the day with us just to make sure she can work together with everyone. If that all works out, I want her to start as soon as possible.'

'I spy a double celebration this weekend. What a great week we've both had.' Jenna beamed at him and he wished he was there with her.

'Seeing you on Friday will be the icing on the cake.'

'Not long to go now, and we only have the one wedding this weekend, so I won't be out that much either.'

'That's kind of good and bad, isn't it, I guess? Good that we can see each other, but not so good that you've only got the one wedding.'

'It goes like that, and although we're into June now, it's still quite early in the season. Maybe it wouldn't hurt to do a bit of advertising. In fact, I have a whole heap of testimonials I could use.'

Jenna's mind was buzzing and Will smiled at her passionate approach to her business.

'Have you thought about expanding your website, sweetheart, from that single page you've got?'

'I have thought about it, but it's another one of those things I've never got round to. How good are you with that sort of stuff?'

'Pretty good, I like to think. Are you thinking about us having a sexy techie weekend?'

'Ha! Sexy is definitely not the word for it, but yeah, if you help me, we could probably get something done quite quickly, couldn't we?'

'Definitely. I'll make a start when you're busy with the wedding if you like. Let me know what else you want to put on it.'

'The wedding's on Sunday, so we'll have Saturday afternoon free to work on it. When will you get back?'

'I'm thinking of taking the Eurostar again. It will take me straight into London and cut out the delay travelling from the airport. I'd hope to get home mid-afternoon.'

'That all sounds brilliant. Take care and I'll see you on Friday.'

She blew him a kiss and as he caught it, he made up his mind it was time for him and Jenna to move their relationship to the next level.

---

## Jenna

Jenna was keen to talk over the proposition from Lulborne House with Greg when he arrived for work. It would mean a lot more work for them if they took on the contract and as Greg had only been employed to work part-time, she didn't know how he would take this new situation.

Greg was in nice and early. After they'd helped Mary set the shop up for the day, and Jenna had caught Greg up on her Nashville trip, they settled in the kitchen for a business chat.

'First of all, I wanted to say thank you and well done for holding the fort with the wedding side of things while I was away. You did a great job, and you managed working with my parents as well.'

'It was no bother, and your parents are lovely too.' Greg smiled at Jenna.

'I have some news about a new contract to supply Lulborne House with flowers for their wedding events. The enquiry came in while I was away and I went up there yesterday to see the woman who does all their organising.'

'Wow! That's a big deal. It would be a big step up for us, wouldn't it?'

'It would, yes. They have weddings during the week, as well as at weekends during the season, so it would more than double our workload. Plus, there would be all the extra driving involved up to the estate and back.'

'Yes, that's going to have quite an impact. Have you definitely decided to take on the contract?'

'I'm seriously considering it, but I wanted to talk it over with you, and also with Will when he comes home at the weekend.'

Greg gave a puzzled frown. 'Why did you want to talk it over with me?'

'I would need someone full-time if I were to take this contract on, and I wondered how you felt about that?'

'I don't know. I'd have to talk it over at home. It would mean more unsociable hours, wouldn't it?'

'I don't think so. It would probably mean we would have to split our time between the weddings we normally have and the ones for the estate. I'm not sure how it would work in practice, but I have to be honest, there would definitely be changes.'

'Okay, let me go home and talk to my boyfriend tonight and see what happens after that. Is that okay?'

'Yes, of course. We should probably check everything over for the wedding we have this weekend, shouldn't we?'

Jenna reviewed her mum's notes with Greg and as everything was very clear, they had easily sorted out the flowers and the decorations by the end of the day. Jenna decided to go and visit her parents to tell them about the new contract on the table from Lulborne House.

'That sounds fantastic, Jenna.' Her mum poured them both a cup of tea from the pot she'd just made and sat down at the kitchen island next to her daughter.

'It's also quite scary because our workload will probably double if we go ahead with it. When I asked Greg if he'd like to go full-time earlier, he wasn't that sure about it. I can't blame him, because the job he applied for was only part-time, and it's me who's moving the goalposts.'

'What about if I helped out while you got started with it? Just on a temporary basis perhaps, until you know what's really involved. And I'm sure your dad would love to carry on driving around for you.'

'It had crossed my mind to ask you both, but are you sure you'd really like to carry on working with us, Mum? You might not get much free time any more.'

'Why don't we see how it goes? If it does need someone permanent, I could stay until you'd found someone.'

'It all sounds good, and thanks so much for offering to help out. I'm going to talk it all over with Will at the weekend and see what he thinks.'

'How's he been getting on back in Paris?'

Jenna filled her mum in on all Will's news too, before reluctantly getting up to leave.

'I'd best make my way, Mum if I want to get home before bedtime.' She gave her mum a hug.

The sound of the front door opening signalled Jenna's dad was home, and shortly after, he called out in greeting from the hallway. Both women turned as he came into the kitchen.

'Jenna, sweetheart! I didn't know you were coming round for dinner.' He gave Jenna a hug and a kiss before putting his arm round his wife and kissing her on the cheek.

'I just popped in for a chat with Mum. I'm on my way now.'

'Are you sure you don't want to stay for dinner? I've prepared a nice home-made pizza.' He wiggled his eyebrows at her persuasively and she laughed.

'That sounds lovely compared to what's in my fridge. I would like to stay. It's just I don't want to be back too late.'

'How about I give you a lift when we've eaten? Go on, love, it will be nice for us to catch up too.'

Jenna sat down again and her dad clapped his hands together. He went to the fridge to retrieve his pizza creation and set it down on the kitchen island while he waited for the oven to come up to temperature.

'That looks fabulous, Dad. You've become quite a good cook in your old age.' Jenna winked at her mum and her dad flicked her gently with the tea towel.

'Less of the old, thank you very much, otherwise you won't be getting any tea.'

## Will

Will arrived back at the cottage in the middle of the afternoon, giving himself plenty of time to prepare for the evening ahead. He wanted to take Jenna out for a romantic candlelit dinner. It was a long time since the two of them had been able to spend time together without worrying about anything else.

With his office manager chosen, Will's job in Paris was almost done, and he was ready to talk to Jackson about his future. There was time for him to do that this weekend, but he wasn't worried about that conversation any more.

Jenna threw her arms round him as she walked into the little kitchen.

'Oh, it's so good to see you. It hasn't been long, but it has felt like it.'

They kissed and all their troubles melted away. As they pulled apart, Jenna looked him up and down.

'Mmm, you look gorgeous. Are we going somewhere special?'

'We are,' he replied, swinging her gently to and fro. 'I've booked a table at Simply Seafood for seven thirty, so you've got plenty of time to get ready.'

'What's the occasion?'

'Do we need one? I just thought it had been too long since we'd been out for the sake of being together and having a delicious meal.'

Jenna went upstairs to get changed and Will took out his laptop while he waited. He'd been thinking about Jenna's website and he was sure he could set up some more pages for her pretty quickly. Once that was done, he would be able to add in testimonials and details about all her different services. He was still sitting there when Jenna returned. She gave a little cough to get his attention.

Will looked up and his mouth dropped open. Closing his laptop and moving it aside, he stood up. 'You look amazing! I can't believe how you've transformed in that short time.'

'Are you trying to say I scrub up well?' She laughed and then her smile faded as she took in Will's look of confusion. There were still a few British sayings he didn't quite get. 'It's okay,' she reassured him. 'It's not rude. It's another way of saying I can look good when I make the effort.'

'I still don't like it. You look beautiful all the time, but you look especially wonderful tonight.' He kissed her tenderly. 'I'm going to call us a cab so we can just take it easy.'

Within half an hour, they were arriving outside the cosy little seafood restaurant they had both come to love. Will remembered Jackson telling him how he'd taken Rachel there on their first proper date, and now it had become one of Will's and Jenna's favourites too.

They ordered prosecco to celebrate being together, and once they'd placed their food orders, they relaxed into the evening.

Jenna took a sip of her drink. 'So, were you still working while I was getting ready?' she asked.

'I was, but this time I was working on your new website.'

Her eyes widened and Will smiled at her surprise.

'That's amazing, and sweet of you to remember as well.'

'It's only very basic at the moment. I'll obviously need more input from you, but it's a start. I had a look at some similar websites online to get the feel of what most of them tend to do, and went from there. The tech side is easy enough for me, now that I've done it a few times for work.'

'Have you ever thought about setting up a business doing web design? You'd be really good at it.'

'No, I've never thought about working for myself. I guess I do have a lot of skills to offer now, especially on the marketing front. I do feel I'd like a change, though.'

'Since when?'

'Since I've been away from you for most of the week, and since I've barely found time to see you at the weekend, due to all your work too.'

Their meals arrived and Will paused to let the waitress put everything down on the table. Jenna eyed her lobster ravioli longingly, making Will laugh. His cod with chorizo also looked amazing. The waitress served their glasses of wine and slipped away, leaving them to pick up their discussion.

'Yes, these last few weeks have been difficult for both of us, but even before then, when you were commuting during the week and I was working all weekend, it was hard. It's probably a good time to review what we want to do next if your Paris job is almost at an end.'

'I agree, and there is something I want to talk to you about.'

Jenna looked up, her face a picture of delight. 'This is so good,' she declared, gesturing at her dish. 'Sorry, what were you saying?'

'Jenna, will you marry me?'

Jenna paused with her fork midway to her mouth. She put her fork down and gave him her full attention. 'Say that again, please?'

'Will you marry me? I know I haven't got down on one knee. I didn't want to embarrass you, but I hope the setting is romantic enough.'

'Of course it is. And, yes, I will.' Her face lit up and she leaned forward to kiss him across the table.

'Oh, Jenna, I wish I hadn't left it so long to ask you. I haven't got you a ring yet. When I asked your mum about it, she advised me to talk it over with you.'

'Wait, you asked my mum?'

'Yes, I spoke to her and your dad earlier in the week to make sure they'd be happy to have me as their son-in-law.'

'And I guess they were?' She gave him a cheeky smile, marvelling at the same time at how her parents had kept the secret from her.

'They were, but not as happy as I'll be to make you my wife, sweetheart.'

# CHAPTER 10

**<u>Jenna</u>**

Jenna left Will working on her new website design while she went off to work on the Saturday morning. She'd given him some testimonials to add to the site and would give him more information on her return. She smiled to herself as she walked through the quiet residential streets leading into town. She and Will were engaged at last, and she couldn't wait to shout it from the rooftops. Mary would be so pleased for her, and her parents obviously were too. She was full of joy, feeling that at last, everything in her world was starting to look a lot rosier.

'Oh my goodness, congratulations!' Mary threw her arms round Jenna when she told her the good news. 'How wonderful for you both. Now we'll be able to plan your wedding at last.'

'Ooh, yes. I will finally be the bride, organising my own flowers, and not just the florist.'

'Do you have any idea of your date yet?'

'We've just settled on as soon as possible. We'd like it to be this year, and nothing too grand. I would like Rachel to be able to come, and that means the timing might be a bit tricky, with her being due in September.'

'Do you have any preference over time of year at all? You could go for spring next year, which would allow Rachel to come more easily.'

'I don't know, Mary. We'll Skype Rachel and Jackson later to tell them the news and I can talk to her about it then.'

What with telling Greg all her news and planning for the following day's wedding, the morning flew by. Jenna popped into the bakery to pick up some lunch for her and Will before walking along the seafront for a while, taking in the colourful boats bobbing in the harbour, and the seagulls swooping about in the hope of some food from the tourists. Then she wended her way up the little streets towards home.

'Hello!' She waited for Will to answer. When no reply came she frowned, puzzled. She popped her head round the doors of the rooms she passed along the hallway but there was no sign of him. On the kitchen table, she found a note.

'Decided to go into town briefly. Should be back around the same time as you xx'

Jenna popped the sandwiches she'd bought onto plates and switched the kettle on. She was staring out the window at their tiny courtyard garden, thinking how she needed to tidy up her flowerpots, when she heard the front door open. She turned round and went out to greet Will.

'Hey, where've you been?' She smiled at him. By the cheeky grin on his face, she knew he'd been up to something. He had a small bag in his hand and was at pains to keep it away from her prying eyes. He came closer.

'Close your eyes,' he whispered.

Jenna did as he asked and he lifted one of her hands and put something velvety there for her. She opened her eyes with a gasp. A jewellery box.

'I know I said we'd talk it over together, but I saw something in the local paper this morning and I thought it was just right for you. I hope you like it.'

She lifted the box lid, her heart pounding. The minute she saw the ring Will had chosen, she released her breath. Inside, nestling on a bed of silk, was a white gold engagement ring with three diamonds set across the top.

'Oh, Will, it's beautiful. I love it.' She looked up at him, her eyes full of unshed tears. 'It's like a modern version of my mum's ring, and just what I would have chosen myself. Thank you.'

Jenna had told Will how much she loved her mum's ring on more than one occasion. It was heartening to know he had been listening so carefully to her.

He took the ring out of the box and lifted her left hand to slip it onto her finger where it fitted perfectly. He blew out a breath too.

'You probably didn't notice, but I sneaked one of your other rings away so the jeweller could make sure it was the right size for you.'

He took her in his arms and kissed her, a deep, lingering kiss with the promise of so much happiness in their married life to come.

Finally, they pulled apart, but Will didn't let her go. 'By the way, your mum wanted you to ring her back so she can, "*squeal down the phone with you about your good news*" was how she put it!'

Jenna laughed. 'Did you tell her we'd be over for Sunday lunch tomorrow?'

'Oh yes, she can't wait to see us and to see Matt's and Natalie's faces when we announce our news as well.'

---

## Will

After lunch, Will spent the afternoon poring over the contract Jenna had been given by Lulborne House. He'd been surprised there was even a contract involved and he wanted to make sure Jenna would be getting the best deal out of it. He heard her tapping away on the computer in the kitchen from his place on the sofa in their lounge. He glanced up and thought about how small the cottage was. It was fine for the two of them, but he did wish they had more space. Maybe that was something they needed to think about as they were now going to be married. He stopped himself there, trying to focus on the legal paperwork in front of him. He'd read a new sentence and moved onto the next, when he realised something didn't sit right with the previous one.

He went through to the kitchen.

'Jenna, did you realise this contract is requiring you to be exclusive to Lulborne House if you sign it?'

She stopped typing in her testimonials and took off her tortoise-shell-framed glasses. 'Huh? Sorry, can you say that again, please?'

He repeated what he'd just said and the look on her face made it clear she hadn't understood that at all. He gave her the contract and pointed to the sentence he was talking about.

'This means you can't do any other weddings if you take on this job.'

'But why? What's the point in that? It would make me vulnerable if I had only that one client.'

'I don't suppose they're that bothered about whether you're vulnerable. I presume they're thinking if they're your only customer, you'll be devoted to them, and not distracted by anyone else. You're right, it's not in your best interests longer term.'

'Damn, Will, that changes everything.'

She looked so disappointed he pulled her up and into his arms for a hug. 'Let me finish looking at it and we'll talk about it again. How are you getting on with the testimonials?'

'Yep, fine and I've started putting in some other details as well.'

'I'm going to do a Skype call with Jackson when I finish reading the contract, okay?'

'Sure.' She still looked worried as he went back to the lounge, but there was nothing they could do to resolve it at the moment.

'Hey, Jackson, good to see you. How's everything?'

'Hey, buddy. Yes, everything's good here. How about you?'

'I have a lot of good news.'

He proceeded to tell him all about the Paris office manager he had found, and his plans to help Chantal settle in.

'So we need to think about what you're going to do next.' Jackson rubbed his hand across his stubble.

'I wanted to talk to you about that. You may want to keep this quiet for now so Jenna can tell Rachel herself, but I asked Jenna to marry me yesterday, and she said yes.'

'Oh, man, that is wonderful news. Congratulations! When are you thinking of holding the wedding?'

'We'd like to do it this year, but we'll fit round you guys. Obviously, we want you both to come, so we can talk about that once your little one is born.'

'That's real good of you both to think about us, thank you.'

'Anyway, I've been thinking about my work a lot recently, because I don't want to be apart from Jenna as much as I have been. To be honest, I've been wondering about striking out on my own as a consultant of some kind.'

'Okay. I didn't see that coming, but I can understand why you're considering this change. Have you given any thought to what kind of consultant?'

'Maybe marketing, PR, website design – the sort of thing I was doing back in Nashville, I guess. I mean, I know I've been doing other things for you as well since I came over here, so I hope if I did go this route, you would still consider me for future projects?'

'Of course. You'll need to tell me what you decide to do and if you are going to leave the company, I'd appreciate some notice. I'll need to talk to everyone about how this changes things for us, but you know I'll support you, right?'

'I appreciate that, Jackson, and I'll be in touch. For now, everything will remain the same, and I'll keep you informed with how things progress in Paris.'

Will sat for a moment thinking about how he might make his new job idea work for both him and Jenna. He was excited but also a little nervous at the thought of going things alone, but he was confident he had the skills. He just needed to give it a try.

'Hey, how was Jackson?' Jenna joined him from the kitchen and sat down in the chair opposite him.

'Yeah, good. I told him about my idea of becoming a consultant and he was all right about it, wishing me well too.'

'He's a great guy and I'm glad he's being supportive of you. I'll speak to Rachel later as well. Did you tell him about our news?'

He looked sheepish but couldn't lie. 'I did, I hope you don't mind too much? I wanted him to know I don't want to be travelling away from you so much any more. It's part of the reason I want to try this consultant idea.'

She stood and came towards him, and he pushed his chair back to allow her to sit on his lap. He slipped his arms round her and she pulled him close to kiss him.

'I love you, and I can't wait to be your wife and partner in everything. I believe in you and your ability to do this. And the work you're doing on my website will be your first testimonial.'

'Have we done enough work for the day now?' He feathered kisses around her jaw, persuading her to his way of thinking. When she moaned softly in his ear, he knew it was only a matter of time before they found their way to the bedroom.

---

**Jenna**

Jenna was up and out early the next morning to pick Greg up, drop by the shop and get off to the wedding in plenty of time. The wedding venue for the whole event was a luxury hotel, so it was a question of dropping the flowers off for the bride and wedding party, and setting up the room where the ceremony was taking place, as well as the reception room. The floral arrangements had been kept cool overnight at the shop so that was their first stop. Within fifteen minutes, they'd loaded everything into the van and were on their way to the hotel.

'Any news about the Lulborne House contract?' Greg asked.

They were driving out of Poole along the coast road, past Jenna's parents' house and towards Sandbanks.

'Yes there is, and unfortunately, it's not good.' Jenna frowned.

'Why's that?'

'If we take it on, we have to agree to work exclusively for them. She didn't say anything about that when I met with her and it was only because I asked Will to have a look at the contract that I even knew about it. It's just not what I want. I feel we've got a great customer base that it's taken me years to build up. I don't want to throw that away now.'

'No, of course not. You could try and negotiate with her. It doesn't have to be the end of your relationship with them.'

'I suppose I could try, but I don't hold out a lot of hope, to be honest.'

Jenna pondered what Greg had said as they continued on their way. She hadn't even thought about negotiating with Lulborne House. Maybe that was naive of her. She'd talk to Will about it and call Lucy tomorrow.

The hotel was located on the beachfront and the view of the sea was spectacular. The wedding couple would have some fantastic photos of their special day, Jenna thought to herself as she and Greg weaved their magic. Two hours later, they were on their way again. The bride looked wonderful and relaxed by the time they'd finished and Jenna was pleased with another job well done. She dropped Greg home and drove back to the cottage in the van for once, rather than walk. They were going to her parents' house for Sunday lunch for the first time in ages and she wanted plenty of time to get herself ready.

Will was in the shower when she returned, and was probably just back from his run. As much as Jenna would have liked to join him, there wasn't time for any of that today. She gathered her clothes and waited for him to emerge so she could take her turn in the bathroom.

'Hey, sweetheart. How's your morning been?' His muscular body was a sight to see. She had a hard time focusing on his face as she took in the towel slung low around his hips and the water drying across his chest.

'Good and bad, I guess would sum it up.'

She stopped daydreaming and came back to the present. 'Why what's happened?'

'I received an email from Mr. Bennett, the lawyer, this morning. I was just enjoying a leisurely breakfast when it arrived in my inbox. Then immediately after that, I received an email from Kim.' He sat down on the bed next to her, drying his hair with a towel as he spoke.

'What did they say?'

'Mr. Bennett has some paperwork he needs to me sign so that he can transfer my share of the money from my stepmom.'

Jenna frowned but let him finish.

'Meanwhile, Kim wants me to take my share of the money. Now she's had a chance to think about it, and to digest her mom's letter, she accepts I deserve it as much as she does. She's asked me to go back to Nashville so we can put things right between us after our last meeting, and, if I do that, I can sign the paperwork as well.'

'Okay, so how do you feel about all that? Do you still feel the same about not taking the money?'

'I have to admit the money will come in handy for us while I get my new business off the ground. It will also mean we can have exactly the wedding and honeymoon we want, won't it? If I have to go back to Nashville, it's not the end of the world, because this ought to be the last time. What do you think?'

'First of all, I don't have to have a flashy wedding or honeymoon. I just want to get married to you.' She leaned over and kissed him. 'But you deserve that money, and as you say, if you have to go back to Nashville to sort it out, so be it. I can even come with you now, with Mum and Dad's help, if that would make it easier.'

After her shower, she changed into clean clothes and did her make-up.

'I told Greg about the Lulborne House issue this morning and he suggested I try and negotiate with them, rather than letting myself be defeated by that one clause. What do you think?'

'Yes, that sounds sensible. Maybe suggest to them that Greg becomes their regular point of contact so he builds a relationship with them. It might put them at ease if they knew they were always going to be speaking to the same person.'

'That's an even better idea.' She finished putting her lipstick on.

Jenna continued thinking about the contract as they drove over to her parents' house, and by the time they arrived, she'd tweaked Will's suggestion with some new ideas of her own.

She was just about to take her key out of her bag to open the front door when it was flung open by none other than her younger brother, Sam, grinning from ear to ear.

'Sam! What are you doing here?' She threw her arms around him.

'Jessie and I have come home for the celebrations. Congratulations on your great news.' Sam let her go and reached out to shake Will's hand.

They all went inside where the whole family was congregating in the kitchen. Jenna kissed Jessie and hugged her, before greeting her other brother, Matt and his wife, Natalie. Her mum was holding Matt's daughter, and Jenna gave them both a quick kiss before hugging her dad.

'This is the best surprise ever,' she said, beaming at them all.

# CHAPTER 11

**Will**

Will returned to Paris on the Monday. He was sad to be leaving Jenna behind again but relieved to have told Jackson his plans and to know his time in Paris would now be limited. By the time he arrived at the office, it was late afternoon. He was pleased to see Chantal working with Bruno to get to grips with her new role.

'So how do you feel after spending the day here today? Do you still want the job?' Will smiled at Chantal, hoping she would say yes.

'I've had a wonderful day, Will. I've enjoyed working with Bruno, which is going to be important in the future, and I think I can make a real difference to Rough Cut's business here in France.'

'That's good to know. And I agree. You'll be a real asset here. I spoke to Jackson about you over the weekend and he's eager to get to know you better. It would be good if we could do a conference call with him tomorrow.'

'Excellent. That sounds like a good idea.'

'The other thing we need to discuss is how long you'd like me to hang around for. I don't want to get in your way – this is your office now – but I don't want to abandon you before you're ready.'

'No, of course. Thank you for being so considerate about my position.' Chantal paused and thought for a moment. 'How about if we see how this week goes? If, at the end of this week, I feel confident enough to get on without you, then we can draw things to a close at that point. Does that work for you?'

Will stood up and stretched out his hand to shake hers. 'That all sounds great.'

Chantal left his office to carry on with her work. Will took the opportunity to review his inbox of paperwork in case there was anything to hand over to her. He wanted to make sure everything was as up-to-date as possible before he left, so Chantal would have the easiest transition. He'd just made a start when his Skype system started ringing. He glanced at his watch, realising it was about ten in the morning over in Nashville, and prepared himself to speak to Jackson. When he switched tabs though, it was Kim.

'Will, hi. How are you?'

'I'm fine.'

'Did you get my email?'

'I did, thank you.' He waited a beat to see if she would say anything else.

'I meant everything I said, Will. I'm sorry we parted on such bad terms after the funeral, and I'd like the chance to put things right between us.'

He softened towards her, appreciating her apology. 'I'll have to make arrangements to come back, and I'll let you know when that's going to be.'

'How is everything? How's Jenna?' Will had the feeling Kim had changed since the last time he'd spoken to her. She seemed much calmer than previously.

'Everything is good and Jenna's fine. We've just got engaged, in fact.'

'That's great news. Congratulations.'

'I'll be in touch again once I know dates and everything.'

Kim rang off, leaving Will full of guilt for the previous argument they'd had, but also nervous about the prospect of seeing her again. He sighed and wondered about calling Jenna, then thought better of it. He'd wait till he got home and discuss it with her then. Instead, he decided to Skype Jackson, as he needed to talk to him about Chantal.

'Hey, Will, I was just thinking about you. How are you?'

'Pretty good. How are you and Rachel doing?'

'We're both good, thanks.'

'I was getting in touch because I'm back in Paris now and Chantal started work today. She's had a really good day. If everything is okay by the end of the week, we've agreed I should let her find her own way from there, without stepping on her toes.'

'Yes, okay, that sounds like a good plan. When can I have a chat with her?'

'We thought a conference call tomorrow would be good, say around this time?'

'Yes, that's fine. Now there's something else I wanted to discuss with you, connected with the conversation we had yesterday about your plans for the future.'

'Was there something specific on your mind?'

'Yes, it's all good, so don't worry. I know you're keen to settle in one place, especially now you and Jenna are getting married, and I've got another proposition for you. I'm going to need someone to oversee the new office managers in London and Paris, and perhaps elsewhere in the longer term. I wondered whether you would be interested in being my European Regional Manager and doing that job for me. In that way, you could be based anywhere you like, as long as you're in Europe.'

Will raised his eyebrows. 'That sounds interesting. I certainly wasn't expecting you to say that.'

Jackson chuckled. 'You know me. I talked over what you'd said with Rachel last night. I would be sorry to see you go, and this was what we came up with together as a way of solving your problem but also helping the company. So, have a think about it, and talk it over with Jenna, then get back to me.'

Will rang off, gathered his things and set off for his apartment across town, surprised by how much he'd have to talk about with Jenna tonight.

---

## Jenna

Jenna could hardly believe they were on their way to Nashville once again. Her parents had happily stepped in and she was relaxed about leaving her team in charge in her absence. She and Will both needed a break and she hoped this trip was going to give them it. The contract with Lulborne House had been re-negotiated and they were due to start working with them at the start of July, in time for the busiest part of the season.

'Hey, what are you thinking about, sweetheart? I can almost hear the cogs whirring in there.'

Jenna laughed. 'I was just feeling grateful for my little team back at the shop, and looking forward to spending time with you. It was good of Jackson to offer us his beach house for a few days, wasn't it?'

'It certainly was, and I can't wait to get there. It'll do us good to spend some time there first, before travelling north to Nashville. I'm feeling pretty grateful myself, for lots of things.' He leaned over and kissed her.

They had a short wait for their connecting flight in Atlanta and just a few hours later, they walked off the plane into the balmy heat of Charleston where Jackson's beach house was located. Neither of them had ever been there before, so from the back of their taxi cab they took in the views of the old port city and its antebellum houses in silent admiration. When the cab pulled up outside Jackson's incredible beachfront home, their jaws dropped open.

'This isn't what I'd imagined a beach house to look like at all,' Jenna whispered as they stood in the neatly tended front garden complete with palm trees, staring up at the pale blue house in front of them, with its magnificent wraparound verandahs on both the first and the second floors.

'Come on, let's go explore.' Will pulled on her hand and led her up a short flight of steps to the front door. He pushed open the solid oak door and stood back to let Jenna go in first.

Jenna set down her bag carefully in the hallway, not wanting to mark the beautifully polished antique pine floors, and wandered from room to room, hardly daring to speak. Will followed behind just as quietly. Will had come from money, she knew, and so he was used to a comfortable lifestyle, but this was on another level. She turned round to look at him. His face was a picture of rapture, as if he couldn't believe his luck.

Picking up her bag as she passed through the hallway once again, she made her way upstairs, eager to find the bedrooms and to see what else the beautiful old house had to offer. When she arrived at the master bedroom, she squealed with excitement, falling on the wrought-iron bed in delight. Will joined her a moment later, propping himself up next to her against the grand headboard.

'Wow! What a sight from the window. This is such an amazing house, isn't it?'

'It truly is. I never imagined we would get to spend time in such a beautiful place.' Jenna sat up and glanced out of the window at the amazing view of the ocean once again. 'I want to go to the beach and eat seafood right now.'

She jumped up and put her bag on the bed, digging out shorts, trainers and a t-shirt for the adventure she had in mind. Will laughed as he did the same. Obviously, her enthusiasm was infectious.

After a long walk on the beach, they ended up at a little seafood restaurant set back from the road. They chose a table outside so they could continue looking at the sea while they ate. They ordered a seafood platter and a bottle of crisp sauvignon blanc and got down to the serious business of tasting all the different seafoods on the dish.

'So, how are you feeling today about Jackson's suggestion?' Jenna asked as she finally removed a piece of crab from the tail and popped it in her mouth.

'I can see it's a generous offer, but I don't know if I want to abandon the chance to explore my own business idea. I suppose Jackson's route is the safe one, and maybe the most obvious one, if we want our future to be secure. It also maintains the link to Nashville, which in the longer term may be somewhere I come back to, despite how I was feeling a week or so ago after everything happened with Kim.'

'Maybe when you see her again in a few days, she'll give you the answers you need. If she has matured as you think, you might want to stay in touch with her after all.'

'Exactly. I do like the sound of Jackson's job, it has to be said. I might ask him whether he'd be happy for me to work four days a week for him, which would give me one day a week to explore other ideas for myself. What would you think about that?'

'It would be the best of both worlds, wouldn't it? Jackson's pretty flexible about most things, so it would be worth asking him.'

'You're right, it certainly can't hurt. We're going to have so much on in the coming year that maybe it would be better to build up my business idea slowly at first to see if I can actually develop something out of it. Whatever I do, I don't want us to be apart any more.' He reached out and took her hand, bringing it to his lips.

Jenna sighed and smiled at him. 'I told you it would be good for us to have a break, didn't I? I feel so much more relaxed already. It would be nice to explore the town this afternoon and see what there is to go and visit over the next few days. Are you up for that?'

'Definitely. A bit of sightseeing will be okay with me. And more lovely food and wine before we get to test out that fabulous bed later.'

Jenna chuckled, assuring him they were of one mind on that front.

## Will

Their week in Charleston passed far too quickly, but it had been a good escape for them both. Now sitting in the cab on his way to meet with Kim and Mr. Bennett again, a sense of peace settled over Will. He didn't want to fight with Kim, and it seemed she might have changed her mind about that too. Hopefully, this would be a simple matter of signing some paperwork and moving on. Will also hoped he and Kim could remain on good terms afterwards, but for that he would have to wait and see. He still couldn't quite believe her change of heart about her mom's will. That was the only thing making him nervous.

When he arrived in the reception area of the lawyer's building, Kim was already there.

'Hi, Will. How are you?'

She seemed more composed.

'I'm good, Kim, thanks. We've been on a vacation break to Charleston so still enjoying the benefits. You look well, too.'

'Yes, I'm feeling pretty good too, thanks. Shall we go in?'

The woman on the reception desk called ahead and they walked along the corridor together to Mr. Bennett's office. The older man greeted them at the door, shaking them both by the hand before showing them in and waving towards two seats opposite his desk.

'Good to see you again, Will. If you're both agreed, the paper-work to be signed today splits your mother's assets between you, as she stipulated in the will.'

He paused, presumably to see if they would object. Will nodded, waiting to hear what Kim would say. When she didn't speak, he released his breath and nodded at the lawyer. Mr. Bennett gave them each a sheaf of papers and a pen. The places where they needed to sign were marked with small, sticky arrows and Will began signing his pages straight away.

'That's mine all done.' He glanced over at Kim as she handed her pages back. She smiled at him as she caught his look.

'Thank you both for making that tedious job so easy,' the lawyer said. 'I have an envelope for each of you here with the details of your respective payments. As you have both sent me your bank details, the amounts will be in your accounts tomorrow. Any other questions before you leave?'

Will looked over at Kim to see if she had any queries, knowing he didn't have any himself. They stood together and each shook the lawyer's hand in turn.

'Thank you for all your help, Mr. Bennett.'

Will followed Kim out of the office and towards the bank of lifts.

'So, what's next for you?' he asked as they headed down to the street.

'I'm planning to move out of the city centre, perhaps to Franklin or thereabouts, and to just see where life takes me.'

The lift door opened on the ground floor.

'Listen, are you doing anything now?' Will asked on an impulse. Kim shook her head. 'Would you like to go for some lunch?'

'I'd really like that, Will.'

As they walked together along the street to one of their favourite cafés near The Ryman, Will experienced a sense of contentment he had almost forgotten. Everything was as it should be in his life, and he was looking forward to the future with a sense of anticipation. He held open the door to the café as they arrived and they found a quiet table in the window.

'You seem much more relaxed now, Kim, than when I saw you last time,' Will told her once their food order had been taken.

'I am. I still battle with my grief after losing Mom, but she's in a better place now. I feel relieved not to have to worry about her any more. Does that sound callous?'

'Not at all. You loved her and you'd cared for her for a long time. Now it's time for you to live your life. Moving out of the city sounds like a good start.'

Their sandwiches came and as Will bit into his shrimp po'boy, a tide of memories came flooding back to him, of happier times spent with Kim when they'd come here straight from school. He wiped his mouth with his napkin and looked over at his half-sister.

'As good as you remember?'

'Sure is.'

'I'm surprised you haven't asked me what made me change my mind about the money. Don't you want to know?'

'Only if you want to tell me. I wasn't going to bring it up again at the risk of upsetting you over it.'

'That's why I changed my mind, right there. You deserve it, Will, especially after the way Mom treated you, and I couldn't be the one to deny you it. When I read her letter, I could see she was trying to put things right with you, even though I was hurt at first. But she told me how much she loved me, and that the money was nothing to do with that. And Chase helped me see that too.' She blushed and Will nodded in understanding.

'How did you two meet?'

'A friend of a friend, but we're so well-matched, it's quite incredible.'

'I'm glad for you, Kim, I really am. I hope everything works out for you both.'

'And I was so pleased to hear about you and Jenna getting engaged. I'm sorry for being rude to her last time you were here. I don't know what came over me, but I know I wasn't myself following Mom's death. I hope she'll be able to forgive me.' Kim looked downcast at the way she'd behaved and Will couldn't be mad at her any longer. He reached out and patted her hand.

'She's long since forgiven you, Kim, that's just the way she is. I'm one hell of a lucky guy.'

---

## Jenna

Jenna beamed at Rachel across the table of the restaurant where they had agreed to meet for lunch.

'I can't tell you how pleased I am to be seeing you again this soon. I didn't imagine we'd be meeting up again before you have the baby.'

'It has worked out so well, and now we can celebrate your good news as well. Show me your ring so I can see it properly.' Rachel oohed and aahed over Jenna's diamond ring before letting her get back to her salad.

'And we want you all to come over for the wedding, so we're totally fine about waiting until you're ready.'

'But you'll have to book a venue, won't you? You won't be able to do that easily with just a couple of weeks' notice.'

'We may have a solution for that actually.'

Jenna told Rachel all about the contract she'd negotiated with Lulborne House, and how much she was looking forward to working with Lucy.

'And Sarah and Dave are working with you as well, now. Is that right?'

'Yes, they covered for me last time and they're doing the same now, while we're here. So with all the new work that will be coming our way, I've asked them to work with me permanently. It will only be part-time so they don't get too worn out. They are supposed to be retired after all.'

'It's fantastic, Jenna. Your business has grown so much in such a short time and you're doing incredibly well. And now you're getting married too. It's all coming together, isn't it?'

'It is. Hopefully, Will and Jackson are going to sort things out too, as far as Will's job is concerned, and everything will be settled. It has been such an unsettling time in many ways.'

Rachel reached out and squeezed her hand. 'It will all be okay. Jackson's very fond of Will and he wants to help him, and you of course.'

'I know and I really appreciate it. We both do.' Jenna paused for a moment before continuing. 'We had a lovely celebration at home the other day, and Sam was there. He sent you his love. He and Jessie are getting on so well. I think they're a very good match for each other.'

'Oh, that's really good to know. Send him my love as well. Jessie seemed like a lovely girl, so I'm glad for both of them. It will be wonderful to come over for the wedding and to see everyone again. This place Lulborne House sounds wonderful. I'll have to look it up on the Internet. With the baby due in September, we'd probably be looking at the New Year before we felt comfortable enough to travel. How does that sound to you?'

'Yes, we might go for early next year or maybe even leave it till spring when it's a bit warmer. That would also give you a bit more time to settle into your new life with a baby.'

Jenna's phone buzzed with a text.

'Oh sorry, that's probably Will texting me to say his meeting's finished.'

She read the message. 'Ooh, he's just had lunch with Kim, so things must have gone very well with her at the lawyer's office. Do you mind if I ask him to come here and join us?'

'Not at all.'

Will turned up a few minutes later, and Jenna waved at him from their table. He made his way over and kissed Jenna and then Rachel on the cheek before sitting down next to Jenna.

'How did it go with Kim?'

'It was all good. She seemed so different that I invited her to lunch. Turns out she has a new boyfriend and this has changed her whole outlook. She's much more relaxed and less self-centred so it's all good. I get the money by transfer tomorrow.'

'Wow! That's great news.'

'And what's more, I had a chat with Jackson just now.' He looked between the two women, keeping them in suspense.

Jenna tutted and rolled her eyes. 'Come on. Don't keep us waiting.'

'I put my idea to him of working as his regional manager for four days a week, and on the fifth day working on my own projects, to see if I really can build my own business. And he agreed. He'll still have me working for him, and I'll be able to start working on my own business with less risk. Most importantly, you and I can be together, Jenna, because I'll be able to work remotely most of the time rather than running around like I've been doing recently.'

'That all sounds fabulous. Well done for coming up with that plan and for working it out with Kim and with Jackson.'

'I'm so pleased for you both,' Rachel said. 'It's been such a lovely thing to see your love for each other grow right from your very first date, and now you're getting married and settling down. Will you stay in the cottage, or do you think you'll want a bigger house now?'

'We'd definitely like to move somewhere bigger. But there is someone else who might like your cottage if you were up for it... Sam and Jessie.' Jenna smiled at the look of surprise on Rachel's face.

'Of course but how has all that come about? I thought they were down in Falmouth.'

'For the time being they are, but by the time we find somewhere new and move in before or after the wedding, Jessie's course will have finished. They were talking the other day about moving back to Poole for work. So it could all turn out very nicely for them, as long as you're okay with it.'

'Definitely. I can't imagine anything nicer.'

Jenna smiled at her old friend, knowing just how far they'd all come together – Rachel and Jackson, Jenna and Will, Sam and Jessie. It had been a long road, but the future for them all looked bright, and she couldn't wait to get started.

## The End

Because reviews are vital in spreading the word, please leave a brief review on **Amazon** if you enjoyed reading this *From Here to You* series. Thank you!

# READ AN EXCERPT FROM THE VINEYARD IN ALSACE

**Fran**

'Here, you can have this back!' I wrenched my engagement ring from my finger and flung it in the general direction of their naked bodies, huddled together under the sheet on the bed. *Our* bed. 'I obviously won't be needing it any more.'

'What the hell, Fran?' The thunderous look on Paul's face as the ring pinged against the metal bed frame almost made me doubt myself. I closed my eyes briefly. *Don't let him control you. You are definitely not the guilty party!*

I took one last look at him and then I turned and ran. I kept on running, as far and as fast as my legs would take me, blood pounding in my ears, my long hair whipping around my face. The whole time my mind raced with thoughts of his double betrayal.

Eventually, my body couldn't take any more and I stopped on the pavement near an underground station, doubled over and panting from the effort. Once I'd got my breath back a bit, I gave Ellie a call. She picked up on the first ring.

'Hey, Fran, how are you?'

That question pushed me over the edge into full-blown sobbing and once I'd started, I couldn't stop.

'What's the matter? Where are you? Is Paul there? Talk to me, please!'

'Hold on a minute,' I managed to choke out, wiping my face on the sleeve of my t-shirt. 'I'm at the Tube station and I need a place to stay. Paul... Paul... well, there is no Paul and me any more.'

I heard her sharp intake of breath before she said, 'Of course you must come here. Will you be okay on your own or do you want me to come and get you?'

'No, I'll be okay. I should be about half an hour. Thanks, Ellie.' I rang off and made my way down into the depths of the Tube, grateful that I would have somewhere to stay so I didn't have to go back home tonight. Afterwards, I couldn't remember finding my way to the platform. I was so distracted by all that had happened and in such a short space of time but the next thing I knew, I was squashed into a seat on a crowded rush-hour carriage, trundling north on the Northern line.

No-one spared me a second glance on the train. It was oddly calming to be sitting among complete strangers in my misery and to know I didn't have to explain myself. I wrapped my arms protectively around my body. *Why on earth had Paul done this to me?* I wracked my brain as the train rattled on, but I could make no sense of it.

When I arrived at Ellie's, she scooped me into her arms at once for a hug, which only made me start crying again. She patted my back comfortingly, and eventually the tears subsided.

'Why don't I get us both a drink and then you can tell me everything that's happened?'

I nodded silently. While Ellie was gone, my phone buzzed with yet another text message. It was from Paul, no doubt trying to find me, but I deleted it along with all the others and set the phone down on the table in front of me. Ellie returned shortly afterwards with two cups of tea. I wouldn't have minded something stronger under the circumstances but it probably wasn't a good idea to get drunk just now. I'd need a clear head for whatever was going to come next.

'So, what the hell has happened?'

And I told her.

'I can't even begin to process it, Ellie. Why would he do that to me in the first place but even worse, why would he do it to me just after we'd got engaged?'

'I don't know what to say, apart from telling you that I never really liked Paul – I'm sorry – and he's proved what a bastard he is by doing this to you. There's no excuse for cheating and you'll never be able to trust him again now.'

I winced at her honesty and at her harsh judgment of Paul.

'In just that one second, my life's been turned upside down. Everything I was planning on – you know, getting married, settling down, starting a family – is now in doubt. I feel like my life is over.' I set down my cup and let the tears roll down my face. My phone buzzed once more with another text. This time, I read it first.

*Where are you? I just want to know that you're okay. I'm really sorry, I've been incredibly stupid.*

'Well, at least he realises that much,' said Ellie, her lips tight with anger as I read it out to her.

My fingers hovered over the keypad but in the end, I deleted the message and turned off the phone.

'I'm going to bed, Ellie. I'm exhausted, and I just can't think straight. Hopefully, things will be clearer in the morning.'

Once I'd climbed into the little single bed in Ellie's spare room, sleep just wouldn't come. I tossed and turned restlessly as images of Paul in bed with this other woman invaded my mind. I thought again about what Ellie had said about never really liking Paul. Had I been taken in by him all this time? I covered my eyes with my hands, embarrassed by my foolishness. I lay there for hours, railing against the injustice of the situation and wondering how I would explain all this to my parents. By the time I finally fell asleep the sun was coming up but I had the beginnings of an idea about what I was going to do next.

# ALSO BY JULIE STOCK

**From Here to You series**

Before You - Prequel - From Here to You

**Domaine des Montagnes series**

First Chance - Prequel - Domaine des Montagnes

The Vineyard in Alsace - Book 1 - Domaine des Montagnes

Starting Over at the Vineyard in Alsace - Book 2 - Domaine des Montagnes

A Leap of Faith at the Vineyard in Alsace - Book 3 - Domaine des Montagnes

**Standalone**

The Bistro by Watersmeet Bridge

Bittersweet - 12 Short Stories for Modern Life

# ABOUT THE AUTHOR

Julie Stock writes contemporary feel-good romance from around the world: novels, novellas and short stories.

She published her début novel, *From Here to Nashville*, in 2015, after starting to write as an escape from the demands of her day job as a teacher. *A Leap of Faith at the Vineyard in Alsace* is her latest book, and the third in the Domaine des Montagnes series set on a vineyard.

Julie is now a full-time author, and loves every minute of her writing life. When not writing, she can be found reading, her favourite past-time, running, a new hobby, or cooking up a storm in the kitchen, glass of wine in hand.

Julie is a member of The Society of Authors.

Julie is married and lives with her family in Cambridgeshire in the UK.

Sign up for Julie's free author newsletter at **www.julie-stock.co.uk.**

Printed in Great Britain
by Amazon

14469905R00308